Praise for
Shadow Kin

"M. J. Scott's *Shadow Kin* is a steampunky romantic fantasy with vampires that doesn't miss its mark."
— #1 *New York Times* bestselling author Patricia Briggs

"*Shadow Kin* is an entertaining novel. Lily and Simon are sympathetic characters who feel the weight of past actions and secrets as they respond to their attraction for each other."
—*New York Times* bestselling author Anne Bishop

"M. J. Scott weaves a fantastic tale of love, betrayal, hope, and sacrifice against a world broken by darkness and light, where the only chance for survival rests within the strength of a woman made of shadow and the faith of a man made of light."
—National bestselling author Devon Monk

"Had me hooked from the very first page."
—*New York Times* bestselling author Keri Arthur

"Exciting and rife with political intrigue and magic, *Shadow Kin* is hard to put down right from the start. Magic, faeries, vampires, werewolves, and Templar knights all come together to create an intriguing story with a unique take on all these fantasy tropes. . . . The lore and history of Scott's world is well fleshed out and the action scenes are exhilarating and fast."
—*Romantic Times*

"A fabulous tale."
—Genre Go R___ ___eviews

Also by M. J. Scott

Shadow Kin

BLOOD KIN

A NOVEL OF THE HALF-LIGHT CITY

M. J. SCOTT

A ROC BOOK

ROC

Published by New American Library, a division of
Penguin Group (USA) Inc., 375 Hudson Street,
New York, New York 10014, USA
Penguin Group (Canada), 90 Eglinton Avenue East, Suite 700, Toronto,
Ontario M4P 2Y3, Canada (a division of Pearson Penguin Canada Inc.)
Penguin Books Ltd., 80 Strand, London WC2R 0RL, England
Penguin Ireland, 25 St. Stephen's Green, Dublin 2,
Ireland (a division of Penguin Books Ltd.)
Penguin Group (Australia), 250 Camberwell Road, Camberwell, Victoria 3124,
Australia (a division of Pearson Australia Group Pty. Ltd.)
Penguin Books India Pvt. Ltd., 11 Community Centre, Panchsheel Park,
New Delhi - 110 017, India
Penguin Group (NZ), 67 Apollo Drive, Rosedale, Auckland 0632,
New Zealand (a division of Pearson New Zealand Ltd.)
Penguin Books (South Africa) (Pty.) Ltd., 24 Sturdee Avenue,
Rosebank, Johannesburg 2196, South Africa

Penguin Books Ltd., Registered Offices:
80 Strand, London WC2R 0RL, England

First published by Roc, an imprint of New American Library,
a division of Penguin Group (USA) Inc.

First Printing, June 2012
10 9 8 7 6 5 4 3 2 1

PUBLISHER'S NOTE
This is a work of fiction. Names, characters, places, and incidents either are the product
of the author's imagination or are used fictitiously, and any resemblance to actual per-
sons, living or dead, business establishments, events, or locales is entirely coincidental.
    The publisher does not have any control over and does not assume any responsibility
for author or third-party Web sites or their content.

ALWAYS LEARNING   **PEARSON**

For Katrina, Jo, and Linda.
I couldn't make up better friends than you.

ACKNOWLEDGMENTS

As always, there are many people to thank. . . .

Miriam Kriss, agent extraordinaire, who knows good writing, how to talk writers down off the ledge, and where the best cocktails and coolest things to do in any city are to be found.

Jessica Wade for a keen editorial eye that untangles plots and slays writerly dumbness with a single glance.

To everyone else in the Roc team, particularly the wonderful, talented art department, who have blessed me with covers of beauty and brilliance. I owe you all more Aussie cookies.

To my awesome family and friends who have seen me through a year that has been somewhat of a roller coaster with cheers, hugs, shopping enablement, champagne, and whatever else I needed at the time.

And lastly to my wee mad torti cat, who has taken over writer companion cat duties with considerable aplomb.

You do not see us, we who hunt the night.
We pass unseen, silent as owls.
Some hunt for food, some for trouble.
Others hunt a different prey.
We watch. We listen.
We find the secrets you would hide.
Knowledge is power, and power has a price.
It takes its toll with no remorse
In gold, in tainted choices, in friends betrayed
And sometimes . . . the price is blood . . .

Chapter One

HOLLY

The clock in my head ticked the seconds too fast. Not literally—the precision of that inner countdown was a hard-won skill—but I was running out of time. It had been nearly ten minutes since I'd let myself into this tiny room and I still had another two charms to place before I could leave. Trouble was, hiding places were scarce.

The room was small to begin with and mostly empty. I'd already tucked a charm into the base of the sole lantern hanging on the wall, hidden another under a creaky floorboard—not ideal for a hear-me, but beggars can't be choosers—and a third into a hole in the wall I'd discovered behind some peeling wallpaper.

Which left few options for the last two. Some would call five charms overkill, but I didn't like leaving things to chance. Particularly not when I had to use charms I'd activated a day earlier, to allow the tiny drops of blood I used to coax them to life to lose their fresh scent. Unfortunately that also meant that they lost power. More charms meant more chance of them working as I needed them to.

Taking another inventory of the room, I made up my mind. There were two chairs in the room, one upholstered in badly faded cheap cotton and the other plain wood. Flicking open my cutthroat, I dropped to my knees and tipped the chair up, slicing a neat seam in the bottom of the upholstery and stuffing the charm inside. Hopefully the fabric would hold.

I used the other chair, plain wood, to reach the top of the window that grudgingly let moonlight through its grimy panes and laid the fifth charm along the top of the frame, behind the decaying curtains. It was a risk . . . if anyone drew the curtains, then it might fall, but I'd layered the hear-me charms with as many layers of protections and ignore-me and fading glamour as I could force into them and it was just going to have to do.

It took another minute to make sure the room was exactly as I'd found it and then I let myself back out after triggering yet another charm to deaden my scent behind me. An expensive night, but then my client was paying me well.

The first part of my night's work achieved, I set off for the vantage point I'd selected earlier to settle down and wait and see what happened next.

An hour later I was wishing that I'd chosen a different profession as I slowly froze solid on the rooftop of the building across from the one that held the room I'd charmed.

I was secure in my little niche next to one of the chimney stacks, yet another charm rendering me safely invisible. But invisibility is sometimes a curse rather than a blessing. For one thing, turning invisible can confound your sense of where you are in space and time. You reach for something and miss, or walk too close to a door frame and blacken an eye. And for another, it doesn't protect you from the elements.

As the current lack of feeling in my chilled-to-the-bone fingertips attested to.

I blew silently on my fingers and huddled closer to the chimney pot beside me, hoping it would somehow magically begin to block more of the unseasonably icy wind. Not surprisingly, it didn't. The brick wasn't even warm. After all, it was summer and not supposed to be so cold. No one who lived in the ramshackle building below the roof I was currently skulking on had money to spare for extra firewood or coal for something as luxurious as heating in summer.

No, they would be wrapped in extra clothing, muttering imprecations at whoever their choice of deity might be and hoping for a return to more seasonal weather, much as I was. I wondered if the grating screeches of the ancient weather vane spinning slowly atop the useless chimney pot annoyed them as much as it was annoying me.

If I spent much longer on this roof, I would be both frozen and deafened. The only benefit of the chill was that the wind whistling around my ears and finding every gap in my clothing didn't smell quite so strongly of rot and garbage as it usually did in Seven Harbors. But that was little comfort as I huddled deeper into my clothes and glared in the direction of the building opposite whilst the muscle in my right calf started to cramp.

Normally I wouldn't have needed to wait so long, but not only had I needed to leave enough time for the charm to erase my scent from the room; I'd also had the misfortune of being tasked to watch for two people who had apparently been detained elsewhere this evening.

One of them had finally arrived about ten minutes ago, and the room I was observing was now bright with lantern light. Through the dirty window, I had a perfect view of Henri Favreau, one of the senior *guerriers* in the Favreau pack, pacing the floorboards. Not known for his patience, he was starting to look as annoyed as I felt.

Rightly so. The person he was supposed to be meeting was late. Almost thirty minutes had passed since their rendezvous had been due to start. Thirty minutes of icy immobility. My calf tightened further, the pain more piercing, and I gritted my teeth.

Time to move.

I gripped the chimney pot and rose cautiously. I wasn't worried about being spotted. My invisibility charm was freshly triggered with a drop of my blood and it would hold. My charms always hold when I use them on myself. Not being full Fae, they tend to be unpredictable when it comes to working for anyone else. A pity, really. If I could spend my days spinning charms for the wealthy, I wouldn't need to earn money sneaking about on rooftops.

But wishing for what might be never changed anything. For now I was rendered safely invisible by the charm tucked through my belt. A useful thing for a spy.

The slate tiles were damp and slick beneath my feet as I straightened one leg then the other, stretching to ease the cramp. Moving made the blood flow somewhat faster, warming me a little. Not much. I would be grateful when I could return to my room above the Swallow's Heart and fill my belly with tea and toast. A hot bath would be even better, but there wouldn't be time for that.

A flicker of movement caught my eye and I turned my attention back to the window.

Finally.

Henri had been joined by his tardy companion. Ignatius Grey. One of the Blood Lords currently battling in the nasty tangle of scheming and violence that was Blood Court politics since Lord Lucius had unexpectedly disappeared six weeks earlier. Ignatius wasn't amongst the highest ranks of the Blood, but he had a reputation for viciousness and had been ruthlessly making his way up in the court even before Lucius died.

It seemed he intended to keep rising.

It also seemed that Henri Favreau was an unhappy Beast who might have decided to rise with him. Maybe Henri was getting tired of being several rungs too low in his pack hierarchy to ever have a real shot at leading. Christophe Favreau, the current alpha, was no friend to Ignatius. Henri was risking a lot being here.

The shift and flow of alliances and power plays since Lucius had vanished was making life very interesting in the Night World. Everyone assumed Lucius was dead. No one knew how. And no one knew who to trust, not that anyone in the Night World really ever trusted anyone else. Everyone wanted information. Hence my unpleasant rooftop sojourn this evening.

Information is what I deal in. Well, mostly. I'm not above retrieving objects as well, but information is generally easier to fence.

And my employer tonight was paying dearly to have confirmation that Henri was talking to Ignatius. I was happy to take the money. It was likely that jobs would dry up for a while soon. The treaty negotiations were getting closer and traditionally the lead up to the negotiations brought a kind of cease fire amongst the four races. No one wanted to be caught doing something not exactly legal under the treaty and be the cause of their own kind losing any of their privileges.

The treaty set the terms of the peace in the City and governed other things to keep balance. Rations of iron and silver, rules of conduct for the Blood and Beasts and Fae outside their own territories. Breaking the treaty, and being found out, could bring serious repercussions.

Of course, bending it a little was business as usual here in the Night World.

I set my feet, seeking purchase on the tiles, finding my balance in readiness to resume my uncomfortable crouch and watch and wait. Hopefully the hear-mes would be doing their job as well, recording the words of the vampire and the werewolf, but just in case, I would wait and watch, reading lips if I could.

My employer would pay well for confirmation of this meeting. She would pay even better for knowledge of what was said.

That was the plan. A damned good one.

Or it would have been if not for the fact that, as I started to crouch, a deep voice bellowed, "You there, halt!" from the street below.

Split seconds can be deadly. So can instincts. Despite the invisibility charm, the accusing tone of that voice was commanding enough to make the deepest reaches of my brain think *Discovered. Caught. Flee.* My head whipped around to see who had found me, and the movement was enough to send one of my feet slipping, just a fraction.

A fraction too far.

I overbalanced, grabbed for the chimney pot, and missed. Instead my hand fastened around the weather vane. And whilst the chimney pot was solidly built, the weather vane was not. It had succumbed to rust and decay like half the things in this benighted borough.

It snapped with a dull twang and I tumbled forward. There was a jerking tear as my invisibility charm caught on the edge of the chimney pot and tore free. My arms blinked into visibility as I tipped over the edge of the roof. I grasped hopelessly for the gutter—missing it by a margin of inches—then my head twisted toward the street four stories below. The only other thing I noticed was a man on a horse. He looked up, shock flashing across his face as I screamed.

Lady knew what good screaming would do. Four stories is *high.* I was about to die.

But I didn't die. Instead, somehow, the man on the horse hurled himself off its back and caught me. I landed in his arms with a thump that knocked the wind out of me. He staggered a little under the impact but kept his feet. I stared up at him, gasping like a gutted fish, unable to believe what he'd done. Tears sprang to my eyes as twin bands of pain burst across my back where it had connected with his arms.

He stared down at me, pale eyes—blue, perhaps—looking as shocked as I felt. How in seven hells had he gotten off his horse and caught me?

"Are you all right?" he said in a deep rumble of a voice.

My lungs finally remembered how to work and I sucked in a huge breath. The oxygen must have reached my brain because I suddenly realized that the reason my back hurt so badly was that my rescuer wore chain mail. And there was only one sort of person who rode the streets of the City wearing chain mail.

I'd fallen off the roof into the arms of a gods-damned Templar.

A Templar who was now looking from me, to the roof, and back again, with a little too much interest for my comfort.

"Yes. Put me down please."

I tried not to look guilty as his gaze fixed on me. Very nice eyes—definitely blue, I decided, despite the muddying effect of the flickering yellow light from the streetlamps—but they looked damned suspicious right now.

Lords of hell. I bit back a curse, mind racing. For a moment I considered trying to glamour him. I could still him for a moment, make him forget he'd ever seen me. The last thing I needed was a Templar poking around in my business. But my success rate with casting a true glamour on others was hardly impressive. Too risky. I was going to have to do this the old-fashioned way. "Down?" I repeated.

His arms tightened. His grip didn't make the pain in my back worse, but it was strong. Too strong for me to break. Apparently I wasn't going anywhere just yet. Any other man and I would've tried for my cutthroat, but trying to fight free of a Templar could only be foolhardy.

"What were you doing up there?" he asked.

I thought fast. "Checking the weather vane. It was making a dreadful racket. Keeping me awake." I followed the words with what I hoped was a suitably dull-witted grateful smile.

The Templar raised pale eyebrows. He wasn't wearing a helm, just the mail and a white-with-red-cross Templar tunic. His hair was light too, even if the gaslight made it difficult to determine exactly what shade it might be.

"In the middle of the night?"

It was barely eleven o'clock. Hardly the middle of the night. But I didn't quibble with his definition. "It was either that or lie awake all night."

"So you thought you'd climb up there and fix it? Very . . . enterprising." His tone suggested stupid was a more appropriate term. Or perhaps it was suggesting that he didn't believe a word of my story.

I tried to remember exactly what bits and pieces were hidden amongst my clothes. Another invisibility charm and a hear-me, if they'd survived the fall. Though the charms resembled metal pendants more than anything, nothing overtly incriminating. True, there was my cutthroat tucked in my boot, but not many people walked around Seven Harbors completely unarmed. The gold chain around my neck gave a clue to my heritage, but being a half-breed wasn't illegal either.

I stifled the surge of relief, focusing on projecting innocence instead. "Yes, that's me. My mother always said not to put things off until tomorrow that I can do today."

Actually, these days, my mother didn't say much at all. Mostly she smiled vaguely and listened when I went to visit her. My father, on the other hand . . .

"Does your mother know you climb around on the roof so late at night?"

"My mother is away just now. Besides, I'm five and twenty. Old enough to direct my own activities."

"So I see." He peered up at the roof again. "You're lucky to be alive."

I nodded vigorously, hoping to draw his eyes down to me, rather than the roof, which could only keep rousing his suspicions. I was quite cognizant of my good fortune in not being a bloody mess on the cobblestones. "Yes. Thank you, sir. I'm very grateful to you. Don't you have to get on with your patrol? Catch some miscreants?"

His eyes returned to mine and I resisted the urge to flutter my eyelashes. That might be pushing the innocent young damsel in distress thing a little too far. Which was a pity, because his face was just as nice as his eyes if you liked big strong males with rough-hewn angles to jaw and cheek and chin.

Which I did. But this was a Templar, I reminded myself. Fluttering eyelashes would be wasted on him.

"I seem to have already caught someone," he said, still not

loosening his grip. His mouth lifted slightly, but I didn't dare assume it was a joke.

"I'm nobody a Templar would be interested in. You were chasing someone, I heard you call out. That's why I fell, you startled me." I said, trying to deflect his attention into guilt.

"My squad will be dealing with that," he said. His expression didn't seem at all remorseful. It stayed alert with a hint of suspicion.

"That's a relief," I said. "We appreciate the work you do, keeping the streets safe," I lied. Dodging Templars made my life harder, not easier. Particularly over the last few weeks with so much unrest. They seemed to be everywhere, but I hadn't expected them in Seven Harbors. It was technically a border borough, but it was more Night World than anything else these days. "Now, if you'd let me down," I continued, eager to be gone, "I'll return to my rooms."

Or see if I could gain another vantage point to observe the meeting. It was probably too late now, but I could at least retrieve the hear-mes and, Lady willing, get some notion of what they'd talked about. "Unless I've broken some law by falling off the roof. I promise, I wasn't trying to do myself an injury. The dam—I mean, cursed—weather vane broke."

His eyebrow—the scarred one—rose at my unladylike language and I tried again for a look of girlish innocence. Not really my forte. I berated myself inwardly for mentioning the law. *Stupid, Holly girl.*

He was no fool, this warrior whose shoulders practically blotted out the light of the gas lamp above us. He suspected I was up to something. But he didn't have a hair of proof and it wasn't as though I were covered in blood or anything else that would suggest wrongdoing.

From farther down the street, there came the sounds of a scuffle. He turned to listen but the noise died away. When he faced me again, he frowned, looking torn. "Are you sure you're unhurt?"

"I expect I'll be a little bruised tomorrow," I said, trying to sound responsible. "If it's anything more than that, I'll take myself off to a healer."

"See that you do. Young ladies aren't built for flitting around the sky like owls."

I stiffened abruptly. The Owl was one of my aliases. Did he

know who I was? Or suspect? "Yes, sir," I said, trying to sound as innocent and ladylike as I knew how, given I'm neither. "I'm quite cured of heights for the foreseeable future." Another lie, but I would make sure to use some of the rope in the supply bag I'd stashed on my way up to the roof to secure myself once I got back up there.

"Good."

He made no move to put me down. Indeed, his expression was reluctant as he glanced once more at the roof, then back at me.

"Are you going to put me down or inspect me all night? I assure you, I'm unworthy of study." I spoke too quickly, heartbeat speeding as I made the stupid comment about inspecting me all night. That could be interpreted in entirely the wrong way. He was handsome, this knight, but a Templar was no one I'd be taking to my bed, no matter how solid his arms might feel around me or how distracting the firm curve of his mouth.

His eyes angled toward the roof again. "Did you fix it? Your noisy weather vane?"

Was he offering help or still testing me? "It snapped," I said, hoping to deter him from either option. "Neatly solving the problem. Please put me down." I was starting to feel a little too comfortable in his arms, breathing in his odd scent of horse and man and leather and iron. Luckily iron doesn't bother me as it does some half-breeds. I don't have as strong magic as some of them, but that was traded for increased tolerance. In my line of work, being comfortable around iron comes in handy.

The Templar finally complied, setting me on my feet on the dampened cobbles. My back throbbed as I straightened, but I concealed the resulting wince. I didn't want him dragging me off to St. Giles or Merciful James or some other hospital. That would take far too much time. I needed to get to the charms before their power faded.

Behind us the horse snorted softly and the Templar turned and clucked a half-soothing, half-stern sound at it. The horse—a massive gray thing—flicked its ears irritably but quieted. My rescuer returned his attention to me. "Let me escort you to your lodgings. The streets are dangerous nowadays."

I shook my head. "It's a matter of feet to the front door." I pointed at the door in question. Not my front door as it happens, but I would be able to get inside, having buggered the lock earlier. Hopefully my hairpins and the lock picks they concealed hadn't come loose in the fall. I could hardly reach up to check. If the Templar insisted on escorting me, then I'd have trouble explaining why I lacked a key to any of the apartments within. "I'll be perfectly all right," I said, trying for that innocent tone again. "Perhaps you could wait here until I get inside? That would make me feel safer."

Playing to his protective streak—I was assuming that someone who'd chosen Templar as a profession had a protective streak—would hopefully get me off the hook.

The Templar looked skeptical. I realized, a little too late, that my clothing was hardly that of a young lady safely tucked up in bed for the night. Most young ladies don't wear trousers, for a start, or hooded tunics. Most young ladies don't wear mottled dark green and gray, though I was hoping that the gaslight would make it difficult for him to determine the color of my clothing.

I'd glamoured my hair before I'd come out so it would look plain old dark brown. When I remove the glamour, it's a richer reddish brown with lighter streaks that sometimes seem copper and sometimes bronze. Almost truly metallic. Not human. Another legacy of my not-so-dear father. I would've preferred a modicum more talent and less distinctive hair. Distinctive features are a drawback in my trade. Which is why I spend a lot of time making charms to alter my appearance and renewing glamours. A full Fae can hold a glamour effortlessly, but for me, it takes work.

The Templar's eyebrow lifted as his eyes traveled down my body to my trousers and boots.

"I didn't think it wise to climb on the roof in a skirt," I said before he could question me. "So I borrowed my brother's trousers." Now I was inventing siblings. Unwise. The more complicated the lie, the harder it is to sell convincingly. I needed to stop babbling and get inside. Something about this man made me nervous.

"Why didn't you send your brother up on the roof to fix the weather vane himself?"

"Oh, he's out gaming," I said, trying to sound disapproving. "I try to stop him but he doesn't listen."

"Young men can be difficult," he said.

So could older ones. He wasn't *old*, this knight, but no one looking at his face would call him young. The scar bisecting his eyebrow had the look of having been there for some years, and there were lines at the edges of his eyes and grooving the corners of his mouth. But it was mostly the weight of his gaze that gave the impression of experience, of survival and solidity. Those eyes had seen things. The sorts of things that make you older than you are.

I shivered suddenly, the night's chill registering again now that the adrenaline rush was finally starting to die away. "I really must go," I said. "Thank you again for, um, rescuing me."

He looked from me to the door. "I'll stay and watch until you're safe inside."

Damn.

"That's very kind of you," I said. I could wait until he'd left before sneaking out again. It would delay my evening slightly, but better than being caught by the Templar for a second time. I had the feeling he wouldn't let me go so easily if I gave him reason not to.

Still, I found myself hesitating, not entirely certain I was ready to leave him behind. Heaven knew I didn't need a man to protect me, but there was something undeniably attractive about him. Not just the physical but something about the man himself.

But the likes of him were not for the likes of me, so the sooner I was on my way, the better. I ducked a quick curtsey at him and headed across the street, hoping he wouldn't come after me.

I needn't have worried. There was a clatter of hooves from down the street and someone called, "Sir? Are you still down here? Someone raised the alarm over in Mickleskin."

The Templar swore and strode to his horse, swinging himself up with one easy move. As he wheeled the horse around, our eyes met for a moment and something strange crossed his face before he nodded at me and then looked away. He didn't look back as he rode off.

And I tried to ignore the fact that I stood there for too long wishing that maybe, just maybe, he would.

By the time I regained my perch on the roof, having triggered my second invisibility charm—and that was a costly waste—Henri and Ignatius were gone. I swore to myself, a steady stream of curses aimed at my clumsiness, the weather vane, Templars, and the capricious whims of the Lady, as I climbed down, crossed to the other building, and snuck into the room they'd used to collect my hear-mes.

Hopefully they had stayed and talked rather than being spooked by the Templars in the street. Hopefully they hadn't noticed me falling off the roof. The charms would tell me either way once I got home to the Swallow and triggered them.

As I stepped into the street again, the sounds of a fight— metal clashing and men yelling and one sharp shrieking squeal from an angered horse—drifted from the west. Several streets over if I were any judge.

Luckily it was in the opposite direction to the Swallow, but still I found myself glancing over my shoulder, hoping my rescuer was not in danger. Then I came to my senses and headed for home at a rapid pace, glad for the charm keeping me safely unseen in the streets.

When I reached the alley behind the Swallow twenty minutes or so later, I paused to let my breath steady. My back ached, two solid bars of pain reminding me what had happened. I wondered if they'd show the imprint of chain mail if I looked.

Bloody hell, a *Templar*.

Close call indeed, Holly girl.

I shook off the unsettling memory of searching blue eyes. I'm not adverse to taking a lover and I hadn't taken up with anyone new since my last gentleman caller had been inconsiderate enough to fall in love with somebody else and excuse himself from our arrangement two months ago, but a Templar was hardly a good candidate for his replacement.

I took another deep breath, ignoring my aching back. Time to forget the knight and focus on the work at hand. I had a client to meet, provided I had information to give her. I touched the invisibility charm to turn it off, still unhappy I'd had to use two in one night. I'd have to spend time and money working new ones, and I was short on the former lately.

The door creaked as it always did, but between the clatter of the kitchen and the sheer volume of the patrons in the rooms beyond, I knew no one would notice me. Not that anyone frequenting the rear halls of the Swallow cared much as to my hours or the company I kept. That was a large part of the reason I roomed here.

It took a few minutes to change my clothes, but soon enough

I was descending the stairs, dressed in black with my hair glamoured to match. The dress—women don't wear trousers to a Blood Assembly—felt restrictive as it always did after a job, the skirts and petticoats too heavy, the bodice too tight. The cloak I carried was heavy and awkward and I longed to be tucked up in my room with a hot brick, tea, and a good book.

But my work wasn't yet done and the Swallow wasn't the sort of place my client frequented. So I would go to her.

The sounds of the assembled drinkers hit me with a roar as I emerged into the main bar. The Swallow, being attached as it is to the rear of the Dove's Rest, one of Brightown's swankier brothels, is a level or two above the standard drinking hell around here. Which meant nicer furnishings, a somewhat wealthier clientele, and gin and beer not quite so likely to send you blind at first swallow as some of the rotgut served in lesser places.

Madame Figg, who, with her husband, runs both the Dove and the Swallow, thinks she has superior taste in decorating. Granted, she resisted repeating the Dove's extravagant red, gold, and black theme, but the Swallow still runs to swooping drapes and swirling paper on the walls and gilt-edged mirrors. All in shades of deep blue and green and bronze. To my mind it looks as though a peacock met with an unfortunate accident, but the clients never seem to mind.

Across the room, I spotted Fen, holding court at his usual table, grinning at some tartily dressed blonde in pink. He caught my eye and raised a hand to beckon me over. The sleeve of his velvet frock coat fell back, revealing the fine iron chain doubled around his wrist. I winced. The chain meant the visions were bad tonight.

I made my way through the crowd, murmuring hellos to regulars. When I arrived at Fen's table, he shooed the blonde away. She looked disappointed, deep red lips pouting, as she departed.

"Hello, lovely," Fen said, bowing over my hand extravagantly. His eyes gleamed as green as the elaborate embroidery that twined over the black velvet of his coat as he smiled up at me.

I smiled back, a little warily. The decanter of brandy on his table was half-empty. I wondered if it had been full at the beginning of the evening. "How's business?"

He flicked his hand dismissively and held out a chair for me.

"Nothing to complain of. Plenty of gulls wanting to know their sparkling futures."

Fen exercised only enough of the powers he hated so much to provide his clients with vague hints of what lay in store for them. Innocuous yet accurate enough that he had quite the reputation amongst those who indulge in that sort of thing. They paid well for his obfuscations. He always said if they knew most of what he really saw, they would pay even more for him not to tell them.

I never knew whether that was the truth. But I did know that more and more he preferred the pain of the iron circling his wrist to facing his visions, so they couldn't be anything pleasant.

His smile broadened as he looked me over, ridiculously attractive, as always, when he exercised himself to charm. His black hair was rakishly rumpled and a chipped green gem swung from the gold hoop in his right ear. A pretty package but I liked him too well to sleep with him. Both of us have few real friends and plenty of offers to warm our beds. We wouldn't risk the former for the temporary pleasures of the latter.

"The more relevant question, my dear spiky one," he continued, "is how's *your* business? Heading out again?" His gaze took in the stark black of my outfit and darkened a little. He didn't approve of me going to Assemblies alone. "You should be careful."

I frowned. "Did you see something?"

His head tilted, smile vanishing as rapidly as it had appeared. He reached for the brandy and refilled his glass. "No. Should I have?"

Blue eyes flashed again in my head. "No." I shook my head firmly, banishing the Templar yet again. "No, definitely not."

The smile stretched back into life. "Why, Holly, you're blushing. I think there's a story here somewhere."

I tried to look discouraging. "Is there a reason you called me over?"

He tilted his glass at me. "Got wind of a commission at the Gilt. Thought you might be interested." Half the brandy vanished in one gulp and he didn't set the glass down. Bad night indeed.

I hid my concern. In this mood, he wouldn't thank me for it. "A commission or a *commission*?" The Gilt is the biggest theater hall in Brightown. Both a hub for gossip and a fairly insatiable consumer of costumes. Sewing is how most of the world thinks I make my living—the ones who don't suspect I have a patron, that is. I need some apparent source of income, even though I earn far more from my runs than I could as a modiste.

"A dress for the new diva," Fen said with a shrug. Another swallow. "Or so I hear."

Excellent. The Gilt was even in the direction I needed to go. Their evening show would be winding up soon. Perfect timing.

"I'll look into it," I said, standing. "Thank you." I leaned across the table and brushed a kiss on his cheek. "Be good," I whispered before I straightened.

Fen blinked at me, expression suddenly shuttered, and reached for the brandy. The look of concentrated determination to reach the bottom of the decanter as he tipped the amber fluid into his glass told me he had no intention of heeding my advice.

But there was nothing I could do for him other than make sure he was poured home safely at the end of the evening. To that end, I had a word in the ear of Junker, one of the bouncers, and tipped him a half crown. Then I headed into the night for the next part of my evening.

Chapter Two

Guy

✠

We were halfway out of Mickleskin when the Beasts attacked.

There was a second's warning when Gray squealed an enraged alarm and then bucked beneath me, lashing out with his back feet. Around me, I heard the swift shouts of my patrol mingling with the snarls of Beasts.

I turned in the saddle, trying to see how many attackers there were. We'd only had a few minutes' respite since the last encounter, which had left one of the novices with a nasty gash in his arm and more of us sporting bruises and lumps. We'd driven that band of humans back squealing to wherever they'd come from—leaving two of their number dead in the street—and I'd only just finished detailing men to carry the dead and my wounded man back to the Brother House and now this.

Hell's fucking balls.

It was too quick. Too soon. Almost as though the attacks were coordinated. But I would have to worry about that later. Gray squealed again and spun as I drew my sword, ignoring the dull ache in my arms from where I'd caught the girl—and that was another part of the night I didn't like at all—and sighting the Beast Gray was objecting to as we circled.

It was in hybrid form, six feet or more of muscle, fangs, and clawed hands. More than able to do damage with the sword it was swinging. Behind it I glimpsed several more Beasts, including a few in full Beast form.

In Beast form, Beasts can take out a horse with one swipe of their claws and they were too low to the ground to reach from horseback anyway. Cursing under my breath, I launched myself from Gray's back, knowing that he would continue to follow his training and do his best to stomp anyone coming near him into oblivion.

The Beast in hybrid form obviously hadn't been expecting that particular move. His eyes widened, but he only had time to get his sword halfway into position to meet my attack by the time I landed. I used the momentum of my leap to carry me forward, thrust my broadsword ahead of me, and spitted him like a pig.

Normally we tried to take prisoners, but when facing an unprovoked ambush, our orders were to protect ourselves and ask questions later.

I yanked my sword free of the Beast, who sank to his knees and toppled over with a dying snarl, and headed for the nearest wolf.

It had seen what I had done to its pack brother and had obviously learned from the experience. Before I could fully close the distance, it feinted right and sprang past me, out of reach of my sword. I spun, trying to follow the path of its movement, but it was fast. Inhumanly fast.

But I was used to fighting inhumanly fast and I was ready as it sprang again before I had fully turned. I dropped to my knees and slashed as it sailed over me. The Beast twisted in the air, almost somersaulting. My sword connected but so did its swiping front claws. But it hit my mail, not my flesh, and tumbled past me.

I struck again as it hit the ground and this time it howled in rage as my sword bit deeper.

I struck again as blood gushed from the Beast's side and, this time, managed the killing blow. The Beast slumped to the ground and I twisted to look for the next opponent.

But around me, my squad had done their job. There were several more dead Beasts in wolf and hybrid forms, and the others had fled. My knights were regrouping quickly, gathering horses and wiping weapons clean. I strode across to where Gavin, my squad leader, was bent over one of the fallen Beasts, searching through the man's clothing with efficient movements.

"Anything?" I asked.

Gavin looked up at me. He'd caught a blow on the side of the face earlier, and his cheek was turning purple under the blood spatters. "Nothing."

"Hell's balls." I swore softly, then bent down and struck a match, trying to figure out the color of the man's eyes. Beast packs tend to run true to type, though of course there are exceptions. And there are those who operate outside the pack structures. The dead man had light brown hair and gray eyes. Two of the three dead wolves were brown too and the third was darker, almost black.

"What do you think?" Gavin asked.

"The black is most likely a Krueger. The brown could be a few packs. I don't recognize this one." I brushed my fingertips over the man's eyelids, shutting away the dead staring eyes.

"With the gray eyes . . . Favreau, perhaps?"

"Maybe." There was no way to prove it if no one came to claim the bodies. "Favreaus usually stay out of things."

"Christophe Favreau used to, under Lucius. He was content with his bite of the gin dens. But things change."

I bit down the desire to swear again. Many things had changed since Lucius left. The former Blood Lord had been ruthless and twisted, but there had been some degree of stability in the Night World under his iron rule. I had agreed he'd needed killing—the secret he'd discovered had been too dangerous, not to mention that he'd been targeting my brother, Simon—but I'd hoped his death would be the end of the City's troubles, not the beginning of new ones.

It had become increasingly obvious over the last few weeks that that had been wishful thinking.

Which meant I had to try again to convince Simon and Lily that they could well be in danger. My brother and his fiancée had met when Lucius sent Lily to kill Simon. Instead—and I still wasn't sure how it had happened—they had fallen in love. And then they'd teamed up to kill Lucius to save Lily's life and to keep the secret of the powers her wraith blood could bestow on a vampire. They'd been convinced that would be the end of things.

I wasn't so sure. For some reason, Lucius had wanted Simon dead. There might be other Blood Lords who felt the same way, not to mention many who had grudges against Lily. The unrest in the City might just provide a tempting cover for someone who wanted to try again.

I straightened, shaking my head. Worrying about Simon and Lily had to wait, as would trying to work out what was driving my growing sense that they were in danger. "We'll take the bodies back to the Brother House, then head back out." If no one claimed the dead, they'd be buried in the common graves maintained by the order. Hardly a glorious fate. But the likelihood of a pack coming to claim these particular dead was small. "Anyone hurt?"

Gavin looked around, counting heads. "Nothing serious."

"Good." As I spoke, I heard the faint tolls of the cathedral bells sounding one a.m. Still three hours to go before our patrol was over. People called the damned city Half-Light, but lately I felt as if I lived only in darkness, guarding the streets while the sun—and the humans we protected—slept. I scrubbed my face, wiping it clean of Beast blood and sweat, and wished desperately for coffee. Tonight was going to be another very long night.

I pulled Gray's saddle from his back, wishing for a shorter horse, food, and anything resembling a bed.

None of which were going to appear any time soon. I blew out a breath, trying to ignore the ache in my arms and shoulders, and hoisted the saddle across the stall door to the waiting groom.

Gray's head drooped. I knew how he felt. The first hints of dawn were starting to lighten the sky—we'd stayed out an extra hour— and the rest of our patrol had been busy. Nothing like the ambush, but more than the usual quota of fights and disturbances in the border boroughs. Hell only knew what was going on deeper into the Night World boroughs. We had no jurisdiction there, so had to confine ourselves to doing what we could on the borders.

I rolled my shoulders again, feeling the bruises where the Beast had clawed me. Once upon a time, I could've patrolled all night, slept for an hour, and set out again after breakfast. But I was no longer twenty-one and foolish.

Not even close.

Still, I wasn't ready to give up patrolling, even if our Abbott General had been dropping some broad hints about promoting me upward again. Upward and inward that would mean. Strategizing and politicking and administrating. All of which were important but about as appealing as a Beast sinking his claws through my guts.

Turning to Gray, I picked up a brush and set to work. Tack I would delegate, but my horse, never. Gray made a halfhearted "where's breakfast?" snap at my hands before he settled and relaxed under the strokes.

Around us, the sounds of the rest of the patrol seeing to their horses rose and fell in a familiar low babble, mingling with the smells of horses and hay and stables. Soothing in a strange way. I blinked as my eyelids drooped, and snapped to a straighter pose. Which made my shoulders ache more.

Nothing I could do about that right now. Nothing I could do about being tired either. There was much to do before I could sleep. I needed to check on the status of the wounded and report to Father Cho.

The City's mood was ugly, restless as a nest of vengeful hornets as the Night World shifted and scrapped and attempted to regain some sort of balance in the wake of Lucius' death. Personally, I'd be happy for the lot of them to kill each other and drag themselves down to hell. Problem was, they'd take a lot of innocent bystanders with them in the process. And protecting those innocent bystanders was my job.

Hell's balls, I even protected the not quite innocent.

Like my brother, Simon, and his fiancée, Lily. The ones who killed Lucius in the first place. That was knowledge that needed to be kept to as few people as possible for as long as possible.

Killing Lucius was a damned good idea, but if the truth that it had been an assassination ever came to light, it had the potential to cause a rain of shit such as the City hadn't seen in a good long while.

Everyone was keyed up, on edge. Quick to flare into violence. And of course, you had the criminal elements—if anyone in the Night World could be considered noncriminal elements—taking advantage of the power vacuum to attempt to gain something for themselves.

And I needed to speak to Simon and Lily again about returning to the Brother House.

I finished brushing Gray, filled his feed bin, and left him to rest.

He was the lucky one. No one was filling my feed bin and sending me off to sleep.

The patrol room buzzed with low conversation when I walked through the door. Too low. Everyone was tired. Pushed too hard. And there wasn't necessarily an end in sight. We were just going to have to bull it out.

I scanned the room, assessing the damage for the night. Apart from the wounded we'd sent to St. Giles, Isaac had a nasty-looking bruise blooming across his left cheek and Sun-Lee's left hand was roughly wrapped with a bloodstained bandage, but everyone was relatively intact. I counted off twenty-four from the other two patrols. No fatalities tonight, then. Relief lightened my mood slightly as I dropped into the nearest chair.

The move jarred my back and I bit down a curse. Beneath the ache, stiffness was setting in. Add a hot bath to the things I needed before I could sleep.

Because of her.

That girl—woman—whoever the hell she was.

And whatever the hell she'd been up to.

Her face floated in front of my eyes for a moment, sharp lines set off with unexpected curves. Big eyes—maybe green, maybe brown—looking up at me, shocked at first, then wary under her charade of politeness. Her eyes tilted slightly, suggested she had some sort of exotic heritage, whether it be an ancestor from the Silk Provinces or even a Fae. She hadn't been heavy, though she'd curved nicely into my arms—

I shook my head. There was a thought almost as crazy as feeling nostalgic for Lucius. She was from the border boroughs, if she wasn't a Night Worlder in truth. She'd been up to something. And I had no time for anything resembling a woman even if she'd been a virtuous flower from one of the finest human families. The ones my mother gave me regular damned updates on.

Simon's pairing off should've assuaged her maternal urge to see us all married—except Hannah, who was still too young—but it hadn't.

But she'd have to stay disappointed. My path didn't include a wife and children. Not while I could still swing a sword.

"Attention," Isaac bellowed, and we all swung to our feet as Father Cho entered the room.

He, as always, waved us to our seats. Not the sort of general who would put the respect due his rank ahead of the needs of tired men.

As we sat, he moved briskly to the front of the room, the silver patches in his close-cropped dark hair looking as though he'd walked through a snowstorm. But it was the rest of us, out there every night walking through the storm. There was too much happening too fast in the Night World. Alliances shifting, players taken off the board and replaced overnight. It made trying to predict where trouble might flare near impossible.

Half the injuries we'd incurred were because of stumbling onto unexpected trouble spots, too-small squads and patrols split up encountering more than we could take on. And now it seemed we might have even more players entering the fray.

Hells, if those Beasts had been Favreaus . . . I rubbed my chin again, not wanting to think about what would happen if more and more factions in the Night World became involved.

We never backed down, but we were paying the price.

And increasingly, we seemed to be just a few steps behind. Tonight's Beast attack must have been planned. It was unlikely a random group of Beasts would decide to attack a Templar patrol just for the hell of it. Question was, what were they up to?

We needed better information. The kind they seemed to have. But the informants we worked with were clamming up—waiting to see which way the dice fell in the power struggles, no doubt.

Somehow we had to find some new sources. And soon.

There was no answer when I knocked on Simon's front door, so I let myself in, intent on raiding his kitchen if he and Lily truly weren't home. I was starving and in desperate need of something to stave off my longing for sleep.

I pushed the door shut behind me carefully. My arms and shoulders still ached. Which summoned *her* again. The girl. Damned lucky neither of us had broken anything, though I had only her word that she hadn't.

The weather vane story was a blatant lie, but we Templars were charged with keeping the peace in the streets, not policing small crimes. Detaining everyone who raised our suspicions in the border boroughs would be a full-time job, not to mention act like a match to kindling on the City's mood right now.

No one wanted that.

"Simon?" I called down the hallway. There was no answer, but the sudden sound of breaking glass from the rear of the house burned away my fatigue with a burst of adrenaline. I broke into a run, drawing my pistol as I pelted down the long hallway.

"Simon!" I shouted again.

There was another thumping crash, a snarl, and a cutoff yowl. I reached the sunroom at the rear of the house. Just in time to see Lily pulling her dagger free from the throat of yet another dead Beast.

"What exactly is going on here?" I demanded.

Simon was crouched by the body of the Beast, his expression an odd mix of satisfaction and regret.

Lily looked up at me, wiped her dagger clean, and sheathed it by her hip. "Hello, Guy."

"I asked a question," I said, trying to keep a rein on my temper.

Simon nodded toward the body. "He broke in. He attacked us. We took steps."

"So I see." I didn't let the string of curses bubbling in my throat free. My gut crawled as I stared down at the Beast. Light brown fur. Like the one we'd killed earlier. "Fuck." I'd never liked coincidences. "Couldn't you have just knocked him out?"

"Dead is safer," Lily said with a shrug.

"But less useful," I countered. "Now we don't know what he wanted."

"I'd say either Lily or me," Simon said.

"Me," Lily said, her voice still calm. "He came for me first."

"He might have just been trying to get you out of the way," Simon countered.

"We'll never know," I said sourly. "I don't suppose you recognize him?" I directed the question at Lily. She had far more intimate knowledge of the Night World and its denizens than either Simon or me.

"Looks like a Favreau," Lily said. "Maybe a Broussard. Hard to tell."

And in hybrid form, the Beast wasn't carrying any useful forms of identification.

Hell's fucking balls. In the back of my mind, I'd been half trying to convince myself that I was being overly concerned to worry that Lily and Simon were still targets. But apparently the suspicious, paranoid part of me had been correct.

"I take it this is the first time this has happened?" I said.

Simon nodded. "Yes. I would have told you."

This earned him a skeptical look. My little brother tended to be pigheaded about his abilities to defend himself.

And now I had to convince him otherwise.

"We need to clean this up." There was a pool of blood under the corpse, but it wasn't spreading. Together we rolled the body up in one of Simon's rugs and mopped up blood. It didn't take long. What that said about our collective experience with dealing with death and mayhem was something I didn't want to think too hard about.

Simon threw an extra ward across the shattered window and we retreated to the kitchen. Lily made coffee and, praise God, took the trouble to add chicory. Maybe that would keep me upright a few more hours.

Simon passed me a mug and I was about to gulp a mouthful when I felt a brush of pressure across my shins.

I sighed, put down the cup, and bent to peer under the table.

Lily's kitten stared up me and leaned harder into my leg.

"Do not claw my boots, catling," I told her sternly.

She blinked, green eyes huge in a gray fluffy face.

"You might as well pick her up," Lily said, entering through the other door to the room. "She'll sit there until you do. And she'll meow."

I scooped up the kitten with one hand and deposited her onto my lap. She curled up into a ball practically smaller than my fist. "You're not getting any of my coffee." The kitten blinked again and commenced to purr at a volume far louder than such a small thing should be capable of.

"Rondel doesn't drink coffee," Lily said with a grin.

"Then explain why the damn thing feels the need to climb all over me every time I drink a cup?"

"Maybe she sees the softer you inside."

I rolled my eyes. "If you wanted a cat who's concerned with people's softer sides, you shouldn't have named her after a knife." As if to emphasize my point, the kitten spread her claws and attempted to dig them through my trouser leg. Luckily I still wore riding leathers.

Lily's grin widened. "It will remind people she has teeth and claws as she grows."

I looked down at the kitten, mostly fluff and purr. "If you say so." Lily had claws herself, even if she kept them mostly sheathed these days. "Tell me more about the Beast."

"There's not much too tell. We were in the sunroom, having breakfast. He came through the window."

I glanced at the kitchen window, where the pale morning sun was just starting to climb over the tree. I didn't think it was an accident that the attack had taken place after sunrise. Daylight was when Lily was at her weakest.

"You can't stay here," I said. No point beating around the bush.

"We're not returning to the Brother House," Simon said in a determined voice. "We're safe here. We're warded."

"So well warded a Beast can come through your window?"

"The ward was down. I was going to move some plants around that wall later. He wouldn't have gotten through otherwise."

"So you assume. Or maybe they're watching you and know when you do stupid things like drop your wards."

"Doesn't hiding us away make it seem as though we have something to hide?" Lily said. "I thought the idea was to make it look as though we're just going on with our lives, like people with nothing to do with what happened to Lucius."

"Obviously that ploy isn't working." Surely they weren't going to play dumb? They had to know what was going on, as I did.

"You don't know that. This could be revenge for someone I killed or general troublemaking," Lily said.

"You're not that naive," I snapped. "This is serious." My mind raced through the implications. If Simon and Lily were under attack, then that was another duty for Templars to handle. Another strain on our forces. And my loyalties.

My jaw tightened. I loved my brother and he'd done the right thing in killing Lucius, but the cost was proving high. If he and Lily were safe in the Brother House, it was one less thing to take my focus off keeping the City safe. I'd done what I could to make sure my parents' home was well protected, and Saskia, oldest of our sisters, was safe enough behind the walls of the Guild of Metalmages. But Saskia and my parents weren't likely to be direct targets. Nor was our youngest sister, Hannah, who was only fifteen.

Simon and Lily, on the other hand, were. And I'd be damned

if I was going to lose another family member to the Night World. The Blood had taken Edwina from us. Her death had almost broken our family. Losing Simon would finish the job. "It would only be temporary," I began.

"No," Lily said immediately. Her voice was even steelier than Simon's. "Not again. I'm not letting anyone control my life again."

Beside her, Simon nodded. "I agree. We can't hide every time there's trouble in the City."

"You won't have to hide if you're dead," I said bluntly. Simon's face stilled but he shook his head.

"No."

"I'm not leaving you unprotected."

"We're not."

"Hell's fucking balls, Simon, this isn't a game. Someone is trying to kill one of you. You need protection."

"Then we'll think of something else," Simon said. "We're not going."

"You'll—" I bit back the words before I could say something stupid. Picking a fight, as appealing as hitting something might be right now, was not going to solve the problem. I forced myself to take another swallow of coffee.

"How was patrol?" Lily asked, expression bland as she changed the subject. "Does anybody seem to be gaining the upper hand?" Her tone was casual, but I knew her interest in the answer wasn't. She'd been enslaved by the last Lord of the Blood. She knew better than any of us what the consequences of the wrong person gaining control of the Blood Courts might be.

"Not that we've heard, but the mood out there is ugly. Most of our informants are clamming up." I met her gaze. "Unless you can think of anyone who might talk to us?"

She shook her head, red braid bouncing. "No one's going to talk to me. Unless it's to try and torture information from me."

"You must know some names?"

"Every Blood Lord and Beast Alpha has their own network of spies and informants. There are some who work for anyone who'll pay, but they tend to guard their identities closely and work through intermediaries. And, if they work mainly in the Night World, they're not going to want to risk talking to the Templars."

Nothing I didn't know. The Night World usually had plenty of people who'd be willing to snitch a little for some ready cash.

But now, with things so chancy, snitching could be fatal. Most people, when faced with the choice of their money or their life, chose the latter.

Which meant we'd have to keep doing what we were doing. Riding into the border boroughs each night hampered by a lack of good information. Might as well ride out with one hand tied behind our backs. We couldn't be sure where to target our efforts or who we should be keeping an eye on.

I drained my coffee and put the cup down, tapping its thin rim restlessly. I had the ultimate spy right in front of me. Lily was a wraith, able to turn incorporeal at will. Undetectable and untouchable. The sensible thing would be to put her to work.

So why hadn't I?

Simon interrupted my thoughts with a refill, then leaned down to kiss Lily, who turned up her face, smiling at him.

And that was my answer, I thought, dropping my gaze to the kitten on my lap. Lily and Simon were happy now. They'd earned their happiness. They'd risked their lives to kill Lucius and end the biggest threat to the City's peace we'd known.

I couldn't ask Lily to put herself in danger, though I doubted she would refuse. The Night World had enslaved and used her all her life. She'd be more than willing to help us deliver a little justice to them.

But risking Lily meant risking Simon's happiness. I couldn't do that. Couldn't destroy the life he was building. After all, I was already in danger most nights. There had to be someone who could carry on the DuCaine name if the worst came to the worst.

"Any ideas why the Favreaus might be getting involved?" I asked Lily.

"With Lucius gone, the packs will be going for either influence or money. An assassination attempt suggests the latter."

I imagined that Lily's head would fetch a pretty price.

"If he was a Favreau," Lily added.

"We crossed paths with some others who looked like that one on patrol," I admitted.

"Well, some packs have always been muscle for hire for the Blood," Lily said.

"Not the Favreaus, though. They have other interests."

"Historically. But right now I'd guess there's more money to be made in fighting than gin. Who knows, it might even be some rogue youngsters, looking to break away."

"That's all we need." Pack wars to add to all the general mayhem. Right now I'd give my right ball for someone who had a line on what the hell was going on in the Night World. I drained the last of the coffee and handed the kitten to Simon. I wasn't in the mood for hours of arguing right now and I needed to report this latest unpleasant development to the Abbott General.

"This discussion isn't over. We'll talk when I get back."

"Where are you going?" Simon asked.

"To talk to Father Cho. And to get someone to help you move the body."

"I thought you'd be asleep," Father Cho said, looking up from the map spread on his desk. His face was drawn, the lines etched into his skin making him look as tired as I felt.

"So did I, sir. But I still have things to do." I stood politely at attention.

He gestured toward the chair beside me. "Sit." He added, "Things?" after I did. He glanced at the map, scribbled a few notes on a paper beside it. I took that to mean "start talking."

"I had breakfast with Simon and Lily."

Father Cho's hand stilled. He looked up, black eyes sharp. "How are they?"

"Better than the Beast they killed this morning, sir."

Father Cho sighed. One hand lifted, rubbed the deep wrinkle between his eyebrows. Maybe his head ached too.

"Any particular reason they're killing Beast Kind?" he asked.

"He tried to break into their house."

"Why?"

"Hard to say. They didn't exactly stop to question him." I tried to keep the disapproval out of my tone but wasn't sure I succeeded. Simon's coffee churned uneasily in my empty stomach, warring with the fatigue and adrenaline stew.

The wrinkle deepened. "I see."

I rolled my shoulders. "This is getting worse. We're losing ground."

"We'll regain it."

He sounded certain. In his position, he had to. But in my position, I had to tell him I thought he was wrong. "I hope you're right, sir. But if things keep going the way they are now, I'm not so sure we will. Not without paying the price."

"It's getting that bad out there? We knew there would be unrest with the Blood having their . . . change of government."

That was a tactful way of saying "after we assassinated their leader." I was fairly sure I'd never be the Abbott General, because I didn't like calling things pretty names. Death was death and no matter how much Lucius deserved it, the fact was that we humans had killed him. "The Blood have had squabbles before. They didn't escalate to this level."

"The death of their lord is somewhat beyond the level of a squabble."

"Still." I rolled my shoulders again, not sure what I was trying to say. "This is different."

"Different, how exactly?"

"It feels like . . . more."

"More?"

"Purposeful. These aren't random fights breaking out."

"You think they're organized?"

"They're not forming ranks and taking up arms. But they are organizing. We were ambushed tonight. By Beasts with the same coloring as the one sent to attack Lily and Simon. That's not something I'm willing to write off as a coincidence. Things should be calming down now that everyone can see the Blood aren't imploding. But they're getting worse."

"And why is that, do you think?"

That was the question that had been playing on my mind. "I'm not sure, sir. But, if I had to guess, I would say that someone is trying to stir up trouble. This close to the treaty negotiations, that makes me nervous. Especially when you add in a Beast attacking Simon and Lily." Father Cho didn't know the true secret of the value of Lily's blood to a vampire—that drinking wraith blood gave them wraithlike powers, including the ability to shadow and pass unseen. Meaning they could go anywhere and get to anyone. But he knew Simon was a target.

Father Cho's brown eyes were intent. "I have a healthy respect for your instincts, Guy. But what good does stirring up trouble do? It would take more than a few brawls to derail the negotiations."

"A citywide riot might do it, though. Or someone doing something that breaks the treaty."

"You think someone is trying to disrupt the negotiations? Or stop them?"

I nodded unhappily. "We both know there are factions within the Night World and the Veiled World who'd be happy with a return to the old ways, sir. And that wouldn't be good."

"I agree. But stopping it is difficult when we lack proof that anything is even happening. You said yourself it's hard enough for us to work out where to patrol."

"We need better information," I said, half to myself. We were drifting off-topic. I was here to see to Simon and Lily's safety. "People are at risk." I leaned forward. Best to get my request over with. "Sir, I'm requesting—"

He cut me off with a gesture. "No."

"No?"

"You were going to ask for protection for Simon and Lily, weren't you?"

I nodded, jaw clenched.

"Then no. They are welcome, of course, to stay in here in the Brother House, but we can't afford the men for a separate detail, Guy. You know that."

"But—"

"I'm sorry." He shook his head. "I can't treat your family any differently than anyone else's."

"Even though they—"

"Yes. I won't say that killing Lucius wasn't a good thing, but we're paying the price now."

"Due respect, sir, but Simon and Lily are a special case. They're being specifically targeted. Whatever Lucius was doing, we haven't seen the end of it. And whoever was working with him has to want Lily and Simon out of the way." Or under their control. That was the alternative I didn't want to let myself think about.

"I can't disagree, Guy." He spread his hands. "But I don't have the men. Unless—"

"Sir?" I didn't like the sudden speculative gleam in his eyes.

"You said it yourself, Guy. We need better information. If we had that, we could be more focused and I might be able to spare a detail. Lily is uniquely suited to—"

It was my turn to cut the conversation short. This was not the way I'd wanted this to go. "No," I said flatly. "No. I'm not asking her to put her life on the line. She's paid enough."

"But you want us to put our lives on the line for her."

"That's what we do, sir."

He looked grim. "I'm sorry. My decision stands. As long as we're stretched so thin, I can't spare anybody."

"I see." There was no point arguing. He'd made up his mind. Which left Lily and Simon exposed if I couldn't convince them to move to the Brother House. Short of drugging them and dragging them here by force, I didn't like my chances.

Hell's balls. I couldn't leave them at risk. I wouldn't lose any more of my family to the Night World. Father Cho wanted information. I was going to find a way to get it.

Chapter Three

HOLLY

The familiar churn of emotion tightened my stomach when I stepped down from the hackney.

Breathe, Holly girl, I reminded myself as I smoothed my skirts and ran a hand over my hair. I looked like any respectable human girl. As far as the staff in the building in front of me knew, I *was* a respectable human girl.

The dutiful daughter visiting her mother.

That part was true.

I hoped they wouldn't ever find out the rest of my story.

The bell by the door made a genteel chime that had always made my teeth grit. It was answered promptly, as usual, and soon enough I was being ushered through to my mother's room.

"How is she?" I asked before the nurse opened the door.

The nurse's brown eyes were sympathetic. "About the same as usual, Miss Everton." She pushed the door open and I took a deep breath before forcing my lips into a smile as I followed her into the room.

"Good morning, Mama," I said.

My mother sat by the window, in a pretty pale green robe, staring out the window. She didn't turn at my greeting. I hid the pang of hurt and continued on into the room, waving the nurse away.

I picked up the hairbrush from the tall chest of drawers that sat against the wall and crossed the room. "It's a pretty day, isn't it?" I said softly.

It was indeed. The chill of the night before had dissipated and the sky was blue, promising warmth, if not heat, later in the day. Still, as I watched my mother, I felt colder than I'd felt back on the rooftop in Seven Harbors.

Nothing new in that. I hated seeing my mother like this. Lost in her own world. Ruined and old before her time, thanks to the gin she'd turned to increasingly over the years. The sanatorium had managed to wean her from that habit, but they hadn't been able to give me my young, beautiful mother back. No, instead, I had a shell, skin too lined and body too worn, housing a mind that had broken with reality quite some time ago. Occasionally my mother knew who I was, but apparently today wasn't to be one of those times.

I hated it and I knew who was to blame, but for now I locked away the emotion and busied myself with brushing my mother's hair. Still silver blond and long—I refused to let the sanatorium cut it—it was the one thing that still matched my memories.

As I brushed, I spoke quietly, telling my mother tales of the life "Miss Everton" supposedly led. A neat, respectable life, working for a modiste and renting a small flat in Bodwell, one of the human boroughs a few miles from Temple Heights where the sanatorium was located.

It was a pretty picture and sometimes I wished I really was that girl, working quietly in a world free from intrigue and violence.

Though I'd probably be bored stupid within days. Nothing ever really happened here. The "doctor" who ran the place wasn't a healer . . . the sanatorium was a place for those the healers couldn't really help, those whose minds rather than bodies were broken. Regardless, he was well trained and his staff was kind. It was the best I could do for my mother—give her a peaceful place to live out her days.

I intended to keep her here, which was why, as far as the sanatorium was concerned, I was Miss Everton and my mother was a widow who'd never gotten over her lost husband. A twisted version of the truth really.

I wasn't ashamed of my past, but this was not the sort of place that would accept a failed whore and her half-Fae bastard daughter as suitable clientele. So Miss Everton I would be.

As long as my mother needed me to be.

*   *   *

The lingering sadness of my morning's visit had almost lifted when I reached the door of my salon around noon. I'd occupied myself on the hackney ride back trying to remind myself of the good news I had to share. My charms had decanted enough information to keep my client happy the previous evening, plus my trip to the Blood Assembly to bring her said information had been blessedly uneventful. On top of that the costume mistress at the Gilt had commissioned not one but three dresses for the new diva.

The last would be welcome news to Regina.

"Reggie," I called as I let myself in, "I have news. Is there tea?" I locked the door behind me. The salon wasn't open today.

"I'm in the workroom," Reggie replied, voice slightly muffled. I made my way across the tiny reception room where we met our clientele and pushed past the green velvet curtain into the back room.

Regina Foss—Reggie to me—stood regarding the half-finished dress on the mannequin in the center of the room with a considering frown. Her lips were pressed around several glass-topped pins.

"Tea?" I repeated, and she waved a hand toward the sideboard where a pot sat steaming gently. I poured myself a cup gratefully. The kitchen at the Swallow didn't really come to life until midday. Between six and midday, one was left to the tender mercies of the assistant cook. Who invariably offered stewed tea and burned coffee. I hadn't wanted to stop anywhere on the way to Bodwell, in case I was late for Mama.

Reggie, on the other hand, made perfect tea, hot and strong.

And sweet, after I stirred in the sugar she wrinkled her nose at. She should've been the one with Fae heritage. The Fae specialized in complicated herbal brews they wouldn't dream of sullying with sugar. But her mother and unknown father were both human. The strange thing was, Reggie, blond, blue-eyed, and sweet-faced, resembled my mother far more than I did. My father had stamped his connection to me clearly. A fact I resented each time I looked in the mirror.

I sipped tea and waited for Reggie to finish making whatever decision she was contemplating. Finally she altered the width of a pleat before placing her pins. When she straightened, pushing wisps of hair back into her neatly coiled bun, I had nearly finished my cup and was considering a second.

Reggie studied the gown for a moment before giving a pleased nod and turning her attention to me with a smile. There were shadows under her eyes, and her plain navy blue dress looked somewhat crumpled.

"Did you work through the night again?" Reggie tended to lose track of time when she was in the throes of creation.

She shook her head. "I got some sleep." Her eyes flicked guiltily to the long, low sofa against the wall. It was intended for our customers to use during fittings. More often than not it was where Reggie catnapped during her all-nighters.

"How much sleep?" Probably no more than me, but I needed less sleep than a human. "Do I have to start sending someone to escort you home again?" I shook my head at her, not entirely joking. "You know you don't need to work so hard. We're doing well."

"I wanted to finish this. Mrs. Bailey is always so pleased when we finish early."

So she should be, the old shrew. Mrs. Bailey was married to the man who owned half of Lower Watt. She did her best to spend the money he made and was one of our best customers, but each new order was a test of Reggie's patience as trims and colors and designs were debated and fussed with endlessly. Which was why I largely let Reggie deal with our customers. I probably would've brained the old bat with the teapot by now.

"Well, make sure you rest this afternoon," I said. "We have a new commission from the Gilt." I rummaged in my carpetbag for my notebook.

I'd finally captured Reggie's interest. She turned away from the mannequin, joining me at the worktable. I winced a little as I sat down. I'd stiffened up in the ride back from Temple Heights. I felt as though I'd, well, fallen off a building. Two bands of livid purple across my upper and lower back had greeted me in the mirror this morning and I ached all over. Some of the bruises had darker patches in perfect circles.

Next time I fell off a building, I would make sure I was caught by someone wearing something far more comfortable than a mail shirt. Or land on a haystack. Of course, the more sensible thing to do would be not to fall off the building at all. Even if that meant missing out on being saved by handsome knights.

"Holly?" Reggie's voice dragged my attention back to reality. "Are you well?"

I blinked, then nodded. "Yes, perfectly, thank you." I spread the notebook open, showing her my sketches. "These are for the new production. *The Courtesan's Lament.*"

Reggie reached for the drawings. "These are for the courtesan?"

"Right. First act, white before she's seduced. Then the purple for the middle and red for the final act." The wardrobe mistress had given me a quick outline of the story. Typical theatrical rubbish, romanticizing life. Being a courtesan was hard, and falling from that position was harder still. It wasn't all beautiful gowns and handsome lovers.

"And the hero?" Reggie asked.

"There are two. A mysterious Beast and the faithful human swain. Three guesses as to how that ends."

"With tears and beautiful singing as one dies?"

I nodded.

Reggie snorted. We had much the same opinion about the appeal of operatic plots. Like me, Reggie was the daughter of a former employee of the Dove. Like me, she'd pulled herself up from that life to quasi respectability. Or maybe near respectability, in her case. After all, she was truly a modiste, not a thief and a spy who mostly pretended to be a modiste.

Though, in fact, our arrangement was a partnership. I drew designs and Reggie executed them, generally improving the dresses in the process. I gave her the lion's share of our income, though she didn't currently know that. My other activities brought me enough income to pay my mother's expenses and mine and I wanted Reggie to have some security if anything ever happened to me. Along with Fen, she was one of my closest friends. I didn't want any of us ending up like our mothers.

"Did Madame Petrovich give you the new diva's measurements?"

"Of course." I nodded at the notebook. "They're on the next page. The diva will deign to be fitted at the Gilt once you've done the muslins."

"I'm sure that will be delightful," Reggie said. She copied down the measurements. "They might take a while . . . that third one is complicated with the train and the cloak and all that beading. Let me make more tea and you can tell me all about last night."

For a horrible moment I thought she meant the Templar and the roof, but then I realized she meant my interview with Madame Petrovich. I summoned a smile. "Excellent plan."

We spent another hour or so going over the designs, me explaining my ideas while Reggie suggested alterations and additions. As I stood to make yet another pot of tea, there was a rattling of the doorknob and a voice piped, "'ullo in there. Looking for Miss Evendale."

I frowned slightly. Most of my customers were women and they, apart from a select few, tended to come here rather than summon me. The kinds of people who looked for the Owl knew to go through the Swallow. So who was looking for me?

I stuck my head through the curtain. A small boy peered through the glass, his expression brightening as he spotted me. Even curiouser. He didn't look like a servant, more like one of the street rats who made a living overcharging anyone they could pester or con into giving them small jobs and errands.

"You Miss Evendale?" he yelled in a squeaky bellow.

I walked over and unlocked the door. The boy stepped back as I opened it a crack. "I can get a message to her," I said, not wanting to confirm my identity.

"I were told only to give this to Miss Evendale herself." He waved an envelope at me and I caught sight of a familiar seal. Damn.

I held out my hand for the envelope. "I'm Miss Evendale."

He looked suspiciously at me from under the peak of his grubby cap, for a moment reminding me of the Templar, then grudgingly handed me the envelope.

"Hold on a moment," I said, and went to get a tip. Street rat he might be, but I didn't like to think of him going hungry.

The boy's eyes widened gratefully when he took the shilling. "Any reply, miss?"

"No. Not now."

He shrugged and left. I locked the door again and carried the envelope into the workroom, laying it on the table beside my notebook. I sat regarding it with disfavor, wondering whether I should have pretended ignorance of Miss Evendale. But the one who'd written this note would find me in the end.

He always did.

Reggie lifted her head from the notes she was making on the diva's dresses. "Is something wrong?"

I sighed. "No. An errand to run, is all."

"Are you sure? You look pale."

"Just tired," I fibbed. "It was a late night last night by the time I was done at the Gilt. And Mama was having a bad morning."

She nodded, eyes full of sympathy, and turned back to her notes. She didn't pry, Reggie. She listened if I wanted to talk, but she didn't demand information. It was one of the reasons I liked her so much.

I gathered up my things. "I'll come back after, if I can. Otherwise, tomorrow. Make sure you get some rest."

She lifted her eyes once more and smiled. "I'll be here."

I blew her a kiss and left. It was nearly noon now and the streets of Gillygate were bustling. As border boroughs went, Gillygate was the least disreputable. Mostly human poor rather than Night Worlders and its shared border with Bellefleurs along the western edge, where the cathedral and the Templar Brother House were, tended to keep things more peaceful than elsewhere.

The streets were safe during the day as long as one was sensible. Which was the reason I'd chosen it for the salon. It was the safest place for Reggie to be, and the location wouldn't deter any potential customers. At least, not any potential customers who were the sort of women who would frequent a border borough modiste.

I ducked around a pie cart and crossed the street to the underground. Gills End Station was a minor one, being so close to Melchior, but it was on the correct line for where I wanted to go. I was unlikely to find a hackney or an autocab willing to take me to my destination, and walking would take too long and be too dangerous even at this time of day.

When I emerged thirty minutes or so later into the streets of Sorrows Hill, the mood was entirely different. Quieter for one thing in the middle of the day. Which made sense when many of the residents would be sleeping the day around underground.

Not that the lack of Blood made the streets any safer during the day. I hooked a see-me-not charm onto the button of my glove. It wasn't the same as invisibility but would make me less likely to draw unwanted attention.

I had my cutthroat under my skirts and a pistol in my bag, but I preferred not to get into trouble in the first place to having to try and fight my way out of it.

Luckily my destination was in the opposite direction to the main Blood warren and not too far from the station. Since Lucius had died or vanished or whatever it actually was that had happened, there had been an increased amount of violence around the warrens and I was more than happy to avoid them.

Still, by the time I lifted the ornate brass knocker on the door of the redbrick town house, I was cursing the one who'd called me here for more than the usual reasons.

After all, he had more than one residence available to choose from in the City. Hell, he could even have summoned me to Summerdale—or one of the nearby villages given he was unlikely to ask a half-breed to actually enter the Veiled World.

Making me traipse across the town and into danger was another way of him making a point. That I would come when he called. Whenever and wherever.

My father is like that.

I didn't know the tall, handsome young man who opened the door so I simply gave my name. He nodded with a half bow and ushered me up the stairs into a sitting room.

"I'm here," I said as my father turned from the window.

Cormen sa'Inviel'astar studied me for a moment.

I gazed back. My father is horribly handsome, in the way of the Fae. His hair is a deep gleaming brown, the color of polished mahogany or very expensive brandy, and his eyes are true bronze, unlike the strange light green-brown shade of mine. It's easy to see why my mother was so enchanted by him. Especially as he looks no older now than he does in my earliest memories of him.

His Family name means "bright night over the hills" or something close enough to it, and I suppose to some he shines like the evening star. I know to my mother he does. Even now, despite everything he's done to her.

But to me, he's simply the bastard who fathered me and destroyed my mother.

He frowned slightly at me and I resisted the urge to rub my chest, where his damned pendant lay hidden beneath my clothes. The gold suddenly seemed cold against my skin. I hated the weight of it. Hated what it represented.

Not an acknowledgment of me as his child, no, for that he would need to give me a Family ring, and one of my fingers would be covered from knuckle to knuckle with a veritable blaze of jewels. No, this was something different. More a brand to my way of thinking, marking me as belonging to him if anyone else should come poaching.

It was spelled, so I couldn't take it off. Which had led to some interesting episodes in bed, but I usually claimed it had too much sentimental value to remove. Hardly the truth, but the men I took to my bed were there for things other than interest in my sentiments.

I was sometimes tempted to wear it outside my clothes, hoping somebody might try to steal it. But they'd have to cut off my head to achieve that aim. So I kept it hidden from view.

Much as my father kept me hidden from the view of the Veiled World. Though, to be fair, most of the Fae who produced half-breeds did that. Some, though, had the decency to leave those offspring alone.

Not my father.

The silence stretched and I realized he was waiting for me to greet him more correctly.

"Sir." I inclined my head politely. No "Father" or "Papa" between us. No, things had to be properly respectful for the bastard and her sire.

He acknowledged me with a nod, much shallower than mine had been, then waved his hand toward the chair. "Sit."

I did so. Things would be over faster if I didn't make a fuss. And I preferred to spend as little time as possible with my father. My mother had mourned and missed him when he'd left. I'd hated him for abandoning us, for what he'd done to her. It was because of him I'd learned to harden my heart, set my eyes on my goals, and let nothing stop me. I'd learned to survive because I'd had to.

But I would never forgive him for changing from the indulgent charming father of my childhood to this distant stranger who seemed to view me as nothing more important than a possession he kept on a seldom-viewed shelf, to be taken out and put to use occasionally.

I had, from time to time, spied for him. For a price. I charged him more than my other clients. I figured he owed me that much. After all, a good portion of my money went toward keeping Mama in comfort at the sanatorium. And it was no one's fault but his that she needed such a refuge in the first place.

I crossed my hands neatly in my lap and stared up at him. I

wasn't going to ask first. No, if he wanted something, he could be the one asking.

"I have a task for you," he said, voice cool.

"Oh?" My stomach curled a little. Damn. It was barely six months since the last task I'd performed for him, retrieving a trinket he'd misplaced in a Beast pack house. Probably while fucking the daughter of the Alpha. That was Cormen's usual mode. Screw someone over or screw something up and call in someone else to clean up his bloody mess.

"There's some information I wish to acquire."

Damn. Not even stealing. Spying. Spying was always more complicated. I set my teeth, forced myself to a politely encouraging smile.

"It involves the humans."

I bounced out of the chair. *"No."*

I didn't spy on the human world. Denizens of the Night World and the border boroughs, yes. Any humans there had made their choices. But the rest of the human world was off-limits. Too dangerous. Human laws were much stricter about transgressions involving the human boroughs. I had no desire to hang or lose a hand.

"Sit down," he snapped.

I stood my ground. "No. Spying on humans is too risky."

"You won't come to any harm."

"Oh? And how do you intend to guarantee that?"

"You keep telling me that you're good at what you do. If you are, there is no risk."

"What if I'm not as good as I think I am?"

He waved a dismissive hand, as if that were of no importance to him. It probably wasn't. He believed that I wouldn't rat him out if I ever fell foul of the law. I wasn't so sure but didn't want his attention to turn to my mother with a vengeful purpose, so I probably would hold my tongue. He wouldn't care what happened to me, of course, only what affect the knowledge of his offspring being so careless and troublesome might have on his standing within the Family and the court.

I stared at him. What game was he playing anyway? Why spy on the humans? The Veiled Queen was a tireless supporter of the treaty and maintaining peace between the races and wouldn't look kindly on those who wished to take a different tack, from what I heard in the Night World gossip mills.

Then my heart sank a little because I realized that if there were those arrogant enough to try and stage some sort of rebellion or coup amongst the Fae, blinded enough by their own sense of self-worth and self-importance to take on the might of the Veiled Queen, then my father would definitely be amongst their number. He had always been astonishingly certain of his inestimable value and exalted place in the world.

"What is so important that you need me?" I asked. I phrased my question carefully. Nothing that could be taken as agreement. Not yet. You had to watch your words amongst the Fae. They didn't lie, but they could misdirect with the best of them. They also considered someone's word to be binding. So I wasn't giving any hint of agreement at this stage.

"You have heard of the sunmage, Simon DuCaine?"

My heart took another little dive south. Shit. If the rumors were to be believed, it was trying to assassinate Simon DuCaine that had ultimately brought about Lucius' downfall. Lucius who had ruled the Blood and the Night World with an iron-spiked fist for several centuries. And now my father wanted to tangle with him?

More to the point, wanted *me* to tangle with him?

"Yes, I know about him." Most people did. Simon was a Master Healer at St. Giles, the biggest hospital in the human boroughs. St. Giles was a Haven, sanctuary to any who claimed it, and Simon was famous throughout the City for treating anyone who sought his help. Plus he was powerful, the strongest sunmage to come along for quite some time. They said he could call sunlight at night. *Please, please, please, let it not be him.*

"Then you must know that he is suspected of being involved in the death of the Blood Lord."

"I've heard rumors," I said cautiously, brain working fast. Did Cormen have proof? That would be worth quite a bit to a number of my clients.

"I believe the rumors to be true," he said. "Sources tell me that he is living with Lucius' shadow. That he is going to marry her."

His tone was incredulous. The Fae hate wraiths, which was what Lucius' former chief assassin was. I've never quite figured out what makes wraiths different from the rest of us half-breeds—for one thing, I've never been able to confirm exactly what parentage a wraith has—but I know that they are abominations to the Fae instead of mere annoying embarrassments or mistakes to be largely ignored like the rest of us.

For a moment I envied her—this woman who had such a fearsome reputation in the Night World for merciless death. If my father would only decide I was an abomination, then he might leave me alone.

For good.

"Is that what you want me to find out? If he is marrying the wraith?" I didn't think it would be. Such a thing would be far too easy to confirm using whatever "sources" he maintained in the human world.

He shook his head, so his hair shone redly in the sunlight filtering through the lacy curtains. He wore it long, past his shoulders, though not so long as the Blood Lords. Vanity.

"No. I wish to find out why it was that Lucius marked him for death."

My mouth went dry. There it was. One of the biggest mysteries in the Night World. What had happened between Lucius and the sunmage? Lucius had apparently not survived it. Yet my father wanted me to poke around and see what I could find out.

I had no illusions that something or someone powerful enough to put an end to Lucius would have no difficulty disposing of me if I came to their attention for trying to find out their secrets. I shook my head. "No. It's too dangerous."

"This is not a request," he said in a low voice.

"The answer's still no. I'm not risking my life by getting in the middle of this. It's got politics and treachery written all over it." My father's interest was the ultimate proof of that.

He cocked his head slightly, looking bored. "I was afraid that you would take this attitude. How many times have I told you that you need to cultivate the proper respect?"

I straightened my spine. "Respectfully, no," I repeated.

He sighed. "Then you leave me with no choice." He made a gesture and suddenly I was frozen in place, my brain recognizing the movement a split second too late to react.

"You wouldn't," I spat.

"If you would be reasonable, I wouldn't have to," he said, making it sound as though this was all my fault.

I tried to move, but everything below my neck had effectively turned to stone. For a moment I wondered, if I said that I would do as he wished, would he release me? But then he made another gesture and it was too late to do anything.

I felt the spell settle over me like an invisible net, feeling sticky and somehow dirty as it clung to my skin. It clogged my mouth and throat so I couldn't even scream the outrage I felt.

A geas. A fucking geas. One of the nastiest forms of Fae magic, one most of them avoided.

Rage flared, hot and furious, made worse because, by some quirk of nature, most Fae magics didn't touch me.

Part of the reason the Fae didn't like half-breeds was that no two of us were the same in terms of what we could or couldn't do. The Fae don't approve of disorder and surprises. Not being susceptible to other Fae's magic had served me well. I could see through glamours and avoid spells. Of course, the other side of that coin was my own talent largely being limited to working on myself and usually fading quickly on anyone else.

But Cormen's magic always worked on me. He said it was because of our shared blood. Another reason I had always avoided going to Summerdale and the Veiled World. I didn't want to discover whether other members of his Family could bespell me at will.

"Holly," he said. It was the first time I'd heard him use my name in years. A geas requires a name. "Holly, you will hear my words and obey."

The invisible net sank a little deeper, burning my skin now as the geas tightened its grip. Tears stung my eyes as I stared at him, hoping the look on my face told him exactly what I thought of him and his stinking magic.

A geas—a binding—overrides free will and forces you to do the caster's bidding. Under the terms of the treaty, the Fae were forbidden to cast them on humans. Lucky for my father, I was exempt from that protection because of my half-breed status.

"You will go to the sunmage Simon DuCaine and you will find out his secret," Cormen said. "You will tell no one but me what you discover."

The geas snapped tight, searing pain, shooting through me as it clasped, snagging me with the sensation of sharp claws shredding my skin and brain. The sensation of something crawling through my brain, leaving a slimy trail, made me want to vomit.

One final agonizing pulse and suddenly the pain vanished,

leaving me free to move. I fell to my knees, retching, still feeling as though my insides were coated in slime.

I didn't actually throw up, much as I would dearly have loved to spatter Cormen's perfectly shining boots. But I couldn't find the strength to stand.

My father continued to speak, this time muttering soft Fae words that I couldn't quite make out. Adding some more nasty tangles to his magic. My stomach heaved, though the pain didn't return.

When he stopped speaking and I was sure I wouldn't fall down again if I rose, I forced myself to my feet, hands clenched. He could drag me through the seven depths of hell before I gave him the satisfaction of one more second of reaction than I was forced to.

"Now what?" I asked. "You can't imagine that he's unprotected, this sunmage. Am I meant to casually introduce myself into his world? I hardly have the right sort of connections for that." The DuCaines were part of the upper echelons of human society, an old family that had both money and magic running through its pedigree.

Cormen actually smiled at me. I resisted the urge to spit in his face.

"As to that, I think the easiest way would be for you to go to St. Giles. That's where he works."

"But I'm not hurt—" This time my brain wasn't quite so slow. I got three steps toward the door before Cormen froze me again.

He walked around me so that I could see his face. "As to that," he said with another brilliant smile, "I have arranged matters." His smile took on a nasty edge. "It will only hurt for a short time. They will heal you at St. Giles."

The door to the room swung open suddenly and a different servant stepped through the door. Not the pretty young man. No, this man was older and harder and, unless I was mistaken, Beast Kind.

"Please, don't," I said, fighting rising terror. "I'll think of another way."

Cormen frowned, smoothing his cuffs as he looked at me. His eyes might as well have been made of the bronze they resembled. They lacked any hint of compassion or remorse. "No. This is faster." He turned to the other man. "I will loosen the hold a little so you can move her if necessary."

Blood pounded in my ears and for a moment I thought I would faint as the man started rolling up his shirtsleeves. For one surreal moment I wondered what would have happened if I had fainted while my father had frozen my body. Then the terror drove any thought other than what was about to happen from my head.

"Not the hands. And try not to damage her face *too* much," Cormen said as he headed toward the door. "She's a pretty thing for a *hai-salai*. There's a shield on the room so no one will hear. Do what is necessary."

As he reached the door, the Beast reached for me with a look half sympathy, half anticipation on his face. He gripped my arm and, as my father left the room, neatly snapped my forearm. I screamed my father's name before the next blow connected with my face. But I knew no one was listening.

Chapter Four

HOLLY

I came to as I landed on something hard. Tears blinded me as I lay, half-winded, struggling to breathe and to adjust to the pain consuming me. Tentatively, I flattened my right hand and felt around me. The pain bit even harder and I froze again, gasping. Beneath my damp palm, the surface was smooth, faintly warm and slick.

Marble, perhaps?

Hospital, something in the far reaches of my brain managed to mutter.

I opened my eyes a crack. That hurt too. But it confirmed that I was indeed lying on marble somewhere out in the open. Sun glared into my eyes, making everything blurred and dazzling through the tears. In the distance I could see more marble—steps leading to a building with a dome rising from the roof.

St. Giles?

My location didn't really concern me. No, what had my attention was the way everything hurt. I wanted to surrender to the waves of dizziness and let them carry me down into the darkness. But I fought them, unwilling to give in. Not when I couldn't remember exactly what had happened. I might still be in danger.

Footsteps tapped across the marble toward me. I curled reflexively into a ball. Which only made everything hurt more. In my next life I was going to try being a boring everyday person who didn't get beaten up. A real live shop girl. Something normal. But even as that thought rose, I remembered my father's face as he instructed the man to hurt me and everything came flooding back with a vengeance.

The beating. The geas. My task.

Bile rose in my throat and I coughed, trying not to retch.

"Miss?" The voice was male. Carefully soft and nonthreatening. Reassuring. "Miss, can you hear me?"

My throat hurt. But I swallowed and somehow managed to croak, "Yes."

"You're at St. Giles," the voice said. "We'll take care of you now."

Good. That was good. More footsteps and then hands lifting me. At which point, the world went black and everything went away again.

When I woke for the second time, I lay on something soft. All right, so that was a small improvement. I still hurt, though, every inch of me aching or throbbing, so maybe I hadn't been unconscious for very long. Surely they would have healed me if I had been? I opened my eyes carefully.

A man wearing a healer green tunic stood at the foot of my bed watching me. His eyes were a summer-sky sort of blue, warm and comforting.

He smiled at me with a friendly nod. "Good, you're awake." His voice was soothing, a warm, low tone that somehow projected reassurance and confidence.

"Doesn't feel good," I managed.

"No, I would imagine that it doesn't," he replied, smile vanishing, eyes cooling. He ran a hand through darkish gold hair, then fished a notebook out of his pocket. "I'll do something about that shortly. Who did this to you?"

His voice was edged with anger. Not directed at me and for that I was grateful. He was tall, this healer. Not quite as broad-shouldered as the Templar but still strong. For a moment I saw the Beast lifting his hand to strike me and had to close my eyes and swallow hard. I was safe now.

"Who did this?" the healer repeated, his tone gentled somewhat.

I felt the geas tighten my throat with greasy claws. Apparently Cormen had indeed included some extra commands in those last Fae mutterings. I couldn't make my mouth work to tell the truth. I ransacked my brain for a plausible story, and the pressure eased when I decided on one. "N-no one. F-fell," I said shakily. "Stairs."

The healer's mouth went flat. "You can tell me the truth. St. Giles is a Haven. If someone's hurting you, we'll keep you safe."

"Stairs," I repeated.

He shook his head at me. "If you insist." He paused and watched me silently, giving me time to change my story. I stayed quiet.

"Do you know your name?"

"Holly." Apparently I was allowed to keep that much. "Holly Ev-Everton." I couldn't get my real surname out. Seemed Cormen had thought of everything. No chance of anyone tying Evendale—the bastardized human form of his name—back to him.

"I'm Master Healer DuCaine. Simon."

Lords of hell. I managed not to react. Just.

Damn. Why did it have to be him?

As much as I wanted to complete my task and free myself from the geas, I hated the thought of giving my father the satisfaction. A pain shot down my arm as I shifted slightly on the pillows, and I bit my lip, trying not to moan.

"All right," Simon said. "Enough questions. I'm going to examine you now."

I eased my head down to the pillow as Simon did various healer things . . . touching my arms and face gently and making rumbly disapproving noises to accompany the frowning disapproval on his face. When the door suddenly opened, we both turned our heads. The motion made me groan. And the groan deepened as I recognized the man who stepped into the room. The damned Templar. What was *he* doing here?

"Simon, I have—" He stopped suddenly and stared at me. "What's *she* doing here?"

One of Simon's eyebrows lifted. "Do you know her?"

The knight nodded, a curt up and down. "We had an . . . encounter last night."

He stared down at me with a look of disapproval far more personal than Simon's. As he did so, I was suddenly struck by the resemblance between them. Both tall, strong. Both blue-eyed and blond though the Templar's eyes were paler and his hair much lighter. Far more like winter sun than summer.

But they had the same square jaw and strong, square hands. The Templar was maybe an inch shorter than Simon but made up for it with muscle. His face, a darker shade of gold than Simon's, had stronger angles that, combined with the scar, made him look far more ruthless than the healer. But the resemblance was unmistakably there. Which meant my mystery knight was most likely Guy DuCaine.

Simon's brother.

A Templar almost as legendary for his unrelenting stance against the Night World as Simon was for his unstinting generosity as a healer.

A man whose dedication to his faith and calling was etched into the very skin of his body.

I stared at the blazing red crosses tattooed on his hands, cursing the Lady and anybody else who came to mind. I'd fallen into the arms of not just any knight but one of the most ruthless of them all. Brother to the man my father had sent me to betray. As Fen would've put it, it seemed the Lady was spitting in my eye today.

I let my eyes flutter closed, trying to look innocent.

"You know her?" Simon said, sounding surprised. "It wasn't the Templars—"

"We don't beat up women, little brother, you know that." The Templar sounded disgusted. His words confirmed my guess at his identity. "She was perfectly well when I left her."

Heavy footsteps approached the bed. "What happened?" he went on.

I wasn't sure if Guy—for it was his deep rumble doing the questioning—was addressing his question to Simon or me. Better to stay silent, I decided. Less chance of messing up while I was muzzy-headed from pain and shock.

"She was dumped outside about half an hour ago," Simon said. I heard him come closer to the bed. If I was following things correctly, the brothers were standing side by side, probably staring down at me. Wonderful. I did my best impression of properly swooned young lady.

"Is she going to be all right?"

"I'm still assessing her. But she's got broken bones. She's going to be here a little while."

Yet another reason for my father to be pleased. I tried not to frown, focusing on keeping up my pretense of insensibility.

"She give a name?"

Guy's accent had shifted a little, become longer and drawn out. Not a City accent. I wondered where he'd picked it up. Simon's voice was standard wealthy educated human without the slang and slurs of the poor.

"Hers? Holly Everton."

"No. Whoever did this to her."

"She says she fell down some stairs."

Guy snorted at this. "I can see you're not asleep," he said, and this time there was no mistaking whom he was addressing. "Might as well open your eyes."

I did so grudgingly. Pale blue eyes bored into mine. I fought the urge to burrow under the covers.

"Another fall?" he said. "What happened? The stairs in your building rusted too?"

"Yes," I said shortly, lifting my chin. Then I winced because moving my head sent fiery spikes down the right side of my face from temple to jaw. What the hell had Cormen's pet Beast done to me? I didn't remember all the details. I hoped I wouldn't remember all the details. I remembered the anger, though. Underneath the pain, that still burned hot and bright.

Guy's expression didn't change. "You should find other accommodations. That place seems . . . unhealthy."

"I'll take it into consideration," I said. He loomed over the bed, making me feel small. He'd left his mail at home today, clad in just a loose white shirt over gray trousers and long, well-worn black boots. Off duty, it seemed. He wore a sword—not the massive one I'd noticed slung between his shoulders last night, thank goodness—at his hip. The sword belt also housed a pistol and some sort of dagger in a sheath. Only three weapons. That probably counted as off duty for a Templar.

But the lack of armor did reduce the sheer physical impact of him. I tried to lever myself up on one elbow, so as not to feel quite so intimidated. Mistake. Everything went swimmy and black again.

". . . off the fucking roof," Guy was saying as I came back to consciousness. This fainting business was growing tiresome. I'd only ever fainted once in my life before. They were going to think I was some sort of weak and stupid female.

Then again, that was what I wanted them to think. People underestimated weak and stupid females. And didn't pay them much attention. Useful if you're a spy.

"That explains the odd bruises on her back," Simon said. "Did she say what she was doing up there?"

"Some nonsense about a weather vane creaking."

"What was she actually doing?"

"I don't know but if she was fixing a weather vane, then I'm a Nightseeker."

I thought it might be wise to interrupt this conversation before Guy could speculate any further. I let out a soft moan.

Simon—well, I assumed it was Simon—laid a hand on my forehead. "Back with us, are you? Good. I'm going to fix some things now and then I'll work more on your arm later, when you've had a chance to rest. You're in shock."

That much I could have figured out myself. I nodded slowly and carefully. Simon's hands moved to either side of my head, and a cool sensation flowed through my skull. The throbbing in my face eased.

"Ohhh," I said in relief. "I like you."

Guy snorted. But it was an amused snort. "He's taken."

I lifted an eyelid. I'm not sure what possessed me. Shock or some deeper instinct that told me there was one way to unnerve the big, strong knight. "That's unfortunate," I said. "Does he have a brother?" Let him think I had really been asleep and hadn't heard what he'd called Simon.

This time it was Simon who laughed. "Yes, I do. Though he isn't a healer." He nodded at Guy. "We had to throw him to the Templars to find a use for him." His tone was affectionate. Guy rolled his eyes, as though this was a very old joke.

"Really?" I murmured. "Well, he does look as though he might be good with his hands."

Guy's face went stiff, blue eyes widening.

"That," Simon said, now sounding highly amused, "is something you'll have to find out for yourself. My fiancée's cat likes him, if that's any help."

The cool sensation flowed farther down my body, and pain receded as it rolled over me. I could get used to this, I decided. I'd never had need of a healer. Another gift of my Fae heritage was an immunity to most of the human diseases that plagued the border boroughs, and I hadn't ever injured myself beyond what some of my half-breed friends could heal before.

I opened the other eye and pursed my lips as I studied Guy. "Good with animals. That's always a promising sign."

Guy's expression went, if anything, even stiffer. "I have to go," he said abruptly. "Let me know if she changes her mind about telling you who did this." He took a step toward the door.

Simon caught his arm. "Wait, didn't you come here for something?"

"One of the novices broke his arm at practice. I'll ask Bryony to take care of it." He made a stiff half bow. "Miss Everton."

The door swung shut behind him as he beat a swift retreat.

Dimples flashed in Simon's cheeks as he grinned after his brother. "Exactly what happened on that roof?" he asked.

"Nothing. I fell, he caught me."

"I see."

"Any more DuCaine brothers likely to come visit me?" I asked, wanting to steer the conversation into safer waters.

"No. He's the only one."

I bit down the instinctive "Thank the Lady," and thought for a moment, trying to come up with what a polite young lady would say in this circumstance. Might as well keep up the charade, even if my ground was looking shaky. "Your mama must be proud of the two of you."

"She'd prefer one of us did what we were supposed to and took over the family business," Simon said with another laugh. He really was a very attractive man. But somehow, it was the other DuCaine who had me intrigued and on edge.

"Ah," I said. "I know that story." Not exactly, but Cormen would definitely prefer it if I did what he wanted me to all the time and toed the line. I wondered what Mama DuCaine really thought of her two sons. Simon's tone was light, so whatever maternal pressure she might be bringing to bear, it didn't seem as though the relationship was strained.

A pang of envy struck. What was it like to have normal parents? A family? Brothers and sisters? I had Fen and Reggie, but it wasn't quite the same thing.

Reggie. Damn. I'd forgotten about her. I needed to send her a note. Maybe I could ask one of the orderlies to arrange it. She'd worry. I didn't want to ask Simon. The fewer clues the

DuCaines had about me, the better. The question was whether an orderly could be trusted not to tell anyone else.

I would think about it later, I decided.

Simon worked a little more of his healer magic, then helped me sit straighter, propped on some pillows. He wrote in his notebook for a minute or two, then tucked it away and pulled a chair up beside the bed.

"All right, Holly. This is how it is. You had some internal bleeding and I've staunched that and eased the bruises. You have three cracked ribs and a broken arm. The arm's the worst and I'll need to do more work on that. But whatever we do, it will take a week or so before everything is properly healed. You're half Fae—"

"How did you know that?"

"I healed you. Fae and humans feel different."

"Oh." So much for keeping my heritage a secret. Then I had a far more unpleasant thought . . . if he could sense I was half Fae, could he by any chance sense the geas? I searched his face for any indication he knew I was here under a binding. But if he did, he wasn't letting on.

"I won't tell anyone if you prefer it not to be known. But it will be on your record here, and the other healers will have to know. It changes how you're treated. Do you heal as Fae do?"

"I heal a little faster than humans, but not much," I admitted. That was one of the reasons my father had chosen this particular ploy, I imagined. He knew if I was injured badly enough, they'd have to keep me here.

Simon nodded. "Is there anyone in Summerdale who should be informed you are here?"

It was a polite way of asking whether I was acknowledged by a Family. I shook my head, trying not to feel the old familiar sting. "No. No one."

His expression stayed carefully professional. "I wasn't sure because of your pendant."

"That's just a keepsake," I lied. I didn't want to explain my father's choke chain to this man, of all people. I might not even be able to, depending on exactly how Cormen had hobbled me with the geas.

"It's bespelled?"

Nerves prickled. He could sense that? And the chain was a tiny enchantment. Not like a geas. "Yes, so I won't lose it." Another lie.

I couldn't tell if he believed me or not, but he didn't ask any more questions. Instead he gave me a strict list of things I wasn't to attempt to do.

When I nodded obediently, he added, "You understood, before, when I told you St. Giles is a Haven?"

"Yes."

"Do you need haven, Holly?" he asked gently.

Can you keep me away from my father? I bit my tongue so I wouldn't ask the question out loud. "No." I shook my head cautiously. Tempting as the thought of haven was, sooner or later I'd have to leave the hospital. After all, I had a life. A business. Two, even. People depended on me.

I couldn't hide from my father in these bright, clean rooms.

And while I was here, I was perfectly positioned to study this man who was being nothing but kind to me. Study him and do what my father wanted to do. Find and betray his secrets. Perhaps even put his life at risk.

Hatred boiled up in me, fresh and hot. If I'd had any power that was useful, I would've killed my father. But at the thought, the geas tightened again, making me suddenly greasily nauseated.

"Are you feeling all right?" Simon asked sharply.

"A little faint," I admitted, leaning against the pillows and swallowing hard until the feeling subsided. Simon's fingers caught my wrist, found my pulse, and he fell silent, a small frown of concentration wrinkling his forehead. I stared up at the ceiling, which was painted the same plain white as the rest of the room, hoping like hell he couldn't sense the magic controlling me.

I didn't know a lot about how one worked a geas . . . it was beyond the reach of my power and therefore something I'd never been taught, but I knew they somehow interacted with your own magic if you had any. So maybe he couldn't sense it. Maybe there was nothing to sense. I fervently hoped so.

As far as I knew, it wasn't unknown in the Veiled Court for a geas to be used as a weapon, so maybe they were truly undetectable.

Simon finally released my wrist. "You need something to eat and drink. Healing depletes your energy stores. I'll get something sent up, and then you can rest for a while before we work on the arm some more. In the meantime, I'll block the pain for you." This time, his fingers rested on my shoulder, three of them positioned in very precise spots. There was another quick cool tingle. Then my arm went dead.

The relief from pain was pleasant even if the overall sensation was unnerving. "Thank you," I said. "You've been very kind."

"It's my job," he said with a don't-mention-it wave of his hand.

"Healing is your job," I corrected. "Being kind is extra."

That won me another smile. I realized I hadn't yet seen his brother smile fully. Simon's smiled made me wonder what Guy's would be like. Would his face lighten and almost glow the way Simon's did? I imagined those blue eyes lit with laughter. It would be a dangerous combination, if I were any judge of men. Which, most of the time, I was. I shifted in the bed slightly. My ploy had worked to keep Guy off balance, but I needed to be careful. Play with fire and sometimes, you end up burned.

Guy
✝

I left Michael, the novice who'd discovered the hard way that fooling around with a mace is not a good idea, in the capable hands of Lady Bryony, the head healer of the hospital, and went to find Simon.

We'd argued to a standstill after I'd gone back to his house to remove the Beast's body, but I was determined to get him to see sense. Even more determined now that my mystery rooftop girl had turned up at the hospital. Her turning up at St. Giles, so close to the attack, made my survival instincts twitch.

I didn't like coincidences.

She was trouble. That much was becoming increasingly clear.

She'd looked different in the daylight, once I'd been able to see past the bruises darkening one side of her face. In the light of the sun, hers was a glistening mass of mixed brown and red. Not entirely human, that hair, the red a shade too red, the brown somehow too bronze in places. Somewhere in her ancestry was a Fae. Her eyes confirmed it. Set at slight angles, large, and, even shadowed with pain, a vivid green-flecked brown. Like something that belonged in a wood, growing free.

Shit. Now I was starting to sound like Simon. What did I care what she looked like? What mattered was what she'd been up to last night and what she was doing here at St. Giles.

My frustration turned my knock on Simon's office door into more of a thump.

"You didn't mention *her* this morning," Simon said as I let myself in without waiting to be invited.

I shut the door behind me. "There wasn't anything to mention." I tried to sound disinterested. I had no doubt Simon was going to have his moment of fun at my expense, but reacting would only inspire him to even further flights of fancy and brotherly harassment.

"Really? You left in an awful hurry back there."

I didn't have to turn my head to see the grin on his face. I could hear it, plain as day in his voice. "I had a novice to take care of. We need to talk, Simon."

Simon ignored me. "She's pretty. Beneath the bruises."

That was a pretty damned obvious change of subject. My hands clenched; I didn't want to start thinking about *her* again. Especially not about those bruises.

Stairs, she'd said. If she'd fallen down stairs, then I'd eat Gray's saddle. She'd been beaten. The only questions were why, and by who? The thought of anyone putting their hands on her made my stomach knot with something uncomfortably close to rage.

Rage I couldn't show or afford to indulge. Holly Everton wasn't an option. She might, however, be an enemy. "I didn't notice," I said. "Stop changing the subject."

Simon shook his head. "My subject is much more interesting than yours. And if you didn't notice that girl, I think it's time you took a leave of absence from the Brotherhood. They've obviously killed your appreciation for the female form."

"My appreciation of the female form is alive and well, thank you. Some of us just have some self-control and don't fall for every female we trip over."

Simon claimed he'd fallen for Lily the moment he'd laid eyes on her, even though she'd been trying to kill him at the time. I had more sense.

Simon grinned. "Looks as though she fell for you."

"Don't cut yourself on that razor wit, little brother. She's part Fae, isn't she?"

Simon's eyes narrowed a little. "Yes. Is there a problem with that?"

Touchy, my little brother. Lily was half Fae. The other half was unconfirmed. I didn't care about that, as well he knew. But I did want to know what I was up against. "No problem, just information." Now it was my turn to change the subject. "I don't like her turning up here today. It seems a little too much of a coincidence."

That caught Simon's attention. "Where exactly did you run into her last night?"

"Seven Harbors."

"Not the Night World."

"It's the next best thing," I pointed out. "And we were ambushed not long after we left her."

"I thought you said that was in Mickleskin."

"It was. But it wasn't that far from where she was."

"Would you be so concerned about her if it wasn't for the Beast attacks?"

I shrugged. "Maybe not. But my gut tells me there's a connection between the ambush and the attack on her, and she keeps appearing near both. It's convenient. Too convenient."

Simon tilted his head. "You're drawing conclusions from thin air. You don't know who this girl is, or what she does. She could be perfectly innocent."

"Maybe. Maybe not. Either way, I intend to find out."

"Don't do anything stupid."

"This from the man who refuses protection when he's being targeted."

He held up a hand. "Before you yell more about that, is there anything I can do for you? That must've been quite the catch. Are you hurt?"

"She doesn't weigh much," I said automatically, feeling the weight of her in my arms again, arms looped around my neck in that instinctive clasp. For someone who didn't weigh much, she was weighing on my mind today. Only because she was up to something, I told myself sternly.

Simon's smile broadened. "Is that so? Still, even a small weight can make quite an impact from a height. That pesky gravity."

"I'm fine, little brother. Save your voodoo for someone else,"

I said, mostly to annoy him. Having spent some years in the heat of the Voodoo Territories, I had a perfectly clear understanding of the differences between Simon's magic and that worked by the Vodouns, with their spirit rituals. Simon had never actually raised the dead, as far as I knew.

Though I'd never actually seen a Vodoun priest do that either, despite the rumors that they could call armies of mindless re-animated bodies to their bidding. Disgust twisted my stomach at the thought. Mindless bodies sounded too close to blood-locked humans. Though the blood-locked had no one to blame but themselves for their condition.

"Are you sure you don't want me to take a look?"

I folded my arms, ignoring the ache as I did so. I'd rather let the bruises heal naturally than put up with Simon trying to inter-rogate me about Holly for the next twenty minutes while he healed me.

"I said, I'm fine. You have patients." Including Holly. Who had all my instincts twitching, and not only the soldierly ones. Still, it was only the soldierly ones that I was going to indulge. Tonight, supposedly my night off, I would being going over to the border boroughs to see what there was to find out about the Favreau pack and a girl named Holly who might have a reason to be climbing around on rooftops at midnight.

In the end, my investigations had to wait a day. I pulled another night's extra patrol and then was forced to sleep. I was tired enough to risk accidentally chopping my own foot off with my sword. Not a good thing to be when I was about to go poking my nose into places that might not take kindly to it.

But when I woke, I was determined to see what I could find out. By the time I reached the fourth tavern, I was starting to think I was on a wild-goose chase. No one I questioned, or bullied—not even my usual sources—was prepared to admit knowing anything about a woman named Holly who might be involved in anything shady. And the few times I'd dropped even a hint of wanting information about a Beast, I killed any conver-sation stone dead and the men whose drinks I'd been buying had rapidly dispersed.

Maybe I was looking in the wrong places.

I'd started in Seven Harbors, scene of our infamous meeting, but the dark and dingy taverns and gaming hells of that borough didn't strike me as her likely haunts. She wasn't the young lady working in a shop she'd pretended to be, but I didn't think she was a streetwalker or a bar doxy either.

So I'd worked my way toward Brightown until I'd fetched up at a slightly better class of tavern called the Goat and Thistle, where I'd finally been given a vaguely worded hint that I might have better luck at the Swallow's Heart.

I knew the place. Big. Flashy. Catering to the young and fast set who weren't quite stupid enough to delve into the Night World proper. Largely human clientele, though, it didn't turn away Beasts or Fae. The Swallow was attached to the largest brothel in Brightown, the Dove's Rest. I had, on the odd occasion, had to round up novices on leave from the depths of both the Swallow and the Dove—though generally the former if we caught wind of their adventures early enough—but I'd never actually spent time in the Swallow as a patron.

As I stepped through the door, I remembered why.

Those who paid for information or muscle had to have money to do so. And money, in Brightown and the upper ends—such as they were—of society in the Border boroughs, tended to flow around the theater halls and the taverns. Not to mention the brothels, which were favored by all four races and weren't as dangerous as the Night World boroughs where the pleasures were more depraved.

Most Templars didn't have a lot of money to throw around in places like this. Plus it wasn't exactly a peaceful place to go for a pint or two . . . it was loud and crowded and flashy.

The place dripped gold and velvet and mirrors and sometimes all three in the same place. Throw in candles and crystal chandeliers and the place glittered like a whore's hangover. And that was before you added all the customers, dressed in typical Brightown fashion. Gaudy for the women, and only slightly less so for the men.

I pulled off my coat—donned against the unseasonable rain—thankful I'd chosen a black jacket and trousers. Close enough to evening dress. Though I lacked the eye-searing waistcoat necessary to truly fit in. Of course, the tattoos on my hands would let anybody who was paying attention know what I was, but Templars weren't monks and, out of uniform and obviously off duty, I shouldn't cause anyone undue concern.

Doing what everyone was doing would improve my odds of blending in. Given that seemed to consist of drinking themselves into oblivion, I pushed my way to the bar and ordered a whiskey. Then I pretended to drink it while I surveyed the room.

The place was crowded but not too crowded. There was a steady stream of men, and the odd woman, coming in from the rear where the Swallow connected to the Dove. Overall, the crowd was largely human, as far as I could tell. There were a few Beast Kind in one corner of the room, but their blond heads meant they weren't Favreaus. And they were not likely to be a good source of information when the questions came from a Templar.

Among the humans, numbers were divided evenly among women and men. The women were drinking as hard as the men, but, apart from the bold few who headed for the archway that led through to the Dove, most of the females in the room seemed to be focusing on a table in the far corner of the room where a young—maybe—man with messy dark hair and a rapidly emptying brandy decanter held court.

Whatever it was he was selling, the women were lapping it up, hanging on his every word, fluttering eyelashes and tugging their necklines lower. Not that Dark Hair was doing all that much to deter them. He smiled and flirted back, judging by the pleased expressions on the women's faces. Still, he seemed to keep the flow moving steadily.

He'd just sent a plump redhead in a shiny yellow dress on her way when he looked toward the bar, caught me watching him, and frowned. Suddenly he looked far less young and far less pleasant.

I dropped my eyes, then looked behind me in case someone else was the object of his displeasure.

No such luck. When I looked again, he had vanished from his table. A minute later he appeared by my side.

"A little out of your way, aren't you?" he asked with a chill to his voice.

This one was dangerous. I reached for my whiskey, using the movement to shift slightly so I had better access to the dagger and pistol on my hip. The dark-haired man was shorter than me by a few inches and more lightly built, but I had lost any illusion that smaller meant weaker very early in my novitiate when Father Cho had regularly pounded me into the mat in the weapons hall.

"What's it to you?"

"That would depend on what you're looking for," the man said.

"Who says I'm looking for anything?" I didn't think I'd be getting any information out of anyone so openly hostile, so best to move him along. Though the set of his jaw suggested he wouldn't be all that amenable to being moved.

"I do," said the man. "And I'm rarely wrong."

I tipped the whiskey glass toward him, pretending a half-foxed salute. "Nice for you."

His attention didn't shift. He wasn't buying my pose. "Not really. You won't find what you're looking for here."

"No? They have decent whiskey and I've heard good things about the girls next door."

"They aren't who you're looking for."

The hairs on the back of my neck stood up. "I think you've got me confused with someone else."

"No. You're the one. And I'm telling you to give it up before anyone gets hurt."

"I'm not in the business of hurting people."

His gaze dropped to my hands, one dark brow arching skeptically. "At least not the ones on your side. Go home, tin man. She—"

I put the glass down a little too hard. Whiskey sloshed over the edge. "She? I didn't say anything about a woman."

The green eyes blinked and I suddenly realized the man was half-drunk even if he wasn't showing it.

"Buggering Veil's eyes." He shook himself like a man casting off a half-remembered dream. "Still. I'm telling you there's nothing for you here."

If he thought he was about to chase me off, he was wrong. For one thing, anybody so overtly wanting to warn me off only confirmed that I was on the right track. He might not reveal anything, but then again, maybe liquor would lead him to another blunder. At this point I would settle for any information at all. "No? Someone told me this was a good place for bird-watching."

The man who'd suggested the Swallow had also muttered something about owls as well, which made no sense, but one can't always be choosy about the bait when casting a wide net for unknown prey.

The green gaze went flat and sharp like a shard of bottle glass. "They told you wrong. Leave. There's nothing but trouble for you here."

I stared at him for a moment, assessing the threat. I didn't want the attention a fight would bring. I had learned a little more. I was on the right path. But if the Swallow did have a connection with Holly, then maybe it was foolish to expect anyone here to talk about it. I needed to go elsewhere. Still in Brightown but not where my quarry actually nested, so to speak.

So I held up my hands, palms out, and nodded at Dark Hair. "All right, I'm going." I pushed coins across to the bar. "Give him more brandy."

HOLLY

By midmorning of my third day in St. Giles, the feeling of being recently trampled by a stampeding bull had receded somewhat. The day before, all I'd managed to do, other than sleep, was coax an orderly into fetching a street rat for me. I'd sent him off with a note for Reggie, telling her that I'd been called away to my mother. But this morning I felt better. I was contemplating attempting to get out of bed when my door opened and Guy DuCaine stalked in.

He looked grim. A winter warrior, all icy eyes and gray clothing.

I straightened against the pillows, trying to pull my cotton robe more tightly around me. It caught on the edges of the light cast Simon had put on my arm to make sure I gave it enough rest. I gave the robe a quick tug and then decided that maybe, if the very mild flirting I'd attempted yesterday had sent Guy fleeing, perhaps I should leave the robe somewhat adrift.

A good spy uses all the weapons at her disposal, after all.

But Guy only gave me a cursory glance before dragging the wooden chair provided for visitors over to the bed. He looked slightly more rested than yesterday. But he wore what could well be the same clothes. Gray trousers, white shirt. A light gray woolen tunic in acknowledgment of the chilly morning. I wondered how he'd look dressed in colors. Blue perhaps, to bring out his eyes. I realized I was staring and forced my wits back to the task at hand. Namely, getting rid of him.

"Sir Guy," I said, taking the opening salvo. "To what do I owe this pleasure?"

He rubbed his chin, scratching at the pale stubble. Perhaps they were the same clothes after all. Had he even been to bed? And if not, why not?

"You look better," he said after a moment.

"Yes," I said warily, "your brother is good at his job."

"So you'll be leaving soon?"

The steely tone made my pulse bump unpleasantly. "Simon wants me to stay here a week."

"Convenient."

"Not really," I countered. "I have a job. I don't know if they'll keep my position if I miss a week of work."

"Is that so?" Guy drawled, his accent suddenly drifting elsewhere again. Wherever elsewhere was, the men were dangerous, I was sure. The drawl was rough yet honeyed, seemingly pitched to scrape just right against female nerves.

Or perhaps to addle their brains. I gathered my wits. "Yes," I replied crisply in what I hoped was an I'm-completely-unaffected-by-you-and-completely-innocent tone. "It is."

"Strange. I wasn't aware that spies kept regular hours."

Chapter Five

HOLLY

Lords of hell. He knew who I was.

First rule of discovery. *Deny, deny, deny.*

I lifted my chin even as my skin chilled with horror. "I'm sure I don't know what you're talking about. I work for a modiste."

He shook his head. "Nice story, but I spent some time in Brightown last night. Looking for someone who might be able to procure some information. After I'd poured enough gin down enough throats, I got a recommendation to contact the Owl. Who, apparently, might go by the name of Holly some of the time. Care to try again?" His voice was dangerously flat and cold.

Stick to the story, Holly girl. "I'm sure I'm not the only female in the City named Holly." I fought not to dig my hands into the counterpane, settling for smoothing it out with brisk strokes instead.

"You're the only one I know who climbs about on rooftops in the middle of the night," he countered. "Seems a strange thing for a seamstress to do."

"Perhaps that was why I was so bad at it."

"Perhaps you were having a bad night. We all have those."

Sometimes we have bad days too, I thought mutinously. If

Guy had figured out my real identity, then Lady only knew what might happen. At worst he'd try to have me kicked out of St. Giles, though maybe I could claim haven if he did. At best, I'd be viewed with suspicion, which would make fulfilling the task Cormen had set that much harder. "I already told you why I was on the roof."

"Yes, and a very unconvincing tale it was too," he said, blue eyes still studying me with a chill that made me want to huddle under the blankets.

Winter indeed.

Cold and potentially lethal.

"Strangely, no one could tell me exactly what this Owl looks like. Female, they agree on, average height, but one man swore red hair and blue eyes and another black with brown."

"Whereas I have hazel eyes and brown hair."

"If you call that brown," Guy said. "I'd imagine a spy can change her appearance. Your hair was darker the night we met."

"That was probably the gaslight. Everything looks different under gaslight," I said, silently cursing the failed glamour that had left me horrified to see my true hair color—odd streaks and all—in the mirror on the first morning I'd woken up here. I could've cast another, but I didn't really have the energy to spare.

"Oh, I'm a fairly good judge of how things look under gaslight," he said. "The one thing that people did seem to agree on is that several of them have seen a heavy gold chain around this Owl's neck. Quite distinctive, they said. Links like feathers. Though no one could tell me what might be hanging from it."

He leaned forward and ran one finger under the collar of my nightgown.

I froze as his finger stroked my skin, and heat rushed through me. My body liked his touch. My brain, however, was flat-out horrified.

His eyes met mine and for a moment he stilled as well, as if he'd forgotten what he was doing.

But then he jerked my chain and the cursed pendant into plain view. The heavy gold key glittered darkly in the light, the amethysts, black diamonds, and deep blue sapphires—sa'Inviel colors—that decorated it sending colored sparks along the walls.

"Something like this, I'd imagine," Guy said, leaning forward. His eyes narrowed as he took in the pendant. "Changing your appearance is even easier if you're Fae."

"I'm not." I hoped like hell that he couldn't read my lineage in the gems.

"Part, then."

"That's none of your business," I said, stuffing the key back beneath my nightgown and trying not to pay attention to the patch of skin still tingling where he'd touched me. If only I'd found a replacement for Stefan Rousselline already. If I'd had a bedmate right now, I wouldn't be acting quite so foolishly over the Templar.

"The Night World is my business," Guy said, settling into his chair. "It seems it's yours as well."

It seemed pointless to keep up the pretense. "So?" I snapped. "I haven't broken any human laws in a human borough. I haven't started a riot in a border borough. There's nothing to interest you here, Templar."

His eyes caught mine for another long second and my heart started to pound. Oh, this man was dangerous all right. Burn-you-to-cinders dangerous. My mother had always taught me not to play with fire. Though, right now, I struggled to remember why.

"On the contrary," he said. "I think I may have a job for you."

I couldn't have been more surprised if he'd knelt down and proposed marriage. "You want to *hire* me?"

"The Most Holy Order of the Knights Templar wants to hire you," he corrected.

"What need does the order have of spies?" I asked, trying to adjust to the rapid turn the conversation had taken. My jaw wasn't actually hanging open, but it felt as though it were.

"We need information, the same as anyone else. We need to know what's going on in the Night World right now. Who's winning the war for power."

"Why?"

"Because it will keep my men safe." He paused, looked as though he was about to continue, then paused again.

"It will help us keep others safe," he continued. "We need to know where the trouble spots are, where we should be patrolling. We need to know who's fanning the flames."

"Don't you already have informants?" I knew very well that they did. But I'd never been tempted to get stuck in the middle of the humans and the Night World. It was complicated enough navigating the Beasts and Blood and Fae and Nightseekers without adding the human world into the mix.

"Our sources are remarkably . . . closemouthed at the moment. Hedging their bets."

He had that much right. The shift and flow of Night World power mongers was as slippery as a greased snake. Which I guess was as good a metaphor for the Night World as any. Deadly. Lightning fast. With fangs. Lots of writhing and flailing and sudden death occurring as the snake tried to grow a new head to replace the one it had lost.

It was good for business even if it increased the risks. But working amongst the Night World was one thing. Working for the Templars against the Night World was likely to result in me being one of those sudden deaths.

"There are others you could hire, if you name the right price," I said. I tapped the cast on my arm. "After all, it's not as if I can do much with this."

"Only if you need to go sneaking around on the tops of buildings."

"What I do tends to involve a certain amount of sneaking around on the tops of buildings. Besides, your brother is keeping me here for a while. Unless you think the Blood are plotting beneath St. Giles."

He looked frustrated, face twisting. "Simon will let you out if I tell him to."

I shrugged, trying not to let the steely determination in his voice intimidate my good sense into capitulation. What he was proposing was potentially lethal. There were those amongst my clientele who would not take kindly to me switching sides. "I'm sorry, it's too dangerous. I can't help you if I'm dead."

"I can protect you."

I laughed, I couldn't help it. The mental image of me sneaking over a rooftop with a Templar in full regalia in tow was ridiculous. "You?"

"What's so funny?"

"Well, look at you." I waved a hand at him, still laughing. Big, solid, blond. Everything about him screamed "human" and "good" and, to anyone who knew anything about combat, "warrior." Plus there were those big red Templar crosses tattooed across the backs of his hands. "Even if you could hide your hands, you might as well have a sign saying 'I'm a Templar' hung around your neck."

"I know how to blend," he said. "I found out about you, didn't I?"

He had a point. But blending in in a few border borough drinking holes and gaming hells was different from actually doing what I did.

"Templars aren't entirely unusual in the border boroughs," I said. "But you won't get far in the Night World. Not unless you're intending to wear gloves the entire time."

"Tattoos can be hidden."

Glamoured, he meant.

"Plenty of Night Worlders can see through a glamour," I retorted. "It's too risky. The instant it was discovered that I was working for the Templars, my career would be over." Or I'd be dead. But I didn't want to actually say that out loud. "I'd never get another commission from the Blood or the Beasts."

He leaned forward suddenly, eyes narrowed. "Do you work for the Beasts often?"

"Why would I tell you that?" I studied his face for a moment. "Is it the Beasts you need information on?" If so, he'd managed to surprise me. I would've thought the Blood were the bigger problem in the Night World right now.

He leaned back. "Why would I tell you that?"

"I thought you wanted to hire me?"

"Does that mean you'll do it?"

"Go spy in the Night World for the Templars?" I shook my head firmly. "I'm sorry, but I'm not giving up my livelihood for you."

"You'd be helping a lot of people."

"I already help people. I have people relying on me and the money I make. People who might die without it. So don't give me your moral higher ground. I don't believe in the greater good."

"Never?"

I met his gaze. Judge me all he wanted, he wasn't going to change my mind. "The greater good has never lifted a finger to help me. Individuals matter."

"The greater good is made up of individuals."

"Yes, and I get to pick which of them I choose to care about. I'm sorry, but my answer is no."

"And if I don't give you a choice?" His voice was still calm but suddenly ominous.

I'd survived in the Night World long enough to recognize a politely worded threat when I heard one. I'd also learned that, most of the time, it was best not to act threatened. "Just how would you do that?" I asked.

"I can throw you in a cell."

"Really?" I tried to sound bored. "Last time I checked, it was difficult to spy on the Night World from a cell in the Templar Brother House. Locking me up hardly helps you."

"You're hardly helping me now," he said, one hand rubbing the cross on the back of the other.

"Anyway, what grounds do you have for locking me up? Being uncooperative isn't a crime. Or do you Templars enjoy locking up the innocent?"

His eyes went even icier and his brows drew down, two pale slashes of lightning above the storm. "This isn't a game, Miss Everton. We're fighting for survival. It's important."

"So is my life," I snapped. His intensity had me somewhat rattled. Were the Templars actually losing ground? Or was there another reason for his urgency? I didn't know why but my gut told me he wasn't telling me the truth. Not that I blamed him for that. But it didn't make me any more inclined to do as he asked.

"I can protect you."

"Didn't we already cover this? How am I meant to explain my new Templar companion?" I didn't bother trying to keep the scorn out of my voice. It was insanity to believe what he proposed would work. "Shall we make everyone believe that you're infatuated with me and can't stay out of my bed? Because that's about the only explanation I can think of that might have any sort of credibility." I expected him to recoil at the idea, but instead his expression turned speculative. And maybe, just maybe, there was something more than professional speculation in those eyes. Something hotter.

Something that could get us both in a lot of trouble.

Me and my big mouth.

"I was joking," I said hastily. "Don't even consider it."

"It's a reasonable idea."

I could almost see the wheels turning in his head. Leading him down precisely the wrong path. "Exactly how much did you have to drink last night? It's a terrible idea. Nobody would believe I could lead a Templar around by the nose. I'm hardly irresistible." I gestured down my body with my good arm.

His eyes moved slowly up and down my body. "Granted,

what you're wearing isn't exactly seductive, but I'm sure you have no trouble making men do what you want."

No. Usually I didn't. And I was careful not to get involved with men who didn't want to play by my rules. Which was why I took my lovers from among the Beast Kind when I could. The younger ones were generally good looking, eager, and inventive in bed but knew ultimately that they would pair up with another Beast. Which prevented them doing stupid things like falling in love with me. One or two of the humans had done so, when I'd been less careful with my choices.

None of them had prepared me for the complexities of trying to convince a Templar knight that playing my lover was a monumentally stupid idea.

"What I want, in this situation," I said with some asperity, "is for you to see sense." I ignored the part of me that was piping up with "no, what I want is to take the Templar out and show him exactly how I make men do what I want." That part was too dumb to recognize that this was the sort of man who made women do what *he* wanted. He wouldn't be so easy to discard or walk away from. So there was no way we'd be starting anything.

Not to mention that dragging a Templar around in my wake was another quick way to destroy my career.

"I am being sensible. You said we needed a cover story and I can't think of a better one."

"And what would be the reason for the great Guy DuCaine suddenly losing his head for a half-Fae Night Worlder?"

He arched an eyebrow. "I'm the great Guy DuCaine?"

I bared my teeth at him. "Oh, don't pretend to be modest. You must know that you have quite the reputation. It's amazing you're not eight foot tall and carrying a flaming sword, the way they carry on about you."

"I leave the flaming swords to the mages." He tapped the sword at his side as if to prove his point. "So it's not completely impossible. Even Templars are corruptible, give the right incentives. We're only men, after all."

"Be that as it may, it doesn't change the facts. You are *the* Guy DuCaine. They'd be calling *me* Holly the Great if I could pull that off. No one will believe it. Somehow I can't see you pulling off crazily love struck."

The eyebrow arched higher and his blue eyes darkened. "Is that so? Why not, pray tell?"

"You're . . ." I waved a hand at him . . . trying to think of something that sounded less insulting than morally uptight . . . "good," I finished lamely.

"Templars aren't monks, you know."

"There's a difference between not being a monk and being able to get people to believe that you're crazed with lust." I caught his eyes, trying to get him to drop the idea. "We'd have to be seen in public together doing loverlike things. Holding hands isn't going to be sufficient. Not in the sorts of places we'd need to go."

"Unless you're actually proposing that we have sex in public, I think I can handle it."

"Oh, really?" I said, exasperated. "You think so? Do you know what goes on in some of the Blood Assemblies and the theater halls and the private balls? Do you know how a woman might greet her lover in such a place?"

He cleared his throat "I—"

"Let me tell you," I continued before he could say anything further. I sat upright, swung my legs out over the edge of the bed. If I couldn't talk sense into the man, then maybe I could scare him off. Show him he was getting in over his head.

"First, you have to imagine me wearing something a lot more . . . revealing than this." I traced a line across my breasts, just above my nipples. Nipples that tingled as his eyes followed the path my finger took as if drawn there by a magnet.

"Something cut down to here. My hair up, so everyone can see." I took a deep breath and stood. "Say that you were seated somewhere as you are now. And I came upon you, my lover." I moved closer until my knees almost brushed against his, waiting for him to flinch, to draw away. To stop me.

He didn't move. Didn't speak. I wasn't entirely sure that he was breathing. I wasn't entirely sure that I was. There was a rush of blood to my head, making me suddenly dizzy. "If I was your lover, in such a place, then I'd probably do something like this." I lifted the edge of my nightgown, thankful that I'd had the fore-sight to don underwear beneath it. Then I swung my leg over his and straddled him. He still didn't move, eyes burning into mine.

Nothing for it now. I was going to have to keep going with the charade. He was warm beneath me, the wool of his trousers soft against my legs. I wrapped my arms around his neck—not easily done with a cast—summoned my best wicked smile, and said, "Hello, lover," and then, hardly knowing what insanity possessed me to start this little charade, leaned forward and pressed my lips to his.

For a moment, I thought I'd won as he stayed still beneath my lips, but then, oh, then, his arms came around my waist and suddenly I was pulled closer toward him, hard against him . . . hard against parts of him that were suddenly hard against me. My head spun and swooped and his mouth opened beneath mine and I learned I'd been right as the taste of him filled my mouth.

Delicious.

Dangerous.

This man was trouble. This man would make you do what he wanted for one more taste of him. This man was suddenly, definitely in control of this kiss and driving us both to a place that we shouldn't go.

This man I wanted.

This man I couldn't have.

Part of my brain screamed at me to stop. But instead I tightened my arms and drank him deep, knowing that it was possible that this would be the only taste of him I ever got. Because sooner or later he would come to his senses and let me go.

And the world might never be quite the same again.

I wasn't sure who finally broke the kiss, wasn't sure which one of us first drew back, both of us gasping. But it was Guy who lifted me from his lap, deposited me gently on the bed, and then turned and walked out of the room.

GUY

"Should've dropped her," I muttered as I slammed through the door to the tunnel that joined St. Giles and the Brother House. Dropped her or dragged her in for questioning and thrown her in a cell there and then.

No. Dropping her would've been simpler.

Not that I'd had any choice in the matter. Throwing myself off Gray's back and toward the falling figure had been pure instinct and not a little luck. And because of that, things were getting complicated.

I quickened my pace, hurrying toward peace. Toward the place that still seemed to simplify things when I stepped through its gates.

I could *think* in the Brother House. Could plan. With thick stone walls to shut out the outer world, I could remember what was important and forget how it felt to kiss Holly.

That *mouth*.

Hell's balls, she was right. I needed another plan. One that didn't involve me posing as her lover or getting any closer to her than strictly necessary. Because there was little doubt that if I did so, I would actually become her lover in very short order.

Which would be simply unholy fucking insane.

I had sworn vows to protect and defend. Which meant I couldn't afford distractions. Even though the order didn't ask us to swear to celibacy, I'd found over the years it was much simpler to pretend they had.

Near the juncture of the tunnels, I almost ran into Simon.

"Where's the fire?" he asked after a tangle of sidestepping narrowly avoided a collision.

I needed a lie. "Noon services begin soon. I'll be late."

"Indeed," Simon said. His expression was vaguely amused. "Perhaps the question then is where are you coming from? Did someone else get injured?"

"No. I didn't patrol last night."

"That doesn't really answer the question."

"No. It doesn't." I went to step around him and he moved to block me.

Then he smiled. "You went to see Holly, didn't you?"

No way in hell was I answering *that* question. For one thing, I wasn't sure I wanted to tell Simon who Holly was. The fewer people who knew, the better. At least until I decided exactly what I wanted to do with her.

Bad choice of words. My brain suddenly conjured up a number of possibilities. None of them involved spying. Or clothing.

Hell's *balls*.

"I'm late for services," I said, and moved again. This time he let me past, though his grin was more than eloquent on the subject of what he thought of my retreat. I took two long steps and then stopped. "Keep a close eye on her."

"On who?" Simon said, still grinning. "On that girl you won't admit you saw? Why, was she feeling unwell?" His smile blinked out suddenly.

"No. But make sure you do."

"Why?"

"Just trust me." I turned to walk on.

"Guy."

The tone was deadly serious now. I turned back. "Yes?"

"You're going to tell me sooner or later." Simon's face was grim, all trace of levity wiped out.

"Don't be so sure. For now, just trust me. After all, I trusted you about Lily."

Simon's eyes lit. "Are you saying you feel about Holly the way I felt about Lily?"

"I am not cow-headed enough to fall in love with a girl I barely know," I said. Lust, maybe, but love? No. What I felt for Holly right now was not love. And I was well schooled in ignoring lust. "I need you to trust me."

This earned me a head shake. "I'll trust you. But you should be careful too. After all, we don't always choose who we fall in love with."

"Stop talking about love. Just because you're settling down doesn't mean I've changed my mind on the matter."

"You can't keep fighting forever."

I set my teeth. This was a subject that I didn't care to discuss. "Why not?"

"Well, for one thing, you're getting older."

Right now I didn't feel terribly old. In fact, I felt very much the way I had at fifteen when a friend's older brother had taken us both to a brothel and introduced us to sex.

Intensely aware of the heat in my body, of the need to touch, to hold.

To take.

Of course, not long after that, I'd realized that I was really meant to become a knight. But I still remembered those first few heady weeks of being completely fogged by the urges of my body, unable to think of anything but the softness of female skin and the heat of—

Fuck. I was doing it again. I really needed to get back to the Brother House. Noon services would help me chase her from my mind.

"I have to go. Watch her," I said again, and left Simon standing in the tunnel.

HOLLY

You need a plan, Holly girl.

It wasn't the first time I'd had the thought since Guy had left. Yet every time I tried to turn my mind to how to get myself out of this particular dilemma that my big mouth seemed to have gotten me into, it drifted instead back to the man himself rather than the problem he represented.

It was impossible to see him purely as an obstacle when I could still taste his kiss.

Maybe, just maybe, I didn't have a problem. Maybe Guy leaving so suddenly was a good sign.

I sighed softly, staring at the stark white walls. I knew a ridiculously overoptimistic thought when I had one. Guy DuCaine was a Templar. A warrior. He was not the kind of man to give up easily on something he wanted. He thought I could help him. He'd be back.

Which meant when he returned, I needed alternatives to offer, to send him on his way.

Having him pose as my lover would be a very, very bad idea.

But could I afford to keep refusing him? He knew the truth about me. If I refused, I was sure he'd be hurrying me away from St. Giles and everyone he was so protective of as quickly as possible.

Which would bring Cormen down on my head with the wrath of hell's furies. And Lady knew what the geas would do to me in the meantime.

The phrase "caught between a rock and a hard place" was finally making sense to me.

I settled back on the bed to study the problem from all sides. Pros.

If I agreed to spy for Guy, I would gain his trust. Presumably, this would also mean I would gain Simon's. And Simon's trust could be key to discovering his secret, if worst came to worst, and I couldn't figure out a way to thwart Cormen. Also it was possible that in spying for Guy I would discover information that other people might well be interested in. Paying customers.

Cons.

Working for the Templars. Which would likely ruin my career if it were ever found out. Or shorten my life span. There was no way I could do it without someone at my back.

Perhaps, before Lucius had vanished, when things had been calmer, there might have been a few others in my business who I would've trusted enough to hire them as part of a team, but that wasn't an option now. It was every man and woman for themselves in the Night World right now, and I couldn't think of anybody other than Fen who I would trust not to decide that they might just make more money selling me out. And I was not going to drag Fen into this mess.

Which left me with Guy's offer of protection. Tempting. If a Templar couldn't keep me alive through all of this, then nobody could.

But try as I might, there was no other way I could think of to explain a Templar at my side.

So I either had to say no and find my own way into Simon's good graces or say yes and think of how to convince everyone that a Templar had fallen for me. All while avoiding ending up dead or letting myself do something stupid like act on the attraction I felt for the brother of the man I was likely going to have to betray.

Easier to stick your hand into a fire and pluck out a live coal without getting burned.

It all twisted around and around in my mind until eventually I fell into a troubled sleep.

Next thing I knew, someone was shaking me awake.

"Wake up," an irritated male voice said.

Fen? For a moment I thought I was dreaming. But no, when I opened my eyes, there he was in all his rumpled glory. Coat wrinkled. Hair wild. Expression a cross between worry and irritation.

Shadows smudged the skin beneath his eyes. I wondered if he'd had a vision. I snuck a glance toward his wrist. The chain was there, its dull black loops not really hiding the bruises beneath. I hid a wince.

"What are you doing here?" Fen had a certain notoriety. Even if the humans wouldn't necessarily know him, some of the Fae who worked in the hospital surely would. If anyone saw him visiting me, it wouldn't be all that difficult to connect the dots between us. Guy had discovered the truth about me, but I didn't want everybody else here to know who I really was.

"You're in trouble," he said.

My heart slowed for a moment, giving one lurching thud as fear cooled my skin. I knew that tone. I rubbed my palms over the counterpane. "I'm fine."

"Who broke your arm, Holly?" His eyes narrowed. "And why do they think your last name is Everton?" He tapped a finger on the neat label on the end of the bedstead.

I folded my arms as best I could with plaster encasing one of them and glared at him. "Mind your own business."

"You are my business," he said. "Particularly when Templar knights come snooping around after you. Who is that big blond one anyway?"

"He came to the Swallow?" Damn, I hadn't imagined Guy had actually found my base. Not that it was likely that it was anyone at the Swallow who had ratted me out. "What did he want?" I wasn't ready to tell Fen that Guy had found out who I was. That would only make him even more difficult to get rid of.

"He was looking for you, asking questions. Who is he?"

It was his "don't make me find out for myself" tone. I wondered what exactly had passed between the two of them but knew better than to ask. No, my task here was to avoid admitting anything and getting Fen to leave the whole mess alone. He was prone to flights of disastrous impulse when he got the bit between his teeth.

"Would you believe my latest conquest?"

He studied me for a moment, green eyes opaque. "Perhaps. Still trouble, though."

"Real trouble?" I asked. "Did you see something?" My stomach flipped. As much as Fen hated his visions, he was seldom wrong.

"A mess of stuff that didn't make much sense," Fen said after a pause. "Which worries me."

"Why?"

"Because it means the future is messy too. Too many possibilities."

My palms went damp. I ran them over the counterpane again, feeling the soft cotton nubs under my skin. It did nothing to soothe me. I had to swallow before I could speak. "What did you see?"

"You here," he said. "That much was clear—and don't think we won't be discussing why you didn't tell me when it happened— but then there was all sorts of things. An owl, which is you, I suppose. A key. Smashed mirrors. A weeping woman. Summerdale. And your big blond friend."

"What was he doing?" We'd return to the Summerdale part in a minute. I hoped to hell Fen hadn't seen me there. I definitely didn't want to go to the Veiled Court.

"I saw him dancing with the owl. Bloody and alone with a sword. And I saw him watch the owl fall from the sky."

"Did he catch it?" I tried not to shiver, throat tightening as fear chilled me. Fen's visions always scared me, and this one didn't sound good at all.

"I didn't see. I saw you crying, though, weeping. Wearing black. It wasn't a good vision, Holly. Whatever you're up to, you should change your plans."

"Believe me, I would if I could."

"I could help you," Fen said. "If you need to get out of here . . . or . . ."

He looked at me, waiting to see if I'd tell him what the hell was going on. I stayed silent. I would *not* involve him. The last thing Fen needed was my father deciding he was a problem. Fen was even more wary of the Veiled World than I was, not wanting to become a tool to some lordly Fae who forced his allegiance.

Besides, if this ended badly, Fen would make sure that Reggie and my mother were taken care of.

"Well, then, keep me in mind." He reached into his jacket and pulled out a leather pouch. "I thought you might want these." Then he nodded to a familiar carpetbag sitting near the wall. "And I brought you some clothes and things."

I undid the complex knot holding the pouch together and peered inside. A small pile of charms nestled together atop a small cloth roll that held another set of my hairpin lock picks. "Fen, you're a wonder."

I didn't ask myself how he knew exactly what I needed. And I was too pleased to take him to task for breaking into my rooms to get my things. No doubt, somewhere in the carpetbag there would be a leather sheath holding my spare cutthroat. Fen knew

I used it for my charms, and if he was worried, he wouldn't want me to be without a weapon.

But even as I relaxed a little as my fingers stirred the familiar shapes of the charms, another thought occurred to me. "I don't want Reggie to know I'm here. I sent her a note, told her I had to go and see Mother. So don't tell her anything, all right?"

Fen frowned. "I won't. How long are they going to keep you here?" He didn't bother asking what had happened again. He knew me better than that.

"I should be out in a few days." Maybe sooner if Guy was actually serious about his crazy plan. "Don't look so serious, Fen. I'm fine, really. Si—the healers have already fixed me. They're only keeping me here to convalesce."

But Fen wasn't stupid. "Simon DuCaine healed you?"

"Yes. He works here, after all."

Fen was scowling.

"What?" I asked.

"In my vision, the sun was shining some of the time, even though it was night. It was shining when I saw you crying. And here you are in the tender care of a sunmage. I don't like this, Holly. You need to get away from here."

I held up my arm in the cast. "I need to stay a few days. This is a haven, Fen. I'm perfectly safe." I hoped it was true, but even if it wasn't, I couldn't leave. For one thing, I didn't know if the geas would let me walk out of here.

His scowl didn't change. "Remember those bodies dumped a few weeks ago? They were dumped right here."

I ignored the sudden sour taste at the back of my mouth at the memory. Thirty-odd human bodies. Blood-locked killed by the Blood at Lucius' order and dumped here in broad daylight by Beasts from the packs he commanded. "Outside, not inside. Even Lucius didn't bring his fight inside a Haven."

"You're assuming that someone from the outside is what you have to worry about."

"Are you telling me it's not? How do you know? You saw me crying, not hurt."

"I know you'd be safer elsewhere."

I worked hard to keep my expression unconcerned. I knew well enough that I should heed any warning Fen had to give. But I couldn't leave the hospital. And he couldn't know why.

"I don't have to stay here too much longer, Fen."

He pursed his lips, tugged irritably at the starched white collar of his shirt, but eventually his expression eased a little. "Is there anything else you need?"

I shook my head. "Just let Reggie know I'll be away a few days. Make sure she doesn't worry. Ask her to visit Mama for me." My mother. A fresh spurt of fury at my father ran through me. I was stuck here, neglecting the people I cared about, the ones who had nothing to do with politics and intrigue, all so my bastard father could play one of his dirty little games.

For a moment, the urge to ask Fen what he knew about bindings made the tip of my tongue tingle. I had to clench my teeth to make sure I didn't. I desperately wanted to be free of the geas and to spike my father's guns if I could, but this wasn't the way. Raising the subject of a geas out of nowhere would be a guaranteed way to make sure that Fen didn't leave until he had the truth—or as much of it as the geas would let me tell—out of me.

"It's just a few days, I promise," I managed when I had myself back under control.

Fen nodded, pushing at the hair that fell into his face with a frustrated flick of his hand. "All right. But any longer than that and I'm coming to get you."

"Thank you," I said.

"This doesn't mean we're not going to talk about how you ended up in here," he said as he stood, smoothing his coat with irritated strokes, eyes intent.

"And that doesn't mean that I'm going to tell you anything other than to mind your own business."

Chapter Six

HOLLY

After allowing myself a moment of "why me?" in which the urge to pull the counterpane over my head and pretend that the world outside didn't exist rolled over me with a vengeance, I climbed out of bed and fetched the bag of clothing Fen had left. I pulled out the selection of clothes Fen had picked for me, suddenly overcome by the desire to wear something that was mine.

Maybe dressing would make me feel more like myself, let me get a grip on the situation. But by the time I had laid out several dresses, I found myself unable to choose and reached instead for the leather pouch, wanting to run the charms through my fingers again, the spark of magic within them and their smooth surfaces strangely comforting. I had barely untied the carefully knotted thongs when the door opened again. I shoved the pouch of charms deep into the bag.

I was proving terribly popular today. More's the pity.

I turned to find Simon watching me with a strange expression. Hells. Had Guy told him about me? Was I about to get thrown out on my ear?

"Hello," I said with a smile. Play the happy, compliant patient. That was the key. Nothing to arouse his suspicions at all.

"How are you feeling?" he asked.

"A little better." So far so good. No "leave this hospital Night

World spy." I lifted the bag down off the bed before Simon could offer to do it for me and pushed it under the bedstead with my foot.

"Is it time for more poking and prodding?" I flashed that innocent smile again and, thankfully, received one in return.

"Just a bit," he said. "Why don't you lie down?"

I obeyed, trying not to let relief spill onto my face. Instead, I focused on Simon, studying him as he moved his hands gently over my arm. There was something different about him today. I closed my eyes, trying to work out what. Over the last day or so, I'd gotten use to the feel of his magic spreading from him. A warm radiant glow like a welcoming fire or a sheltered patch of sunlight on a cool day. Different than how a Fae or Beast felt. But today there was something unfamiliar about that glow . . . something slightly off.

I let my senses reach out.

There.

About halfway down his body. Oddness, like a dissonant note in a song. A little chill spot. That felt . . . like Fae magic. A charm. A very familiar feeling charm at that.

I frowned. What need did Simon DuCaine have for an invisibility charm within the walls of St. Giles?

"Sorry, did that hurt?" Simon said.

I smoothed my expression, opened my eyes, winced at the light. "No. I was thinking of something else."

"Nothing bad, I hope."

I summoned a smile. "No, nothing bad." At least, not from my father's point of view. This was the clue I'd been looking for. Something to work with, to maybe lead me to the answers I sought. The clue that might bring trouble and pain to this man who had, if not saved my life, then patched me back together. Brother to the man who kissed so dangerously and knew my secrets. It left a bitter taste in my mouth. "Just woolgathering."

I wished it were true.

But I'd learned a long time ago that wishing for something didn't help.

"You're doing fine," Simon said. "I'll keep you here another few days, but after that, you'll be free to go."

"Oh. Good," I said. Not good. Once I left the hospital, my main opportunity to discover Simon's secret would be gone. Guy would, no doubt, be watching closely to see what I did if I left.

"Are you sure you don't want to tell us what happened?" Simon said as he straightened. He asked me the same question every time he saw me. "I don't want to send you home into any danger."

If only he knew.

"There's nothing to worry about. I'll be perfectly all right."

Just as well I was only half Fae. A true Fae would have been undone by the tower of lies I was piling up. *Who would you prefer to betray today, Holly? Simon? Your father? Or yourself perhaps?*

If I had to choose one of those three, it would be Cormen. Problem was, to do that, I needed to break the geas. Which I had no idea how to do. "To tell you the truth, I'll be glad to get back to work."

Simon looked slightly taken aback. "Has there been something amiss here at the hospital?"

"Oh no." I summoned my best polite young lady tone again. If I only had a few days, then I needed to get on with the task at hand. I needed out of this room. "It's only that being stuck in this room all day is a little . . . boring."

"Ah. You must be feeling better." He smiled approvingly. "I'm satisfied with your internal injuries, so as long as you're careful with the arm and take things slowly, you can walk around a little. There's a nice garden near the children's wing."

It wasn't the garden I was interested in, but I nodded politely, delighted with the prospect of being able to get to work. My gut told me that whatever secret it was that Simon was keeping, it most likely involved the hospital. I couldn't see him sneaking around embroiled in political plots that took him far from his work.

"That sounds lovely," I said.

"Good. Any of the nurses or orderlies can direct you. There are a few places to avoid, but they're all clearly marked. You don't want to pick up an infection and have to stay here longer."

No, I didn't. But I imagined I was going to have to go some places I wasn't supposed to be. Hopefully the charms Fen had brought would prove helpful. Using them in a hospital full of Fae was risky, but I was confident in my work. I'd always been able to make my charms near undetectable. Even to powerful Fae who could make charms as slick as the one Simon carried. I couldn't see it with my eyes at all, even though I sensed it. To someone without my gift it would be as invisible as it rendered the person carrying it.

Whoever made it had done a good job. And I wanted to know what Simon was using it for. But first things first. Wait for him to leave, inspect my charms, and then see how much I could actually physically manage to do. The cast would hamper me somewhat—climbing would be out—but I was hoping I'd recovered enough of my strength to do some serious reconnoitering.

It was slow progress to find the garden. My legs, once I started moving, were surprisingly shaky. Simon had told me healing took energy, but the only thing I'd been doing besides sleeping was eating like a horse. Apparently I should've eaten like two horses.

It was frustrating. It takes strength and stamina to spy, to wait patiently for an opportunity to overhear the perfect piece of information. I was no good to anyone if I couldn't walk the hospital corridors without needing to pause every fifty feet or so and wait for my heart to stop pounding.

I eventually reached my destination. Nothing I saw on the journey gave me any clues as to what Simon might be doing with an invisibility charm. As far as I could tell, the rooms I passed were wards or offices or examination rooms. No one had been kind enough to leave a sign pointing to the secret Simon was hiding.

I couldn't even sense any trace of his charm amongst the general low-level aftertaste of Fae magic that permeated the corridors.

I passed quite a few Fae as I walked, most of them in healer green. None of them went out of their way to speak to me, but no one turned away either. Apparently the Fae who worked here at least knew how to pretend not to share the general Fae prejudices. I hadn't reworked the glamour on my hair. I didn't see the point when I'd already been revealed as half Fae, so any of them would be able to see the lines of my heritage clearly. My pendant was firmly tucked beneath the high neck of the dress I wore, though.

The garden lay between two of the hospital buildings, set to catch the morning sun and provide shade later in the day, sheltered from the wind by the white marble walls. A large expanse of lawn was edged with benches and there were some toys—raggedy dolls and a few wooden blocks—lying abandoned on the grass.

The air was warm and soft as I stepped into the space. Apparently the cold spell had passed while I'd been out of commission.

Bright flowers filled the flower beds enclosing the grass. Near one of them knelt a slim woman with red hair caught up in a knot of braids, digging in the earth with a small fork. A flat basket of small green plants rested beside her.

As I stepped onto the grass, she swung around, her reaction a little too fast to be human. And a little too cautious for your average gardener. Not to mention a human wouldn't have heard my careful footsteps.

As our eyes met, I saw her make an effort to relax her alert stance a little. Obviously I didn't appear to be a threat. Maybe it was the cast. But even as she eased down, her eyes tracked me as I looked around the space and then wandered across to a garden bench near her.

"Hello," I said, taking a seat.

"Hello," she said with a nod. She made no move to turn back to her planting.

"It's a pretty day to be out," I said, turning my face up to the sun and closing my eyes for a moment. Best to appear as non-threatening as possible.

"Yes."

I opened my eyes again, let myself release a pleased sigh before I smiled at her. I was half playing a part, but that didn't alter the fact that the warmth of the sun and the soft air did feel lovely after being cooped up for so long. "I've been inside for a couple of days."

She cocked her head, then nodded at my arm. "What happened?"

"Fell down some stairs."

Her gaze sharpened. She wasn't buying my story any more than Guy and Simon had. "I've fallen down some stairs in my time," she said softly. She looked regretful for a moment. Then shook her head as if banishing a bad memory.

"Healer DuCaine mended my arm," I said. "I'm fine now. I have to rest a few days until everything finishes healing."

"Simon?" Her face brightened, her smile radiant.

The change was extraordinary and I suddenly realized who this must be. Lily. My hand curled around the top of the bench in sudden caution. Lucius' assassin. Simon's fiancée, if the rumors were true.

A *wraith*.

More dangerous than Guy, in her way. He might stop to consider the moral implications of killing me, but I didn't think that Lily would pause for even a second to defend the man who put that expression on her face.

"Yes. He's very good." I fought the urge to flee, focusing on calming my speeding pulse. Wraiths couldn't use their powers in daylight. She had no reason to suspect me of anything. I was safe.

She could still kill you with her gardening fork, a part of my brain whispered.

And therefore I shouldn't give her any reason to want to kill me. I straightened my shoulders and lowered the arm with the unwieldy cast into my lap. Look harmless, that was the idea.

"Do you work with Simon?" I asked, seeking confirmation that she was who I thought she was.

Her smile dimmed a little, her expression suddenly wary. Her eyes were gray. A deep clear gray like light reflecting off water or the early signs of a storm rising. I hoped I wasn't about to find out just how stormy she could be as she studied me. This woman was a trained killer. No one to be taken lightly or trifled with. I needed my wits about me.

"I work here in the hospital," she said neutrally. "Everyone knows Simon."

Not volunteering information. Cautious. I should go slowly. Trouble was I was running out of time. Once I was discharged, finding what Cormen wanted would become that much harder. Of course, getting killed with a garden fork because I'd aroused the protective instincts of an assassin would also be counterproductive.

"He seems a very good healer."

That warmed her smile again. "He's one of the strongest sun-mages in the City."

"Are you a healer too?" She wore a pale green shirt with black linen trousers. The shirt wasn't healer green, but close. The trousers were unusual for a woman, here in the human world. I wondered if Fen had packed any of mine. I hadn't gotten that far in the bag before Simon had interrupted me.

"No. Just a gardener. Maybe an herbalist one day."

Lucius' executioner was now a gardener. Now, there was a difficult concept to wrap one's brain around.

"It must be nice to be around all this every day. Those colors are lovely." I pointed to where she was planting out pansies. The flowers were a bright purple, blending in with the others—lavender and pale violet—to make a sweep of color shading from dark to light in a graceful arc. "I work for a modiste," I added. "I tend to notice colors. Did you design the bed?"

Her smile widened just a little, though her gray eyes still studied me carefully. There was tension in her shoulders, and her hand shifted on the handle of the fork, easing and tightening in nearly imperceptible movements. I wondered if she was uncomfortable making small talk or still just wary. I was good at reading people, but I couldn't decide.

Which made sense. You didn't do anything without thinking in the Night World. Not if you wanted to survive. Anyone who'd grown up in Lucius' court would've learned to control their emotions and reactions as naturally as breathing.

"Yes, I designed it. I'm still learning." She looked down at the flat basket, still half-full of plants waiting to be settled into the earth. "But thank you."

"It must be peaceful working here."

"Not when the children are let loose," she said. "But it's nice to make somewhere for people to come and rest. The hospital isn't always a happy place."

"No." I couldn't help the reflexive shiver that slid down my spine as I remembered Cormen's face as he left me to the mercies of his Beast.

I blinked and came back to myself as I realized I was staring into space. Lily was watching me. "I'm Holly," I said, wondering if the obvious might just be the thing to get me the confirmation of her identity I was seeking. "Holly Everton." The fake name was coming more easily now.

Lily cocked her head. "It's nice to meet you, Miss Everton. But if you'll excuse me, I need to get on with this."

I knew a dismissal when I heard one. Lily was not going to be an easy nut to crack. And it was better not to push and arouse her suspicions. No. It would be better to try and work my angles with Simon than Lily.

Still, I would return to the garden another time if I could. Lily interested me. For one thing, she'd won free of Lucius and survived. Not many left the Night World, let alone the Blood Courts. I wondered how she'd managed it. Was it true what the rumors whispered? Had she killed Lucius herself? And if so, why? For Simon, or for some darker reason?

Whatever the truth, she was here now. Here with no one making her dance to their tune. Here and free to sit in the sunshine and plant a garden.

For a moment I felt a pang of envy so deep I almost gasped. I'd always told myself that one day I would retire, move away. Start again and live in peace in a little house where no one would be interested in me and where my mother could live out her days in comfort. But the reality was that, unless there was a miracle, my mother was more likely to live out her days in the sanatorium. Which meant I needed the money to pay for it. The Owl wouldn't be flying away to a cozy fantasy nest any time soon.

Plus, to get beyond my father's reach—somewhere where he couldn't reach out and try to use me whenever it suited him—would mean going farther than I wanted to.

Would mean leaving everything I'd ever known, not to mention Reggie and Fen.

So there was no point sitting on a bench feeling sorry for myself. I had a job to do unless I could beat the geas. Which would require a miracle as much as curing my mother would. So most likely I would have to do as Cormen had commanded. That would at least give me some small degree of freedom until he decided to remember my existence again.

Fulfilling his wishes was the one sure way to free myself from his stinking geas. And I would make damn certain that I learned more about the disgusting things to see if there was anything I could do to avoid him trapping me with one again.

But that too had to wait until I had done what I'd come to do. I nodded politely to Lily and climbed to my feet, still feeling slightly unsteady. Time to go exploring.

Unfortunately my explorations didn't yield anything useful. I was starting to tire rapidly by the time I'd covered most of the main wing. Still, I forced myself to try one last corridor before giving up.

I retraced my steps from the ward where I'd hit a dead end to the place where the corridor I traveled intersected with four others. I had tried four of the five now. The last one lay straight ahead. It branched around a corner not far down its length and I couldn't see anything beyond that point.

I drew a deep breath. "One more try," I said softly, and walked slowly into the corridor. It didn't take long to reach the corner. So I took the turn. So far the corridor had been just that, a plain empty passage without even doors leading from it. The other corridors had held offices and wards, but this one was blank. Maybe that was a good sign.

I had walked for about five minutes when the corridor ended abruptly in a landing. A wooden staircase curled in a spiral both up and down.

Down? I peered out the window behind the stairs. I was still on the ground level of the hospital. So, what lay beneath? Laundries and kitchens and the usual, I supposed, but when I leaned cautiously over the railing I couldn't hear anything that suggested any such thing. No voices or water or the clatter of a large kitchen. I knew those noises well from the Swallow. And St. Giles was far bigger than the Swallow. Its kitchens and such would be massive. There was no smell of soap or steam or cooking. So, unless the hospital used magic to hide such things—and I couldn't think of why it would be worthwhile doing so—that wasn't what was down there in the bowels of the building. My instincts tugged at me. Down.

I hesitated. I hadn't brought any charms with me. Nothing to disguise myself or the traces of my passing. It seemed too risky to investigate while it was daylight and the hospital still hummed busily. No. I should go back. Try again later tonight with a charm to hide me.

My stomach growled suddenly as if agreeing with the assessment. I needed some food and a nap or I would, I suddenly realized, quite possibly fall over. I was pushing too hard.

A relapse wouldn't help me. I peered down over the railing again.

No.

Time to retreat. Tonight I could return with my charms and investigate properly. Fen had packed some trousers and shirts in the dark colors I used for runs in amongst the dresses and girl things. I would do a better job with the right tools.

I made my way back the way I had come, walking slowly to

ease the slightly woozy feeling in my head. When I met Simon coming the other way around the corner, I jumped like a startled cat.

"Miss Everton?" he said, eyebrows shooting upward. "What are you doing here?"

"I got turned around," I said. I'd thought of my cover story before even setting out. "This place has so many corridors, and they all look the same. Still, I knew I'd gone wrong when I reached the staircase. So I turned back." I smiled up at him, doing my best to charm. "Can you tell me how to get to my room? I think I need to lie down."

By the time Simon guided me back to the ward, I wasn't pretending any longer. I did need to lie down. In fact I fell asleep and didn't wake for several hours. My dinner was cold on a tray by my bed when I woke, but I was hungry enough to eat it anyway, stuffing roast lamb and vegetables into my mouth and slathering bread with a thick layer of butter and jam.

I felt somewhat better after I'd devoured the last of the food. But after finishing the meal, I knew I had a choice to make. It was late now. There was no clock in my room, but the sun, which stayed high for longer this time of year, had vanished a while ago and the sky outside my window was true night dark. The hours for visitors were well and truly over and the hospital was growing quiet. Well, quiet as a hospital got. It was never completely silent, but that didn't bother me. I'd grown up sleeping above a brothel. Compared to that, St. Giles was silent as a grave.

And I was wide awake.

There was nothing for it. If I was going to go risk those stairs and whatever lay below them, it should be now. I fetched the charm pouch from where I'd carefully wrapped it in the folds of one of the dresses Fen had brought, and upended its contents onto the counterpane.

Fen, it seemed, was to be thanked. There were not one but two invisibility charms bundled up with three hear-mes, a look-away, and a forget-me. I picked up one of the invisibility charms, feeling the faint buzz of it, waiting to be sparked to life.

I laid the charm in my lap and reached for the cutthroat. As many times as I'd pricked my fingers to draw blood to feed a charm, I'd never quite gotten used to the sensation. But I gritted my teeth and made the tiny cut. Blood beaded on my fingertip and I pressed it into the charm, feeling the sudden spark as it flared to life while I sucked my finger waiting for the cut to stop stinging.

When it did, I slipped the charm around my neck, threading the leather thong around the gold links of the chain holding my pendant where it hung, vibrating silently to my senses.

I pulled my hair back and tucking it around itself into a loose knot . . . the best I could do with my arm in a cast. The lock pick pins slid into place more easily and I felt the familiar sense of calm settle over me as I readied myself to work.

I touched the charm again to activate it, felt the edges of the world fizz and sparkle slightly as they always did before the sensation faded to the merest tickle in my skin. It was always somewhat eerie to see myself fade from view, but I took a deep breath, tidied everything away, messed the counterpane up so it looked as if I had just risen to perhaps use the facilities, and then slipped out the door.

I rapidly found my way to the staircase and, as I had earlier, stood for a moment trying to listen for anyone approaching. The stairs were narrow and I was invisible, not incorporeal. Anyone brushing past would feel me.

But it seemed for now, the stairs were deserted, so I took a last deep breath and headed down.

The stairs took me down three levels before they came to an end in another anonymous empty corridor leading straight ahead. At least it made deciding which way to go a little easier. I walked slowly down the tiled floor keeping close to the left-hand wall.

I reached the end of the corridor. This time it led off in two separate directions. If my sense of direction wasn't letting me down, then one ran back toward the front of the hospital and the other across the grounds. That way, my sketchy knowledge of the area told me, lay the Templar Brother House, though I wasn't sure why there would be a tunnel between the two.

So, where did the other branch lead? St. Giles was made up of seven or eight large buildings, so there were quite a few possibilities.

I hesitated. The corridor leading toward the hospital felt as all the others I'd traversed. Smelling faintly of hospital smells and the strange hot and cold mix of Fae and human magic. But the other direction . . . it felt different. Nothing I could put my finger on but somehow muffled.

That way. I followed my gut.

About a minute later I wished my gut might have had the foresight to warn me that I was about to run into three Templars walking in the other direction.

I froze in place, pressed against the wall, willing myself to breathe silently. All three of them were dressed in full mail and white tunics emblazoned with a red cross. Two of them half carried the third, a younger-looking man with deep brown skin whose tunic was covered with more red than just the cross. He'd been hurt, a rough bandage binding his right arm. It too was stained red. Bright, bright red. Rapidly spreading.

He looked as though he was half-unconscious and the two men escorting him looked grim, their clothes also spattered with blood.

I felt an instant of guilt. This was what Guy was facing every night. Danger. Injury. Death perhaps. All because they tried to keep the peace.

But keeping the peace wasn't my business. No, I was more concerned with keeping me and mine in one piece. Still, my gaze followed the Templars, as they passed me, wondering what they'd come up against.

I didn't take sides in Night World politics. I couldn't afford to. Another Blood Lord would rise to take power and fill the void that Lucius had left behind. It was hard to believe that whoever it was could be any more vicious than Lucius himself. The main issue would be whether they were progressive or one of those who thought we should return to the old days before the treaties. The latter seemed unlikely despite Guy's concerns.

The Blood had it good with the laws that allowed them free rein to drink amongst the Nightseekers—the humans who sought them out to chase the addictive pleasure of vampire blood. Hells, they weren't even punished if they *killed* Nightseekers. Why would they want to stir up trouble with the humans? Humans might be physically weaker, but they still had magic. And they had the Templars. Warriors prepared to defend their race unto death.

It was the Templars who'd helped win the battles that had led to the first treaty negotiations, leading attacks into the Blood and Beast territories until all parties were forced to negotiate. Once they'd won their way that far, the Fae queen had lent her support to the process.

As for the Beast packs, well, they varied. Some allied themselves with the Blood and some were more distant. Some just wanted to live their lives like the rest of us. I couldn't see that they would want war with the humans either.

None of this political musing was helping me fulfill my current mission. I schooled myself to silence and stillness until the Templars vanished around the corner and then set off again.

Luckily no more Templars appeared to give me further heart palpitations. There were, however, seemingly never-ending tunnel branches. I took the simple approach of choosing a right, left, right, left pattern. That was easy enough to remember and I could try other variations later if I needed to.

I was beginning to think the tunnels must run halfway across the City when I turned down another branch and the unexpected smell of iron and magic prickled my nose like a handful of black pepper.

My stomach tightened. Iron? Down here? Under a hospital half-full of Fae? That was something out of place.

Something hidden.

And I was looking for hidden things.

I set off down the tunnel. It was darker than the others, fewer torches lighting the way, but my eyes adjusted and I continued forward, the peppery, spiky taint of magic—human magic—and iron growing stronger in the air. Along with a gradual feeling that I was doing the wrong thing.

I ignored that.

Most likely, if there was something hidden down here, then there would be keep-away spells, designed to make anyone who stumbled upon the tunnel turn away. But they didn't stop me as I moved through the dim light until I came to an abrupt halt.

A massive door barred my way. A massive *iron* door. The air fairly reeked of it. If I were full Fae, I'd be feeling ill and heading rapidly in the other direction by now.

But I was a half-breed and immune to iron. Not that that meant I was getting through the door. The iron might not hurt me, but the wards shimmering over its surface almost certainly would. The colors of them swirled and sparked, interlocking lines of magic that spoke of protection that was beyond my abilities to defeat. Simple wards I can get around easily enough—I wouldn't be much of a spy if I couldn't accomplish that much—but these were far from simple. If I wasn't mistaken, both Fae and human magic had raised the layers of defenses and I didn't even know where to begin to unravel them. I clenched my hands, resisting the urge to pound on the door in frustration.

Iron to keep out the Fae. Whatever was down here was definitely a human secret. Simon's secret? Who else might be hiding something under St. Giles? Simon was, as Lily had mentioned, one of the strongest sunmages in the City. Surely it had to be him?

I could feel the geas straining within me, urging me on like a hunter who has finally tracked his prey to its lair. It made my stomach churn with a mix of the magic's anticipation and my own revulsion.

The problem was that I couldn't get any farther. Not without knowing more about the wards. I stared at the flickering shimmers, jaw clenching. I'd been hoping this would be easy. I should have known better. If the secret was easy to discover, then Cormen wouldn't have sent me. He would've used one of his own spies.

At least I knew there was definitely something to discover. Now I merely had to determine how to find out just what the bloody hell it was.

Chapter Seven

Guy
✠

You never get used to the dead.

I'd been in many battles, killed many men. Had many fall beside me but still, it never rests easy. Alone with the dead, with the smell of drying blood and cooling sweat and the stink of death, everything always felt too loud, too jerky, too . . . wrong. Even my own thoughts.

I knew I should be happy that they'd gone to God, gone to eternal grace and light. But yet every time, the stillness, the lack of life, is almost unbearable.

Tonight was no different. Tonight my hands were clenched as I stared down at the sheet-draped bodies in front of me. Two of my men. Rohan, only recently sworn to full knighthood, and Lenny, who was one of the knights who'd taught me to fight. Good soldiers. Good men. Lost. Cut down in a few minutes of out-of-nowhere Beast Kind attack.

Their deaths were the highest of the costs but not the only. Our sunmage, Liam, had been taken straight to St. Giles with a vicious wound to his arm I feared might cost him its use. And what the fuck my squad was going to do with our sunmage out of commission was something else I had to figure out.

"Are you still determined not to ask Lily for help?" Father Cho's voice came from behind me, ringing loud in the too-quiet room.

He didn't need to say more. Didn't need to speak of ambushes, of misdirection, of culpability. I knew who to blame.

I was the one who hadn't yet found a way to gather the information we needed. I was the one who'd led my men into another ambush, leaving these two dead amongst the bodies of more brown-haired or brown-furred Beast Kind.

Why the fuck were the Favreaus attacking us?

How the fuck had I managed to let things get so bad?

My fault, yes. But I wouldn't add to my guilt by letting my brother and his lover join the tally of the dead. But neither would I let that tally continue to grow.

"Lily isn't who we need," I said, not moving.

"She's a bloody better option than anyone else we have," a second voice chimed in.

I turned. Patrick. Another of our squad leaders. His brown hair stuck up in dried sweat spikes, and blood smeared his face. Had he lost people tonight as well?

His face bore the same rage consuming me.

"Lily is not an option," I said flatly. Patrick and I were friends. We'd entered the order together, fought together, drunk together, but friendship has its limits.

"You'd let our men die to protect a wraith? A half-breed God knows what?" he snarled.

My hand closed over my sword hilt. "Hold your tongue."

"Stand down," Father Cho ordered.

I eased back, just enough to appear to be obeying the order. "He doesn't get to talk that way about Lily, sir."

Father Cho nodded. "You're right. But he's also right. Unless you have a viable alternative, then this matter will be taken out of your hands. I'll ask her directly."

I didn't like the way "ask" sounded in his too-calm tone. Much too much like "order." Father Cho was another one of the few who knew Lily and Simon had killed Lucius. He had a blade to hold to her throat if he wanted. I didn't doubt he would use it to protect the City.

Beside him, Patrick looked triumphant. My hand curled again, the hilt hard against my hand. I wanted to hit something, and right now Patrick was a tempting target. But hitting a brother knight was likely to get me confined to the Brother House.

"There's another option, sir," I said. "Give me a few hours to get it set up." I saluted him, fist to heart, then headed for the door. This time I wasn't taking Holly's no for an answer.

HOLLY

The next morning I'd barely gotten dressed before Guy appeared in my doorway. He looked tired. Unshaven and his face streaked with grime. He smelled, quite frankly, of sweat and horse and the streets. Still, there was a part of me that pricked up its ears at the sight of him. Truly, I had no sense of self-preservation.

Be polite. Be calm. "Sir Guy. What brings you here?"

"I came to see if you'd changed your mind." He came farther into the room, shutting the door with a little too much force. He loomed there, in his stained tunic and trousers. Wrath incarnate. Suddenly it felt as if the air had been sucked out of the room.

"You mean have I decided to commit suicide?" I asked.

Anger rose from Guy like wings, stretching across the room to launch him at his prey. Which seemed to be me, if the intentness of his gaze was anything to go by.

But I'd learned a thing or two about dealing with predators in the Night World. With most—with the Blood and humans at least, as Beast Kind protocol is a very different animal—it's best not to give in to their threats. That only makes you seem weak. I straightened my spine. "No. I haven't."

"That's too bad," he said in a flat tone, gaze not moving.

I fought the urge to step back. "Oh? Are you here to cart me off to one of your cells, after all?" I felt sweat break out in the small of my back, fear tightening my throat.

If I called out now, would anyone hear me? Would they interfere if Guy did drag me out of the room? "What do you think Simon will think of that?"

"This isn't Simon's business," he said, but his voice sounded less cold. His hand strayed down from his sword to his right thigh, rubbing it as though it pained him.

"Are you hurt?" I asked despite myself.

His hand stilled as he shook his head. "No. But two of my men were killed last night." The rubbing started again and I wondered if he was even aware he was doing it. I should call

for Simon, but something in the bleak tone of his voice caught
at me.

Do not be foolish, Holly girl. He had problems, yes. The whole
city had problems. But I couldn't help him. I had to help myself.

"I'm sorry," I said softly. I could offer him that much at least.

"Sorry doesn't help me," he said, anger thrumming beneath
his words.

"I'm sorry anyway."

"They were good men," he said. If ice could burn, I'd imagine it would look like his eyes. "Good men who were trying to
protect others. They died because we walked into an ambush."

"That's not your fault." My throat was even drier. I swallowed, trying to ease it and the churning wave of nausea that
rose at the images his words conjured.

"It's my duty to protect. To keep the peace. I swore an oath."

"You can't promise to succeed all the time," I protested.

The heat in his rage turned chill. *Veil's eyes.* Did he really
think he had to do exactly that? Not many shades of gray in
Guy's world. What I knew of the human faith seemed very
black-and-white. How high did he set his standards?

Far above anything you'll ever measure up to, Holly girl.

I gritted my teeth at the sardonic voice in my head. I didn't
want to measure up to his standards. This man wasn't for me.
Particularly if he only saw me as a means to an end. I'd had
enough of that from my father. Anyone who wanted to use me
paid. And did so on my terms. "No one succeeds all the time," I
repeated. "Not even the famous Guy DuCaine."

"If the Templars don't succeed in this, then we all lose," he
snapped. "This isn't just the Blood jostling for power. If it were
just that, everything would be settled by now. This close to the
treaty negotiations, everyone should be focused on that. But instead, we have murder and riots and trouble as far as the eye can
see. The Night World may as well be on fire. Someone is stirring
things up."

My spine crawled. "What do you mean?"

"This isn't just the Blood playing politics. Someone has a
larger game in mind."

I sat down on the bed abruptly, as I tasted bile. "Such as?"

"I don't know," he said. Then his mouth tightened. "But if I
had to guess, I'd say that someone was trying to gain control of
the City. Break the treaty."

"Oh." My mind filled with unpleasant possibilities. Everyone in the City was brought up on the tales of the Old Days and why we shouldn't return to them. But apparently someone didn't agree. At least if Guy was correct.

And Cormen has you spying on a human, the voice whispered. Why would he want to do that? Gods, was Cormen really that stupid? To stand against the Veiled Queen?

Maybe not, but he might just be that arrogant.

"Exactly. Which is why I need your help."

"I can't help you, Guy," I said, then regretted the slip of the tongue that set his name free on my lips. "You'd just wind up with my death on your conscience too. Neither of us would be happy about that."

"You can help. You're a spy. Presumably a good one if you've survived this long. You know the Night World. You could find out who's doing this."

"What if it's not any one person? What if it's just a combination of things going wrong? The Blood being in turmoil. The Beasts taking advantage. And the Fae—" I paused for a moment, feeling the geas tighten my throat again. "Well, who knows what the Fae might be up to? But they seem the least likely to try and abandon the treaties. The iron rations make it easier for them to be in the world, not harder."

Guy's mouth set in deep carved lines as if he'd been up for days rather than just a night. As if what he'd seen had turned him to stone. "Even if it's more than one, we'd still know more than we know now. I need to know who's behind the attacks on the Templars."

"Attacks?"

"I told you. Ambushes. Beast Kind ambushes. At least one attack a night for nearly a week. Since the night I caught you, in fact."

Beasts attacking Templars? That meant either an alpha making some sort of power play, proving his loyalty to one of the Blood, or else someone had deep enough pockets to buy Beast muscle.

My mind flashed back to Henri and Ignatius. An unlikely pairing. Up to something. The conversation I'd recorded between them had been unhelpful. Caged in the broadest of terms. Nothing definitely incriminating or specific. Damn. My client had wanted confirmation they were meeting mostly. Now I wished she'd paid me to find out more.

What—I pulled myself out of my reverie. There was no point speculating. I was not going to throw myself into the middle of this and get myself killed.

"Do you know which pack?" I heard myself ask despite my good intentions.

"A mix. But the majority are wolves with light brown fur. Men with brown hair. Gray eyes."

Favreaus. Most likely. True, there were several packs that ran to light brown coloring, but the gray eyes . . . that was a Favreau trait. I looked down at my hands, mind still whirling.

The Favreaus . . . or Henri and a subfaction of the pack? Christophe had no love for Ignatius. Henri had ambition. Gods. There was no way of knowing. Not while I was here.

And here is where you're staying. You have a job to do.

I knew it was the truth. But I wanted to know more. If my father was involved in this mess . . . and the tingle in my gut—a well-honed instinct I'd learned to trust over the years—told me that he might just be . . . then knowing more might just be the opportunity to bring him down I'd always wanted.

But there was the little matter of the geas to consider. Not to mention the general insanity of wading into Night World politics right now.

I looked up at Guy. "Even if you knew which pack was behind this, what good would it do you? Are you going to wage war on the Beasts? Isn't that against the treaty?"

Guy's jaw clenched. "What we do with the information is not your business right now. Getting it is the first step. It's our duty to protect the City. We can't let it fall. *I* won't let it happen."

I noticed the change of pronoun at the end. Lady's eyes. Did he really think it was up to him to save the whole damned city? What sort of man thought that?

A good one. A very, very good one.

A crazy one, I retorted to the annoying whisper in my head. "You and your brother seem to have a thing about saving people," I said, trying for lightness in the face of his pain and frustration. I couldn't afford sympathy. Couldn't afford to want to soothe him. It would come at far too high a cost. "Perhaps you should've been a healer too."

"No." He shook his head, then stood. "No. This is my calling. I'm a warrior. And I'm sorry, Holly, but I have to do what I think is right to fulfill my oaths."

The crawling sensation in my spine redoubled. This wasn't good. But before I could protest or form any sort of plan to escape, the door flew open again. I jumped. Guy merely spun around.

Fen's tall form filled the doorway.

"What are you doing here?"

Guy and I spoke at the same time.

Fen scowled as he stepped into the room. One hand drifted to his hip where I knew he would have a pistol. "I could ask you the same question, tin man. I told you to stay away from her."

Guy folded his arms. "Sorry, I don't take orders from civilians. Particularly not crackpot drunks."

Buggering lords of hell. I stretched my hand toward the knife on my breakfast table as masculine aggression smoked the air. I would stab someone to stop a fight if I had to. I'd done it before.

Say something before this gets ugly.

"Fen, what are you doing here?"

He looked to me and his frown eased. But the expression that replaced it was one of worry.

My stomach dropped a little. "Fen?"

"I have some news," he said. He looked at Guy, and then jerked his head toward the door.

"I'm staying right here," Guy said, steel edged. "Holly and I were having a conversation."

"Holly?" Fen said.

I hugged my arms around myself, not liking the chilled queasiness that filled my stomach. "He can stay." I looked at Guy. "For now. What is it?"

"It's Reggie," he said quietly.

My mouth went dry. "What about her?" I asked.

"I can't find her."

"I don't understand."

"I went round to the—" He broke off, looking at Guy, obviously unsure how much he knew. "To see her. She wasn't there. And she wasn't in her rooms last night."

I looked at him, knew he was thinking the same things as me. Reggie didn't do one-night stands. She didn't go off without letting anyone know where she was.

"Maybe she worked through the night. Did you—"

"Yes, I checked again this morning. There was no one there."

Not good, Holly girl.

I wanted very badly to pretend that I couldn't put the pieces together, that I didn't know what this meant. But I did. I bent my head to my knees for a moment, breathing deep. Reggie was missing.

"Holly." Fen spoke softly, but something in his tone chilled me further.

I dragged my head upward, though it felt heavy on my neck, dread weighing it down. Fen's eyes were a dark sorrowing green instead of their usual merry gleam. Beside him, Guy's face was still grimly icy, but he stayed mercifully silent. "There's more, isn't there?"

Fen nodded. "Yes. When I couldn't find Reggie, I went to the sanatorium. Your mother isn't there."

Sweet lords of hell. *Mama.* My hands started to shake.

"What do you mean, she's not there?"

"Dr. Salinger said somebody came to collect her two days ago. Reggie was apparently visiting her and she went with them. Whoever it was didn't leave a forwarding address. He seemed quite confused about it all. I think somebody glamoured him."

I dropped my head down, beating my head against my knees. Stupid. So, so stupid. Why hadn't I seen this coming? I should've known Cormen would have a backup plan, another way to tighten the leash around my neck. Damn him to the depths of hell. Fen came over to me, crouched by the bed, and laid a hand on my arm. "Do you know who it was?"

I looked at him, tried not to sound as terrified as I felt. "Who do you think?"

Fen's mouth went flat. "Since when has he been poking around you again?"

"Who?" Guy demanded. "What's going on?"

How to explain Cormen to Guy? I wasn't sure I would even be able to speak his name with the geas controlling me. I wasn't sure I wanted to. "It's complicated."

"Someone has taken your mother away from a sanatorium along with your friend. Is your mother sick?"

I didn't particularly want to explain my mother either. "As I said, it's complicated." My tongue felt clumsy in my mouth and I didn't know whether it was the fear or the geas. Cormen had my mother, that much I was sure of. I had to assume he'd taken Reggie as well. That was how he'd found my mother, no doubt— set someone to follow Reggie and swooped them both up in one go. Surety for my good behavior.

Which meant he would be willing to do more than just take them to ensure my complicity with his little scheme.

My mother was old now, worn out beyond her years by the grief my father had caused her and the gin she'd drunk to forget. Cormen wouldn't think twice about hurting her. To him, she was no longer the beautiful human who'd caught his attention for a few years. Now she was just a tool.

Reggie would be even less to him.

My hands clenched involuntarily, my short nails digging into my skin. He would hurt them. Kill them maybe. And who knew if he would set them free even if I delivered Simon's secret?

He wanted this secret badly. Badly enough to want to ensure that I was bound to his will. And what better leverage than keeping my family hostage? I couldn't let him hurt them. But I had no idea how to go about finding the information he wanted. Or how to stop him.

"Holly?" Fen broke the silence. "What do you need?"

I looked up into the green eyes that understood all too well what it was to be cast off by a Fae lord. To be viewed as a possession to be discarded or picked up according to another's whim. And then I found myself looking past green to blue. To the warrior whose strength I suddenly needed.

"I need to speak to Sir Guy," I said to Fen. "Could you give us some time alone please?"

He didn't look happy but he gave in when I insisted.

"Well?" Guy said as the door closed behind Fen. "Are you going to tell me what's going on?"

I wanted to. The problem was that I didn't know how much I would be able to tell him. And I definitely didn't want to have to explain going into some sort of paroxysm if I involuntarily triggered the geas. "I can't," I said. "Not all of it."

"Why not?"

"Because it's dangerous," I said. There. That sounded plausible. Plus it was true.

"Are you going to tell me any of it?"

"Perhaps." I forced myself to look him straight in the eye and not give in to the panic still beating at me every time I thought of my mother and Reggie left to Cormen's not-so-tender mercies. "But first I have a proposition for you."

"Yes?" He sounded wary now.

"I'll help you—I'll spy for you—if you help me."

"Help you with what, exactly?"

I stopped for a moment, not sure that what I was about to say made any sense at all. But right now I couldn't think of anyone else who might actually be able to help me take on Cormen and succeed. "I need you to help me get them back. My mother and Reggie."

"From who?"

"I can't tell you that. Not all of it. One of the Fae. That's all I can say." Even that made my skin crawl a little under the sting of the geas. There was no way I could say "my father."

"Do you know where they are?"

"No."

"Do you have a plan?"

"No."

He folded his arms. "Do you have any idea what it is you'll need me for?"

"No." I was starting to feel vaguely stupid. And hopeless.

To my surprise, Guy smiled. A somewhat grim smile but a smile nevertheless. "Good. Sounds like my kind of situation."

I gaped at him. He sounded as though he was looking forward to it. "Excuse me?"

"Hopeless causes. It's what the Templars do best."

I forced my jaw shut. "Are you making fun of me?" My rule was more to run away from trouble when I could. But I wasn't a Templar. This attitude was exactly why I needed him.

He shook his head. "No. I'm being honest. It is what I do best. Now, how are you going to find out where they are?"

That much, I did know. The prospect didn't exactly delight me, but the only other way to find out where Cormen had taken my mother was even less appealing. I squared my shoulders. "The same way we're going to find out what you want to know about the Beasts. We're going to go play in the Night World."

Guy's blue eyes turned intent. "You said that wasn't a good idea."

"It's not a good idea," I said. "But I don't have a better one. You want information. I want my mother and Reggie. So we can make a deal. But the Night World is our only option." Which meant we both better start praying to whatever petty saints and deities looked after hopeless causes, because it would take a miracle or two to pull this off. "So if you can't deal with that, say no."

"Oh, I can deal with the Night World."

"Can you? Because this means you can't go in waving your sword."

"I know that."

"It also means," I continued before I could stop to think too hard about what I was about to say, "that you need a cover story. Tell me you've got one. Other than playing my lover." It was a vain hope that he might have come up with something else that made sense when I hadn't been able to. Even if he could come up with a story to explain why Guy DuCaine was suddenly slumming it in the Night World, I couldn't think of anything that explained the two of us spending time together other than us being lovers. I had no time to waste to come up for other ways for us to meet and exchange information without anyone knowing. Not with my family in Cormen's hands.

"I haven't," he admitted. "But you're right, it is the only thing that makes sense."

Lords of hell. *Bad idea, Holly girl.* But I didn't have another. I was just going to have to make certain that playing lovers didn't go any further than that.

Which might be another vain hope, when even now there was a part of me that wanted to touch him, to try and ease some of the pain and weariness I saw in his face, despite my better judgment. I curled my fingers into my palm, determined to keep my hands to myself. "You still need a reason that people will buy for you being there with me in the first place. They need to think you're not a Templar any more or nothing else will matter."

He nodded. "Leave that to me."

His expression did invite any questions on my part, so I just nodded in return. "How long will it take?" Every hour that Cormen had Mama and Reggie was an hour they were in danger, an hour closer to the point where his temper might snap.

"Plan on leaving tonight," he said.

Guy
✝

"Are you sure about this?" Father Cho asked gravely. He leaned across the desk, as if proximity could persuade me to abandon my plan.

"As sure as I can be, sir."

"You trust this girl? This Night Worlder?"

An interesting question. Did I think I should trust Holly? No. Did I somehow feel that perhaps I did, despite myself? Yes. And, in truth, she wasn't a true Night Worlder. But I wasn't going to be foolish enough to let myself be swayed by my instincts. "Not particularly. But she needs my help. I believe that will keep her in line. At least until she gets what she wants."

"And after that?"

That was a bridge I hoped I wouldn't have to cross. "I intend to see to it that we get what we want first. It's worth it if we can get to the bottom of these ambushes and stop them," I said firmly.

Father Cho shook his head. "I don't like this, Guy. We need you here."

"We need the information more. I'm not letting her go after it unprotected."

We stared at each other.

"There is another way."

"Lily is not up for discussion, sir. Besides, I need to use Simon and Lily for my cover story."

"I don't like that either. If you make your brother knights doubt you, believe what you want them to believe, it might take a long time to win back their trust. You might never get it back fully."

I wasn't going to think about that. The order was a part of my family. But for family, you made sacrifices. Did things they might not like to keep them safe.

Paid the price willingly.

So I would pay. And hope that God, at least, would grant me forgiveness if my brother knights wouldn't. In the end, that was all that mattered.

"I'm aware of that. I'll live with it."

Father Cho's dark brown eyes were sorrowful. "I know you will. That's why I wish you wouldn't. You're a good man, Guy. But you're stepping into darkness here."

"I've come through darkness before, sir. I'll find my way, with God's grace."

"I really can't convince you otherwise?"

"No."

He pursed his lips, bowed his head for a moment. Considering my fate. If he refused to grant permission, I didn't know exactly what I would do. I believed I was choosing the right path. Would I step onto it against the order's wishes? I waited, ignoring the tension riding my gut.

"Very well," Father Cho said. "I will let you do this thing. I will pray for your success." His tone suggested he thought I would need his prayers.

I hoped to hell that he wasn't right. "Thank you, sir."

He straightened, all business now that he'd made his decision. "When do you want to begin?"

"I need to speak to Lady Bryony first." I glanced at the clock on the wall. It was just after midday. The Night World was asleep. If Holly and I were going to make a splashy entrance, then we needed to arrive after it had come to life. After dark. "And I have some other things to arrange."

Lily to convince, as a starting point. She and Simon were going to be just as unhappy with me as Father Cho was.

"How long do you need?"

I calculated time against the list of things to do forming in my head. "I think if we set things in motion after the afternoon services, that should work."

"All right. Go do what you have to do."

I nodded. "Yes, sir." I saluted him and turned to leave.

"Guy?"

I turned. "Yes, Father?"

"Make sure you don't forget who you are."

Chapter Eight

HOLLY

The pile of charms was awfully small. One invisibility charm, three hear-mes, the look-away, and the forget-me. Worse, I didn't have any of the things I needed to fashion more.

Charms are odd beasts. Peculiar, contrary, and volatile. Everyone fashions them uniquely. Some use metal, some wood, some fabric or even leaves and grasses. The material isn't actually important, it's just a place to store your magic, but everybody has to find the way of coaxing that magic that works for them. I work with metal and glass and use leather and oils.

And blood.

Just trappings, Miss Evendale. I could almost hear the prim tones of the reluctant tutor my father had hired to teach me when I'd first shown signs of having power. We hadn't gotten very far past the rudiments before it became evident that my charms only worked well on me. Not useful in Cormen's eyes. No point wasting any more coin on my education.

But the basics had been enough and I picked up the rest myself over the years, honing the craft until I could make almost anything I needed.

Anything *I* needed. I'd never been able to produce something that I could rely on to work consistently for somebody else.

Which was exactly what I needed now.

I swallowed against tears of frustration. I needed this to work. I was leaving St. Giles tonight. But I needed a way to keep doing what the geas wanted me to do. Otherwise, for all I knew, it would force me to turn around and come straight back as soon as I stepped over the boundaries of the hospital.

I needed a way to spy on Simon when I couldn't actually be here to do it.

And, in the almost endless few hours since Guy had left to do whatever it was he was going to do, the only option I could come up with was a charm. Something to be my eyes and ears. Something to get through those wards guarding that iron door so far below.

I didn't want to do it. Not if I could find my father and get Mama and Reggie back first. Not if I could figure out how to rid myself of his hells-damned geas.

But I'd run out of time. So I had no choice.

I stirred the charms with a finger.

Think, *Holly girl.*

The charm I needed wasn't anything I'd ever thought of making. Or even heard of anyone else making. The most reliable charms did one thing and one thing only.

I needed one that did many things and hid itself as well.

Question was, could I conjure the impossible?

GUY
✝

"Sir Guy," Lady Bryony said with a nod, straightening from the plant she'd been tending. "What can I do for you?"

She wore a dark purple dress, which almost matched the unnatural Fae shade of her eyes, her black hair piled on her head. The light caught the sapphires in her Family ring as she beckoned me forward.

"A favor, my lady," I said, feeling awkward. Simon thought I had a "thing" for Lady Bryony. Perhaps I did. She was undeniably beautiful, but it was a dangerous beauty. Sharp and deadly like a knife's blade. She could heat a man's blood, sure enough, but like as not she could also boil it dry in his veins with a look. And beyond that, she made the air prickle around her. As though she had a thunderstorm under her skin.

Wiser to keep away. Not risk the lightning strike.

The Fae were nothing to trifle with. Nor beg favors from. A debt to a Fae was dangerous. Lady Bryony spent most of her time in the human world, and her affection for my brother might mean that she treated me as she would him and would take no obligation from me. But then again, it might not.

I waited while she considered this, head tipped to one side, one hand toying with the ever-changing chain around her neck. Behind me, I heard the door close firmly. Another reminder of her power. "Go on," she said.

I held out my hands. "I need to go into the Night World for a time. These are going to cause problems. Can you glamour them?"

"You want to hide your tattoos? Why?" Her voice sounded genuinely shocked. "What does the Abbott General have to say about this?"

"The Abbott General is well aware of it," I said. "But I can't tell you why. And I must ask for your word that you will not speak of this."

The chain around her neck darkened a little as her brows drew down. "Secrets, Guy? Haven't we had enough of those lately?"

"Troubled times, my lady," I said. "This way is safest."

"Is it that you don't trust me or you're trying to protect me?" she said, the frown still marring her face.

"Father Cho and I agreed that this is necessary," I said, trying to avoid the question. I wasn't going to tell Bryony I didn't trust her. And she'd probably laugh in my face if I told her I was protecting her.

Bryony pressed her lips together as though she wanted to argue, but knew better than to question me further if I had Father Cho's blessing.

"Hold out your hands," she said.

I did so and she took my hands in hers, inspecting them closely. "How old were you when you got these?" she asked.

"I took my final vows at nineteen."

"I see." Her grip tightened and something tingled through my skin, like the brush of icy feathers. Then Bryony looked up at me, shaking her head.

"These will be hard to hide with a glamour, Guy. They're part of you now. I think you would fight the magic. Besides, in the

Night World there will be many who'll be able to tell you've glamoured your hands. Some won't question it, but there will be those who do. Those who are capable of seeing right through the spell."

I bit back the curse. Holly had said as much the very first time I'd proposed going with her into the Night World. I'd hoped she was wrong. "Is there something else you can do?"

The chain around her neck slid rapidly through several colors before settling on greenish silver. "That depends on what you're going to be doing."

I shook my head at her. "Nice try, my lady. But I can't tell you that."

She let go of my hands, smoothed her skirts, and sat down. "There's no easy way to hide these. They're old and the color is deep. I could come up with something to change the color, but it might do permanent damage to your skin."

I looked down at the crosses, familiar to me as my reflection. Imagined them scarred and distorted. My gut twisted.

"Guy?"

I looked at Bryony, anger and disgust mingling as I realized what I was going to have to do. Father Cho had been right. This path was going to take me places I didn't want to go. But that wasn't a reason to turn around. I could live with a little darkness if I got what I wanted, if it protected my family and the order. "Thank you," I said. "Looks as though I might have to do this the old-fashioned way."

HOLLY

I was running out of time. Guy had said "tonight." It was already midafternoon; the sun through my window was turning languid, losing the bite of the hottest part of the day. If I was going to act, I had to act now.

So, then. A charm to do what no charm did. Simple.

A threefold charm. To listen. To disappear. To protect itself. Any one of those alone I could do. But how to turn three into one?

My hand froze over the charms. Could it really be that simple?

Maybe not. But it wasn't as though I had endless options available to me. I scooped up the invisibility charm, the hear-me, and the look-away. Three dangling circles of metal and glass glinted in my hand, their leather and silk thongs twisted around them.

I had no flame to melt them, to combine them, so I was going to have to do something more basic. More primal.

Three into one. I let my mind go blank, seeking that place where the magic flows without thinking.

I stood, carried the charms over to the window, let the light pour over them as I untied the thongs and then twisted the three onto a single loop, pressed tightly together.

The feel of them changed slightly under my fingers but not enough. They needed something more.

Change. Combine. Connect.

The old ways would say that the most basic key to bind something to your will is blood. Yours or theirs. That was, as far as I could tell, the reason that Cormen could bind me when nobody else could. Blood ties.

Charms weren't flesh. They didn't have blood of their own, though they did have a strange sort of life. Usually it took a tiny drop of blood to spark that life.

This time I would need more.

I thought for a moment. The cutthroat cut finely, but that didn't feel right. Magic requires power. Desire. Emotion.

I needed something that would bite me deeper than the razor.

I looked around the room, trying to think what I could use. Then went to the bed and the bag Fen had brought me. Along with clothes and charms, he'd brought me my hair brush and various things scooped pell-mell off my dressing table. Amongst them was a small mirror, a pretty gilt thing that had been my mother's.

One of the last things she'd given me before she'd drifted into whatever place it was she went to in her mind. I remembered her laughing as she tossed it to me, telling me that I needed such things more than she did now. The mirror's glass was small but hopefully large enough that if I smashed it, it should yield a shard or two big enough to slice a finger.

I wrapped my hand around it, fighting tears again. I didn't want to destroy it, but that was exactly why I had to. A sacrifice would add to the power of the charm. I pressed the mirror quickly to my lips. Then, eyes stinging, I wrapped it in the folds of a skirt and bashed it hard against the metal bed frame. There was a rapid *clink* of breaking glass and I felt the shape of it bend beneath my hand.

Mama. Biting my lip, I unwrapped the folds quickly. Several large shards of mirrored glass glinted up at me and I picked one up carefully to carry to the window.

I gathered the charms and reached for the magic again. Nothing but my will and my blood to help work what I needed. I took a deep breath, slashed my forearm with the glass, biting down the protesting cry that rose in my throat at the sudden pain.

Blood welled. Came fast and red. Too fast. I fought for breath as the room wobbled a little around me.

I held my arm over the charms, letting the blood drip until I judged there was enough. Then I closed my fingers around them, feeling blood-dampened metal and leather and glass.

My arm throbbed as I closed my eyes and concentrated.

Change. Combine. Connect.

Sweet Lady, let this work.

The song of the charms under my hand altered, a chord resolving. Three distinct notes hummed into one and I opened my hand cautiously. They still looked the same. Still a mess of thongs and metal and glass, but the bright red blood had vanished and only that single note sounded in my head like a benediction.

So I'd achieved something. Whether or not it would do what I needed was another matter entirely. As was how in seven hells I was going to be able to plant it on Simon before I left.

GUY
✠

"Simon isn't here," Lily said, scooping the kitten off her lap as she rose to greet me with a smile.

I didn't think the smile would last very long once she heard what I had come to say. "I came to see you."

The smile vanished. "Yes?"

She had good instincts; she knew trouble when she saw it. Growing up in the Blood Court will do that to a person.

"Can we sit?"

She considered me for a moment, then turned on her heel and led the way to the kitchen. She pulled out one of the kitchen chairs and nodded at me. "Sit. Talk."

"We had trouble again last night," I said, trying to think how best to appeal to this woman who was still largely a mystery to me. The one thing I knew for certain about her was that she would defend what she considered hers. Simon fell into that category. I thought I did too but wasn't entirely sure. "Men died," I continued.

"I'm sorry," she said gravely. "In your squad?"

"Yes, two."

Sympathy flashed in the clear gray eyes. "The City is troubled."

"The City," I said, figuring that, when it came right to it, the truth was easiest, "seems to be under attack. Or the treaty is."

Lily shifted in her chair, one hand straying to her hip as it did when she felt uneasy. She still wore her weapons, even here in the house where she felt safest. "How do you know?"

"There's simply too much trouble. If it were just the Blood, there'd be a new lord by now and things would be calming down."

"You don't know that for sure."

"No. But I don't know that I'm wrong either. These attacks . . . there's a reason for them. Just like there has to be a reason for the Beast that tried here."

Her eyes darkened at the memory. "They haven't tried again."

"Yet," I said bluntly.

Lily nodded. Good. I wasn't going to have to argue. Lily was a fighter, like me. She saw things clearly.

"If these ambushes keep happening, then the Templars are going to be weakened before we even get close to the treaty negotiations. If that happens the whole damned city is going to go down in flames. I need to find out who's behind them and stop them."

Lily went very still. "You want me to spy for you?" Her tone was flat, every emotion stripped from it, buried under control that went down to her bones. This was how she'd been when Simon and I had first taken her from Lucius. Before Simon had somehow connected with the woman beneath the killer. A creature of ice and shadow. No way to know what she was thinking. Or what she might do.

"No. I want to keep you safe. You and Simon. I want to make sure that you're not dragged into this. You know what the risk is if one of the Blood did catch you. A Blood Lord with wraith powers is the last thing we need. But I won't lie to you, Lily. There are those in the order who think we should be using you."

"I don't belong to the Templars." Her voice if anything was colder. Lily had been a slave for the first thirty-odd years of her life. I knew she had no intention of letting anybody control her ever again. She'd die first.

"I know you don't. And I won't let them try to claim otherwise."

"Why do I feel as though there's a 'but' at the end of that sentence?"

"Because there is. To keep you out of this, I have to use somebody else."

"Who?"

"There was a girl brought into St. Giles a few days ago."

"The one who fell down some stairs?"

My eyebrows rose a little. "How did you know about her?"

"Simon told me. And I think I met her in the garden a few days ago. She's half Fae, yes?"

"Yes. She's also a spy."

"A Night Worlder?"

"More a neutral party. From what I hear, she works for whoever has the price. Blood or Beast or Fae or maybe even humans."

"None of whom will appreciate her working for the Templars," Lily said. "So why is she helping you?" There was a dangerous gleam in her eye now.

"I'm not forcing her," I said before her temper could rise too high. "We've come to an agreement. I'm helping her with something she wants and she'll help me in turn."

"Then what's the catch?"

"As you said, it's dangerous for her to do this. And I'm not going to leave her unprotected."

Lily's mouth formed a perfect O for a moment, then she pressed her lips together disapprovingly. "A Templar can't go into the Night World, Guy. You won't get anywhere. If they let you live."

"I know," I said grimly. "That's where you come in."

*   *   *

I left Lily with Bryony and returned to the Brother House just as afternoon services were beginning. I slipped into the chapel, taking a seat near the rear of the high narrow room, and closed my eyes.

God, let me be doing the right thing.

Not much as prayers went, but I'd never been one for fancy prayers outside of the order's rituals. So far, God didn't seem to mind.

I didn't really pay attention to the service. The familiar cadences washed over me, leaving me alone in my head with my simple prayer as my body and mouth moved at the correct times and formed the correct responses. As always, a sense of calm settled over me as I sat surrounded by the sounds of worship. A sense that I was doing the right thing. A feeling unique to this place.

I swallowed, the next response dying on my lips. How long until I would stand here again, in this place that had always been a refuge and a homecoming? The place where I stood with my fellow knights and my God and felt welcome.

Would it ever be that way again?

God, let me do the right thing and please, God, forgive me.

The last chants ended and I stood, adrenaline combining with the lack of sleep to leave me feeling detached and vaguely sick. As Father Cho moved past me, he nodded slightly. I squared my shoulders. All right, then. Time to begin.

I waited until everyone else had left the chapel, wanting a few more moments of peace. When I finally emerged, one of the novices was waiting for me.

"Father Cho needs you to attend the afternoon report, Sir Guy," he said respectfully. I looked at him, struggling for a moment to remember his name. He was young and gangly and eager, like most of the novices. As I had been at his age. Several lifetimes ago.

"Thank you, Robert," I said.

"In his office, sir."

I nodded. Nothing out of the ordinary. Not yet. No one would suspect what we were about to do. "On your way," I said to Robert, and started for Father Cho's office, feeling not a little like a novice on his way to a punishment myself.

Father Cho stood, as usual, behind his desk, studying the map spread across it. Ranged around him were the five early patrol squad leaders, red-eyed, dust-stained, and rumpled. Patrick was there too. He obviously hadn't gotten any sleep yet either. And he didn't look as though his mood had improved any.

I'd half expected him to be here—Father Cho always did know how to pick his audience—but I wished I'd been wrong.

However, the more people who witnessed this, the better. I joined the others at the desk, taking position opposite Patrick.

Father Cho lifted his head, his expression inscrutable. I wondered if he was giving me a chance to change my mind. I merely stood silent. He looked around the group, then at me. "We lost another man today," he said.

Hell's balls. Three in one day? At this rate there might not be an order to return to. "Who?" I asked.

"Kendrick." It was Patrick who spoke, and anger turned his voice gravelly. "Another ambush. Fucking Beasts."

Kendrick was another of the novices. I tightened my jaw, determined not to show any reaction. I was here to be contrary. "Too bad," I said casually. "He would've been a good man, eventually."

Stuart, Kendrick's squad leader, shot me an incredulous look. "He *was* a good man," he snarled. He turned to Father Cho. "We can't keep going on this way. It's suicide."

"You think we should just give up? Hide away?" Patrick shot back.

"I think we need a better plan," Stuart said.

"What we need," Patrick said with a dark look in my direction, "is better information."

"What we need," I said, mimicking his tone and his look, "is for you not to think, Patrick. Never was your strong point."

Patrick's hand slipped down to his sword hilt. "You—"

"Enough." Father Cho's voice snapped out, and we fell silent, too well trained to ignore that particular tone of command.

"We need intelligence," he said into the silence. He looked squarely at me. "I'm sorry, Guy, but we're going to have to use Lily."

"No," I said flatly. "You're not."

"You have a better idea?" Patrick said, his hand still wrapped around his sword.

"No," I said, feeling sick at what I was doing. Patrick was playing into my hands exactly as we needed him to. But it didn't feel good. No, seeing the anger and pain in him felt more like being covered in battle gore, the kind that clings to your skin and fills your nose with the stink of pain and death. The kind you can't wait to scrub away but are never sure you truly can. "No, I don't. But you're not having Lily."

"Yet you'd put us at risk to protect your brother's Night Worlder whore?" Patrick snarled.

My sword was out and pointed at Patrick's throat before he could blink. "I believe the term you're looking for," I drawled, "is *fiancée*. Apologize."

"For speaking the truth?" Patrick said. "I don't think so."

There was a hiss of metal as he started to pull his own sword free. I pressed my point closer, just at the point of drawing blood.

"Guy! Stand down," Father Cho snapped.

I shook my head. "No, sir, I don't believe I will. Patrick here insulted a member of my family."

"You do not draw a weapon on a brother knight in this house. Stand down!" Father Cho thundered.

My fingers gripped the sword tighter as I fought the instinctive urge to obey. "No," I repeated. "He's not my brother when he would happily send someone under my protection into danger."

"Guy, don't do this," Father Cho said. "I won't have discord in the order. We can't afford it."

"Then I suggest you tell Patrick that Lily is not a weapon to be deployed at his whim," I said, still watching Patrick. I didn't think he'd actually attack me in front of Father Cho or else we'd have one more disgraced knight than I'd been planning on to deal with.

Father Cho looked furious. Enough that part of me instinctively wanted to follow his order. Years of training bit deep, but I ignored them, held my sword steady.

"I'm the one who decides what weapons we will or will not use, and right now we need all of them. I'm sure Lily will understand why we need her," Father Cho said flatly.

She probably would at that. In fact, she'd argued with me for a long time before agreeing to do things my way because she did feel she owed the humans something. But her sense of obligation wasn't enough for me to agree to let her throw away what she and Simon had built together. Or let whoever was pulling the strings behind this whole mess get their hands on her so easily. If indeed it was her they wanted.

"No, sir," I said, wondering if my voice sounded as strange to them as it did to me. I felt as though I were listening to myself from a distance or watching a play. One where I knew what happened, knew I couldn't change it, but still wanted to scream at the players to make the ending come out differently. "I don't think you can. I think you'll find that Lily has been granted haven at St. Giles. As has my brother. And not even you can make them set one foot over the threshold against their will, sir."

"You warned them?" Father Cho sounded both furious and incredulous now. I'd not realized he was such a good actor. Then again, leading men is partly a performance. "You knew that I wanted to ask for her help and you warned her? Against the interests of the order and the whole bloody city?"

You could have heard a pin drop. Stuart and the other four squad leaders were frozen in place, not knowing where to turn. Patrick stared at me as if I'd just smeared dog shit across the chapel altar.

"So it would seem. You forced me to choose. Well, I choose my family." I left off the "sir" with an effort of will.

"Once upon a time you would have said the order was your family, Guy. You swore oaths. Oaths of obedience. I'll give you one last chance. Go and talk to Lily. That's an order."

"I can't do that."

"Guy, we're fighting a war. Right here, right now, we're under attack. The people we have sworn to protect are dying. I just gave you an order."

"And I'm declining it. I won't do it." I steeled myself for what came next.

Father Cho drew in a breath. "So be it."

I turned my head at that, meeting his gaze, dark with pain and anger. "The six of you stand witness here. Guy DuCaine, for forswearing your oaths to this order, I hereby banish you from its ranks. You are stripped of rank and commission. I want you out of here in one hour."

I stepped back, sheathed my sword. "Suits me just fine," I said. "I don't belong here anymore."

Father Cho's mouth was flat and grim. "So let it be done," he said, completing the order. "May God have mercy on your soul. Because if we find you working against the order again, Guy, we will not."

Chapter Nine

HOLLY

I heard the cathedral bell toll five o'clock and wondered how much time I had left before Guy returned. Not much. I had to plant the charm. Which meant seeing Simon. He usually checked in on me sometime during the afternoon. So, did I chance waiting or did I go looking?

My palms were damp as I slipped the charm into my pocket. Making it was the first step. Getting it into place would be another thing entirely. I didn't know if a glamour would even work on a sunmage.

If it didn't . . . if I tried and failed, then Lady knew what might happen.

Don't think about that. Just get to work. I took a shaky breath, then made up my mind. I would go find Simon before I ran out of time. I was just about to leave when Simon opened my door and smiled at me.

Guilt squeezed my heart. This man had been nothing but kind to me, yet here I was, trying to betray him. But kind or not, he wasn't family. My mother and Reggie were. They were depending on me. I had no choice. And perhaps my father was wrong. Perhaps Simon had no secrets to be discovered.

"How are you feeling today?" Simon asked, studying me with those guileless blue eyes.

Do it now. I had to try. No more time for doubt or indecision. If I hesitated, I would lose my chance and my mother and Reggie might be lost.

"Actually, I wanted to talk to you about that," I said. I held my arm. "I need you to take the cast off."

"What?" He came toward me as I had hoped he would. "You're not ready for that. Your bones will still be fragile." He laid his hand on the cast and frowned. "Is it hurting you?"

"Simon," I said softly, and he looked at me. I laid my hand over his, skin to skin.

Do it now. No more thinking.

I gathered my magic and threw the glamour at him. Simon's eyes went soft and dazed.

"Simon," I said, testing exactly what control I might have over him. "Let go of my arm."

He obeyed.

"Good. Now, I'm going to do something and you're not to remember it." I stood slowly, but he stayed where he was, not moving, not reacting.

Cautiously, using every pickpocket skill I ever had, I came around to his side and slid my hand under his tunic, to where I sensed the invisibility charm, like a tiny cool beacon. This was the tricky part. This charm wasn't mine, but I had to piggyback mine onto it. And hope that no one would notice the difference.

Simon's charm was tied to a loop inside the waistband of his trousers. Feeling ill, I gently pulled it free from where the fabric pressed it against his skin. Like mine, it was fashioned from leather and metal, which made my task a little easier. I studied the charm for a moment, feeling its buzz against my skin.

It didn't feel completely alien. So maybe this had a chance of working. Of course, I had no idea what the charm felt like to Simon, or indeed if he could feel it at all. He wasn't Fae, after all. While human mages could work glamours and wards, they didn't do charms as far as I knew. They were a peculiarly Fae thing.

When I was sure the charm wasn't going to do something odd in protest of being removed from its owner, I reached into the pocket of my jacket and pulled out the hybrid charm I'd fashioned earlier. I plaited the two charms together, trying to hide the metal disc of mine behind the more oval shape of Simon's. Then, with another whispered plea to whichever deity might be listening, I triggered my charm, after pouring still more power into it in the hope it would last as long as it needed to.

Inside me, I felt the geas buzz with something that felt like approval. I choked back the revulsion that greased my throat in response.

The charm shivered in my hands and suddenly I could only see Simon's. I could feel the slightly thickened thong under my fingers, but I couldn't see my charm. So the invisibility part, at least, was working. Now I just had hope that the hear-me would do its part too. And that the look-away would be enough to keep the whole thing safe. Plus the completely unknown factor of whether there would actually be anything for the hear-me to hear.

Too late now. I was out of time. I fastened the charm in place and slid into position on the bed.

"Simon," I said gently, easing his hand back onto my cast. "Forget."

His eyes drifted slowly shut for a moment and I dissolved the glamour with a slow breath, releasing him gently.

"Simon?" I said in a more normal voice.

He shook his head for a moment, and then yawned. "Sorry," he said, sounding somewhat embarrassed. "It's been a busy day. Now, what were you saying about your arm?"

Relief made my pulse pound in my ears for a moment. It seemed I'd gotten away with it. At least for now.

"I said, I need you to take the cast off," I said, acting as though there'd been no break in our conversation.

"But why?" he asked.

Before I could answer, the door was flung open and Guy stalked in.

"Because," Guy said, shooting a "don't argue" look at Simon, "she's coming with me."

"What are you talking about?" Simon said. "She's in no shape to go anywhere."

"Nevertheless, we're leaving. Take off her cast." Guy folded his arms. He looked tired and tense. I wasn't sure exactly what he'd just done, but whatever it was, he wasn't happy about it.

"Where are you going?" Simon asked.

Guy frowned at him. "No time to explain, little brother. Go find Lily. She'll explain."

Simon's face was starting to move from confused to angry. "She's not working today. Why is she here?"

"She's seen the light. She's going to be staying here for a while. Bryony has granted her haven."

"What? Gods and suns, Guy, what is going on?"

"Talk to Lily," Guy said shortly. "We have to go."

"Holly?" Simon said.

"Take it off, please," I said.

The brothers stared at each other for a long moment, hands bunching, scowling identically. I wondered if I was about to have to break up a fight.

Simon finally shook his head, looking disgusted, and focused his attention on me. "You know you're doing this against my advice?" he asked. He stood at the end of the bed, holding the slim leather book, which he scribbled his notes into with both hands as if he might prefer to knock some sense into me with it.

I nodded and held out my arm. Despite the roil of guilt and fear in my stomach and my inability to convince myself that this wouldn't all end in disaster, I would be all too happy to have the cast off. It was heavy. And beneath it, my skin itched. "I know. Take it off."

Simon looked from me to Guy and shook his head. "This isn't a good idea."

"She wants the cast off," Guy said flatly. "Take it off."

"And if I refuse?" Simon said.

Guy shrugged. "Then I'll take her somewhere else. It's her choice."

Simon's face turned stubborn. "This really isn't a good idea."

"It's my decision," I said, giving my arm a little jerk. I was careful to keep the other arm—the one with the gash from the mirror that I'd bandaged as best I could with a strip of petticoat—back a little. I didn't know if Simon could sense a minor wound if he wasn't actually trying to, but I didn't want to risk it. There was no good explanation for how I'd managed to cut my arm. Simon frowned but bent to the cast. "What's so important?"

"That's my business," Guy said, arms folded against his chest. He looked forbiddingly grim. Simon was braver than me to argue with him.

"Your business or Templar business?" Simon's gaze shot to me. "Holly? You're doing this of your own free will, aren't you?"

I nodded. "Yes. Don't worry, he isn't coercing me."

"Just as well," Simon muttered.

He and Guy exchanged another of those inscrutable looks, but Simon didn't make any more protests. He did something to the cast that made it neatly divide into two parts and lifted it gently from my arm. Then he washed the remaining bits of plaster off my skin and slathered on a strong-smelling salve. I wrinkled my nose. "Thank you." My arm smelled of garlic or . . . no, not garlic exactly but something stingingly pungent. "What is that stuff?"

"Healer business," Simon said shortly. "It will help your skin and wake up the muscles. You've only had the cast on a few days, but there's always some wastage." He fixed me with a stern glance. "So don't go doing anything stupid. You'll need to strengthen the arm. Slowly. Your bones are still fragile."

"I will," I said, not sure whether I meant yes, I'd let it rest or yes, I'd do something stupid.

Given where Guy and I were headed, the latter seemed almost inevitable. Just wanting to go spy in the Night World was a fair indication of stupidity.

Generally I skirted around its edges as far as possible. The border boroughs provided plenty of jobs for me without getting too deep into the night. But stupid or not, I had need, in this case. If there was any information about where my father was and what he might be plotting to be had, it would be the Night Worlders who knew.

Simon put the jar of salve on the bed, on top of the bag of my things, and then turned to Guy. "Look after her. And be careful. I don't want to have to come after you."

"I'm always careful, little brother," Guy said easily. But there was tension in his neck and shoulders as he shifted against the wall he was leaning on. "You know that."

"I mean normal-person careful, not Templar careful," Simon said. "I don't want to be stitching both of you back together next time I see you."

"You worry too much," Guy said. Then he looked at me. "Ready to go?"

HOLLY

Guy didn't speak as we marched out of St. Giles. I held my breath as we crossed the threshold, half expecting the geas to freeze me in my tracks, but nothing happened.

I didn't know whether that was because a geas couldn't do that or because what I was doing now was in some way playing into what Cormen wanted—a thought that didn't make me any happier about the situation—but at the moment I couldn't afford to worry too much about it. Right now I had to focus on what I'd agreed with Guy. Somehow find out if it was the Favreaus who were behind the ambushes on the Templars and, if so, who was pulling their strings. And then save my mother and Reggie.

Guy bundled me into the first hackney that came along and directed it to Brightown. The hackney clattered along the cobbles, turning right and driving past the Brother House. Guy stared out the small window at the gray stone buildings, sitting so still I wasn't entirely sure he hadn't turned to stone himself.

But once the Brother House was out of sight, he seemed to remember he wasn't alone. "Brightown is right, isn't it? That's where you live, at the Swallow?"

I nodded slowly, not entirely sure what to say. Guy was outwardly calm, but he was almost vibrating with whatever it was he was suppressing. I wasn't sure I wanted to risk an explosion.

Still, best to know what I was dealing with. "It worked, then, whatever it was that you cooked up with Father Cho?" He'd been sketchy on the details of how he was going to get the Abbott General to agree to our plan.

He looked toward the window for a moment, hands flexing where they lay on his thighs. "Yes. As far as the Templars are concerned, I'm no longer a knight."

"Oh, Guy, *no*." I couldn't help the reaction. What had he done? He'd spent his life serving the order and now he was willing to let them believe he'd abandon them?

"Yes," he said, still not looking at me. "It was the only way."

My fingers clasped the chain around my neck. Damn Cormen. Damn him to something worse than hell. Then another thought occurred to me. Exactly how bad were things in the City for Guy to be willing to go so far? My fingers tightened as I shivered slightly. "Will they take you back?"

Guy's head swiveled back to me. "First things first, Miss Everton. We have a long way to go before we can even think about that." His voice was cool.

I stared at him. Then nodded. He was right. We had a job to do. Two jobs. I had to think about that, not the man in front of me. I had to stay in control. I had to not let Guy DuCaine get to me. I had to keep the upper hand. "Don't you think you should call me Holly, given you're about to start living with me?"

His blue eyes were inscrutable. "If you wish."

Fine. If he wanted to play it cool, then I could accommodate him. "We need to talk about what happens when we get to the Swallow," I said. "You haven't changed your mind about playing my lover?"

He shook his head.

"Good. Then we have to get it right from the start."

"Yes," he said. His hands flexed again and he stared down at them for a moment. "Which reminds me. We can't go straight there. Is there a sigiler in Brightown? A good one?"

"A sigiler?" Nerves curled uneasily in my stomach. "What do you need a sigiler for?"

He held up his hands. "You were right, I won't get far in the Night World with these. Plus everyone outside the Night World needs to believe I'm an ex-Templar."

He was going to do something to his tattoos. *Oh, Guy, no.* This time I managed not to say it out loud. "Isn't there another way?"

"No. I asked Lady Bryony. She couldn't come up with anything that wouldn't damage my hands. She agreed with you that a glamour was too risky. So, do you know where there's a sigiler or not?"

"Yes," I said, trying not to let my voice sound anything other than professional. "There's one in Gleaming Street."

Guy leaned forward and rapped on the hackney wall. When the driver answered, he gave our new destination.

I leaned against the worn leather seat, feeling sick. He was going to change his tattoos. Change the very thing that showed the world who he was. "Was Bryony sure?" I had to ask.

"Yes," Guy said. "She said they were too old, too deep. I was nineteen when I took my final vows."

My head twitched toward him. So young. Nineteen. Too young to decide something that would seal the rest of your life. Then again, at nineteen, I'd been forced to put my mother in a sanatorium and then try to figure out how to support her and me without becoming a whore. I didn't remember feeling particularly young back then. Maybe Guy hadn't either.

Still, what made a man choose to become a Templar?

I wasn't entirely sure I understood faith. There'd never seemed to be a God looking out for me particularly. In fact, I suspected, if there were deities up there . . . be it the Lady of Fate or Guy's God or the more esoteric beings who populated the Fae's belief system—of whom my understanding was sketchy at best—then I was somehow not on their lists of favored daughters. Surely favorites of the gods didn't end up in my situation or feel as though betrayal awaited them wherever they turned.

But Guy didn't share my doubts. He believed in something. He'd shaped his whole life around those beliefs. Even now he was prepared to risk his reputation and the very thing that was the embodiment of his faith to keep pursuing what he believed was the right thing to do.

Not an easy way to live, perhaps.

His face was unreadable as he swayed with the jolts of the hackney. I couldn't help looking down at his hands. He'd worn those crosses since he was nineteen. From what I knew of him, he was at least a few years past thirty now. They were part of him.

And now, because of the deal we'd made, he was losing that most public symbol of his belief. Permanently.

A fresh wave of anger at my father washed over me. Everyone he touched seemed to end up worse off, and I hated the fact that he'd turned me into his instrument.

Geas or no geas, he and I were going to have a reckoning at the end of this.

GUY
✠

Holly paused on the grimy doorstep of the sigiler's shop. "Are you sure you want to do this?"

I flexed my hands, trying not to think too hard about it, and took another pull on the bottle of whiskey she'd procured for me after the hackney had dropped us near Gleaming Street. She wouldn't take no for an answer when I'd tried to refuse.

Now I was glad of her insistence. The plan called for me to be drunk and angry when we finally reached the Swallow. That wasn't going to be difficult. "I'm sure," I said, and pushed past her to open the door.

The sigiler's shop was small, sparse, and dimly lit. A short wooden counter was bare except for a small brass bell. In front of it were three plain wooden chairs. Behind it a moth-eaten green velvet curtain cloaked whatever might lie beyond.

The walls were covered with scraps of paper displaying detailed designs in all the colors of the rainbow. I ignored them. I didn't need a design. I knew what I was here for. I took a breath, trying to ready myself. The place reeked of the incense burning in a black china dish set on a bracket on the wall behind the counter.

The smell didn't sit well with the whiskey and rage filling my stomach. I sat on the nearest chair and tried not to think.

Thoughts crowded in anyway. I knew the cure for that. More whiskey. I tilted the bottle. The liquor burned my throat, and my stomach twisted. Not from nerves but from revulsion at what was to come.

"You can still change your mind," Holly said.

"There isn't any other way." I jerked my chin at the bell. "Ring."

As she lifted the bell, the jangling noise grating against my ears, I put the bottle down on the floor. Too much now and I wouldn't feel what was about to happen. And I needed to feel it.

A few seconds after Holly rang the bell, a short, dark-haired woman appeared from behind the curtain's folds.

She looked from Holly to me with intelligent black eyes. "Yes?"

"My friend . . ." Holly paused for a moment and looked at me as if asking one last time if I really wanted to go through with this.

I stayed still. Stone.

"My friend has need of your services."

"Yes?" the woman repeated again. Her voice had a faint lilt. Echoes of the Silk Provinces? Or somewhere even more exotic? I didn't care. I brushed off the sudden burning wish to be in the hells-damned Silk Provinces, or anywhere away from the City really, and stood. Two steps and my hands were flat on the desk.

"Yes," I said. "I want to do something with these."

The woman arched dark eyebrows. "Templar? Templars have their own sigilers."

I forced myself to shrug. "Was a Templar. Now I'm not. So I don't give a fuck what they do."

The eyebrows rose higher, but she didn't press her point. Good decision.

"What do you want?"

"Something simple," I said. "They put their goddamned mark on me and the useless healers tell me it can't be removed, but that doesn't mean it can't be remade." I slashed a finger across my hand, trying not to think about what I was doing. "Black. Whatever you think best . . . as long as it makes it clear I'm not one of theirs anymore."

Beside me, Holly was very still. Very quiet. But the way she'd folded her arms tightly across her chest spoke volumes. She was unhappy with this turn of events.

Well, that made two of us.

It's for a good cause, what you swore to do, I reminded myself. *And it doesn't actually change who you are.* The last part I was finding hard to believe just now.

The sigiler peered up at me. "You been drinking?"

"A little. Not enough to change anything. Do you want the work or not?" I pulled a gold sovereign from my pocket. More than ample compensation for what I was asking.

She looked at the coin, then at me. The coin vanished into her pocket. "On your head, then," she said, and beckoned us to come around the counter.

The room she led us to was hardly bigger than the outer one. It reeked of the same incense mixed with the acrid tang of the inks. I remembered that smell from my investiture.

The sigiler told me to sit. Holly hovered in the background at first, and then sat beside me when the woman hissed impatiently at her. The sigiler took my hands in hers, studying them for a long time. Finally she nodded once and let go of me. With neat, precise movements she set out inks and needles. Then she poured some clear liquid from a bottle and swabbed down the back of my hands. The liquid tingled and the smell of herbs and alcohol cut through the other scents.

Another smell I remembered.

Don't think.

I forced myself to stay still as the sigiler turned her attention back to ink and needles and the dull brass hammer, changing the way she'd laid them out a little.

I remembered those too. Remembered how brightly the needles and hammer had flashed in the light pouring through the cathedral windows as the order's sigiler had lifted them to be blessed.

What I didn't remember, I realized as the sigiler placed the first needle and set to work, was the pain. I fought the urge to pull my hand away as the woman worked with her inkpot and the sharp biting needles, her black hair—black as the ink in the pot before her—falling forward to hide her face. I gritted my teeth and stared at Holly, not wanting to see what was happening to my hands.

She watched the sigiler, eyes intent and unhappy. She didn't flinch at the sight of blood at least. But she hadn't looked directly at me since I'd taken my seat at the sigiler's bench and spread my right hand flat on the table.

That was fine with me. I was in no mood for small talk. But the silence, broken only by the tap, tap, tap of the sigiler's long, thin hammer against the needles and my own forcibly smoothed breath, started to close in around me as the pain spiked my skin.

Just pain. Nothing I hadn't dealt with before.

I saw myself for a moment, kneeling in the chapel at the Brother House at nineteen, surrounded by the sounds of the brothers' voices chanting as I raised my hands to the sigiler to be marked. Then I'd been filled with joy and the pain had been nothing. I barely remembered the sensation other than fierce pride and knowing that I had taken the right step.

So young. So certain.

Now I was old. I'd known more pain than I'd imagined possible. I'd borne most of it, as I would now, with set teeth and God's grace.

"You want a rest?" the sigiler asked abruptly. I realized the pain had stopped, other than the deep throbbing burn in my hand. The black eyes watched me with professional concern.

"No. Just get on with it." I didn't look at what she'd done. The back of my hand felt as though she'd set it alight, but the pain would fade. I reached for the bottle, the fire redoubling as

I curled my hand around the neck and took another swig, then laid my left hand on the table. The still-whole cross seemed even redder than normal and beside me, Holly sucked in a quick breath as I spread my fingers.

"Talk to me," I said to her, dragging my eyes away from the cross and up to her face.

She turned her head to meet my gaze. "What do you want to talk about?"

I wanted to ask about her mother. About where we were going. About how she was going to find the information we sought. Wanted her to tell me that this wasn't all going to be for nothing. But we were supposed to be establishing my cover. So I forced myself to reach for the drawl I could slide into at will and shot her a smile.

"How 'bout we talk about exactly what you're going to let me do to you once we're done here, sugar?"

Her eyes widened for a moment, the pupils flaring. Then I saw her remember the game too. She tossed her head as the sigiler snorted softly and drove the needle into my hand.

I didn't let my smile falter.

"Who says I've decided to let you do anything?" Holly said with a suddenly dazzling smile. She'd dropped her voice low and smoky. The female version of my drawl. It worked. My attention was arrested by the sudden shift in her posture, which went from tense to "come and get me" in an instant.

Spy, I remembered. Game player. She had to be a good actress to do what she did. So I shouldn't be stupid and let myself believe that any of it was real.

Still, we had to play the game. So I kept the grin on my face and managed a wink. "Darlin', you know you want to."

Chapter Ten

HOLLY
🗝

It was risky, this game we were playing. The force of Guy's grin hit like a blow. Some might think Simon was the more handsome of the two, but not once they saw Guy smile. He could fell legions of women with one of those smiles.

I couldn't afford to be one of them. Because it was all just a game. But at least the game meant I could indulge myself a little. Give myself a moment to pretend there were no problems in my life, nothing more important than the man in front of me and the pleasure we could share.

I leaned closer, put a hand on his cheek. "I think you're the one doing the wanting," I said, flexing my fingers slightly, so the stubble starting to shadow his face pricked my skin.

Flirting was a kindness. It would take his mind off what the sigiler was doing to him with those bright flashing needles and the pot of night-dark ink.

I had watched the transformation—desecration maybe—of his right hand with a churning stomach. Watched the darkness blot out most of the red, changing a symbol of faith to one of violence. Watched the blood well and Guy's arm tense as his face went blank and distant, his eyes looking anywhere but down.

I didn't want to watch anymore, but if he was strong enough

to have this done, then the least I could do was bear witness without flinching. And distract him.

I leaned in farther. "Are you wanting anything?" I whispered when my lips were close enough to his that it would only take a little movement to bring us together.

Our eyes locked, his blue as the heart of a candle flame, burning into me. Making me forget that this was supposed to be a game.

Making me want something more.

Careful, now.

I pulled away. "Like more whiskey perhaps?" I reached for the bottle near his free hand, careful not to bump it.

Guy's eyes followed my movement and he froze, staring down at his hand. The skin no longer bore a cross . . . well, not just a cross. Now there was a snarling face—a wolf or a dog or some hellbeast—black and jagged with eyes and mouth burning red, from the ruined cross beneath.

The ends of the arms of the cross framed the head, but now they were joined by a row of black thorns. It was striking and beautiful in a horrible way. Rage and violence limned on skin and given life.

My stomach rolled as I looked at it and I desperately wanted some of the whiskey for myself. But one of us should stay sober, and Guy deserved to be the one to wash away his pain.

"Here," I said, snatching up the bottle and holding it to his lips. The bleak look in his eyes as they met mine made me wonder if it wouldn't just be kinder to knock him over the head with it. "This will help."

"I know something that will help more," he muttered before taking a swig of the whiskey. Then he pulled me forward to kiss me fiercely. He tasted of whiskey, rich and warm, and the answering swirl of dizziness that swept through felt much like taking a gulp of the finest malt.

Addictive.

Potent.

Enough to knock me off balance and make the world spin momentarily.

Dangerous.

I tried to remember who I was and where we were. I just about remembered that we were meant to be playing lovers. So instead of staggering backward to try and catch my breath and my wits, I forced myself to tap his nose and smile. "Not just yet," I said. "I want you to have use of both hands when we get to that part."

As if in answer, Guy winced, glancing down at his hand, then reached for the bottle again. A third of it had already vanished.

I hoped he had a good head for liquor. Playing the drunken, embittered, recently ousted Templar was different from actually being a drunken, enraged, recently defaced Templar. But I couldn't bring myself to warn him off. Couldn't bring myself to do much more than look at him, trying to read what was going on behind his outward calm and not think too much about how much I wanted to kiss him again.

"Finished," the sigiler announced suddenly as Guy and I stared at each other.

She poured something pungent onto a cloth from a small blue bottle and wiped both of Guy's hands. "This will keep them clean." She shoved the bottle toward him, then did the same with a small jar. "Helps you heal. Use both, three times a day for one week. Keep dry as much as possible. No infection."

I nodded when Guy said nothing, and reached for the bottle and the jar, putting them into my bag. "Thank you. It's beautiful work. Do we owe you any more?" I expected her to say no, given Guy had already paid her a sovereign, but her black eyes narrowed speculatively.

I tried to stare her down, but she named a somewhat startling figure. I was tempted to haggle, but another look at Guy staring at the beasts now snarling from his hands made me rethink.

I dug in my purse, put the money on the table, and stood. "Come on, big boy," I said to Guy, trying to break the trance he seemed to have fallen into. "The night's still young."

He got to his feet and followed me out into the street, whiskey bottle dangling from one hand.

His knuckles were white and I wondered how much his hands hurt.

"Are you all right?" I said in a low voice when we'd walked a little way down the street. He still hadn't spoken. It was making me nervous and I was trying to decide whether or not to tell him we should call off the whole thing and send a note to Simon to come take him home.

But that would make a mockery of what he'd just done, so I bit my lip and waited for him to speak.

"Yes," Guy growled. He flexed his empty hand, angling it under the gaslight to look at it. I winced. It had to hurt. And the physical hurt was probably the least of it.

"Come on, then," I said. "Let's keep moving. It's not safe this time of night."

He shot me a look, reminding me that he knew as much as me about the dangers of these streets at night. He had fought and bled here. Lost comrades here. His lips peeled back in what some might have called a smile. I thought it was closer to a snarl and hoped like hell that nobody did challenge us tonight. A fight would offer the perfect opportunity for Guy to take out whatever frustrations he was battling. But I didn't want him to have to deal with hurting or killing someone for no good reason in addition to everything else.

"We'll go to the Swallow," I said. "I'll buy you another bottle of that." I nodded at the whiskey. "You can sleep."

"I thought we were meant to be working," he said, his tone still low and underscored with a rumble of anger.

"We're meant to be establishing your cover," I said. "Me dragging you through the Swallow and up to my room should start that process quite nicely."

"I can think of other things that would help with that," he said, moving toward me suddenly.

"Such as?" I tried to keep my voice light, but nerves quivered in my stomach. I knew I should move away, should keep walking, but I was frozen as he reached for me in the lamplight, big and strong and in pain.

"This." The whiskey bottle dropped to the cobbles and shattered as his lips came down on mine again. I knew how it felt. My own grip on common sense fractured as well, splintering into glittering shards of delight that scattered in all directions.

His mouth was hot and fierce. Demanding and seeking at the same time. His hands curled round my waist and gripped fiercely as if he could pull me inside him completely. There was desperation in his kiss, the taste of a man seeking oblivion. I'd come across it once or twice before. Men in pain will drink or fight or sometimes seek to shut it out or ward it off by other means. I'd taken hurting men to my bed before.

But I didn't want that to be the reason this man came to my bed. I pulled away. "No. Not like this," I said, feeling my heart pound. "If we do this it will be because we both want pleasure. Right now you just want escape."

His brows drew together. "I—"

"Don't," I said. "We need to get to the Swallow." I stepped carefully around the glass. "Now you definitely need more whiskey."

Guy
✚

I followed Holly down the street, trying to clear the fog from my head. My hands burned as if someone had rubbed acid into the skin. And my head throbbed. Not as badly as my cock, though. Hell's balls. What was I thinking? Three times I'd kissed her now and every fucking time it had been a mistake.

Not that my body agreed with that assessment right now. No. It knew what it wanted. It wanted the woman stalking down the road in front of me, her back ramrod straight and her skirts swishing with the angry taps of her boot heels. I'd managed to annoy her with that last kiss. I couldn't blame her. She'd been right. I hadn't been particularly thinking of her. I'd just wanted something to make me stop thinking altogether. In her place I'd be pissed too.

I was feeling pretty pissed myself. This had been my idea, true, but I hadn't bargained on feeling this way when I'd seen what the sigiler had done to my hands. It had made me want to vomit, seeing the symbol of what I believed turned into mere pictures.

Made me long for hot water and the chapel in the Brother House. Anything to feel clean and whole again.

But that wasn't Holly's fault. We needed each other if we were going to survive this mad scheme. Which meant I needed to find my footing and get on with it and my body needed to just get used to the fact that it wouldn't be getting any more tastes of that mouth any time soon.

Playing lovers was one thing. Actually becoming lovers with a Night World spy could only lead to trouble.

And we already had more than enough trouble on our hands.

I kicked the neck of the bottle across the street, where it hit the gutter and shattered. Then I followed Holly. The least I could do was make sure that no one accosted her between here and the Swallow. I was still a Templar. Losing my crosses didn't change that. I was oath-bound to protect. And so I would.

Still, I couldn't help feeling disappointed when we reached the Swallow without anyone trying anything. Beating up a would-be cutpurse or thief might have made me feel better. Plus surely a street brawl would add to the story we were meant to be building.

Holly turned as we neared the front door. "Right," she said. "This is it. Once we go through there, we're in this. No going back. Last chance to back out."

I held up my hands, showing her the snarling beasts once more. "I didn't do this on a whim," I growled.

"My mother and my friend, remember?" Holly said, lifting her chin. "They're just as important as your information. We're trying to do both."

She was fierce, this one. Single-minded in pursuit of what she wanted. Protecting what was hers.

I recognized that. Respected it. But I wouldn't let it stop me from protecting what was mine.

I nodded. "Yes." Did she really think that I'd forget about her mother? Holly still hadn't said much about who it was she thought had taken her mother, but it couldn't be anyone good. Nice people, as a rule, didn't kidnap sick old ladies from sanatoriums.

"All right." She reached up and tugged at my shirt collar, doing something I couldn't quite figure out to it. "So drunk or lustful?" she asked.

"Excuse me?"

"Drunk or lustful? There are two ways we can play this." She moved in closer to me as a couple of men came down the street. To a casual observer it would seem we were about to embrace, or had just finished doing so, the warmth of her body temptingly close. Drunk seemed the sensible option, but the whiskey I'd already drunk rode uneasily in my stomach. I felt the way I did when I'd fought too long on too little sleep. I needed food, not more alcohol.

"Lustful," I said with a stern warning to certain parts of my body that this was only an act.

She blinked, her changeable eyes dark in the gaslight. "Are you sure?"

"Yes."

Her mouth twisted, but then she stepped back. "All right, then. Lustful it is." She did something at the front of her dress and there was suddenly quite a bit more of her flesh on show than previously.

The gaslights at the front of the Swallow were bright, and I had a perfect view down to the curves of her breasts. My hands flexed as I went hard again and even the pain of the new tattoos wasn't enough to kill the surge of lust.

Oh yes, this was a really stupid idea.

Still, I didn't argue as Holly tucked her arm through mine and tugged me toward the Swallow, leaning into me and laughing as if I'd just said something brilliant. Two large bully boys stood guarding the door, but their menacing stance relaxed as Holly turned her smile on them.

"Evening, Miss Holly," one of them said with a grin. "What's that you've got yourself, then?"

"Boys, this is Guy. He's going to be staying with me for a time." Her voice was practically a purr, and I fought to keep the surprise off my face.

Lustful. I was meant to be lustful, not stunned. Though as I looked down at Holly and caught another glimpse of lush round breasts spilling out of her corset, maybe stunned by lust would do just as well.

"You're a lucky man," the other bouncer said to me with a nod. Then his hand drifted down to his coat, flipping it back to reveal a pistol and a wicked-looking truncheon. "But you be good to Miss Holly. We'll be watching you."

I managed to nod. "Oh, don't worry. I intend on treating her very well." I snaked an arm around her waist and pulled her into me. "Good is hardly the word."

Holly managed to roll her eyes in a way that seemed flirtatious. "My, my." She made a little fanning motion in front of her face. "I do hope you're going to live up to these expectations you're setting, big boy."

She winked at the two men who were watching her with approval. I noticed their gazes stayed on her face. Either they had better willpower than me, or they'd known her long enough to not be knocked sideways by her body.

"After all," she continued with a toss of her head that some-how managed to make her dress slip lower still. "I have very high standards." She pulled away and took a few swaying steps through the doors before turning back. "And I hate to be disap-pointed."

HOLLY

"This is where you live?" Guy stood just inside my doorway, his eyes taking careful inventory of the room.

I paused, not sure how to take the question. Was he disap-pointed? Or surprised? Or neither? "I don't spend a lot of time here," I said, trying to sound as though I didn't care what he thought.

I put the bottle of whiskey I'd bought downstairs—part of our act—down on my dresser. My rooms were small but not tiny. Over time I'd convinced—well, paid—the Figgs to allow me to have two of the chambers converted into one. I had enough room for a decent bed, a table and chairs, a desk, and a wardrobe with some floor space in between. It was all I needed for now. One day I'd buy a house and have all the rooms I wanted.

One day.

But not today. No, today, I wondered what Guy saw.

He moved from the door, still looking around him. "It seems like you. Nice."

I relaxed slightly. Though maybe I should be insulted . . . what exactly had he been expecting? "Thank you." I didn't spend much money on rent, but I had splurged a little on the rugs and my bedding. Not too much—even with wards as strong as I could make them, it was foolish to have anything too valuable in a place like the Swallow.

Reggie had pushed me toward deep pinks and blues and reds, insisting jewel tones suited me best. I liked my very female little cave, but for once, standing here with Guy, made me feel some-how uncomfortable. He seemed too austere in his gray and white. Too big. Too male.

Looking away from him, I pushed the bags, which had been delivered while we were making our way here, against the wall, then moved around the room, checking my wards. I could tell Fen had been in here, but there were no echoes of anyone else.

Guy looked around one more time and then sat by the table. "Now what?"

His hands rested on his knees. I tried not to look at the snarling faces, but they drew the eye. They'd had an interesting effect downstairs when he'd put them flat on the bar and demanded whiskey.

Fen's face from across the room had been a picture of dismay and confusion. I had the feeling that he and I would be having a long heart-to-heart lecture sometime very soon.

But I couldn't think about Fen. Instead I fastened the buttons at the neckline of my dress and sat primly on the nearest chair trying to think.

I'd dragged Guy through the Swallow, flirting outrageously, and he'd played along, even planting another mind-melting kiss on my mouth in the middle of the room, to the rowdy applause of the patrons. Then he'd topped his act by being suitably brutish and snarly at the bar. The very image of a lust-addled, angry warrior. No point blowing all that hard work now.

"You mean we should start jumping up and down on the bed to convince everyone we're busy making wildly passionate love?" I tried not to look at the bed and picture just that. "No need, I've always had aural shields around my room."

Though right now I was regretting that fact a little. Some bouncing on the bed with Guy might have been fun.

Focus on the job, Holly girl.

"What they make up in their own heads will convince them more than anything we could do." I thought fast for alternatives. If Guy had chosen drunk as his cover, I would've been perfectly happy holing up in my room for the night and letting him drink as much as he wanted. But he hadn't and now he seemed wide awake, watching me as I prowled around, feeling restless.

I wasn't sure that staying here with him under such circumstances was a good idea. The bed seemed to loom large with him in the room, and *that* really was a bad, bad idea. But with Guy full of whiskey and obviously spoiling for a fight, this wasn't the time to take him out into the Night World. No, he needed just a little time to get used to what he'd done tonight.

And I needed a little time to think.

I looked down at his hands, where the snarling faces looked

somewhat swollen, the edges reddened. They had to hurt like hell.

That, at least, I could do something about. I had no real talent for healing, but Fen did. Enough to soothe minor bumps and scrapes and cuts anyway. He should be able to do something to ease Guy's hands. And, hopefully, the cut on my arm, which had started throbbing again.

I poured whiskey into a glass and passed it to him. "Drink this. I'll be back in a moment."

His eyes turned suspicious. "Where are you going?"

"Just drink it."

It took more than a moment for me to convince Fen to come back upstairs, but it was still no longer than five minutes or so before I let us back into my room.

Guy sat by the table, his glass still full. Or maybe that was refilled. The level in the bottle seemed to have dropped a little farther. I had to hand it to him. He definitely seemed to have a head for liquor.

"What's he doing here?" Guy asked.

"Fen can heal, a little. He's going to take a look at your hands."

Fen, for once, wisely kept his mouth shut as Guy's brows drew down, making the scar that slashed one of them stand out more strongly. "My hands are fine."

I rolled my eyes. "Your hands have to be hurting. If Simon was here, you'd let him heal them, wouldn't you?"

Guy jerked his head at Fen. "He isn't Simon."

"No, but he's as close as you're going to get for tonight. Don't be difficult. You'll be more use to me with both your hands in good working order." I pointed at the bed. "Come over here and sit down where the light is better and let Fen help you."

For a moment I thought he was going to argue some more, but instead he got up, lifted the whiskey bottle in one hand, and moved to the bed. His steps were slow but steady, though I got the feeling he was concentrating hard to make sure they were.

He dropped down onto the bed and held out his free hand.

"Do your worst."

I shot a look at Fen, making sure he wasn't going to rise to the bait. He returned a "you owe me" gaze of his own before he moved to where Guy was on the bed.

"Can you bring a candle over please, Holly?" Fen said in a casual tone as he inspected Guy's hand. He turned to me, his brows lifted as if to ask what the hell was going on. I frowned at him and fetched a candle.

Guy didn't seem to be paying any attention to what we were doing. He gazed into the fire, still taking mouthfuls of whiskey from the bottle, his expression fixed in impassive lines.

"Sleep?" I mouthed at Fen, and he nodded fractionally before he bent back over Guy's hand. A shiver of magic swept through the air, and Guy flicked his gaze back to us, the lines in his face easing.

"Other hand," Fen said in a calm tone, and Guy switched the bottle over.

This time the pulse of magic was stronger. It continued in a wave, like the beat of a heart, and I was relieved to see Guy's eyes begin to drift shut. The pulse continued and suddenly Fen leaned forward, easing the bottle free of Guy's hand as the bigger man fell gently backward onto my bed.

"Will that do?" Fen asked, passing me the whiskey bottle.

"How long will he be out?" I stared down at Guy. It didn't look like the most comfortable position to sleep in, with his legs dangling down to the floor.

"How much did he have to drink?"

"Half a bottle, maybe."

"Well, then I'd say you're safe until morning." Fen's eyes glinted—half amused, half frustrated—as he spoke. "Are you going to tell me what's going on?"

I shook my head. "Not yet. Help me move him."

Manhandling six-foot-plus of solidly built knight was no easy feat, even for two of us, but we managed to drag him farther up the bed and roll him onto his side. I draped the counterpane over Guy.

"Where are you going to sleep?" Fen asked.

"The floor will do. I have spare blankets. But I'm not going to sleep just yet."

"Oh?"

I looked at Guy again, his face peaceful in sleep, the first time it had looked that way all day. Fen's magic and the sleep would hopefully give him some ease. And it had given me the time and space I needed to do what I had to do.

"Yes," I said. "I'm going out."

Chapter Eleven

HOLLY

Guilt lingered in the pit of my stomach as I hurried away from the Swallow. Guy wouldn't be happy if he woke to find me gone, so I just had to hope that Fen was right and that I had hours before that happened.

Fen had worked his magic on my arm—healing the cut I'd made with Mama's mirror—before he'd reluctantly let me go. I knew I couldn't hold off telling him at least part of the story too much longer. Fen's patience would last only so long and then he would do some snooping of his own to find out what I was up to. I didn't want him blundering into Cormen's path or, for that matter, the path of whoever might be setting Beast Kind to mess with Templars.

I took a hackney to the edges of Sorrow's Hill, then slipped out of the carriage and paid the driver. Once the cab had clattered out of sight, I found an out-of-sight place to trigger the invisibility charm in my purse. This time of night, Sorrow's Hill was no safe place. I wanted to move unseen through the streets.

As much as possible I kept to the alleys and lesser-used lanes. It meant negotiating my way over rubbish and rubble that was messy and stank of dead things and piss and decay, but it was better than blundering into the path of a Beast or Blood Lord out searching for some fun.

Though it seemed that the Lady was smiling on me and the Beasts and Blood were keeping mostly indoors. Which only increased the nerves turning my stomach to acid. When even Night Worlders were nervous to be out on the streets, things were indeed getting bad.

When I neared Cormen's house, where the houses tended toward rows of terraced town houses, I left the streets altogether, climbing up to the rooftops where I felt much safer though no less nervous.

Soon enough I was perched near the chimney of the town house next to my father's, studying the wards. I hadn't in the past paid much attention to the wards here. This wasn't the house my mother and I had shared with Cormen, and the few times I'd come here to answer Cormen's demands, I had been more interested in getting out as fast as possible rather than how I might one day get in.

From my vantage point, the wards looked simple enough. Another demonstration of Cormen's arrogance that he would consider basic defenses all he needed, as if it were unthinkable that anyone could want to move against him. But then again, as far as I knew, he spent most of his time in Summerdale, only venturing into the City in search of entertainment from time to time. Perhaps he just didn't think it was worth his while to expend effort on more elaborate wards when he rarely slept here.

Or maybe he increased the power of the wards when he was actually in the house. I traced the lines of the wards again, hoping that my luck was holding and that indeed my father was not at home tonight. I suppressed the part of me that wondered whether my mother and Reggie might be inside the house. Cormen was arrogant, but I had no doubt he would not be so foolish as to stash his hostages here in the first place I was likely to look.

And if he had, the wards would be much, much, stronger.

Still, I had to bite my lip for a moment, blinking back the sudden sting of salt as my faint hope was extinguished.

Concentrate. There was no time for falling apart.

I narrowed my focus back to the wards, reading the lines of them, deciphering what they might do. I thought I had the lay of them now, but still, I lingered, double-checking and considering my options.

Overly cautious perhaps, but these wards were tinged with traces of Cormen's magic. If he had set any clever traps, they were far more likely to catch me than anybody else's tricks and pitfalls might.

The ward lines spoke of protection and alarms but, try as I might, I couldn't see anything more subtle woven into them. There was the usual knot of anchor points near the doors at the rear and front of the building—places where recognition spells were built into the wards so that those who were most often in and out of the house did not have to bother with taking down the wards to enter or leave and where temporary gaps could be opened to admit visitors—and it was those that I would be targeting.

If my father wasn't at home, I doubted there would be many staff inside. Maybe a housekeeper to keep the place ready at a moment's notice, but otherwise Cormen generally traveled with his retinue of retainers and servants and guards. He wouldn't waste money paying for human servants here in the City if he didn't have to.

No lights showed through the drawn blinds or curtains in the windows that I could see, so I would take my chances that if anyone was within, they would be safely asleep.

I slipped down from the rooftop and into the yard behind the town house. Even invisible as I was, the rear door, out of sight of the street, was the safest choice. I found the anchor point easily enough. I hovered my hand nearer to the ward, getting a closer read on the tangle of magics. Then snatched it back, as another thought occurred to me.

Maybe I didn't need to take down the wards. Maybe they could be coaxed to let me in. After all, if they'd been keyed to let members of Cormen's Family in, as would be usual, perhaps I could pass. But how to test my theory?

The answer sprang to mind fairly quickly and, sighing, I pulled out my cutthroat. I was getting sick of the sight of my own blood. At least, for this, I only needed a few drops. A quick nick from the razor and I flicked a drop toward the ward.

It faded a little but not completely. So perhaps my theory was correct. Though, maybe, I was taking the wrong approach. The wards couldn't taste the blood of anybody who entered after all, and I had another more easily accessible talisman of my connection to my father.

With a grim smile, I drew my pendant from beneath my shirt. True, it wasn't a Family ring but it was set with the same stones as a ring would be and the magic that made it impossible for me to take off was woven by Cormen's own hand. The Fae used similar protections on Family rings to ensure that they couldn't be lost or stolen.

Maybe my father's little choke chain might come in useful for once.

Tentatively, I stretched the key toward the ward, ready to pull back and flee if I was wrong and the wards reacted. I needn't have worried. The key glimmered once as it touched the shimmering ward, and then the ward peeled back from the door like smoke.

I yanked my lock picks from my hair and made quick work of the lock. The door opened silently and I slipped inside, easing it shut behind me. I paused a moment, stretching my senses, but heard nothing but silence.

I didn't want to waste time doing a sweep of the house; instead, I headed straight for the stairs and my father's second-floor study.

I wasn't sure exactly what I was looking for . . . but Cormen was up to something and any hint at all as to what that might be would be welcome. As would anything that might tell me where he was hiding himself. He'd put the geas on me to get me to find out what Simon's secret was and maybe I wouldn't be able to avoid doing what he wanted, but I was sure as seven hells going to try and make life difficult for him in whatever way I could. If he was up to something and I knew what, then I had a bargaining chip. Something to use against him.

Something to get my family back.

The study was dark, the curtains neatly drawn, cutting out the light of the moon and the gaslights in the street below. My eyes adjusted slowly until I could make out the outlines of the desk and furniture dotted around the room, but it wasn't going to be enough. I tugged a tiny glow charm from the pouch at my waist and pinched the nick on my finger, hoping to squeeze a little more blood out of it.

Glows don't take much energy and luckily this one warmed to life without me having to do any more damage to my fingertips. The light was enough to see the detail I needed and I set about working the room over. Donning gloves, I checked the less obvious places first, sliding my hands over the shelves and into cupboards, feeling for papers or hints of protection wards.

I gained little for my troubles other than a sheen of the lemon-scented furniture polish on the thin leather covering my fingertips.

I moved onto the safe. It was only a small one with a straightforward combination lock. It took me a few minutes of listening and twirling to crack the required combination. I opened the door cautiously, wondering if there would be any nasty surprises inside, but there weren't. There was a buzz of a ward around the inner chamber. I recognized the feel of it. It would only be activated if I removed the contents of the safe. Otherwise, I was safe.

I peered into the safe. Empty save for a midsized leather pouch. Wriggling my fingers, I reached for the pouch, touching its surface with practiced ease. Small hard lumps rolled under my fingers.

Gems, if I wasn't mistaken. It was a moment's work to undo the ties and confirm my impression. The pouch held a small fortune in diamonds and sapphires, glinting rainbowed silver and deep inky blue at me in the thin glow light.

A small whistle escaped my lips. Gems were worth a lot of money in the City. Small, more portable than gold, plus prized for their use in charms.

So, what was Cormen doing with enough diamonds to fund a small army?

My stomach turned suddenly cold.

Fuck. Maybe he was doing exactly that?

Or maybe I was leaping to conclusions. I tied the gems back up carefully and locked the safe. I wasn't here to steal from Cormen. Tempting though the gems were, I didn't want him to have any reason to come looking for a thief.

But the gems had piqued my interest and set my intuition humming. So I crossed the room to the big desk where Cormen conducted his affairs, such as they were, whilst in town and commenced my search again.

Sitting in Cormen's chair made my spine creep. Maybe his scent was soaked into the leather or maybe it was just my imagination, but I could smell him for a moment and had to catch myself as I jerked around, expecting to see him standing behind me.

But the room was still empty and I took three deep breaths to slow my racing heart and turned my attention back to the job at hand.

There was a thick stack of heavy cards on a small metal tray to my left. I lifted the glow and flipped through the cards. Invitations. To parties. To the opera at the Gilt. To other theater halls.

The last few in the pile were from three different Beast packs. An invitation to dine with Pierre Rousselline, yet another suggestion for opera with a Krueger whose first name didn't ring any bells with me, and the last for a night of cards with Etienne Davidoff. No Favreaus. Of course, if one was doing something underhand with a Beast pack, one wouldn't necessarily want to be seen in public with them.

Still, three different packs. My father had never spent a lot of time with the Beasts that I knew of. So, why now? I memorized the details of the invitations and resumed the search.

No incriminating letters or neatly set out plans revealed themselves. There were a few bills to do with the running of the town house and some letters written in the Fae language. I didn't read Fae, but given that neither did Beasts or Blood usually, I doubted the letters were the key to the puzzle.

I was sliding the letters back into place in the drawer from which they'd come when my hand brushed a small rectangular shape.

By reflex, my fingers closed around it and I drew out the object to look more closely.

At first I took it for a plain black box, but then I felt something embossed on the underside. Flipping the box over, I stared down at the elaborate H stamped into the cloth-covered card. This time it wasn't just my stomach that grew cold. No, this time a shiver ran through my whole body. I knew what the box was. I knew where that H belonged.

Halcyon.

Lord Lucius had favored that particular Blood Assembly over the others. It was Halcyon where he held court on the nights he wanted to show his face on the edges of his world, rather than at the Sorrow's Hill warrens or any of the Blood-only gathering places.

And where, if he wanted to show favor and admit anyone to the upper levels, he would send out black metal tokens in small boxes just like this.

My hand clamped around the box. I forced myself to let go, to slide it open. No token lay within. I had expected as much. They weren't the sort of thing one left lying around.

A token to Halcyon meant a more than a casual acquaintance with the Blood . . . which again, was something I hadn't expected of my father. Or it meant that your favor was being sought. That was even more disturbing.

The question was, who had sent the token? Had my father had it from Lucius himself or was it a more recent acquisition from the man who was setting himself up as the new master of Halcyon and using it as a base in his quest for control of the Blood Court?

I didn't know which was worse. That my father had had dealings with Lucius was a terrifying enough thought. But Lucius was dead and therefore the association should be dead too. But as for Ignatius Grey . . . power hungry, vicious, determined . . . the thought of my father being involved with Ignatius was somehow even worse. Because that would mean that whatever he was doing was happening now, was linked to all the trouble in the City most likely.

If it were true, my father was playing a dangerous game.

And my mother and Reggie might be right in the middle of it.

Come to think of it, so might I.

The sky was starting to show the first hints of dawn light when I finally returned to the Swallow. I had taken the time to go over the rest of the rooms in Cormen's town house, hoping to find a trace of either my mother or Reggie. But despite the faint hint of rosewater in one of the bedrooms—a scent Reggie favored along with half the female population of the City—there was nothing to give me any reason to think Cormen had brought them there.

A side trip to the salon in Gillygate had proved similarly fruitless. So really, all I had to show for the night, other than the discovery that my father possessed a Halcyon token, were eyes that felt as if they'd been dipped in sand, a fervent desire for sleep, and an increasing feeling of desperation.

I opened the door to my rooms carefully and slipped inside. Guy still lay on the bed, looking as if he hadn't moved from where I'd left him. Somehow in the few hours I'd been gone, he'd left a stamp on the room—a masculine scent of leather and soap and faint hints of whiskey mingling with my own perfumes.

A momentary hint of insanity made me want to crawl in beside him, but I pushed it away. Instead I stole across to my wardrobe, pulled a blanket from the top shelf, and curled up on my small sofa to steal a few hours of sleep myself.

Guy
✝

"I thought Templars would be early risers."

The voice swam through my consciousness accompanied by a strong scent of coffee. But it didn't help me break through the fog of sleep holding me down.

"*Guy.*"

The voice was sharper now.

"We have work to do."

A finger poked my shoulder. That was enough to kick my instincts into action. My hand snapped up and grabbed as my eyes snapped open.

"Guy!" Holly's face was outraged. "Let go."

I loosened my grip, still somewhat confused as to where exactly I was. "Never wake a sleeping soldier."

"I called you several times," Holly said, rubbing her forearm ruefully. I belatedly remembered what Simon had said about her bones still being fragile, and winced.

"Next time," she continued, "I'll use a bucket of cold water."

I doubted there would be a next time. I was usually a light sleeper. Which made me wonder why I wasn't today.

"What time is it?" I asked while I sorted out my recollections of last night. I reached for the coffee Holly held out, and froze as I saw the snarling beast on the back of my hand. Memories crashed back with a vengeance. I swallowed coffee so I wouldn't start swearing.

"It's close to three," Holly said.

"In the afternoon?" The sunlight pouring into the room made this somewhat a stupid question. But the habit of rising for dawn services was so ingrained that I couldn't even remember the last time I'd slept past sunrise. "What did you do to me?"

Holly tilted her head, little rivers of sunlight gleaming on her hair. "Me? You're the one who drank most of a bottle of whiskey last night. If you're feeling sorry for yourself this afternoon, I'd imagine that might have something to do with it."

I inhaled more coffee, considering. Perhaps she was right. There's only so long you can go without enough sleep, after all, and adding more alcohol than I'd drunk in one sitting for a long while to the mix couldn't have helped any. But I was rested now, or at least some semblance of rested, the coffee scalding away the cobwebs in my head quite nicely. "You should have woken me earlier. We have work to do."

"Most of the people you're interested in are asleep right now," Holly said. "Besides which, I'm not letting you go anywhere near them until I'm sure you understand how to behave."

"I know how to behave."

"In your world, you do. This isn't your world. Mistakes could get you—or both of us—killed."

"I—"

"Don't argue. You wanted someone to help you find out things you can't find out on your own. So it would make sense if you'd listen to me and let me do just that."

I regarded the dregs of the coffee in my mug for a time. She had a point. I didn't particularly like it but it was nonetheless a valid point. I drained the coffee and held it out for a refill. "Fine. Start talking."

HOLLY

By the time the sun had set and the Night World was beginning to think about stirring, I was just about all talked out. I had given Guy a crash course in surviving the border boroughs and the edges of the Night World but still wasn't sure that either of us was truly ready for what faced us.

Trouble was, after almost a week in St. Giles, I was out of touch myself. Things were shifting fast enough in the Blood Court that five days might as well be five months. Which was why I had decided that our first port of call had to be the Gilt.

Now I just had to convince Guy. Who, after a day cooped up in my room, was prowling around like a dog too long on the chain. The fact that he looked very good prowling was one I was trying to ignore.

"Can we go yet?" he asked as he finished his latest circuit of the room.

I looked over at the tiny carriage clock on my dressing table. "It's early yet. It will be a few more hours before things pick up around here."

"So we just sit here?"

"No." I shook my head. I didn't think that being confined to quarters with Guy for much longer was a good idea. Or my good intentions might just decide to decamp. "No, now I get changed and we'll go out and make a spectacle of ourselves. Show everyone that I've caught myself a fine new man." I managed to sound careless as I said it. But it was far from the truth. The longer I'd talked today, the more nervous I'd become about what we were trying to do.

That little black box I'd found at Cormen's weighed on my mind. Veil's eyes, if he was mixed up with some Blood plot . . . I'd swung from worrying about my mother and Reggie and what the hell Cormen was involved in to trying to ignore the effect that proximity to Guy was having on my baser instincts all day.

The combination was making me distinctly seasick.

And there was no one to throw me a life preserver.

I'd gotten myself into this mess and I was going to have to get myself safely to shore again.

"Where exactly?"

Guy's question broke my spiral of worry once again. I considered his point. The more time we spent in public, the better. It would give people a reason to talk and keep both of us occupied. We'd spent the better part of a day in my rooms. People would already be assuming that we'd put the bed to good use.

"Dinner first," I said.

"Here?"

"No. The Swallow's clientele is mostly human. We need somewhere with more . . . scope. Somewhere with Night Worlders. Where we can see what there is to see." And be seen ourselves, more to the point. See what the Night World made of Guy DuCaine out on the town with a half-breed Fae like me. See if that rattled any cages amongst those who knew what I did. Then our dangerous charade could begin in earnest.

"Where, then?"

"We'll go to Justine's. Always plenty of people there. And then we'll go to the late show at the Gilt." Friday night, the Gilt started its mostly respectable opera a little earlier and then, after that was done, put on a more risqué show to keep the crowds in their seats and spending money on wine and food.

"Opera?" Guy looked as though he'd swigged a mouthful of soured wine.

"The late show isn't opera. Just singing and dancing." I hid a smile, wondering exactly what my straitlaced knight would make of the sorts of songs and dances he was about to be subjected to. "It will be fun. Besides, the Beast packs are fond of opera."

That sharpened his gaze.

"The Favreaus?"

"Christophe is often there, yes. And where the alpha goes, so go others in the pack." Of course, we didn't know if the Favreaus were behind the attacks on the Templars or if Christophe knew anything about it, but it was as good a place as any to see what might come crawling out of the woodwork.

"Will he be there tonight?"

"I don't know. Even if he's not, we're sure to learn something useful. Trust me."

"We don't have days to waste on frivolities." Guy's mouth was set. Unconvinced, the Templar.

"I know," I said. I knew it better than he did, most likely. "But you still need to trust me." I gave him a stern glance, then crossed the room. "And we both need the right clothes." I threw open the wardrobe and studied my choices. Not black. Black was for Blood Assemblies. The Gilt required something showier. More flamboyant. I reached for Reggie's latest creation, lifting it carefully from the rack and holding it at arm's length.

Definitely showy. Heavy silk in a bronze gold shade like the edges of a peacock's feather, it fit like a snake skin, apart from the bustled rear of the skirt, which billowed and flowed down in tier after tier of small ruffles that swayed when I walked, drawing the eye to my behind.

The neckline plunged and swooped, doing the same for my décolletage in the front. Reggie had beaded and embroidered long curling feathers here and there on the skirt and bodice, picking out highlights with a deeper green like a real peacock.

Reggie, who'd never actually seen me wearing the dress in public. Reggie, who might never see it. *No*. I pushed the anxiety away. I couldn't afford it just now. I needed all my wits about me.

I forced myself to focus back on the dress. It was spectacular and tarty and, really, just what the Gilt required. Of course, it required a ridiculous corset to make it fit. I would have to send for someone to help me put it on.

"What's wrong?" Guy asked as I laid the dress carefully across the bed.

"I'll need help with my laces. I'll just—"

"I can do it.

My eyebrows shot up. "You?"

"Don't look so shocked. I have dealt with women's underwear before," he said.

I wasn't shocked that he knew; I was shocked by the flutter in my stomach at the thought of him lacing me up, his fingers on my back and waist.

"It looked busy downstairs. Why pull one of the servants away from their work when I can help?" He leaned back in the chair slightly, a challenging gleam in his eyes.

So we were back to our little dance, were we? I contemplated the flutter in my stomach for a few more seconds. Guy thought he was calling my bluff. Let him continue to think that.

But I was rapidly realizing that there was only one likely ending to this particular waltz. Eventually we were going to give in to whatever it was that caused the flutters in my stomach and the heat I felt in his kisses.

One of us would fold. And then we would end up in bed. It was inevitable. Even if I was going to do my damnedest to delay as long as possible, I was also going to enjoy the dance.

"If you're sure you don't mind," I said, letting my own voice turn lazy and female.

"Sugar, if you're meeting men who mind helping you with your underwear, you're meeting the wrong sort of men."

"Are you *sure* you're a Templar?" I said as I returned to the wardrobe to fetch the corset. It was a thing of beauty, like the dress, but I still regarded it with reluctance. The corsets I wore under my day dresses were designed to be done up by a woman alone and laced more loosely than the ones that went with Reggie's confections, which could leave me feeling light-headed if I wasn't careful.

"Turn your back," I said, feeling suddenly shy.

"Won't that make lacing you up difficult?"

"I'll tell you when I need your help." I wasn't sure that if he stood there watching me take off my clothes, I wouldn't just give in right now and throw myself at him. We had a job to do tonight. Which meant doing what we'd come here to do rather than what my body wanted to do.

Guy rolled his eyes but obeyed, standing and turning around, arms folded across his chest.

I unbuttoned my dress, unlaced my normal corset and slithered into the silk drawers that went with the gown before picking up the corset.

"You can turn around now," I said when I had the front secured. I was devoutly thankful that the silk of the drawers was the same color as the dress rather than a more revealing white or pale pink. Maybe Reggie was psychic.

Guy's footsteps made the floorboards creak softly as he came to me.

"Pretty," he said. I hoped he was looking at the dress lying across the bed rather than at my behind.

"Just lace me up."

"How tightly?"

Hmm, maybe he had done this before after all. "Tight. The dress needs tight."

"Rather you than me," he muttered, then added, "Breathe in."

I obediently sucked in air and pulled my stomach muscles tight. Guy started tugging on the laces, wrapping the corset closely around me. He did it deftly. I'd never considered the fact that brute strength might come in handy when dressing, but apparently it did. Maybe the Templars should start hiring out as ladies' maids. I giggled a little at the thought of Guy in a maid's uniform.

"What's so funny?" He yanked again at the laces and I felt the pressure on my torso increase to a familiar degree of discomfort.

"Nothing. I think that's tight enough."

"Whatever you say," he said, but he continued fussing with the laces for a few more seconds before he tied them off. His fingers felt hot through the satin and silk and boning, and a flush raced across my cheeks.

Distraction. That's what I needed. Anything to overcome the

fact that his hands were separated from my skin by just a few thin layers of silk. Silk he could probably rip from me quite easily.

Definitely in need of a distraction. I stepped away from him and picked up the dress, pulling it down over my head with a rush.

"Do you need a hand with that?"

I started to say no but then realized I probably did. The dress was tight and I could tear it if I rushed trying to tug it on. Plus there were further fastenings at my back. I sighed. "Yes, please."

To his credit, he didn't try to take advantage of the situation. He just eased the dress into place and dealt with the rest of the buttons and fastenings efficiently before retreating. I didn't know whether to be relieved or insulted again.

Instead of trying to determine which it was, I did some retreating of my own over to the dressing table. My pendant was hidden between my breasts, just covered by the fabric of the dress. The old gold shade of it went well with the fabric, so I didn't bother to glamour the chain.

But the chain alone wouldn't be enough. I found heavy earrings of bronze and green glass and fastened them into place. Then I stared into the mirror and muttered the words to glamour my hair, changing its shade to a rich golden brown that toned with the dress and didn't scream "Fae" quite as loudly as my own color. It shaped itself obediently into curls and waves that looked as though I'd spent hours with a coiffeur, and I twisted the mass of it, tying it up and away from my face in a tumbled bun. Thanks to the glamour, the curls rearranged themselves obediently.

"Nice trick," Guy said.

"It has its uses." I wasn't going to defend my magic to him. I reached for a rouge pot. I could glamour my face too, but that took effort. Simple makeup was easier.

"What else can you do?" he asked.

I froze for a moment, and then forced myself to keep moving. I sat back in front of the mirror and picked up a brush to dip in my rouge. *He doesn't know,* I reminded myself. He had no way of knowing what I had done to Simon. "Bits and pieces. My magic always works better on me than anyone else." Hopefully that would satisfy his curiosity. A girl couldn't afford to give away all her secrets, after all. "This won't take long."

"That I'll believe when I see it."

Was that something close to a joke? I could see him in the mirror. He'd taken a seat on the end of the bed, his hands once more resting on his knees, throwing the new shapes of his tattoos into prominence. Apart from the slight awkwardness of his position, he looked far too at home on my bed.

Paint, not paladins. I bent to my cosmetics, dragging my eyes away from his reflection. I dipped the brush and started working the rouge into my cheeks—all the better to hide the flush riding my skin.

"Do you go to the Gilt often?" he asked.

"Often enough," I admitted. "Mostly for work. I told you, it attracts all sorts of people. A good place to see who's talking—or not talking—to who."

I didn't mention the fact that it was also a good source of income for my shop. The less he knew about my life, the better. He knew about Fen. He knew about Reggie. He knew about my mother, but he didn't know the details and I wanted to keep it that way. I doubted I'd be able to keep Fen completely clear of it. He was at least fifty percent curiosity and most of the rest of him was meddle and mischief mixed with a strong portion of protectiveness when it came to women. He would definitely be poking around trying to see what we were up to.

Especially as now I'd turned up at the Swallow voluntarily with the man he'd seen in his vision.

He was probably already champing at the bit to try and pry the truth out of me, but he knew better than to come to my room when I had a man here.

I finished my cheeks and reached for eye paint and kohl. "Do you like theater?" I didn't imagine he'd have much time for such things as a Templar, but he came from a prominent family. He must've been exposed to such things as a child. Not that I found it easy to imagine him as a child. He seemed so big and solid and strong. I couldn't picture him small and vulnerable.

He shook his head. "Not opera."

"Why not?" I caught his glance in the mirror.

"I don't mind listening to the music," he said, looking away. "But the costumes and the plots are fairly ridiculous. It's distracting."

I guessed that was understandable coming from someone used to the austerity of a Templar's life. "What about other entertainments. . . . how do Templars entertain themselves?" I asked.

"We go out in the night and fight things," he said.

My eyebrows shot up and he grinned. "No. Well, yes, we do but that's work really. We don't get a lot of free time, but we spend it as most would."

"What, you sit around drinking and gaming? Isn't that what most men do?"

Guy shook his head at me. "You need to meet some different men. Not that Templars are saints." His smile widened as he ran his eyes over me again, and my stomach tightened.

"How disappointing," I said, trying for a teasing tone. "I like my men saintly." I turned back to the mirror, angling so I couldn't see him behind me. My hand trembled slightly as I reached for a brush to finish my eyes. Ignoring him made my stomach ease a little, but I was still far too aware of him behind me.

But there's only so long you can draw out applying eye makeup. Eventually I finished and had to face him again. "Now," I said. "We just have to deal with what you're going to wear."

Chapter Twelve

HOLLY

Turned out that putting Guy into evening clothes was both a good and a bad thing. Good that he owned them and we didn't have to cobble something together from clothes left behind at the Dove and good, yes, that he'd thought to bring them with him. But the sight of him in immaculate tailored black-and-white was not helping me with my "let's not tumble immediately into bed" plan.

I wasn't the only one admiring my escort. He attracted glances left, right, and center as we walked into the foyer of the Gilt, just as he had at Justine's earlier. I had the feeling that if I hadn't been actually hanging on to his arm, some enterprising young thing would've swept him away.

Guy seemed mostly oblivious to the attention, though I wasn't sure if that was actually the case or he was pretending to be polite. Either way I was relieved. After all, it would be hard to sell "this man is completely besotted with me" if he was ogling every other female in the vicinity.

Fortunately we secured seats in one of the boxes in the first balcony. Expensive, but the point was to be seen and the boxes were prime territory for gossip-worthy activities. We even had it all to ourselves, which was unusual. And also somewhat problematic—private boxes were traditionally used by lovers for trysts during the show.

If Guy and I were alone, people would expect us to put on some sort of display of passion to add to the spectacle.

But while the lights were up, at least we could maintain some semblance of propriety. Still, I made sure to let my gloved hand fall onto Guy's knee once we were both seated, sending him a smile. "We're meant to be madly in lust, remember?" I said softly. "And we're on show."

He was quick on the uptake; I had to give him that. He smiled at me, then leaned in and pressed a kiss to my shoulder, left bare by the dress. "Is this the sort of thing they're expecting?" he asked, trailing his lips across to my neck.

I tried not to let my eyes cross as pleased shivers ran over my skin. "It will do for now," I managed.

"See anyone interesting?" he said, as he continued nibbling his way up my neck.

I let my head loll back for a moment to give him better access, then forced myself to laugh and push him away, tapping his leg with my fan in admonishment. I opened my purse to find my opera glasses, hoping no one—least of all Guy—would notice my hands were trembling a little and that I fumbled the ties.

The opera glasses were the excuse I needed to move a little farther away, shifting my skirts as I pretended to seek a better angle for viewing. "Why don't you order some champagne, darling?" I said, pitching my voice to carry to those in the next box. "We need to celebrate your freedom." There. Let them chew on that.

The other boxes were occupied, though the crowd was thinner than usual. Still, there were enough people that the hum of their voices rose loud enough to make quiet conversation difficult. Along with the sound, the mingled scents of several hundred different perfumes and gaslight smoke and greasepaint filled the air. The smell of possibility.

I leaned a little farther forward, gazing down into the stalls, wishing I knew more about what had been happening while I'd been in St. Giles. It would be easier to read the crowd if I knew who was currently siding with who. Still, I could make some useful guesses until I could talk to some of my contacts. I raised the glasses from the stalls to the semicircular double tier of boxes.

"See anyone interesting now?" Guy asked quietly, leaning close to me again.

"Not yet," I said. I hadn't spotted any Favreaus I recognized, though there were three people in Christophe's usual box. No Ignatius Grey. And no Cormen, thank the Veil. I'd been half afraid he'd be here. If he saw me with Guy, he would no doubt require an explanation of why I wasn't still in St. Giles. Though hopefully Guy's presence would be enough to prevent him from pushing a confrontation.

Guy tapped the glasses. "Can I look?"

I shook my head at him, forcing a giggle as though he'd said something droll. "No, too obvious."

"I know how to observe," he said.

"I'm sure you do. From a vantage point on a battlefield or down in the streets. This is a different art."

I lowered the glasses, to demonstrate my point. The box attendant came with our champagne and I fussed with my hair a little while he poured two glasses, situated the bottle in a bucket of ice, and retreated soundlessly.

Guy raised his glass to me with a wicked grin. "Why don't you educate me, then?"

I pursed my lips, gave him a considering glance. "It takes subtlety. Templars aren't big on subtlety."

"Oh no?" He leaned closer, breathed a soft puff of air onto my throat, sending a shiver down my skin, despite myself. "I can be subtle."

Subtle enough to melt me, apparently.

I snapped my fan open with my free hand and waved him back. "Most people here are watching the crowd more than the opera," I said when I had my breath back. "And they know they're being watched in return."

"Which means?"

"You can't be too obvious," I said. "It's a game. No one wants to be caught out studying anyone else too closely. So. Glances. Glimpses. It's like a flirtation. Looks that are long enough, but not too long."

His eyes seemed very blue in the flickering lights of the myriad chandeliers that lit the theater. "And what exactly are we looking for?"

"Conversations. Lack of conversations. Proximity. Invitations. Patronage." It was hard to explain to someone who wasn't used to riding the undercurrents of this world.

"Politics, in other words."

"Yes. With *subtlety*."

He drank champagne, glanced out over the crowd, then hit me with another smile. Another casual touch, this time his finger tapping my earring and managing to stroke the curve of my ear at the same time. "Politics requires context," he said.

"Yes," I managed.

"So. Give me context, then. Show me what you see."

I wasn't going to give him all my secrets. "That would take longer than the length of the show to explain."

"You have to start somewhere. After all, isn't this why you spent all afternoon lecturing me?"

He had me there. I'd agreed to do this. I needed him. I tilted my head slightly toward the front of the box. "All right. Don't look immediately but the fourth box to the right of the stage, on the first tier. That's Christophe Favreau's. In a moment you can look. Then tell me what you see." I opened my fan again, made long, lazy movements while I sipped more of the champagne. The very picture of "please seduce me" to anyone watching.

Guy reached for the bottle to refill his glass. "There are three people in that box. Two men. One woman in a green dress. The men—one is older, graying hair—are sitting one each side of her."

Champagne caught in my throat as I sucked in a breath, surprised. "You didn't look."

"I told you I know how to observe." His smile was pleased.

I narrowed my eyes at him. "So, what does it mean?"

"They could be guarding her," he said.

I shrugged, fanned myself. "Perhaps. Or they could be rivals for her affections. Or arranging a liaison. Or father, daughter, and son. More importantly, who isn't in the box?"

"Christophe Favreau?"

"Yes."

"And that's more important?"

"It could be. They're sitting near the front of the box. Prime position. Normally the alpha would sit there. So for them to feel comfortable doing so, they're either valued guests or maybe they have a hold over him."

"Or Christophe could be running late and they'll move when he arrives."

"That's less likely. Beasts would normally wait for their Alpha before entering his box."

"Are they Beast Kind?"

"You're the observer, you tell me."

"Both the men are tall. Strong. Even the older man. I'd say they are."

"I'd agree. I'm not so sure about her, though." It was always harder to tell a female Beast in human form from a distance. They tended to be not quite so out-of-the-usual tall as the men, and without proximity to catch a scent or their warmer-than-normal body heat, it was easier for the women to blend in with a human crowd. Which made them more dangerous in some ways.

"So you think Christophe isn't going to be here tonight?"

I smiled at him, pleased. "Very good. And that means there's more to be found out in where he might actually be."

Guy frowned a little. "Let me guess. More watching."

"And a little discreet inquiry." I toasted him with my glass.

"I'm guessing that leads to more questions."

"It's a tangled web." He was quick, the Templar, and I hoped he was starting to see why he needed me. The Night World was indeed an intricately knotted and entwined complex of relationships—only the Veiled Court itself was more difficult to traverse—and a blundering outsider would get nowhere fast. If indeed he survived the experience.

Guy squared his shoulders. Nodded just once. "All right. Tell me more."

I raised my glasses again, judging a suitable interval had elapsed since my last survey of the room. The crowd was thickening a little and, to my surprise, I spotted Henri Favreau, sitting almost directly across from us. On the opposite side of the theater to the Favreau box. He was amongst a group of men his own age. Several of them had the same Favreau coloring as him. The others . . . I skimmed my gaze past, then returned. A Rouselline, at a guess. Two more who could be from a number of packs. No Kruegers. And another face I recognized. Antoine Delacroix.

Now, that was interesting. Antoine was distinctly out of favor with his alpha. Almost as out of favor as one could be without actually being outcast from the pack. A disgruntled young *guerrier* with ambition. He and Henri would have much to discuss perhaps.

The group of them bore further study, but I'd seen enough for now. Who else had joined the throng whilst Guy and I talked?

Still no sign of Ignatius, though he was no connoisseur of opera, and one had to think Henri and Ignatius would be avoiding public appearances in the same places, if they were up to something. I wasn't sad to miss Ignatius. He made my skin crawl even from the careful distance I'd managed to maintain from him whenever I'd had cause to be anywhere near his haunts in the Blood Assemblies and Night World boroughs.

I settled back in my seat, pondering the possibilities of Henri Favreau and Antoine Delacroix. Guy offered me a fresh glass of champagne, mouth opening to ask me something, when there was a stir in one of the boxes three to the left of Henri's. I raised the glasses again, then stiffened.

Damn. Adeline.

Now, that was someone I hadn't been expecting to see.

Adeline Louis was another of the Blood Lords engaged in the current power struggle. One of the few females vying for top spot . . . and the reason I'd been on the roof in Seven Harbors the night I'd fallen.

Was it just a coincidence that she was here the same night as Henri?

"Something interesting?" Guy murmured as I kept a weather eye on Adeline whilst she and her retinue situated themselves in the box with a flurry of silk wraps and rearrangement of furniture. Guy was still playing relaxed, but a sudden sense of alertness ran beneath the outward ease.

"Perhaps," I replied in the same low tone, lowering the glasses before my gaze became rude. But I was a fraction too late. Adeline had seen me. Her mouth—a painted red slash—against the icy white of her skin curved upward slightly. She lifted her fan, an extravagant thing of black feathers and jet that matched her frilled and beaded black dress and flipped it toward herself just ever so slightly. A small gesture, but the intent was unmistakable.

"Damn," I said softly.

"What?"

"I've been summoned." I drained the champagne and inclined my head a fraction toward Adeline to let her know I'd received her message.

Her own white head tilted in reply and even from this distance, the bright blue of her eyes glinted at me.

The eyes of the Blood are unnerving. After the Turn, their

skin and hair fades to white, losing all traces of human color, but some quirk of the magic or power or whatever it is that enables human to become vampire leaves their eyes untouched. The effect is uncanny. Not striking the way the odd colors of the Fae can be but chilling somehow to see that one remaining hint of their humanity in colorless faces.

They play up their oddness, dressing solely in black and white, though the more powerful sometimes add touches of bloodred. Lord Lucius had always sported something red, most usually in the form of the heavy ruby and iron rings he favored. Rings that I'd heard he'd used to strike flesh from bone on occasion.

Adeline was more circumspect, only rouging her lips, but even that hint of color was a display of her status. I didn't trust her, but she paid very well.

Well enough that I was going to have to go and see what she wanted.

"This won't take long," I said to Guy as the houselights dimmed.

"Darlin', I can't bear to be parted from you for even an instant." He smiled, but his tone was deadly serious. He rose from his seat and offered me his arm. "I insist on escorting you wherever you need to go."

The overture was starting as we made our way along the corridor behind the boxes toward Adeline's. Guy tucked my arm firmly through his, keeping me close. I hadn't been able to convince him that I was perfectly able to handle this by myself.

The stretch of carpet outside Adeline's box was crowded. Two Blood stood closest to the door of the box, a man and a woman, their pale skin stark in the lowered lighting. Guarding them was a group of three male Trusted, the humans who serve the Blood, providing food, protection, sex, and anything else that might be required. All in the hope that one day they might be chosen to be turned.

All three men were tall, dark-haired, and handsome. But it was a fool who mistook beauty for weakness among the Blood. Adeline's protectors were more than capable of defending her.

A very pretty young girl with blond hair and bite marks on her neck stood next to the two vampires. She wore a soft pink gown that somehow made the red of the wounds stand out more than usual. Jet-beaded cuffs circled her delicate wrists, signaling her status for anyone who cared to look.

I hid a shudder. They were obviously feeling bold to bring . . . refreshments. Still, the girl was a Nightseeker and there wasn't anything we could do about that.

It was perfectly legal for the Blood to feed on a willing human. In fact, the treaty guaranteed them the right. The girl's face bore a glazed look of pleasure that told me either one of the Blood had been using her for sex or she was a true seeker and one of them had been feeding her their blood. The blood of a vampire.

Addictive and nearly always fatal for humans who allowed themselves to be ensnared by it over time. The only escape for a human addicted to the blood was to be turned. Which Nightseekers rarely were.

Guy stiffened, his arm turning to stone beneath my hand. I glanced up, thinking that it was the Blood who had him on alert, but he was staring at the girl. She looked at us for a moment before turning to stare at the female Blood with a worshipful look. That solved the mystery of exactly whose little morsel she was. Adeline wouldn't feed in public. The older Blood rarely did. Sometimes they might indulge at an Assembly, but then, they didn't really consider those to be public, more an extension of their court.

I dug my fingers into Guy's forearm, trying to remind him to control himself.

"I believe Lady Adeline wishes to see me," I said to the nearest Trusted. He nodded and opened the door to the box after a moment's hesitation in which he studied Guy and Guy stared back. I'm not sure what silent male communication passed between them, but it had obviously been made clear that Guy wouldn't be letting me enter alone.

The music swelled louder and the nape of my neck prickled as I stepped into the dark. I had never overcome my dislike for being in close quarters with the Blood, though I frequently had to be. I liked having them behind me even less, but having Guy with me eased my nerves somewhat.

And, as the Blood went, Lady Adeline was relatively civilized. She had always treated me with courtesy. She paid promptly and had never tried to seduce me into letting her feed. I'd always been glad of it. But that didn't mean I enjoyed our encounters.

"Holly, how pleasant to see you." Adeline rose from her seat and walked to where we were hovering in the rear of the box. Hers had fewer seats than the one Guy and I were using. Only one row of chairs was arranged near the front of the box. The rest of the space was filled by several low sofas. Sofas to make feeding easier. I made a note not to sit on any of them.

"Won't you take a seat?" Adeline tilted her head at Guy. "Who is your charming companion?"

"This is Guy," I said.

Her eyes widened for a moment and her gaze flicked down to his hands. He'd refused to wear gloves, pointing out that they would defeat the purpose of letting people know he was no longer a Templar. In the darkness his tattoos were partially obscured, but the Blood can see far better in the dark than I. No doubt Adeline could see what adorned Guy's hands. Even with the work of the sigiler, anyone who knew Templars would be able to see the original design beneath the new ink. I wondered whether it had been a mistake to bring him. If Adeline interpreted his presence as a threat, who knew what she would do?

But she didn't move or bare her fangs. No, instead her mouth just curved in the darkness. "How . . . interesting. Sit down, please, both of you." She ushered us toward the nearest pair of sofas, where we would be mostly hidden from the view of the rest of the boxes.

Which meant Adeline didn't want everyone to be able to see. Interesting indeed.

Was she hiding me or Guy? She wasn't stupid. I had no doubt she knew exactly who he was. But I didn't think she was quite so certain about what he was doing with me. Her eyes, lit with curiosity, studied us closely.

"Did you have a task for me, my lady?" I asked softly when Guy had eased himself into a seat. He'd picked the one closest to the aisle, the one between Adeline and me. It had a clear path to the door. I'd made the same calculations in choosing my seat but had decided to let him have the best vantage point. After all, if this did go wrong, it would be his strength and fighting skill that was our best defense.

"Perhaps," she said, snapping open her fan and setting it gently wafting. The movement of the air made her perfume, something laden with musk and herbs, drift toward us, turning the air cloying.

I resisted the urge to grit my teeth. The Blood turn everything into a dance of careful negotiation and tiny drips of information, always trying to keep the upper hand. I kept my tone carefully polite. Annoying the Blood most likely to assist me would be ill advised.

I opened my own fan, matching the indolent pace of her movements. "May I ask how the situation stands at present?"

Adeline flicked her fan toward the front of the box. "No particular change. Things have been relatively quiet this week."

I doubted that was the whole truth. "Does that mean things have settled?"

The fan snapped shut as she shook her head. "That would be an overly optimistic interpretation. Indeed, this particular lull is making me somewhat uneasy. It is unlike my beloved brethren to pause for breath, so to speak."

"Do you think there is a play about to be made?" I hoped not. The last thing we needed was a full-out Blood war in progress while we tried to find my father. Though it might reveal the information Guy sought more easily.

Adeline shrugged and smiled slightly, red lips not revealing her fangs. "That remains to be seen." She tilted her head at Guy. "Does your friend need to hear our conversation?"

"My friend is . . . protection," I said. "He stays." I snapped my own fan shut to emphasize the point.

"Oh, but not merely a bodyguard, surely? He is too delicious for that, Holly." Adeline's smile widened. She was probing now and I had no choice but to reply. The Night World had to think Guy and I were lovers.

"He has other talents," I replied silkily. I hoped it was clear enough what those talents might be.

"Quite a coup," Adeline murmured. "I had heard there was some . . . unpleasantness at the Brother House yesterday. But we had not expected . . ." She tilted her head at Guy again.

News traveled fast in the City. I'd hoped it would, that word of Guy's expulsion would have reached certain ears before he appeared at my side, but I couldn't help wondering how he felt about it. He looked calm enough, sitting there in the half-light watching Adeline, but who knew what was underneath that trained facade?

Time to change the subject. "I know a good thing when I see one. In truth, it has made things easier for us."

"You knew him before?" Adeline's brows arched high.

I gave a tiny shrug and what I hoped was a coy smile. "A lady doesn't kiss and tell, my lady. Now, before we get down to business, may I ask for some information on my own behalf?" I phrased my words carefully. She was not a Fae to trap me in obligation, but the Blood were nearly as tricky to deal with. They liked nothing better than to hold a debt over your head.

"You may ask."

Well, that was as much as I could hope for. Ask the question and she would decide whether or not to answer. Plus she would gain the knowledge of what exactly it was that I was seeking. Still, I had to take the gamble. I straightened in the chair. "I'm trying to determine the whereabouts of Cormen sa'Inviel'astar," I said.

"Your—"

"Yes." I cut her off before she could say any more, the geas flaring with a wave of pain. I hadn't known for certain that Adeline knew of my relationship to Cormen. Now I had to make sure she didn't reveal it to Guy or I wasn't sure what the geas would force me to do. "Yes. Has he come to your attention lately, my lady?"

She cocked her head, considering, and then her smile spread wider in a way that made my neck prickle even more. "Why, yes. And how fortuitous because I do believe he is invited to attend a gathering at Halcyon tomorrow night. Ignatius is throwing a party. And it was Ignatius I needed you to watch for me."

"Is Ignatius a concern, my lady?" Her interest had given me an opening to ask.

"He grows bolder, yes. He's always been ambitious, but it takes more than ambition. He is young yet. Previously he lacked the necessary resources."

Money, I took that to mean. Sheer force of personality and willingness to kill weren't enough to hold the Blood. No, it also took money to build alliances and secure a position. "Previously? Has he acquired such resources now?"

Adeline pursed her lips. "He has grown more extravagant lately. I believe he is obtaining funds from somewhere. I would like more definite information."

Which was where I would come in. If Adeline didn't know who was bankrolling Ignatius, then the source was either beyond her reach within the Blood or, more likely, coming from outside the Blood.

The thought made me shiver as I remembered the pouch of gems in my father's safe. I didn't like coincidences. "I will see what I can do, my lady. I assume you can acquire an invitation for us?"

Anger roiled off Guy as Adeline's entourage disappeared into her box, leaving us alone in the corridor. The sound of the music rising faintly through the walls of the boxes was the only reminder we were in a building full of hundreds of people.

I didn't look at him. The corridors of the Gilt were hardly the place for a disagreement and I could tell he was spoiling for an argument.

I was beginning to wonder if this had been a ridiculous idea. If Guy was going to let his temper get the better of him here at the Gilt, the first time I agreed to something he didn't want to do, how was he going to cope with the other much worse things we might do or see as we moved more deeply within the Night World? Maybe his Templar instincts were just too deeply ingrained and he wouldn't be able to pull off the charade after all.

But I didn't know how to broach the subject. How does one tell a warrior knight he might have to let someone else lead him into unfamiliar territory and that he couldn't just attack the enemy head-on?

I had no idea.

Maybe he just needed time to calm down. But time was a luxury we didn't have.

"I'm going to the—" I gestured down the corridor toward the bathrooms, figuring that, at this point, leaving him alone for a few minutes might be the safest ploy. "I'll meet you back at our box."

He didn't argue, just turned on his heel and walked away. For a moment I let myself admire the view as he stalked down the corridor. For a large man, he moved beautifully—even as tightly controlled as he was now in his anger. Like a dancer or, I supposed, the trained warrior he was. A man in charge of his body. One who knew how to use it.

I tapped myself on the forehead with my closed fan. I shouldn't be thinking about Guy's body and what he might or might not know how to do with it. I should be thinking about how we were going to find my father, how to find out more about what the Favreaus might or might not be about, and how I was going to navigate an angry knight through the perils of a Blood Assembly without any bloodshed tomorrow night.

I forced myself to turn away and head to the retiring room. Given that we were still in the early stages of the first act, it was deserted. No one had had time yet to grow bored or consume too much champagne.

But no flashes of blinding insight occurred to me as I stared at myself at the mirror and delayed returning to the box by fussing with my makeup.

Settling my own armor in place for the battle to come. I recognized what I was doing even as I went through the motions. I needed Guy to do what I wanted. There was one obvious way of increasing my influence over him. Take him to bed.

My body approved of the idea even as my brain cringed at the calculation behind the thought.

Curse Cormen to the seven depths of hell. His machinations were going a good way to turning me into the one thing I'd always sworn I wouldn't become.

A whore.

Though was it whoring if all I got in return was the usual willingness of a male in lust to please his bedmate?

It would be if the only reason I bedded Guy was to get him to do what I wanted. I curled my lip at my reflection. If only it could be that uncomplicated. But it wasn't.

Stupid, Holly girl.

I needed to be hit in the head with something far more effective than the fan. Then maybe I wouldn't find the idea of Guy in my bed so enticing.

But if I didn't use sex, then my alternatives appeared limited. Guy wasn't the sort of man to be persuaded to something he didn't want to do easily. One only had to spend a few minutes in his company to realize that. And it wasn't as if there was no attraction between us. The kisses we'd shared were ample proof that we shared an attraction. Both of us would be willing participants.

Wasn't sex always a battle on some level?

Perhaps it was, but I preferred to be on the same side as my bed partner. I scowled at the thought.

"What a pretty sight."

The voice came out of nowhere. I whirled, heart hammering. My father leaned against the door, his eyes fixed on me like an eagle tracking a mouse. I hadn't heard him come in. Or noticed the door opening and closing. He'd concealed himself somehow.

My spine prickled. I forced myself to act relaxed, let my hand stray to the fan on the table. There was a dagger hidden in its handle. A thin, sharp stiletto. Iron mixed with silver. I'd use it on him if I had to.

"I'm surprised to see you here tonight," Cormen said, his voice ice edged as he continued to track me with those emotionless eyes. "I set you to a different task."

"I am working on that," I said. It wasn't a lie. Not outright.

"Is that so?" He took a step toward me and my hand tightened on the fan. "I told you to watch Simon DuCaine, not bed his brother."

Gods. He knew who Guy was.

"And how better to gain Simon's trust than to win his brother's?" I retorted.

"I don't have time for you to use your dubious charms to win over the DuCaines. I want that information."

The words ended with a crack like a whip, and pain suddenly clawed my stomach. Cormen tugging on his leash. I steeled myself, trying to remember how to breathe, and stared him down. The urge to attack him in return, to hurt him until he told me where my mother and Reggie were and if they were still alive, pounded through my veins. But Cormen was fast and his magics were stronger than mine. My only hope of defeating him in a face-to-face fight would be a lucky strike. One that killed him.

Leaving me without the information I needed and possibly damning Mama and Reggie to rot in whatever hole he had stashed them in.

For now I needed him alive.

Alive and unsuspecting.

"You wanted me to do this because I'm good at what I do. You need to let me do it."

"I don't *have* to do any such thing." He moved closer still and I had to fight not to back up. My throat dried and I suddenly recalled his face as he ordered the Beast to beat me. My stomach clenched against a wave of nausea. I wouldn't give him the satisfaction of knowing how much he scared me.

"You will deliver what I asked. You will deliver it quickly or you will pay the price." His voice was whispered ice, turning me to frozen fear.

I'd always hated Cormen since he'd abandoned us. That hate had grown over the years, and the beating had only set it burning fiercer. But I hadn't realized that the beating had planted fear too.

He'd ordered someone to hurt me with no more thought than one might give to throwing away a broken piece of crockery. And with no more remorse than one might show for that act. He would do it again—and worse—if he had to. I knew that much for sure.

"I *am* working as quickly as I can. It's not as if I can walk up to Simon DuCaine and demand that he tell me his secrets."

"You were at the hospital for days."

"And most of that time I was bed-bound, thanks to you. Your thug was overly enthusiastic. The healers at St. Giles are very conscientious. They don't let patients who are recovering from being severely beaten wander around out of bed."

"That is not my problem. Perhaps all that is needed here is to provide you with some additional motivation." He reached into his pocket and drew something from it. A long glittering chain, twin to mine. The pendant dangling from it was a stylized heart set with black diamonds and sapphires.

I knew that pendant as well as my own. I'd seen it hanging around my mother's neck every day since I'd been born. The fear stalking my nerves blossomed into something nearer to terror. I couldn't breathe.

So. Here was the proof I'd been seeking, the proof some small broken part of me had hoped not to find. Cormen had my mother and likely Reggie too. "Where did you get that?" I hissed.

The pendant glinted in the light of the chandeliers, the jewels set in the gold sending sparks of black and blue dancing across the walls.

"Your mother let me borrow it."

"You bastard," I spat. "You leave her out of this."

"Why should I? She belongs to me."

"She does not. Neither of us does. You walked away from us. You cut us off and left us to rot in the gutter. I swear, Cormen, if you've hurt her I'll—" The words cut off as pain choked me, acid claws wrapping my throat, burning down to my belly.

"You'll what exactly?" he said with a sneer. "Don't get above yourself, little *hai-salai*." He grabbed my chin as I sputtered, unable to talk. "Now. Listen closely. I want the sunmage's secret." His bronze eyes gleamed malevolently as his nails dug into my cheeks. "I want it fast."

He let go of me abruptly, stepped back, and lifted the pendant once more. "And if you disappoint me, this will be the last time you see this or your mother."

I still couldn't speak, though I no longer knew if it was the geas or sheer rage and terror stealing my voice. My cheeks stung from the bite of his nails, and my heart raced. I ached to move. To reach the fan and stab him, cut him. Anything to hurt him. To rid myself of him. But all I could do was stand there and listen.

"Do we have an understanding?" He shoved the necklace into his pocket, then carefully smoothed down the lines of his frock coat.

I nodded. There wasn't anything else I could do. My bastard father had the upper hand. But as I watched him turn and leave, I was determined that he wouldn't keep it for long.

Chapter Thirteen

GUY

✠

"Ignatius Grey?" I demanded as Holly slipped through the door of the box. "Are you insane?"

She scowled, eyes sparking green as the jewels in her ears. "Keep your voice down. People will hear."

We were still well to the rear of the box, so I didn't know if that was a valid point, but she had been to the theater more than I, so I reluctantly let her go. I pointed at the nearest seat, forcing my voice to a more loverlike tone. "Won't you have a seat, *darling*?"

Holly sat facing the stage. Her eyes glittered in the dim light. I stopped for a moment. Tears? No. She wasn't crying. Her face was pale under the paint, her mouth set. Angry.

That made two of us.

"Ignatius Grey?" I repeated, lowering myself into the chair opposite and angling my body toward her as though we were having an intimate tête-à-tête.

Those glittering eyes fastened on me. "Yes. This is what I do, Guy." Her fan snapped open, then closed again, her gloved hands moving restlessly over the carved sticks.

"I thought you crawled around on rooftops, spying on people."

"Sometimes the information isn't on rooftops. Sometimes

it's at the theater. Or the Assemblies. Which means I have to be there."

"In Blood Assemblies." I heard my voice go flat. I tried to rein back the temper rising within. Of all the places . . . an Assembly. I loathed them and everyone who willingly attended them.

But everything Holly said was true. She was a spy. A professional. Good enough for Blood Lords to hire her. She knew what she was doing. And I'd known we might have to venture into the Night World when I'd started this. So why was I fighting the urge to punch someone at the thought of her parading through a Blood Assembly?

I hated the Assemblies, that was true, but this wasn't that feeling. This felt different. Sharper somehow.

"When the situation requires it, yes," Holly said, still tapping her fan restlessly. "I've done it before. It's safe enough."

I tried not to think about the last time I'd been in a Blood Assembly. Because that had involved a riot, killing a few Beasts, and Simon kidnapping Lily. Hardly a recommendation for the safety of such places. "You have an interesting definition of safe."

"I'm not an idiot, Guy," she snapped. "This is how I make my living. I'm not going there to drink vampire blood or get myself chewed on." She lifted her chin defiantly. "You don't see any scars on my neck, do you?"

"No." I'd kissed that neck . . . that skin. I knew it bore no scars.

Anger flared again. Hotly possessive.

Hell's balls. *No.* I reined myself in with a heavy mental hand. Holly was not mine.

I didn't want the ties such emotions brought.

But I did want her.

That much was clear. Inescapably clear. Much as I'd have to be blind not to know she wanted me too. I'd felt it in the tiny reactions of her skin under my lips, in the catch of breath. In the heat of her eyes.

She was a spy, yes. A game player. But whatever it was flaring between us, it wasn't a game.

I needed to resist it.

Of course, given her current mood, if I tried anything, I would suffer something worse than a refusal. I didn't doubt she had weapons somewhere on her person or that she knew how to use them. She was a fighter. A survivor. She would do what she had to do. I needed to remember that that might not be the same as what I wanted her to do.

Hells, I needed to remember that she might just turn me down regardless of what mood she was in. Perhaps she still had a grip on her common sense. She was practical, I knew that much.

But I still couldn't quite help looking at the slim column of white throat, rising from the silk, framed by the chain that arrowed down to where her breasts rose from the dress in smooth curves and disappeared below the ruffles as if its sole purpose was to draw the eye there. To her skin. Warm, that skin. My hands remembered. And it smelled of . . . well, Holly and flowers and something subtle that seemed to seep into my brain whenever I got near her. It tasted good too.

Too good.

Hell's balls, what was I doing thinking about kissing her when we were talking about the stupidity of going to an Assembly?

Another yank on those mental reins was required.

I studied her. Her fan swished angrily, like a cat's tail. She hadn't been angry when we'd parted outside Adeline Louis' box. No, then she'd been almost too well pleased with herself.

And yet by the time she returned to me, she'd been angry.

So what had happened in between?

"Why are you angry?" I asked.

The fan stilled. "Why are you arguing with me?"

Deflecting a question with a question, I knew that technique all too well.

"Something happened," I said flatly. "Before you came back here."

She was very good. The fan snapped back into action with a dismissive flutter. But not before I saw the small flash of surprise in her eyes. I was right.

"Nothing happened," she said.

"You're lying."

"You're still arguing. Nothing happened, Guy."

"We can't do this if you're going to lie to me."

"I'm not lying." Another flutter of the fan. "It was nothing." She looked at me, then away.

"It?"

She bit her lip. "If you must know, I ran into someone."

"Who?"

Her eyes came back to me. "If you must know, someone I once . . . kept company with."

Shared her bed with, she meant. I felt another hot surge of anger. "And?"

"And he was unpleasant about you," she said. "I sent him on his way. As I said, it was nothing. Or rather, it's something that can work for us. He'll no doubt be talking about me."

I wasn't sure if I believed her. Even if I did, I wasn't sure that I *should* believe her. She had her own agenda here; I needed to remember that. I wanted something from her and I believed that she would hold to her end of her agreement, but I'd be a fool to think that her only priority was finding her mother and her friend.

Silence hung between us. I could push her, but I doubted she'd give away anything she didn't want to. I'd only make her angrier. More likely to do something reckless.

So I would hold my tongue. Bide my time. For now. "Your Lady Adeline is concerned about Ignatius Grey. He's bad news. Particularly if he's gotten his hands on some money," I said, trying to return to the topic at hand.

Exasperation flashed over Holly's face before she restored her tight social smile. "I'm well aware of that. I imagine I have a far better understanding of Ignatius and his particular peccadilloes than you do."

"If you did, you wouldn't—"

"Wouldn't what? Go near him?" She leaned closer, smile tightening further. "I'm a spy. And a thief. I'm not some delicate little flower that you have to protect, Guy. I can handle myself. The question seems to be whether you can cope with what we're doing. If you're going to start throwing your weight around whenever we come across a Blood Lord or a Beast or the Fae, then we might as well give up now."

The words were almost a slap. And stopped me short. I drew in a breath, ignoring the scent of her that drifted with it. "I can behave myself if you can."

I certainly wasn't going to let her do this alone. Maybe she had done these things before, but now she had me. I looked down at my hands, at the beasts snarling there. Just because I bore them didn't mean I had to become them. I'd agreed to go along with the plan. I'd defaced my *tattoos*, for the love of all that was holy. I needed the information she could uncover. I wouldn't abandon the path—or Holly—now.

Even if I did want to shake her until her teeth rattled.

"Good." She turned away from me slightly, flicking a curl that had fallen over her shoulder. "Let's watch the show."

I changed seats, moving beside her. We had to keep up the pretence. And more than that, I needed to be closer to her. The tension riding me wasn't just the knowledge that half the people in the theater were Blood or Beasts, setting off every instinct I possessed. No, part of it was just being close to her.

I wanted her. Wanted to peel that dress from her and lay her down and take her until we both forgot who we were and what we were doing.

You couldn't fake actual desire. You could resist it and I knew that she, just like me, was resisting mightily, but you couldn't conjure the spark from nothingness. You couldn't make the air prickle when someone else walked into the room.

It was either there or not.

And, because God apparently had a nasty sense of humor right now, it was there between us.

The question was whether we could both keep our heads and resist.

It would be good between us. It had been a long time since I'd allowed myself the distraction of giving in to this kind of hunger. We didn't swear celibacy, but my life was simpler without sex.

My Brother knights chose their own paths. Some largely ignored women, some found women willing to satisfy their hungers. Some even fell in love and married as the Church would prefer.

Love. I didn't even want to think the word.

Because there was no place in my world for that emotion when it came to a woman.

It came at too high a cost.

But I was used to guarding myself. Planning liaisons as carefully as I planned campaigns in battle. I wasn't going to let her slip through my defenses. I was going to stay in control.

Take charge.

Starting right now.

And the first thing any good soldier did when taking charge of a campaign was to get the lay of the land.

In my case, that meant understanding the woman sitting beside me, looking as though she was listening happily to the shaky soprano currently gracing the stage.

But she wasn't just listening. No. Her eyes studied the crowd, searching it.

Spy. Thief. What did she see with those eyes? What did she see when she looked at me?

I leaned closer, felt her jump in surprise. "Looking for someone in particular?" I said, mouth close to her ear.

"N-no."

Another lie. "I can't help you if I'm walking blind, Holly. You want me to understand this world." I gestured at the audience. "Time for another lesson."

She looked somewhat chastened. "I'm sorry. I forgot. I usually work alone." She offered a quick smile. A real one this time.

"And I usually work with fifty other men. I can adjust if you can."

The corner of her mouth quirked. "I'm not sure I can replace fifty Templars."

"You don't have to. Who are you looking for?"

She looked down, smoothed her skirt where it wasn't wrinkled. "No one in particular."

Lying again. All right. I knew when to hold position rather than attack. "Then what?"

She looked back up. "I was just watching the dance."

"The dance?"

"I told you earlier. The Night World isn't simple. Everything shifts and moves and turns in an instant. It's a dance, only you're never quite sure what song might play next or if there's a new set of steps everyone else but you knows."

"Battles are that way too," I said.

"I guess." She shrugged a shoulder. "I've never seen a battle."

"They're unpredictable." And violent, bloody, and horrible. So perhaps a good metaphor for Night World politics after all.

"So maybe I can follow your dance. I might even let you lead." I grinned at her and she relaxed, a little. "Good. How about you smile at me while we talk? After all, we don't want to disappoint our audience."

"I'll smile if you will." She grinned at me and then lifted the fan to her face. The air stirred the curls around her face and she brushed them back into place with her free hand. The movement settled her dress even lower on her chest, baring more of the curve of her breast to my view. My mouth went dry. I knew she was acting, but the effect was very real.

Keep your mind on the task at hand. I summoned an answering smile. "Seems fair."

Holly angled her body toward me so that her skirts brushed my knees. "So. The dance." The fan was still for a moment as she looked out over the theater.

"What do you know of the Favreaus?" she asked.

Right this minute, I chiefly knew that she smelled very good and that her skin almost gleamed in the half-light. *Favreaus, Guy. Beast Kind. Ambushes.*

I took a breath. "Mostly what you told me this afternoon. Not known to cause trouble. Kept their noses reasonably clean until Lucius died."

"Was killed, if you believe the rumors," Holly murmured.

I paused. Was she digging for information? Or just commenting. She wasn't the only one with secrets, after all.

"Died. Since then the Blood have been trying to determine who might take his place. Which also leaves the Beast Kind packs scrambling for territory and position."

"That's a polite way of saying the entire Night World is tallying up quite the body count."

I smiled. "Darlin', a gentleman always strives for politeness."

"Are you a gentleman, then?"

"My mother would like to believe so."

The fan dropped, revealing her wide smile. "Well, I have heard that knights are meant to be chivalrous."

"There is that," I agreed. "But we were talking about the Night World, not me."

"We were." She sighed. "A pity, really." She slanted a glance at me with those very green eyes that made me wonder exactly what she meant. But I wasn't about to ask.

"You'll have noticed that Christophe Favreau's box still has no sign of Christophe himself," Holly continued.

I nodded. That much I had taken in while I'd been waiting for Holly to return.

"There is a Favreau here, though. In the box across from us.

There are a number of Beasts. Do you see?" She waved her fan idly and smiled, as though we were discussing the weather.

I found the box she meant and the man. Light brown hair neatly tied back in a queue and pale eyes. Too far to see if they were gray without Holly's opera glasses. His head was bent toward the blond man sitting beside him, discussing something with an intent expression. "Which one is he?" I asked.

"That's Henri. He's a *guerrier*, though a low-ranked one."

"If he's a *guerrier*, why is he here when his alpha isn't?" *Guerriers* were the pack warriors. And most often, their job was to guard the alpha.

"A good question," Holly said. "He may merely have the night off."

"Do *guerriers* get nights off?"

"Do Templars?" She arched a brow at me.

We did. Though in the current unrest, time off had been scarce.

"So you think he's just out on the town?"

"Maybe. Though he keeps interesting company. That's Antoine Delacroix he's with."

I knew that name . . . though I couldn't quite remember why. The Delacroix pack was another that had been closely allied to Lord Lucius. Though, if I remembered rightly, Christophe Favreau and Paul Delacroix didn't much like each other. "And Antoine is?"

"A troubled young man," Holly said. "Very much out of favor with his pack right now. He narrowly avoided being cast out a while back. His father is a senior *guerrier*, which may have saved him."

I turned my attention back to the two men. True, the younger Beasts did sometimes ignore pack boundaries while out carousing, but would a Favreau *guerrier* usually hang around with a member of another pack who was in disgrace? The packs didn't poach from each other. A cast-out Beast would find no home with another clan. As I watched, the singer onstage reached a crescendo, and a wave of applause echoed around the theater. Henri raised his head and our eyes met. His brows drew down before his face smoothed and he moved his gaze away.

I made myself focus back on the stage, trying to look interested in the caterwauling of the soprano. Something about Henri set my teeth on edge. But this wasn't the place to try and discuss how we might learn more about him. That could wait until we were somewhere more private.

"So, do the Favreaus support anyone in particular? Do they have a favorite candidate for Blood Lord?" I asked. The soprano hit one last high note and the crowd broke into more rapturous applause. Holly clapped politely and I followed her example. The orchestra struck up again and a group of acrobats tumbled onto the stage.

"No. Not that I've heard. They gained a lot under Lucius. I'd think they'd be looking to support someone who wanted to keep the status quo. One of Lucius' lieutenants."

"Like Ignatius Grey?"

Her face went carefully blank. "Ignatius was one of Lucius' circle, yes. But Christophe doesn't like him."

"Can he afford to dislike Ignatius? From all I've heard, Grey is doing well for himself. And he's captured your Lady Adeline's attention, it seems."

I had heard a little of Lucius' court from Lily. She didn't like to talk about him and I'd only managed to coax information out of her a few times. Ignatius' name had come up more than once. Lily despised him. She'd once said he was as vicious as Lucius but not nearly as clever. Not someone you wanted in control of the Blood. It took an iron fist and a keen mind to hold the Blood Court together.

Holly shrugged. "As Adeline said, Ignatius bears watching. And any smart alpha will be hedging his bets right now."

"Any idea what his views on the treaties are?"

"Ignatius or Christophe?"

I held out a hand, trying not to look at the tattoo snarling at me. "It's not exactly a secret that Lucius would've been happy for us to return to the old days." Where the Blood could feed at will and had come close to enslaving the humans entirely. "Does Ignatius share his politics?"

"I don't know," Holly said, biting her lip. "No one who was trying for such a thing would talk about it."

"And Lady Adeline?"

"Adeline has always been . . . courteous to me. Don't get me wrong, she's Blood, but I can't imagine her wanting to return to a dog-eat-dog world. She's too fond of her comforts."

"So you trust her?"

"Trust might be too strong a word. But she's definitely not on Ignatius' side."

"I see." My head was throbbing dully. Too many threads to try and pull together. The noise of the orchestra and the audience grated on my nerves. "What about the man you asked her about . . . Cormen, was it? Who's he? A Fae?"

Her face returned to that careful stillness. "Yes, he's Fae." Her voice sounded slightly hoarse and she didn't say anything else. Instead she looked down at her hands where they'd twisted together in her lap.

Nervous? Or no, not nervous. *Scared.* A connection finally clicked into place. "Wait. Is he the one you think took your mother and your friend?"

She nodded slowly. "Maybe. Yes."

"Why? What does he want?"

She flinched. "I'm not sure. Not yet." Her voice still sounded rough, as if she'd been shouting. Which she hadn't.

"Do you need a drink?" I looked across to where our abandoned bottle of champagne sat in a bucket of half-melted ice.

"No. No, I'm all right."

She didn't sound convincing. She'd turned pale. Too pale. Maybe I wasn't the only one who needed rest. I suddenly remembered that I'd dragged her out of St. Giles too soon.

"Do you want to leave? How long does this thing go on for anyway?"

"A few more hours," she said, sounding slightly more normal. "We can't leave until interval at the earliest. It would be very bad form."

I shrugged, an escape plan forming rapidly in my head. There was information to be learned here at the Gilt, but I knew when to retreat so as to refine a strategy.

"Guy, I was serious," she said. "If we go, everyone will notice."

"Isn't that half the purpose of us being here? To be seen."

"To be seen, not cause a scene," she retorted.

"Darlin', no one expects a drunken, lustful ex-Templar to behave." And before she could protest, I bent, scooped her up in my arms, kissed her soundly when she gave a surprised shriek of protest, paused so that everyone could turn and see exactly who was interrupting the show, then swept her out of the box.

*   *   *

Holly was still giggling when I put her down, finding myself strangely reluctant to let go as she found her balance. So I offered her my arm as we walked down the steps toward the street.

The courtyard outside the Gilt was strangely quiet. It had bustled with 'cabs and hackneys and private carriages when we'd arrived. But, as Holly had pointed out, we were leaving early, so none of the drivers would be expecting customers just yet. The night air was warm, so it wouldn't hurt to wait for a while.

"Told you we were early," Holly said. As she spoke, I caught a movement out of the corner of my eye. A small red light flared in the darkness to the left of the stairs, and a waft of cigar smoke curled into the air.

Just a theater patron who'd stepped outside for some fresh air? Maybe. But I pulled Holly a little closer, and felt for the pistol at my hip.

Where were the damn 'cabs?

The smell of cigar grew stronger and then someone walked into the light, heading toward us. No, not someone. Henri Favreau. Holly went stiff beside me.

Henri smiled, too-white teeth flashing like knife blades. "Good evening," he said. "Is the show not to your taste tonight?"

He was looking at Holly. Which didn't ease my nerves any. She was the more vulnerable target.

"It wasn't their finest production," Holly said. Her voice was vaguely bored, a good imitation of a pampered society girl unimpressed with the entertainment on offer. She slipped her arm free of mine but didn't move away.

"True," Henri agreed. "But it's always interesting what one can see at such things, isn't it?"

"I guess." Holly shrugged. "But if you'll excuse us, we have another party to attend."

Henri tossed his cigar down onto the stones, grinding it with his foot to extinguish the glowing end. "For instance," he said as though Holly hadn't spoken, "it's very interesting to find a Templar at the Gilt."

"I'm no Templar," I said. I put a little growl into the words. A clear enough "back off" signal if he wasn't a fool.

"A Templar only a few days clear of the order is still a Templar." A second voice came from behind us. I twisted to see

Antoine Delacroix standing a little above us on the stairs. Damn.
I'd forgotten that Beasts move almost as soundlessly as Blood
when they want to. I moved back a pace, taking Holly with me.

"Perhaps you shouldn't be so quick to tell us that," Antoine
said easily. "After all, a Templar has protection. A curious disgraced knight, however . . ."

"I'm not curious," I said flatly. "We came to see the show."

Antoine tilted his head. "You were watching us, Templar."

"Everyone watches everyone at the Gilt," Holly said. Her
voice was perfectly calm.

"Anyway, why should we watch you?" I said. If this was going to end badly, might as well make it quick. "Were you doing
something noteworthy?"

Antoine bared his teeth.

"Not a smart place to start a fight," I said to him. "There are
plenty of people around."

"Not near enough," Antoine replied. A knife suddenly glinted
in his hand. "It wouldn't take long."

The pistol appeared in my hand before I realized I'd drawn it.
"Think you're fast enough?" Beside me, Holly sucked in a breath
and I saw the glint of metal in her hand too. The pistol she carried
was smaller than mine, but it was pointed across me at Henri.

I hoped she had silver bullets.

Antoine had gone very still, but his knife was still held at the
ready. Beasts are fast. He could throw it before either of us could
react. I risked a quick glance at Henri. He looked worried. A
smarter man than his companion, then.

"Do you think you're fast enough to get both of us?" Antoine
asked, his hand beginning to move.

"Maybe not," I said. And I fired just as his fingers loosed the
blade, sending it winging toward me. Antoine jerked backward
and collapsed as the bullet tore into his chest. I threw myself into
a crouch and the knife cut the air above my head before clatter-
ing to the cobbles. There was another shot and Henri yelped too.
I didn't stop to see what Holly had hit, simply fired another shot
into Antoine's knee, grabbed Holly's arm, and started to run.

We ran for a block or so before it became clear no one was
following us. Still, I maintained our speed, heading toward the
nearest station, praying that a cab or hackney would come into
sight soon.

Holly kept pace, her face grim. When a cab finally did rattle

into view, the driver had barely pulled to a halt before I bundled
Holly inside, climbed in after her, and yelled for the driver to get
moving.

HOLLY
🗝

"I can't believe you did that," I said as the autocab jolted and
hissed to a shuddering halt outside the Swallow. Beside me,
Guy's expression was alert but unworried. As if nothing had
happened.

I shivered beneath my light wrap. Beasts. We'd shot two
Beasts. There'd been silence between us during the journey
here, both of us watching for pursuit. But now that we were
safely back under the gas lamps outside the Swallow, I wanted
to talk.

"It was us or them," Guy said. "Besides, they'll live. Antoine
was still breathing. You didn't kill Henri, did you?"

I shook my head as I shivered again. I'd never shot anyone
before. Slashed a few with my razor to get out of a tight spot, but
I'd never actually fired my pistol at someone and seen the bullet
pierce flesh. "No," I managed. "I hit his shoulder."

Guy nodded. "Good. Then they've learned a lesson." He
opened the door and swung himself out of the 'cab.

"Or we've earned ourselves two enemies," I muttered, but I
let Guy help me out of the 'cab in turn and stood blinking and
still shivering as he paid the driver.

"I have plenty of enemies," Guy said easily. "Two more
won't hurt me."

I wished I shared his confidence. I did my damned best to
stay neutral. I didn't go around shooting Beast Kind in broad
moonlight. And we'd left them alive and knowing who we were.

"Let's go inside," I said. I wanted my rooms. My bed. My
wards. Safety.

Guy's arm came around me. "All right," he said. "But smile,
please. Or everyone will want to know what's wrong."

I summoned a smile from somewhere. "I just want to be in
bed," I said as we walked toward the Swallow.

"Hear, hear," said Junker, from a few feet away where he

stood at the main door. "You treat that boy right, Miss Holly." He coughed, elbowed Benny beside him, and winked ostentatiously.

I managed to smile back while Guy made a noise suspiciously like a laugh hastily turned into a cough and tucked his arm around my waist. "I'm sure she will," he said with a half bow at the boys. "You heard the man, Holly darlin', time's a-wasting."

Play the game. "No good ever came to a girl from a man in a rush," I said, tapping him on the nose with my fan. As his expression turned indignant, I wriggled out of his grip and beat a hasty retreat through the door.

Unfortunately, the first person I saw was Fen. Who frowned thunderously, put down his glass of brandy, and stalked toward me.

"We need to talk," he said, taking my arm just as Guy came through the door behind me and joined us.

Guy looked at my arm, then at Fen, and scowled. Fen scowled back. Wonderful. The last thing I needed right now was the two of them butting heads in the middle of the Swallow.

"Not now, Fen," I said.

His hand stayed firm on my arm. "Yes, now."

His tone was so flat I glanced involuntarily down to his wrist. The chain was still in place. Still, had he had another vision? If he had, I needed to hear what he had to say. "All right," I said.

"No," Guy said firmly.

Fen and I both looked at him.

"I said no," Guy said, blue eyes chilling rapidly. "It's late. And you're tired. You need to sleep."

He and Fen glared at each other. Just what I needed.

"She won't admit she needs to rest, she's stubborn," Guy said. "You know that."

Fen nodded. "All right, tin man. In the morning, then."

He and Guy exchanged another long inscrutable-male look and I knew fought the urge to knock their heads together. Guy held out his arm and we left Fen behind.

Chapter Fourteen

HOLLY

8━

"You're making me dizzy," Guy said. "Stand still."

I paused in my pacing. Guy half sprawled on the edge of the bed looking far more relaxed than I felt. Then again, he was probably used to shooting people.

I wasn't. Every time I stopped pacing, I saw Henri's face again and felt ill. And when I did pace, my brain was a whirl of Cormen and my mother and Adeline and the geas and—

"You're thinking so hard your head might explode. How am I supposed to explain that to Fen?"

The lazy drawl was back in his voice. The extremely sexy lazy drawl. The one that did nothing to ease the tension driving me to pace in the first place. It did, however, refocus it slightly on him.

"This isn't a joke, Guy. What we did could cause trouble."

"I won't let anything happen to you."

"It's not just me!" I heard my voice go shrill and clamped my teeth together.

Guy frowned. "You're overreacting." He studied me for a moment. "Oh, hell's balls, you've never shot anyone before, have you?"

"N-no."

"Fuck." His tone was gentle despite the language. He stood

and crossed to the mantelpiece, poured a glass of whiskey, came back, and held it out. "Drink this. It will help."

I looked down at the whiskey. What the hell, it couldn't hurt. I tilted my head back and drained the glass. The whiskey hit my stomach in a fiery rush, making my eyes water even as warmth bloomed through me. I coughed.

"I didn't say drink it all at once," Guy said, still using that gentle tone. He led me over to the bed. "Here, sit."

I sat, leaned into him. He was warm, like the whiskey heat spreading through me. "How many people have you shot?"

"Too many," he said. "Don't think about it."

"How do I do that?"

He laughed, a soft rumble. "More whiskey?"

"Not a good idea." Whiskey had never been my drink. Spending half the night vomiting wasn't going to make me feel better about what I'd done.

What *we'd* done. I closed my eyes, trying not to think. The scent of warm male mingled with the faint scent of the liquor and the lingering traces of the perfumes and greasepaint smell I associated with a night at the Gilt floated up around me, soothing somehow.

Not just soothing. Enticing.

I moved a little closer to Guy, felt him tense.

"Darlin', unless you want a whole different kind of distraction . . ."

My eyes flew open. Something wary yet wicked glinted in Guy's eyes. Did he mean what I thought he did?

"What does that mean?" I asked.

Was he flirting with me? Here where there was no need for pretense? Flirting deliberately? Surely he hadn't had enough champagne at the Gilt to make him do something crazy? Or was he reacting to the aftermath of the fight as well?

Or just to me? My pulse stuttered.

Guy cocked his head. "Do you really want to know?"

My heart bumped. *Don't be stupid, Holly girl.* But it seemed I wasn't listening to myself. "Yes."

"You really want me to . . . distract . . . you?"

I froze again. There was no mistaking the invitation in that sentence. I knew the sound of a man who was asking to put his hands on you. Perhaps he was drunk after all. And maybe I was because I wanted to accept the invitation. "Yes. But it's not a good idea."

"Right now it sounds pretty good to me." Smoke and night and heat tinted his drawl now. It made my skin prickle hotly.

"After all, everyone thinks we're sleeping together. If our reputations are going to be ruined, we might as well enjoy it."

"You think sleeping with me will ruin your reputation?"

He laughed, then shook his head. "Darlin', I think it can only improve my reputation. You know what I meant."

I bit my lip. "I don't know—"

He pushed off the bed. "Neither do I. But it seems today's the day for the world to be a little crazy. And I don't see why that crazy has to be all bad." He stopped when he was maybe half a foot away, so that I had to tilt my head to keep watching his face. "Want to make the bad things go away?"

I swallowed as a shiver ran down my spine. Actually I did. Quite desperately. Wanted to let him take me over to the bed and then just take me over. But I didn't know if I wanted all the associated complications that would come with that choice.

"Holly . . ." He reached out and drew one of the pins from my hair. "It's been a hell of a day. And you've been the only good thing in it." Another pin and a lock of hair fell down against my shoulder. The shiver in my skin blossomed into a shudder as his finger traced the place where it lay. "Come to bed."

"It's not that simple."

"It could be."

I looked away. Ah, it would be easy to let myself believe that, but Guy wasn't the usual sort of man I took to my bed. And I wasn't the sort of woman he took to his. Not for more than a night anyway.

I wasn't fooling myself that one night with him would be enough for me. Which was exactly why I should be running in the other direction. If I wanted him again before I'd even had him the first time, what hope did I have of keeping my head around him?

How to explain what I was feeling? "Guy—" I lifted my head.

Then he kissed me and I forgot.

Forgot anything but the feel of his lips on mine. Sweet lords of hell, the man could kiss. A bloody Templar knight and yet he kissed as if he'd done nothing but practice kissing women all his life.

Sweet, hot, drugging kisses that stole through my veins as

though he were the whiskey I'd poured into him. Making my skin heat and my resolve melt until I was pressed against him, hands pulling him closer, one word swirling through my head.

Inevitable.

That's what we were. I'd known it from that first time I'd kissed him at St. Giles. I wanted him in my bed and he wanted to be there. If I was going to have to watch him walk away from me when all this was over, then at least I wanted to have the memory of him to keep me warm.

I pulled my hands from around his neck and pushed on his chest. Back toward the mattress, trying to slow my breathing and the reckless ache under my skin. I could sleep with him, but I couldn't let myself think it was anything more than that. I needed to keep some last piece of control. Anything else would be true madness.

"I'm your one good thing?" I asked as he broke off the kiss in response to my hands.

He nodded slowly.

"Well, I think we can improve on that score."

"Does that mean what I think it means?"

I let myself smile at him, at the heat in his eyes and the way it made my stomach curl and twist in time with the ache that was starting to beat lower down. "Do you need me to spell it out?"

His smile widened even farther. "I think a gentleman should always make sure that he understands what a lady desires."

My smile widened. "Is that so? Well, then. How's this? You helped me into this dress. Perhaps you'd be so kind as to help me out of it now?"

"How attached are you to it?" His voice was no longer a drawl, more like a purr.

"It's silk. Expensive."

"I'll buy you a new one."

I laughed and felt my heart crack a little that he could make me feel so giddy amid the chaos. Then I ruthlessly pushed my doubts away. No more thinking. "It's a one-of-kind design. Besides, patience is a virtue. Aren't gentlemen meant to be virtuous?"

He laughed then. "Not when they're removing a woman's clothes, they're not."

"Touché. But perhaps I'm in the mood to take things slowly."

"You're in the mood to kill me."

"No." I let my smile widen, and then stood, turning slowly so he could reach the fastenings on my dress. "If you die, then we won't get to have any fun at all."

"But I'd die happy."

"You'd be happy. But where would I be?"

His hands moved to the first button, then paused and stroked my back. "True. A gentleman is meant to see to the well-being of others before himself."

I laughed again, a bubble of delight rising within me. I'd known I'd wanted him, known the physical yearning for him, but this new playful side of him was as enticing to my mind as the rest of him was to my body. I'd never imagined that a laughing lover might lurk beneath the steel and serious nature.

But apparently I was lacking imagination, because with each silly, teasing exchange I could feel my worries dissolving and a bubble of happiness rising around us where we could just be. Worries could be dealt with in the clear light of day. Right now I wanted the laughter and the pleasure.

Maybe that was selfish but I couldn't bring myself to care.

"Not too slowly," I admonished as he started on the buttons, his fingers moving with infinite care on the silk.

"Bossy little thing, aren't you? Why don't you just relax and let me take care of this?"

"I. Am. Not. Bossy," I said, only half pretending outrage.

"Oh, really? That's not how it seems to me. You've been ordering me around all day. You like being in charge, don't you?" The last of the buttons slipped free and he pushed the dress down off my shoulders so it pooled at my feet. His mouth drifted down to my neck, alternating kisses with wickedly gentle bites that set my nerves alight. "You'd probably like nothing better than tying me to the bed and having your wicked way with me."

I opened my mouth to deny it, but somehow my tongue was frozen as the image of Guy naked and bound on my bed sprang to mind. All that muscle and hardness mine to do with it as I wished?

Oh *my*.

My nipples went hard against the silk of the corset, the restrictive pressure making them almost painful. Almost, but not quite. I sucked in a breath, shook my head to clear it.

"Thought so," he said with a chuckle. "Not tonight, though. Tonight, I think we'll start with something simpler before we start deciding who gets to be in charge. Like me inside you. How does that sound?"

I wasn't sure I could answer as his words echoed around my head and my body tightened in response. His fingers worked the laces of my corset and before I knew it I was left wearing my shift and stockings while Guy circled around me. "Very nice," he said, taking me in.

I wondered if he was expecting me to blush and shield myself as a polite and proper lady might. If he did, he was going to be disappointed. I enjoyed the expression on his face as he studied me. Though, I had to admit, if he kept looking at me that way for too much longer, I might do something pathetically proper-lady-like and collapse because my knees had given way.

I tossed my hair back over my shoulders, knowing that the thin silk of my chemise wasn't concealing much at all. "Surely gentlemen don't wear evening clothes to bed?"

"Darlin', the only thing I want to wear tonight is you." He tugged his shirt over his head and it flew across the room somewhere. I didn't watch where it landed; I was too busy gazing at what its absence had revealed.

Oh. My.

He was beautiful. There was no other word for it. Muscle carved his chest and arms and turned them into living sculptures. The male personified. But it wasn't a perfect unearthly beauty. No. This body had fought and struggled. There was a long scar across his ribs, and faded white lines from other wounds crossed the gold of his skin of his arms and shoulders.

This man had fought. And won.

He was strong and true.

And if I didn't have him very soon, I was going to scream

"Very nice," I said. "Now the trousers."

"You're taking charge again."

"Someone has to."

"You're the one who wanted to go slowly."

"I've changed my mind. I want fast. And hard. And really, right now would be just fine with me."

It was his turn to go still. He sucked in a breath. A breath that turned into a groan. "Don't joke about that."

I backed toward the bed. "Who said I was joking?"

His shoes practically vanished from his feet and his trousers fell to the ground. Apparently what Templars wore under their clothes was really not much at all. Thin linen drawers that looked as if they'd rip off quite nicely.

"Sweet lords of hell," I said softly.

His face turned serious. "I'd rather they didn't have anything to do with this," he said.

"I'd rather we stopped talking altogether."

"Fine with me." He moved fast when he wanted to, and before I knew quite what happened I was lying on the bed with him on top of me. His mouth came down on mine again and suddenly there was no more thinking. There was only sensation.

Heat streaked through me as I felt him hard between my legs, hot beneath that linen barrier. I arched against him, wanting more of the pleasure beating at me. We turned and twisted and my shift disappeared with a silken rip as we bit and kissed and tasted in a frenzy, rolling across the bed in an attempt to find the place where we were closest together.

"Holly," Guy groaned. "We should slow down."

"Guy DuCaine," I growled in response. "If you slow down now, I really will kill you."

That earned me another dose of that smile and a "if you say so, darlin'," in that velvet drawl that made me want him even more.

Then, to my consternation, he pulled himself away from me.

"Where are you going?" I demanded. "Don't make me hurt you."

He chuckled. "Just trying to take these off." He stuck his thumbs in the waistband of his drawers and pushed them down slightly. Trouble was, with his erection standing proudly, they were never going to slide down willingly.

I rocked up to my knees and reached to help him. "Buttons," I said. "Buttons are important." And cooperative. They slipped free and so did he. Hard male flesh bared to my gaze and grasp.

"Sweet lords of—" I broke off, remembering his request. "All that's holy," I said in the end, and wrapped my fingers around him before he could remonstrate. "Come here." I slid my hand up, then down, then back up.

He sucked in a breath. "Holly, if you keep doing that, I won't be able to move at all."

I lifted my hands. "All right. I'll behave. Or misbehave rather. If you care to join me?"

"Don't mind if I do, at that." He reached out and pulled me

closer effortlessly. Strong, this man. I wasn't small, but he could lift me as if I were no more than a feather. It made me feel protected somehow. And powerful, knowing that right now all that strength and power were focused on me and that I could bring him to his knees with a touch if I chose.

Of course, he could pretty much bring me to mine the same way.

I wrapped myself around him and pulled his head down to mine, pressing my mouth to his to taste him again. It made my head spin and the room sway and I almost didn't notice that we were moving. By the time we broke for breath, I was lying on my back once more and Guy was above me with nothing between us this time. He liked being on top.

Fine with me for now, but later, I'd see how he liked the tables being turned. I had no illusions that having him once would be enough. It was going to be a long night if he lived up to my expectations. I smiled at the thought.

He looked half-dazed as our eyes met. As if he weren't quite sure what he was doing there. I decided to remind him and hooked a leg around his thigh, pulling him closer still. I ached for him. I'd had enough of kisses and caresses. Crazy, given we'd barely started. Usually I'd want to take my time, but right now all I knew was the fact that I wanted him inside. Wanted to know him in that primitive way. Wanted nothing between us at all.

"Veil's eyes, Guy," I said desperately, "I want you. *Now.*"

He laughed then, long and low, and slid himself against me. It wasn't enough. We could do slow and teasing later. Now I needed him, needed his weight against me, and his hands on me, and him inside me. I arched my hips, changing position. "I said now." And angled myself over him.

He slid home and I felt a satisfied wash of pleasure that went all the way down to my bones. Guy groaned.

"Don't be gentle on my account," I whispered in his ear before biting it none too softly.

"Whatever my lady commands," he said, and then he moved. Fast. Strong. And oh so right. Heat flared and bloomed between us until the lights behind my eyes turned red and I couldn't think anymore. Couldn't do anything but move with him as he took me—as I took him. Fast and hot and hard, both of us gasping and struggling to get closer, nearer, deeper.

Pleasure built and washed and built, over and over, until suddenly, one of us—I couldn't tell anymore who—cried out and one last wave took me and broke over us so I came screaming his name.

When I woke, the room was mostly dark, only the faintest light coming through the window. The other side of the bed was empty, no warm male body filling it. I struggled up, trying to work out what time it might be. I didn't feel as though I'd slept very long. We'd been busy, my Templar and I. My body stilled hummed pleasantly from the aftermath. "Guy?" I said softly into the darkness.

There was a rustle from the direction of the window. "Did I wake you?"

My vision adjusted to the darkness as I turned toward the sound of his voice. He stood near the window, the faint outline of a man, head bowed. "What are you doing over there?"

"Sorry, old habits die hard."

"Old habits?"

"We have dawn services every day. I'm pretty much programmed to wake up at this hour."

Damn. He hadn't been just standing there; he'd been praying. He'd climbed from my bed after we'd spent hours doing things I didn't think his God approved of and he was standing in the dark, praying. Offering up whatever it was he offered.

"Do you want some light?"

His head turned to me, his face a pale blur. "No. Go back to sleep. I don't need the light to do this."

That seemed wrong somehow. I'd dragged him into my world, into the darkness—and likely would drag him deeper before we were done—but that didn't mean he had to be cloaked in it. I fumbled toward the small table at the side of my bed, found matches, and lit a candle.

The bright flame made my vision blur all over again. I squinted until it cleared. Guy wore just his shirt and gray Templar trousers. His feet were bare. I swung mine down out of bed and carried the candle over to him, wrapping the sheet around me as I walked. "Here."

He took it and nodded. "Thank you. But I'm nearly finished."

"But it's not dawn yet."

"I don't think God minds if I'm a bit early." His mouth quirked. "And what the brothers don't know can't hurt them. It's the same as being on a campaign. Pray where you can and let God worry about the rest."

I cocked my head at him, not believing him. He'd given me peace last night. Peace and pleasure in the darkness of the bed we'd shared. But now, with the light, reality came creeping. Along with guilt and worry. "I disturbed you. I'll go back to bed."

His hand snaked out, caught my wrist. "You could join me."

"I don't think we pray to the same God." Religion wasn't something that occupied much of my time. As far as I could tell, the gods weren't that interested in me either.

"Praying is praying. Father Cho would say all gods are the same."

"A lot of people would disagree with him. The entire Fae race, for instance."

"Well, the Fae are peculiar, we all know that."

I didn't point out that I was half Fae. "So are you." It didn't matter if he thought I was odd. He was never going to be a permanent fixture in my life. This could only be a temporary interlude. Some snatched moments of pleasure. Before the darkness caught up with us both. I shivered, knowing the cool dawn air wasn't entirely to blame.

His hand loosened. "You're cold. Get back into bed."

"You must be cold too." But I'd yet to see him show any sign of noticing the weather. In bed, he'd radiated heat—almost as much as a Beast.

"Are you trying to distract me?"

"Would it work?"

"Perhaps. There aren't usually any mostly naked women around at our dawn services." He was smiling properly now.

"I'm sure there's a good reason for that."

"Yes. It seems they're distracting."

First I'd made him pray in the dark and now I was distracting him from praying at all. If his view of the world and what came after was the correct one, then I was probably in for some trouble. I climbed into bed and pulled the counterpane up around me. "Sorry."

"Don't apologize. Distraction is a choice."

"That sounds like Templar talk again."

"Don't tell me you don't have to focus when you're doing what you do."

He had me there. I was good at ignoring whatever wasn't important to accomplish the job at hand. But right now what *was* important if I was going to accomplish anything was the man standing by my window. I needed to understand him better. I knew him physically but he was still a mystery.

The Fae say that you can't use a tool properly until you understand it. I didn't want to think I was using Guy, but I couldn't claim to be completely innocent in that regard. Then again, neither could he.

So, understand the man. Come to grips with what he was. A Knight Templar. A holy warrior. Someone who believed in God and redemption and all the things I had no time for.

"You've gone quiet," he said, not moving from the window. "Did I say something I shouldn't?"

"No." I pulled the counterpane closer, letting my chin rest on the soft velvet. "Just thinking."

"That's rarely a good sign."

"What, women thinking?"

He laughed. "I have no problem with women thinking. My mother and sisters are cleverer than I am."

"Then what did you mean?"

"I meant that a lover sitting in bed telling you she's thinking is not usually good news."

I wasn't sure how I felt about the fact he'd had enough lovers to have learned that particular lesson. And that was very much the pot calling the kettle black. It wasn't much of a reach to think that I had probably had more bed partners than a man who'd become a Templar at seventeen.

"You think I'm going to throw you out of bed after only one night?"

"Wouldn't be the first time." In the candlelight his eyes seemed very blue as they watched me. Waiting for my verdict perhaps?

"Well, those particular females must've been crazy." Or possessed of a better sense of self-preservation than I. "Anyway, I wasn't thinking about that."

"What were you thinking about?"

I glanced at the candle, watched the flame dance for a few seconds. "Why did you become a Templar?"

"Why did I become a Templar or why do I believe what I believe?"

"Are those two different questions?"

"Maybe. Sometimes. But the latter is often what people want to know when they ask me about being a knight."

I cocked my head. "Both. Either. You decide."

His brows lifted. "You want to talk theology?"

"It seems appropriate. If you're usually in church at this time of the morning, then anything else would be vaguely . . ."

"Sacrilegious? As I said, I don't think my God cares when I pray."

"Are you avoiding my question?"

"No. Do you really want to know?"

"Yes."

"Why?"

"Because I'm curious. You didn't have to do this. Your family is wealthy. You could have been anything. Or done nothing. Yet you chose to do something dangerous because of your belief in one God. I don't understand it."

"God? Or choosing to believe." He set the candle in its holder on the windowsill and settled himself onto a nearby chair.

"Both. But the first seems to be a subject we're unlikely to agree on. Tell me why you dedicated your life to danger when you didn't have to."

"Is that the only reason for doing something? Because you have to?"

I pulled the covers tighter. Different worlds, this man and I. "For doing something dangerous, it's the most compelling reason."

"You're a spy. That's dangerous."

"Do you think I'd be a spy if I had had a choice?" Would anybody? I risked my life doing what I did. Traded terror and danger for cold, hard cash. Guy did it for devotion. How could he understand?

"I don't know. Would you?"

"No."

"Yet you chose to become one."

"I had to."

"There are other ways to earn money."

"That's easy for someone with your background to say. Try being poor in the border boroughs. See how far that gets you.

My mother was a whore. Not many people tend to give you a chance when your mother sells her body for money. Of course, Madame Figg would have given me a chance to follow in Mama's footsteps."

"So you made a choice because you didn't like the other options?"

"Yes."

He shrugged. "So did I."

"I don't understand."

"I don't know how to explain it. But I looked around me and I saw things in the world that weren't fair. Or good. Or just. People getting hurt."

"You could've been a doctor or an advocate."

"Did I mention the thought of being locked up in school for years made me want to punch somebody?"

"Yet you chose to be locked up in the Brother House."

"Not exactly. It's not being locked up if you want to do it. I wanted it."

"Why?"

"Because it felt right. I knew this was how I could make the world a better place. Save it."

"Save it for humans, you mean."

"We're the most vulnerable. But no. I don't wish the Fae or the Beasts ill. I can't say I'm crazy about the Blood, but if they obey the rules, then I'll leave them alone too. But if they hurt those I want to protect, then they're fair game. As other humans would be too."

"God wants you to protect people?"

"That's what I believe, yes."

"By killing others?"

"By keeping the peace. And yes, sometimes by bringing others to justice."

Or delivering that justice, as far as I could tell. A Templar's sword was an executioner's sword. If he killed, it was in the name of his God and no one would gainsay it. No one human, at least. "By giving your life?"

"If that happens, then yes. But believe me, it's not something I want to happen. In fact, I've spent a good deal of time learning how to make sure it doesn't."

"No one can make sure of that."

"You can be the best you can be. Minimize the risk. Surely

you understand that. After all, you climb about on rooftops and consort with the Night World. That's not exactly taking the safe route."

"I don't plan on doing what I do forever."

His eyes sharpened, he leaned forward. "Neither do I."

"Templars don't retire."

"No, but neither do they actively fight all their lives. Eventually I guess I'll be a commander."

"Or the Abbott General"

"Bloody hell. I hope not."

"What would be wrong with that?"

"Too much politics."

Templar was an interesting choice of occupation for a man who didn't like politics. After all, part of the reason for their existence was to enforce the treaties the politicians negotiated. But best to leave well enough alone for now. I turned the conversation to a slightly different path.

"And what about life outside the order?" This was skating perilously close to things that it was dumb to ask a man who'd spent a total of one night in your bed. Most men would construe it as a question about families. Or marriage. I had to admit to a reasonable amount of curiosity as to what Guy's views were, but it was a dead-end discussion. He and I were strictly temporary.

"Outside the order? Are you asking about my hobbies again?" His eyes glittered in the candlelight; he knew very well what I meant.

"Other than chopping off people's heads, you mean?"

He smiled suddenly. "I don't believe I've ever actually decapitated someone. Usually sticking your sword in them does the trick. Or shooting them."

I didn't want to think about shooting people. "I'll keep that in mind. But no, I wasn't asking about your hobbies. I was asking whether you ever wanted something more. Templars do marry, don't they?"

"Some do. It's allowed," he admitted.

"You sound as though you'd rather be decapitated."

"It's not something I think about terribly often." He grinned. "Anyway, now that Simon has Lily, Mother will be able to fixate on them producing offspring rather than me."

"But you're the eldest."

"Legally, if the courts had to rule, that's not true. To join the Templars you forfeit your worldly possessions."

"To the Church?"

"Sometimes. But I was seventeen, not of age. My worldly possessions amounted to clothes, a horse, and some armor. Plus my sword. Come to think of it, that hasn't changed much. I'm not sure I'm a terribly marriageable prospect."

He obviously didn't look in the mirror very often. I stayed silent. "You don't want a family?"

"I have a family. I have two, in fact. My blood family and the order."

I tried not to be jealous. Two families. I had perhaps, if one thought about it in generous terms, bits of one. Mother, Fen, Reggie. Cormen wasn't family despite our shared blood. He was almost the opposite of family, in fact.

But I wasn't completely envious. Families were risky. They exposed you to the possibility of hurt and betrayal. Plus a family implied tying yourself to a man for life. I didn't want to do that. Didn't want to give my happiness to someone who might treat me as cruelly as Cormen had treated my mother. So perhaps Guy and I weren't so different after all.

But I did want a life. I wanted freedom and to not have to keep living the life I did. One day I would have enough money. One day.

Thinking about one day didn't help much. I shivered again. "Tell me about your family." Maybe a tale of normality would take my mind off everything that worried me. Give me hope that some people did live happy lives.

Guy straightened in his chair, cocked his head at me. "What do you want to know?"

"Tell me about your sisters. And your parents." Over the years I'd heard a lot about Simon—a sunmage as powerful as him was inevitably the focus of Night World speculation—but I didn't know a lot about the rest of the DuCaines.

"There's not much to tell." He looked down for a moment. "Saskia's the oldest. She's a 'prentice metalmage. And Hannah— she's the youngest—she's still in school. Edwina. She died."

His face was suddenly stony, his voice bleak. Somehow I knew that whatever had caused his sister's death, it hadn't been anything simple like an illness or an accident. "Oh." I hugged my arms tighter around my knees.

"You're cold."

"You could come and warm me up." I no longer wanted to talk. Our conversation had made me melancholy. I wasn't sure I understood him any better, but I couldn't deny that I wanted him. Right now he seemed the perfect way to chase away the chill of the morning. "If you're done," I added.

"Perhaps I am, at that," he said with a nod. He pulled his shirt over his head and sat still for a moment studying me.

In the candlelight, he was curved muscle and hard planes that flickered smooth gold and shadow as the flame shifted. It made his hair a brighter shade and his eyes deep and unfathomable. I was suddenly very glad that he didn't want to get married. That meant that some girl couldn't win his heart and take him away before I was done with him.

I let the counterpane fall away from my shoulders, baring myself to his gaze.

He didn't need a second invitation.

Chapter Fifteen

HOLLY

AS I'd feared, with daylight came reality. When I woke a second time, my mind was churning. My mother. Cormen. The Beasts. Ignatius. A visit to Halcyon.

Henri and Antoine. The more I thought about it, the more it puzzled me. We hadn't done anything confrontational at the Gilt, yet there had been a confrontation. Why? Who had they been trying to warn off? Guy? Or me?

One of us, that much was clear, which made me nervous. And I didn't like it any more when I turned to thinking about Cormen and why he'd been at the Gilt. He too had tried to intimidate me, but why was he there in the first place? In his position, I'd be safely in Summerdale, pulling strings via my lackeys. He didn't need to threaten me. The geas should control me well enough for his purposes.

And how had he even known I'd be at the Gilt?

He couldn't have . . . which meant he was there for some other reason.

Why?

Was it just a coincidence that Henri and Antoine were there too?

That they had tried to attack us after my encounter with Cormen?

Was there a connection?

Or was I just building stories out of shadows?

I felt tired contemplating it all. Tired and lacking in ideas about how to proceed. I flopped down on my pillow with a sigh.

"What's wrong?" Guy asked.

I rolled to face him. "Just thinking."

"I thought we discussed that earlier," he said with a smile. "No thinking allowed."

"I'm serious. There's a lot we need to do."

He hoisted himself up on one elbow. "Does your list include eating breakfast?"

Men. I was wondering how we were going to survive the next few days and he was wondering where his next meal was coming from. "You're going to be expensive to keep, aren't you?" I said, matching his pose. "Eating me out of house and home."

"I think I earned breakfast, at least."

I didn't want to think about that. I willed myself not to blush. I didn't blush.

Particularly not over this man.

Not when I was starting to think letting him into my bed had been a mistake. Not because I hadn't enjoyed it. No, I enjoyed it too much. Now, lying next to him, when I should be thinking about tonight and what I needed to achieve, I was thinking about how good he smelled and the way his face looked in the morning shaded with pale stubble and his hair spiky from sleep.

Thinking that way could only lead to disaster.

I sat up. "We should eat. We have work to do."

"Halcyon won't even open its door until the sun sets," Guy objected, yawning. "We have plenty of time."

That was the tone of a man hopeful of coaxing his woman back into bed.

No. I didn't want that to happen. I threw back the counterpane and reached for my robe as I stood. "Not that much time. We need weapons and clothes and charms and—" I stopped, frustrated when I couldn't find my slippers.

"Charms?"

"Yes, charms," I said. "I'm half Fae, remember?"

Guy sat up, leaning forward, arms draped around his knees. "I hadn't forgotten." He sounded slightly puzzled. Probably because I was behaving like a shrew.

I didn't know why I was so flustered, but the last of the languor of the previous night left my body in a rush, forced out by a rising tide of fear and worry. I needed some time to regain my composure or I would be picking a fight with Guy for no reason. Which would only risk letting him see how off balance I felt.

"And most of all," I said, not looking at him, "I need a bath." With that brilliant statement, I left the room before he could say anything else.

GUY
✠

I put down the book I hadn't been reading when Holly returned. She closed the door, the long wet ringlets of her hair dripping onto her silk robe.

She'd fled the room in such a rush, I still wasn't sure what had happened. Did she regret what had happened? Did I? I didn't know the answer to either. But I did regret the empty space in the bed beside me.

So while she'd taken an inordinately long time to take a bath, I'd prowled around the room. I was tempted to snoop, but Holly was a spy. I was fairly sure she'd have ways of telling if her things had been disturbed. So I picked a book from her shelves and tried to read.

In the clear morning light, her face free of paint or glamour, Holly looked young. Young and beautiful, her Fae blood sculpting the curves and arches of her face into something far from ordinary. Something arresting.

Guilt twisted in my stomach.

Foolish.

Foolish to give in last night, to take her to bed. Foolish to think we could both walk away from this unscathed when I'd spent half my time alone trying not to think about having her again.

Foolish was something neither of us could afford.

But I couldn't quite bring myself to raise the subject, to chase the happy look from her eyes, to bring back the shuttered expression she'd worn last night in the cab back from the Gilt. Twenty-five was too young to be so grim. How long had she been spying and thieving and fighting to make a life for herself?

Walking a tightrope above the razor edges of the Night World. Too long.

The City shouldn't be that way. People should be safe to live their lives.

And if they were, I'd spend my days with nothing to do but pray and teach young men how to use weapons they wouldn't need.

"Penny for your thoughts?" Holly asked as she wrapped a linen towel around her head.

"I was thinking about Halcyon," I said.

"Serious thoughts." She crossed the room, unlatched the window. The sun was indeed bright in the sky. The day promised to grow warm, if not hot. Perhaps we'd seen the last of the unseasonable cold weather that had grayed the days so far this season. Or maybe we were all moving closer to hell.

"Blood Assemblies are serious places."

"We'll be all right. We just need a plan. We can talk after breakfast." She came back to the wardrobe, peered in as though considering her choices. "I've been to Halcyon before and I've survived."

"The last time I was there," I said, "there was a riot and I killed a couple of people."

Her mouth fell open. "When were you ever in—oh. Of course, the night Lily disappeared. I heard about that. You were the Templar with Simon that night." She looked vaguely disapproving rather than concerned. Maybe she was critiquing our lack of stealth. Well, let her try kidnapping Lucius' pet assassin out from under his nose and see how well she did.

"I was."

"You're not planning on starting another riot tonight, are you?"

"Not unless I have to." I didn't think it would be wise to mention any of the other times I'd had to cross the threshold of an Assembly. Most of those had involved violence as well. Of course, each of those had been sanctioned searches for somebody who'd broken the law.

She started to smile, then paused and frowned instead. "You're serious, aren't you?"

"Of course. I'm here to protect you."

"By starting a riot?"

"If that's what it takes."

She shook her head. "I really don't recommend it."

"Then don't do anything that would make it necessary."

"I can't think of much I would do that would make it necessary for you to start a fight in a Blood Assembly."

I could. Starting with what she was likely to wear. The thought of her parading through an Assembly wearing a dress like the one she'd worn to the Gilt, half her body on display, made my fingers itch for a sword. And the fact that that was my first thought was an indication of just how foolish I'd been last night. "Good. Let's keep it that way."

HOLLY

A CLOSED FOR FAMILY EMERGENCY sign hung on the door of my salon when we arrived in Gillygate. Fen's elegant black handwriting turned my stomach to acid. Reggie should be here, safe, working at making the dresses she loved. Instead, because of me, she was gods knew where. Captive. Possibly hurt.

I set my teeth. No. I wasn't going to think about that. I couldn't think about that. I needed my head clear. No time for emotions. I couldn't think about Mama and Reggie and I couldn't think about Guy and what had passed between us in bed last night.

The door opened easily to my key. The place smelled vaguely dusty and the air was warm and stale. It needed airing out. I would have to check the fabrics too. Reggie was very particular about how they were stored, babying the fine silks and satins and velvets. At least it wasn't winter when, in such an old building, a few days of cold without anyone here to light the stoves to warm the air could set damp and mold to growing in the rolls of material before you could blink.

Guy followed me into the room, shutting and locking the door behind us. When I asked, he opened the small window above the door slightly to let in some air.

"So you were telling the truth, about working for a modiste?" he said as I led the way toward the back rooms.

When had I said that? I had to stop and think, and then it came to me. Our conversation in St. Giles. When he'd first tried to hire me. Not so long ago really, but it felt like forever. "Well, Reggie's really the modiste. And I don't work for her. She works for me."

"You own this place?" He sounded startled and I turned around. He looked startled too.

"I get paid well for what I do," I said, not willing to apologize for that. "I needed an explanation for where that money comes from. And Reggie needed somewhere to work. She's very talented. I didn't want her slaving away for someone who would pay her nothing and steal her designs."

"I see." He looked around the room. It was his habit in any new place, I'd come to realize. He studied the layout, the exits. Probably could already tell me a plan for getting out of here in a hurry if he had to. A soldier's view of the world.

My view was somewhat different. My view was slightly inclined to giggle at the sight of him, so big and solid in the midst of all the female trappings of Reggie's workroom. The dressmaker's forms, draped with half-finished dresses or toiles, the piles of lace and feathers, the neat rows of ribbons in all shades of the rainbow hanging on a tier of racks in one corner. Plus the pretty feminine furnishings Reggie had chosen.

Guy looked both out of place and strangely at ease. "I gather Reggie made that dress you wore last night?"

"Yes, she makes all my gowns."

He raised an eyebrow. "Then you're right, she is talented. How did you two meet?"

"Her mother worked with mine," I said, and waited to see how he reacted. So far he had seemed fine with the fact that my mother had been a whore, but I wasn't entirely convinced he wasn't just too polite to let his disapproval show. He came from money. From the upper reaches of human society. The women he knew didn't have to scrape for survival. And the Church he served didn't exactly approve of selling sex for money.

"You grew up together?"

"Yes. She's two years younger than me." There weren't many children in the brothel. Most of the girls and women took care not to catch. Those who did had ways of taking care of the results. But Annie, Reggie's mother, had refused to take that path. My mother, of course, had me in the rosy period of her relationship with Cormen. When he'd been too taken with her beauty to object to anything she wanted.

I was an only child, though. Mama was smart enough to realize that Cormen wouldn't take kindly to too many other demands on her time once I'd arrived. So I'd lived a solitary life, a
petted child among adults. Until Cormen left and Mama, after
the money started to run out, took up work at the Swallow. Until
Reggie and Fen.

My family.

"My workroom is through here." I waved at the door at the
far end of room. "You can wait here or out front. Reggie has
books. And tea."

"Can't I watch?"

That stopped me. I hadn't performed magic with an audience
in years. Building charms took focus and concentration. The
thought of Guy watching me didn't seem all that conducive to
either of those things. But perhaps it wouldn't matter. After all,
even if he were sitting outside, I would still know he was there.
"I usually work alone," I said slowly.

"You won't even know I'm there."

Doubtful. "It's not all that interesting," I said. After all, he
couldn't actually see the magic. The rest was more like making
jewelry.

"Even so, I'd like to see." His expression was hard to read,
his pale eyes intent on mine.

Did he really want to see me work? Or was he just being
protective? Or was he going to try and talk to me about tonight
again? I had fobbed him off after breakfast, insisting we come
here first. I knew that discussing plans for Halcyon would only
make me nervous and I needed my concentration for the charms.
Regardless of his motives, I found it hard to resist him. "All
right." I nodded. "But if it turns out you interfere with what I'm
doing, I'm tossing you out."

He smiled then. "Fair enough."

He was as good as his word. He followed me silently into my
little workroom, took a seat on the chair I pointed out, and sat
quietly as I poked around the baskets and shelves of materials,
letting my instincts guide my hands.

The basic materials for each of my charms are similar but
never exactly the same. Different oils, different colors, even different ways of joining each element together. The magic told me
what it wanted on any given day.

Today its mood seemed somber. I kept reaching for black and

silver. Dark blues and purples. Lavender oil, sage, and rosemary. Dull chips of night-dark agate. The colors reminded me of Cormen's Family ring, making my stomach curl uneasily.

"Can I ask a question?"

I started, having half forgotten Guy was there. He knew how to be silent. How to fade into the background—not a bad trick for a man of his size and coloring. He'd make a good spy. Maybe he had been one. "Of course."

"How does it work?"

"Making a charm?"

He nodded.

"It's hard to explain to someone without magic. Does Simon use charms?"

Guy frowned. "He does wards. He's always been hopeless at glamours."

"Sunmages are best at healing, from what I understand. Or fire." Human magic was a different beast. Fed by whatever element they had affinity with. Fae magic simply was. Part of us, part of the earth, fed by the life force of everything around us. Or so I'd been told.

The Fae believed that was why they were so long-lived, that the connection with everything sustained them. And their connection to life was why they had a historical distaste for the Blood. Who should be dead.

"What are you good at?"

I gestured at the tabletop, littered with everything I'd gathered. "This. To a degree. My charms work well for me." I wasn't going to tell him everything. "Otherwise, my powers are fairly basic. Wards. Glamours."

Full Fae could do much, much more than I. The Veiled Queen could shape Summerdale itself—or at least the Veiled Court, which lay below its hills—to her will. Other Fae could use their powers to hide or disguise or change their own territories in the Veiled World, but the queen could dissolve those magics if she chose. Her power held the court for her. To claim the crown, someone would have to be strong enough to defeat her. Or convince enough of the court to band together to remove her. That hadn't happened for a very long time. Over a thousand years.

Hopefully it wouldn't happen any time soon.

Guy shifted on his chair. "You still haven't answered my

question. About how the charms work." He gestured at the table. "What are you making?"

"Tools of the trade," I said lightly. "A few invisibility charms—"

"You can turn invisible?" Guy looked startled. "Like Lily?"

"Lily's a wraith. Wraiths aren't invisible, they're incorporeal. I can't walk through walls. More's the pity." I shot him a quick smile, to let him see I was joking. I had no desire to be a wraith. It was bad enough being a normal half-breed without being something that the Fae actively abhorred.

"Walking through walls would be useful for someone in your line of work."

"Yes," I admitted. "But I'm pretty good with locks and wards anyway."

"What else?" Guy asked.

"Look-aways—those distract people so they won't notice something. Or someone. Hear-mes. Those are the basics I use the most." I stirred the small pile of crystals I'd gathered together.

There was something else that would be useful tonight, I realized. Something to connect Guy and Fen and me and let us know if one of us needed help. I didn't make alert charms very often. I didn't need them, working alone. Fen had one he shared with Reggie, given he was usually in a better position to stop what he was doing and come to her aid than I was. She didn't always remember to wear it, despite our warnings. She mustn't have been wearing it when she was taken or Fen would have had a warning of Cormen's ploy, at least.

I'd only ever made alerts to connect two people. Three would be a different thing again.

Well, I would try, and if it didn't work, Fen would be able to come up with something. I would breathe easier in Halcyon with some way to call for help. Ignatius Grey was no one to be trifled with. Even more so now, if he was climbing the ranks fast enough to make Adeline nervous.

He was obviously confident enough to throw a soiree tonight.

The only part I hadn't figured out was why my father would be attending the party. I couldn't see what he would gain from it, and Cormen rarely did anything not to his own advantage.

There were always some Fae who traded and dealt with the Blood Court, but my father's Family—the sa'Inviels—and his particular branch of it were, from what I understood, amongst the more conservative Fae. They kept to themselves, mainly staying in Summerdale. Some of the younger members, Cormen included, had started to spend more time in the human world and the social whirl of the border boroughs, but I didn't think any of them were moving toward the Night World.

I paid attention to their movements, when I could, mostly to keep track of where Cormen might be so I could avoid him.

"Holly?" Guy's voice interrupted me.

I blinked. "Sorry, I was thinking. About the charms. I told you it takes concentration." A lie. But there was no point in sharing my uneasiness with Guy. He would try and find a way for us not to go to Halcyon. "Was there—"

Guy
✠

Holly broke off, jumping as the jangle of a bell interrupted her. She frowned. "The sign says we're closed. Why would someone ring?"

I stood. "I'll go see. You stay here." She was right. Who knew we were here? Reason enough to be cautious.

I didn't recognize the man and woman—dark-haired and dark-eyed, dressed in sober clothing of gray and brown for the man and a dull blue dress for the woman—standing outside the door, but when he saw me, the man smiled.

I didn't open the door. "Can I help you?" I asked, knowing my voice would carry through the open window.

"Guy, it's us. Let us in." Simon's voice. But a voice could be faked.

"Us?" I queried.

The woman rolled her eyes and pulled a chain out from under her dress. A finely wrought thing of iron and silver and gold. I knew that chain. "You're getting paranoid in your old age, Guy. Let us in."

That voice I knew too. Saskia. Eldest of my sisters. Metal-mage in training. Not known for her patience or her respect for her elders. I unlocked the door. "What are you doing here?"

They walked past me, Saskia winking at me. I pulled the

blind down to cover the glass of the door and locked it. "Hell's balls, Simon, don't you have any sense?"

"We—" He stopped, staring down at my hands.

Beside, him, Saskia gasped. "Gods, Guy. Your *hands*."

She sounded horrified. The glamours that disguised their appearances shimmered and vanished, leaving me facing two pairs of accusing eyes. Saskia's green-gray gaze even angrier than Simon's blue.

"What did you do?" Simon demanded. "Lily told me your plan, but I didn't think you'd go this far." He came forward, reaching for my arm.

I stepped away. "I'm more interested in what the two of you are doing here," I said. "I told you to stay away."

"I'd like to know that too." Holly appeared behind Simon and Saskia, who both spun around as she spoke. Simon's hand dropped to his hip while Saskia's lifted, palm out.

"Calm down," I snapped. "It's Holly."

Simon had the grace to look slightly sheepish. Saskia's narrowed gaze stayed on Holly as Holly moved to my side.

"What were you thinking, Simon?" I continued. "And why on earth would you drag Saskia into this?"

"Because with Lily stuck in St. Giles, thanks to you, she was the quickest way to find you," Simon said.

Fuck. I'd forgotten about that. Saskia could find any of the family. Had been able to since her powers rose. No games of hide-and-seek at DuCaine family gatherings anymore. Simon said it was something to do with her affinity for iron and us being related and there being iron in our blood. I didn't understand it, but it was damned annoying.

"You could have asked her and then left her at the Guild," I pointed out.

"I thought you'd prefer I was incognito," Simon said.

"I'd prefer you'd stayed away altogether," I retorted. "You're supposed to be staying out of trouble."

"So Saskia offered to glamour us," Simon continued as though I hadn't spoken.

"You're the metalmage," Holly said from beside me.

Saskia nodded. "And you're a spy, or so Simon tells me."

I glared at Simon. Holly just said, "Yes, I am," very coolly.

"Can you teach me how to pick a lock?" Saskia said with a grin.

"No, she can't," I said firmly. I gave Simon a "now look what you've done" look over Saskia's head.

"I wouldn't think locks would be a difficulty for a metal-mage," Holly said, with an answering smile.

"That depends on whether or not they were built by another metalmage," Saskia said.

"No one is teaching anyone to pick locks," I said again. "I asked you why you were here."

"I wanted to make sure you were all right," Simon said steadily.

"We agreed that I'd contact you, if I needed to," I said. "It's only been two days." I stopped, studied Simon for a moment. "What happened?"

"Someone set a fire at St. Giles last night," Simon said. He held up a hand to stop me before I could speak. "No one was hurt. The wards took care of things."

That didn't exactly comfort me. Wards will fail if enough power is thrown at them. "Any idea who was behind it?"

"Lily thought she smelled Beasts, but with the smoke and water, she couldn't be sure."

Beasts again. I didn't like it at all. First they'd tried for Holly and me. Now they were targeting St. Giles. Which boiled down to targeting Simon and Lily.

"The wards held, Guy," Saskia said. "The Masters of the Guilds are there now, reinforcing them. It's still safe for Lily and Simon."

I let out a breath. I hadn't noticed I was holding it. "All right. Then that's where you should be. Back there. It's safest." I wished I could send them to the Brother House, but it would risk revealing that my expulsion was a ploy.

"What about you?" Simon asked.

"We're fine," I said. Holly was silent beside me. I hoped she would stay that way. I didn't want Simon knowing what had happened at the Gilt or that we were going to Halcyon tonight. If he did, he'd never leave. Even now his blue eyes were skeptical.

"Truly," I said.

He moved fast, catching my wrist and twisting my hand so he could see the tattoo more clearly. "You certain about that?"

"They're only tattoos," I said, pulling my hand free. "I have a job to do. This is what it takes."

"Lily would have helped you. *We* would have helped you," Simon said.

"Which is exactly what I didn't want. Our family has been through enough."

"Since when do you get to decide what's right for us?" Saskia said.

"I'm the eldest."

She made a dismissive noise. "Simon and I are mages."

"You're a 'prentice, not a mage. And Holly and I don't need any help. I'd tell you if I did. If you want to make this easier for me, then you'll stay away. Stay safe."

Simon looked torn. I knew that the last thing he wanted was to put Lily or anyone else at risk. But the list of people he wanted to protect included me. "Are your hands all right?" he asked finally, and I knew I'd won the argument for now.

I held out my hands, knowing he'd want to check them no matter what I said. "Yes. I had a healer." As expected, Simon took my hands in his anyway and his eyes took on that peculiar look of focus he wore when he healed.

Saskia stood to one side, one hand twirling a piece of her hair—a sure sign she hadn't yet made up her mind whether she was going to do as I asked.

"I swear, Sass," I said to her. "On my oaths. I'll ask for help, if I need it." I intended that to be never.

"The order banished you," she said, eyes unhappy. "You don't have any oaths."

Ah. So Simon hadn't told Saskia the whole truth. Wise man. Saskia was more stubborn than a mule with its feet glued to the ground.

"They might have released me, but I didn't," I said gently. Saskia hated feeling helpless. She'd only grown more fierce since Edwina had died, determined to do her part to protect our family. "I'll ask. When it's time. If you go back with Simon now and don't make this harder on everybody."

She nodded slowly. "All right, but if you don't, you know I can melt your sword and your mail and all your other precious bits of Templar metal into slag, don't you?"

Holly laughed, then turned it into a more diplomatic cough. Simon released my hands with a satisfied nod. His eyes were amused. He knew Saskia was perfectly capable of making good on her threats.

"I know," I said diplomatically. "And I will, I promise. But you two have to go now. Holly and I have work to do."

HOLLY

Guy was silent as he closed the door behind Simon and his sister, his movements very deliberate as he locked the door behind them. He stayed for a minute, looking through the glass, no doubt following their progress down the street. Back to St. Giles.

I stayed where I was, trying to think. The sight of Simon had made my stomach burn, the geas waking with a greasy swirl. I didn't think it could force me to actually walk out of the building and follow him, but seeing Simon had been a harsh reminder of Cormen.

Of the fact that I was running out of time.

And the stark truth that this situation was getting more dangerous by the minute. Veil's eyes. Someone had set a fire in a Haven.

A *human* Haven located right next door to the Templar Brother House. A bold move indeed.

It couldn't be a coincidence that it happened while Simon and Lily were there. So, was someone else also curious as to what Simon's secret might be or was Cormen—and whoever else might be involved with him—making some sort of double play?

My stomach swam again at the thought. If Cormen managed to find out what he wanted from somebody else, then he didn't need me. And he didn't need my mother or Reggie to control me.

I had to get it first.

Which meant working out how to get myself back to St. Giles. After tonight, of course. If I could find out what Cormen was doing attending a party at Halcyon, it might just let me foil his plans.

"Let's get back to work," I said to Guy.

He turned from the door. "Yes. We need to talk about tonight."

I nodded and led the way back to my workroom. When we were both safely inside, I triggered the ward, wanting the added safety of knowing nobody could be listening in on us.

Guy took a seat near my workbench. I stirred the pile of crystals nervously. "Do you think the attack on St. Giles is connected to what happened at the Gilt?" I asked.

"It would be stupid not to at this point," Guy said.

"Revenge for what we did to Henri and Antoine?"

"Or just a continuation of the campaign against the Templars. After all, St. Giles is next door to the Brother House. The order will always defend it."

He was more optimistic than me. This was starting to feel far too orchestrated. Too personal.

It had started with attacks on the Templars, yes, but Guy was a Templar. And a DuCaine. What better way to distract him from protecting Simon than to keep the Templars occupied?

But I couldn't ask him about Simon, or if he thought that might be the reason. Just the thought of raising the subject made my throat tighten. The geas wouldn't let me speak of it. I was sure of that much.

So time to focus on what I could talk about. Starting with what had happened at the Gilt. "I still don't understand why Henri and Antoine came after us last night," I said. "We hadn't done anything to provoke them. It seems like a big risk for them to start something in so public a place."

"Unless somebody is making it worth their while to do so," Guy said. "Someone with cash."

"Ignatius." Or whoever was funding him. "But why would Ignatius be attacking the Templars? If we could prove it, the Veiled Queen would end him."

"Maybe he does share Lucius' politics after all. Anyway, we have no proof."

"Someone is behind the attacks on your squads," I said. "And it seems far more likely that it's a group of young Beasts like Henri and Antoine than one of the alphas. The younger ones have far less to lose."

"And far more to gain," Guy said. "If I was Ignatius—or whoever might be behind this—I'd use people like them as well. Young men can be easily led into stupidity." His words sounded bitter, as if they were cutting too close to something in his own past.

But he spoke the truth. And it wasn't just young men who could do stupid things. Women were just as susceptible. My mother had taught me that. Even Cormen . . . he was young by Fae standards. From a less prominent branch of the sa'Inviels. Arrogant. Another with much to gain perhaps.

"All right," I said. "So we need to find out more about Henri and Antoine. We have to go to Halcyon tonight. We can start there. If we don't find anything, then we'll look elsewhere. Fen will be able to find out more about their habits for us." Starting with whether they'd both survived last night. I'd ask him when we returned to the Swallow. He was probably itching to stick his nose into my business by now anyway.

"And speaking of Fen," I added, "I think we should bring him with us to Halcyon."

"Why?"

"Three is better than two," I said. "And he's not without his own talents."

Chapter Sixteen

HOLLY

The dress made only the faintest pretence of having sleeves. In reality, they were two wide straps with the tiniest of ruffles along the edges. My neck and shoulders and décolletage were on display for the world to see, though I did have the, for once, comforting weight of my father's chain obscuring a little of the view.

Not that the chain would be any protection against a vampire. But by proclaiming me a Fae by-blow who had at least some notice from her sire, it had always given any Blood tempted in my direction cause to stop and reconsider their choice.

I had enough to worry about tonight without having to fight off unwanted advances from vampires.

Now if only I could come up with something that would ward off Henri or Antoine or any of their friends.

To complete the requisite Blood Assembly "dinner is served" ensemble, I had pulled my hair up and glamoured it a brown near enough to black. Out of some small sense of rebellion, I'd left one bronze streak at the front.

Guy had donned evening clothes again, though this time his shirt—hastily procured by Fen—was black, not white. He looked ominous.

I liked the effect. Ominous would keep everyone at bay.

Fen was waiting for us as we came downstairs. Unusually there was no bottle of brandy within reach. Instead he was drumming his fingers against the mahogany surface of the long bar, earning himself a look of displeasure from Mr. Figg.

Like Guy, he wore all black, his hair tamed into some semblance of civility with a black satin ribbon that matched the trim of his velvet frock coat. The only color came from the deep green jewel winking from his cravat.

He gave me an assessing glance and a small nod. I lifted an eyebrow. I didn't need him to approve my dress. Reggie had a faultless eye. I looked like sin poured into black satin and jet. Just what the Blood liked best. The problem was going to be convincing them that I was for display only. No touching. That was where Guy and Fen came in.

I didn't like looking as though I were offering myself up on a platter, but anything more conservative would make me stand out at an Assembly. And the last thing I wanted was to draw attention to myself. A good spy knows how to blend in.

"Evening," Guy said to Fen. They nodded at each other but neither made any further attempt at conversation. We'd said everything that needed to be said earlier when Guy and I had returned from Gillygate. Each of us had one of the alert charms sewn into an accessible spot on our clothes—easier for Guy and Fen than for me—and my evening bag was loaded with several other charms just in case.

I had a cutthroat strapped to one thigh where I could get to it through Reggie's strategically placed pocket. It wasn't my usual silver—that wouldn't be allowed into the Assembly—but deadly honed steel would do the job as well. Guy and Fen, I assumed, had their own weapons.

In short, we were as ready as we would ever be.

Fen had secured a carriage, and the journey was completed in short order. Halcyon was in Lesangre, only two boroughs over from Brightown. A short distance, but now we were truly in Night World territory and all the rules changed.

Here we were fair game if we let a vampire play with us. We could be killed and no one would be able to do anything to the one who did so. Of course, that meant we could do our own killing if necessary as well. If anyone objected to a vampire trying to snack from them, then they were within their rights to defend themselves.

It didn't happen very often, though. Mostly because the sort of people who came to the Assemblies wanted to be snacked on, or wanted the exotic thrill of sex with a Beast or Blood, or, worst of all, wanted to drink vampire blood and know the ecstasy it could bring. They were unlikely to object to getting their heart's desire. But the other real reason was that vampires were pretty hard for humans to kill. Attack one and you were likely to end up dead if you weren't very, very good.

Even if you did manage to kill one of them, the Blood might try and avenge the death. So you had to be willing to stick to the human boroughs and avoid going out after dark if you succeeded.

The driver pulled the horses up with a jingle of harness and a stream of soothing words. They must have been fairly used to coming here, as they weren't going crazy the way horses often did around Beasts and vampires. Instead the pair merely stamped their hooves now and then, ears flicking nervously in the direction of the flaming torches burning outside the massive metal gates guarding the Assembly.

I pulled the invitation Adeline had sent from my evening bag. The elegant black card was enough to see us whisked ahead of the line and through the front doors with speed.

Once we were inside, I took a moment to rearrange my skirts, fussing with them while I focused on bringing my breathing under control as much as possible. The Blood and the Beasts would be able to hear my hastened heartbeat and I didn't want to seem too nervous.

That would only serve to draw attention.

I snapped my fan—one of Reggie's flamboyant creations of black-dyed ostrich feathers, carved ebony, and silver and black glass beads—open and turned to Guy and Fen.

"Remember the plan," I said. We were here to find out as much as we could. About Ignatius. About Henri and Antoine. And, particularly, from my point of view, about Cormen. Fen nodded and turned on his heel, pushing into the crowd. Guy held out his arm, making it clear we would be staying together.

I was perfectly happy to oblige him. I took another breath, as deep as I could in the cursed corset—even tighter than the one I'd worn under the bronze dress—and let him lead me into the main room.

It was less crowded than normal. Obviously Ignatius was

keeping his guest list select tonight. The smaller numbers made it easier to move through the room, scanning faces.

"You know the rules, yes?" I asked Guy in a low voice. "The alcoves"—I tilted my fan toward the rows of small rooms whose doors lined two walls of the main room, illuminated by the ornate red privacy lamps hanging above their lintels—"are for sex or feeding. So don't go into one unless you're ready for one or the other. Or both," I added. "We'll try to get upstairs later. Lucius had his office up there and many of the Blood have private rooms. If Ignatius is holding court, it will be upstairs. But it's too early for that. We want to stay here and mingle."

The main room was huge. On a normal night it held close to a thousand people, enjoying the spectacle, crowded around the small tables or pressed up against the many bars that plied them with liquor to lull inhibitions and dull nerves. The huge hexagonal dance floor was occupied tonight with rows of couples in all combinations of races working their way through the old-fashioned Blood Court dances.

Damn. I hadn't asked Guy if he knew how to dance. The dances were an excellent way to overhear useful information. And Cormen loved dancing. Most Fae did. Though in Cormen's case, it was more to do with him being a vain bastard who wanted to display himself than any true love of music and movement.

Beside me, Guy flexed his hands, then ran them down the front of his frock coat. "Define mingling."

"Talking. Dancing. No killing anyone," I said, not entirely joking. Guy's ability to keep his temper and not revert to warrior mode if something minor happened was going to be crucial.

"I can do that," he said dryly. Then his voice lowered. "As long as anyone doesn't do anything to deserve killing."

"Just remember that this is their territory, their rules," I said tightly. "Otherwise we'll be the ones getting killed. Now, how about we actually act as though we're here to enjoy ourselves?" I lifted a glass of champagne from the tray of a white-clad server and drank half of it in one gulp to calm my rising nerves.

"Certainly." Guy didn't take a drink but he did bow to me and offer his hand. "Would you care to dance?"

Apparently Templars could dance. Or at least, this one could. Perhaps he'd been taught before he'd become a knight, though his skills didn't seem rusty. The small orchestra played a series of waltzes after the last set of court dances, and Guy partnered me expertly.

Dancing with him was exhilarating, being whirled around in those strong arms, knowing that all I had to do was go where he led. Though I had a job to do, so I tried to keep my head and watched the other couples on the dance floor as we moved. I didn't see Cormen anywhere. Or Henri or Antoine. Nor any of the Beasts who'd been at the Gilt with them last night, even though there were a reasonable number of young Beasts moving through the throng.

Ignatius I didn't expect to see. He'd be holed up somewhere above us letting those who wanted his good favor or support come to him in supplication. Enjoying disappointing most of them or wringing more out of them than they were willing to give if the stories I'd heard about him were true.

After the third waltz, the orchestra took a break. Guy and I stepped off the dance floor.

"Now what?" he asked.

"More mingling," I said. "It's easy enough, you stand there looking big and gorgeous and that will distract people enough so they won't notice me."

His eyes swept over me. "Anyone who doesn't notice you in that dress is either blind or dead."

"Technically the Blood *are* dead." Or had died, I supposed. They rose again after the Turn.

"Yes, but they're not blind. No one could fail to notice you, dressed that way."

"What way?" I bristled at his censoring tone.

"Like a Nightseeker."

"That's the point," I said through a fake smile. "We're blending in. Stop acting like a jealous lover. Or rather, stop talking like a Templar and pretend to be my lover. My lover would like this dress."

His scarred brow lifted. "Who said I didn't like it? I just don't like everyone else seeing you in it."

Heat swept over me with a rush. I fanned cool air toward my face. It didn't help much. The whole room was too warm, heated by the hundreds of candles in lamps and chandeliers hung around the room and the crush of too many bodies.

I tried to recall what it had been like up on the roof in the freezing wind in Seven Harbors, but it didn't help. Not when

Guy's eyes were watching me, his expression dark and possessive.

Concentrate on business.

"That's better," I said, lowering the fan and summoning a smile. "Keep looking at me like that and no one will doubt we're sleeping together."

He didn't answer, simply held out his arm. We moved through the crowds, stopping to speak politely to those who greeted us.

There were only a few Fae amongst those gathered here and no one I recognized. I started to doubt that we would find my father here, despite what Adeline had told us.

If he was helping Ignatius in some way, surely he wouldn't flaunt the connection?

After half an hour or so of carefully navigated small talk and avoiding contact with any of the Blood, Guy steered us toward an empty table.

"What is this achieving?" he asked as we sat down. "We've learned nothing."

"Not nothing," I said. "You need to be patient. These things are never straightforward."

"Our men are dying out there," he said.

"Don't you mean their men?" I frowned at him. Now wasn't the time for slipping. "I understand, Guy, but we need to do this carefully." I pitched my voice low. "We can't tip our hand to whoever might be involved. We need to get deeper in, and that takes time."

"What takes time?" Fen asked, suddenly appearing at the table. His hair looked rumpled and his tie was somewhat askew.

"What have you been doing?" I said, arching my eyebrow.

"Information gathering," he said shortly. "No sign of your— Cormen," he amended. "But that doesn't mean he's not here somewhere."

"I haven't seen many Fae at all," I said.

"That's because most of them have more sense than to come to Blood Assemblies," Fen said. He straightened his tie, his fingers moving sharply. The movement made his sleeve ride up, revealing the iron chain wrapped tight around his wrist.

I frowned. Was he having visions? I tried to remember the last time I had seen Fen without his chain and failed. Which made me suddenly cold amid the heat. He'd told me once he saw more in times of trouble or uncertainty. Which described the City near perfectly right now.

But this was hardly the place to discuss it with him. I wasn't sure I wanted to know what he was seeing for a start.

What had we been talking about? Fae. Yes. "We're not interested in the ones who have more sense," I pointed out. "We're trying to figure out who's pulling whose strings, remember?"

"I remember," Fen said. "That's why I've spent way too much time in one of those stinking alcoves with a serving girl, charming a list of the Fae who are here tonight out of her."

"And?"

He rattled off a list of names. None of them from my father's Family. Frustration tightened my throat. The problem was that I didn't know enough about the Veiled Court. I was sure there were clues in that list of names, but I couldn't spot them. "Do they mean anything to you?"

"They're mostly from minor branches," Fen said. "As one would expect. We need an insider. We should be poking around in Summerdale."

"No." I wasn't going to have this argument again. "No going to the Veiled Court." Not unless we absolutely had to.

For one thing, as *hai-salai*, Fen and I could be pulled into a world of family obligations and duties from which we might never escape if we let anyone from either of our fathers' families gain a hold over us. And for another, the Veiled Court itself was perilous, if the tales are to be believed. Much safer to deal with the Blood here in the City than the Fae in the seat of their power.

The Fae guarded their lands ruthlessly. It was difficult to gain admittance to Summerdale, let alone the Veiled World beneath its hills. The Fae could hide themselves, disguise themselves, and make the very earth change around you to confuse, trap, or kill you. And that was before you started to deal with their politics and their impossible-to-untangle webs of Families and obligation.

"Well, unless Cormen is going to make a late appearance, I suggest we turn our attention to other things," Fen said.

"It's early yet," I pointed out.

"Or he may be upstairs already," Fen added.

"I don't suppose your serving girl was forthcoming about who is controlling access to the upper levels tonight?" I said.

"No."

Of course not. Luck couldn't be with me tonight. I needed to think.

"If we're settling in for a long evening, then I'm getting a drink," Fen said. "Anyone else?"

I considered asking for lemonade but doubted they served any such thing here. "Champagne," I said eventually, hoping that a little alcohol might take the edge off the frustration building in my gut. Guy asked for whiskey and Fen went to fetch the drinks.

Over the next hour we drank enough to keep up appearances and Guy and Fen both danced with me, but my father still didn't arrive. More people joined the festivities, making the room grow warmer as the press of bodies—human and Blood and Beasts—warmed the air.

But amongst the myriad faces and conversations I didn't see or hear anyone or anything useful to our cause. Leaving me with a growing sense of unease that not even Guy's arms around me as we danced could dispel.

Eventually, feeling the need to do something before I started screaming in frustration, I excused myself from our table, on the pretence of going to the retiring room. I moved restlessly through the crowd, trying to work out my next move.

Soon enough I reached the staircase to the upper levels. I drifted past, acted uninterested. How hard would it be to slip upstairs? I had one of my freshly made invisibility charms in my bag. With so few Fae in the crowd, it would almost certainly be safe to use.

But that left the problem of the three male Blood guarding the mouth of the stairs. As I watched out of the corner of my eye, a human couple approached the three and were firmly rebuffed.

From the protesting conversation, I gathered that only those with tokens were being admitted upstairs tonight.

Three Blood actively on the watch for interlopers was too chancy a proposition, even with an invisibility charm. They could smell me or hear me and I'd be caught.

I craned my head, trying to locate Guy and Fen through the crowd. I could just see the top of Guy's blond head back at the table. Both he and Fen were watching the dancers. Not looking for me. Yet.

Time to think of another approach.

My head had started to ache from the heat, and the sticks of my fan dug into my palm through my glove. As I hovered around the staircase, trying to work out what to do, movement on the staircase caught my eye. The man—Beast—descending was someone I knew.

Christophe Favreau.

He was frowning as he straightened his cuffs. Two younger Favreaus—neither of them Henri unfortunately—trailed behind him wearing angry expressions. I turned away, heart beating fast.

What was Christophe doing here? He didn't like Ignatius. His disgruntled expression suggested nothing had changed that fact.

What had just happened upstairs? What might still be happening?

I'd never know if I didn't get up there myself. I turned my back on the main staircase and moved deeper into the Assembly. There must be other staircases. The ones the Trusted and the servers used.

I spotted a serving girl, dressed in filmy white gauze like the rest of them, not far from me. Time to see where she went.

I trailed her a little way, ready with a story of overindulgence and confusion if I was confronted. Soon enough, the serving girl vanished between a thick set of black velvet curtains.

I looked down at what I was wearing. If I moved behind the scenes, there was no way anyone would mistake me for a servant. Nor a Trusted. The Blood tended to dress female Trusted as scantily as the servers. No, I was clearly a guest.

On the other hand, the Trusted and the servants were generally human. Far less likely to detect me if I used the invisibility charm.

Now or never.

I yanked the charm out of my bag and activated it.

Then I stepped cautiously through the curtains and set off once more.

Behind the velvet, Halcyon was far less sumptuous. The wide hallway had black-painted walls and gas lamps bare of the elaborate decorations of the public rooms. I hugged the wall and moved forward cautiously.

The kitchens, I reasoned, would be toward the rear of the building. And, presumably, the servants' stairs to the upper floors would be close to the kitchens so that food and drink arrived promptly when required.

The hallway turned a corner and I caught a waft of roasted meat in the air. Good. I was headed in the right direction.

As I got closer, the halls got busier. But most of the servers using them were laden with trays of drink and food, or were returning empty ones, and they kept to the middle of the hall except when they passed each other. I was safe enough if I kept to the edges and moved carefully, keeping my breath silent and easy.

It seemed to take a long time to reach the kitchen, though I knew it to be only a few minutes. I poked my head around the corner of the hall where it branched in either direction. Straight ahead was the kitchen. Two big doors stood open, giving me a perfect view of the many cooks hard at work. To my right, two servers moved away from the kitchen, their trays laden, and I saw them enter another doorway. That had to lead to the stairs to the upper floor.

I craned my neck in the other direction before I moved off, checking for threats. The left branch of the corridor was shorter, ending in a heavy door that was ajar. In the doorway, a male Trusted in the clothing of a guard was talking to someone. Just before I turned away, the Trusted moved a little and Henri Favreau's angry face came into view before the Trusted moved to block my line of sight again. Relief poured through me. I hadn't killed him. But just as rapidly, curiosity replaced it. Why was Henri trying to come through the back door?

"No, sir, I cannot admit you," the Trusted said.

Now, here was a conversation I needed to hear more of. The upper floors could wait a few minutes.

I had hear-mes in my purse. I moved as fast as I dared down toward the door, bringing one of the charms out as I did so, taking care to keep it close.

I stopped a few feet away, not willing to chance coming any closer. The Trusted wouldn't scent me, but Henri just might. But my hear-mes have a decent range. It was close enough.

The Trusted had one arm against the door frame. Brave man to stand against a Beast, but the Trusted are fiercely loyal to their Blood masters.

"No, sir," he repeated.

"Let me in, you insolent moron. I have a token."

"I have express orders not to admit you, sir."

"To hell with that, I got shot. I am *owed*." Henri's voice rose indignantly.

"Then I suggest you discuss that another time," the Trusted said. His tone was still scrupulously polite but steel-edged. Henri was going to have to go through him to get in, that much was clear.

"My lord won't thank you for causing a scene," the Trusted added. "You should leave."

"I . . ." Henri's voice sputtered and then died as the Trusted drew a pistol from his belt. "All right," he said in a low, furious tone. "But this is not the end of it."

"I'm sure you'll be more than welcome on another occasion, sir," the Trusted said. He stepped back and slammed the door closed, affording me another pleasing glimpse of Henri looking outraged before he disappeared from view.

I shut the hear-me down and pressed myself back against the wall as the Trusted came back up the hallway.

"Idiot," he muttered as he passed, and I fought the giggle that rose in my throat.

I waited a minute longer, half expecting Henri to pound on the door and demand admittance a second time, but the corridor stayed quiet. I looked down at the hear-me. *Proof*. Proof of a connection between Ignatius and Henri.

True, no names had been used, but Halcyon was clearly under Ignatius' control tonight. The Trusted had referred to his "lord." Tonight that could only be Ignatius. Henri's voice could be identified from the recording. Hopefully it was enough to tie them together.

I should take the charm back to Guy and Fen. This was the start of the proof Guy needed. But if I left now, I doubted they would let me come back to try for the upper floor. And I still needed to know if Cormen was here.

I didn't yet have the proof *I* was looking for. Was he involved in whatever it was Ignatius was up to? More important, was he still in the City? Did he still have Mama and Reggie hidden here somewhere? If he did, there was still a chance I could discover where. And with a Templar knight at my disposal, surely we could get them back?

If I could steal them back, send them somewhere safe, then everything else became simpler. Even if I couldn't avoid giving Cormen what he wanted, my family would be all right.

I couldn't lose this chance. Guilt curled through me, but I

pushed it away. Guy could wait. I put the hear-me back in my purse and continued back the way I'd come.

I had to wait another few minutes for the stairs to be clear of servers, but eventually they emptied and I ran up them as lightly as possible. At the top of the stairs was a small foyer with curtained doorways leading left and right. I paused, trying to guess at the layout from what I knew of the building.

Left, was my best guess, so I stepped through the curtains carefully, shrinking away as the fringed velvet brushed over my skin like tiny ghost fingers.

The hallway beyond was dimly lit and I couldn't hear anything. In fact the whole upper floor was eerily quiet. Too quiet. Almost . . . dead feeling. Which either meant nothing was happening in this part of the floor or that Halcyon had excellent aural shields.

I suspected the latter. I considered my options. Go with instinct or try the other way. I decided to stick to my original decision and moved farther along the corridor. Up here, the floor was covered in a thick carpet of black with fine traceries of white.

The walls were papered in a dark red with little vignettes bordered in fine black lines forming a diagonal pattern enclosed by flourishes that looked unpleasantly thorny. I didn't look too closely at what the images actually depicted. Nothing terribly pleasant, I would imagine.

I moved cautiously, nerves stretching to catch a hint of sound. Up here, the air smelled like the Blood. A mix of the incenses they favor and blood and other smells I didn't want to identify.

I was definitely back in their territory, not the more human world belowstairs.

Which meant, I realized, that I needed to turn off the invisibility charm. My stomach twisted uneasily, but I knew the instinct was right. Dressed as a guest of the Assembly, I might pass in unchallenged up here—after all, if reaching this level required a token, there would be no reason to suspect me if I looked as if I belonged. But if a Blood smelled or heard me while I was invisible, then my purpose here would be crystal clear.

I doubted I would survive such a discovery.

Still, it took me quite a few seconds to convince my suddenly frozen fingers to reach for the invisibility charm and deactivate it.

Fortune favors the brave, I reminded myself, trying to calm my racing heart. *Sweet Lady, be with me tonight.*

I had only walked a few more feet before I turned another corner and ran into one of the Blood.

He looked at me with cool gray eyes, one white brow lifting. "Lost?"

"No. I was just returning to the party," I lied. .

"Really? Then in that case, let me escort you."

A cool hand clamped around my arm before I had a chance to react.

"That is most kind of you." I managed to keep my voice calm with an effort. There was no way for me to break free of a vampire's grip, but perhaps if he thought me unconcerned, he would let go. "I would hate to miss the entertainment."

The vampire looked down at me, face neutral. "Is that so?"

"Yes." I smiled up at him, then faked a stumble. He caught me, then, as I had hoped, let me go.

"My apologies, my lord. My shoe." I bent for a moment, tugged at my shoe beneath my skirts. When I straightened I made sure I was a little farther away from him. Not that I could react fast enough to block a vampire.

"If you would be so kind, my lord." I inclined my head at him and gestured for him to lead the way.

My fingers gripped the strings of my bag tightly. I couldn't help tracing the edge of the flower that masked my alert charm. If I triggered it, Guy and Fen would come.

The question was whether they would be fast enough.

Not yet. Not before I'd found anything.

The vampire seemed to come to a decision. "Follow me." He turned on his heel, moving too smoothly, in that eerie way the Blood do, and led the way down the hallway.

There was the same dead silence as we walked. The carpet muffled my footsteps, and the Blood made no noise as he moved, which only made me more unsettled.

The smell of incense grew stronger, heavily spiced with cloves and sandalwood and smoky herbs. It made my nose twitch as if some part of my brain were trying to tell me that there was another smell being hidden by the smoky odor. A less pleasant smell. Blood maybe. Or fear.

There was a sudden burst of laughter from farther down the corridor. Was this Ignatius' private party?

Apparently it was. We reached another curtained doorway where the laughter came louder. The vampire held the curtain aside and gestured me through.

"After you, lady," he said smoothly as I moved past him. The noise in the room cut off abruptly, leaving an eerie silence. Like stepping into a dark cave and knowing something lurks in the dark but being unable to hear anything.

It was too late to change my mind, so I kept walking. The conversations started again, though, to my ear, the tone now had a nasty edge to it. Avid, almost. The room was brightly lit and larger than I had expected. There must have been thirty people standing or sitting on the low sofas. Mostly Blood, though there were a few barely clothed human women and men kneeling by some of the sofas or curled into laps. No Fae. No Cormen.

Just vampires and those who came willingly to them.

Fuck.

I looked away from the humans. Nightseekers or Trusted, either way they had chosen to be here. As had I. I forced myself to look calm as I scanned the room.

There. At the far end of the room, seated in a chair that bore a strong resemblance to a throne—carved from some heavy black wood, its cushions made from an equally black satin brocade that gleamed sullenly in the gaslight.

Ignatius Grey, his long white hair falling free over his shoulders, sat in the chair, his posture a lesson in studied power. He wore black-and-white, the only color in his face the strange light brown of his eyes. Which were full of satisfaction as he surveyed his surroundings. Several of the half-naked humans sat around his feet, waiting to serve. The rest of the party seemed to keep one eye on him as they talked and laughed.

No hiding his ambitions here apparently.

As I approached, Ignatius stopped his contemplation of the room and stared at me. I dropped my gaze politely, stopping a little distance from the naked back of the woman closest to Ignatius' feet.

"Well, well, what have we here?" he said. His voice had a rough burr, even though his accent was very correct. A little too correct, I thought. Rumor had it that Ignatius Grey had been a Seven Harbors pickpocket when he'd been human. He would have worked hard to lose the traces of the gutter from his voice.

I wondered if the rasp had been there before he had turned. It wasn't entirely unpleasant, much as he was not unpleasant to look at, if you liked rough and brawny. The Blood do not, as a rule, turn those who are unattractive.

I dropped into a curtsey, felt the comforting weight of the razor strapped to my thigh. It wasn't much, but it made me feel a little less vulnerable. "My Lord Grey." Not Lord Ignatius. Not yet. I looked him in the eye as I straightened.

His gaze sharpened. "And where did you spring from?"

"My lord?"

"Come to offer yourself, have you?" He gestured around the room. "As you can see, we are not lacking in morsels this evening. Tempting though you may be."

I hoped the shiver of disgust crawling down my spine didn't show. "No, my lord. That isn't my interest."

He frowned, white brows drawing together. "Truly? Then you're wasting my time."

"I—I have a message, my lord."

"From whom?"

I drew my pendant from beneath the neckline. Time to roll the dice and pray the Lady was on my side. "From the one who gave me this."

Ignatius leaned forward, face gone still. "Go on."

"He sends his regrets, my lord."

"Does he indeed?"

I bowed my head, feeling triumph surge beneath my fear. Ignatius knew my father.

"Interesting that he feels it necessary to send them twice," Ignatius continued in a flat tone.

Fuck and double fuck. I'd screwed up. Question was, could I talk my way out of it? "Twice, my lord?"

"The sa'Inviel had already sent a message. So, what are you? My consolation prize?" There was heat in his eyes now and anger in his voice. I clamped my mouth shut, trying to think.

Ignatius leaned farther forward. "Does he think he can buy me off with a *hai'salai*? He knows half-breeds are no use to me."

I definitely didn't like the sound of that. My fingers slipped to the flower, pressed the charm. Time for backup. "I was only told to give the message. And his assurances that all your needs will be met."

"And if my needs include you?"

Fear arced through me.

"Ah, he didn't mention that part to you, did he?" Ignatius' eyes narrowed. "You must be trusting, to walk in here for him. You must think much of him."

"Yes, my lord." The lie stuck in my throat, but I would do anything to stall for time. Guy and Fen would find me. They would get me out of this.

"So, what will you give to walk out of here again?"

Ignatius stood. I steeled my spine. I would not step back. No retreat.

"You need the evening star's goodwill, my lord," I said.

"Oh? And does he value you so highly? That it would offend him if I . . . indulged myself?"

"He protects what is his," I said with a false smile. Bravado. When surrounded by predators, you don't survive by acting meek. "He said you were an honorable ally."

Surprisingly, he laughed. Less surprisingly, it wasn't a pleasant sound. "I don't know who has been telling him tales about my honor," he said. "But I think they have led you both astray."

"Perhaps you don't know yourself, my lord." Around us, the room had grown very quiet. I didn't dare look away from Ignatius. He moved closer to me, close enough that I could see the tiny pinpoints of red starting to flare in his pupils.

"Oh, I think I do. Much as I think he knew what would happen to you."

Chapter Seventeen

HOLLY

My pulse started to beat far too fast as the scent of vampire—blood and something acidic that couldn't be masked by the cologne Ignatius wore—filled my nose. "And that is?"

He leaned in, close to my ear. "A taste. That is the price of exit, little *hai'salai.*"

His voice was edged with more than its usual rasp. There was threat in that tone. I moved backward; I couldn't help it. *"No."* The denial was instinctive.

Ignatius leaned closer. "So fast, with her refusal." Around me, I felt the silence, if anything, grow deeper. Bottomless. A endless pit waiting to swallow anyone who made a wrong move. If the other Blood were chilled to silence by Ignatius' tone, what should I be? My pulse sped. I had to lock my knees against the urge to run.

"He will pay more. If I am unharmed," I said, trying to slow the pounding in my ears with a deep breath. This was about Mama. About Reggie. I had to get out of here. I had to save them.

"I do not bargain. You will pay. Or you will not leave."

I swallowed slowly, trying to ease the acid in my throat. "Is there nothing—"

His lips drew back, baring his fangs. "I said I do not bargain. I meant it. Make your choice, halfling. I have named my price."

This was why I avoided the Blood. They were ruthless. And I had nothing to counter with. My fingers itched toward the razor, but there was no way to attempt to hurt a Blood Lord here and survive the experience. Maybe if I were a wraith, I could manage it. But I wasn't. The only way to survive was to comply.

My blood. How bad could it be?

Very, very bad, unless you are very, very careful. For once, I had no argument with that little voice in my head. One dealt very carefully with the devil or paid the price. Ignatius might not be the Lord of the humans' hell or any other, but he was dangerous beyond my reckoning. I needed to tread very carefully. Remember what I had been taught about bargaining with vampires. "There must be limits. That is the law."

He smiled and behind me I heard murmurs from those watching us. I had no idea what that might mean.

"Such bravery. What limits are you proposing?"

Anything I could think of that would keep me alive and let me walk out of here. I was glad of my gloves, hiding the dampness of my palms. There was a trickle of sweat in the small of my back, and fear biting at my stomach.

There was a protocol. The treaties allowed for a human or Fae to control how much he or she was willing to offer a vampire. Of course, if the vampire managed through guile or the taste of their own blood to get you to forget protocol, then all bets were off. I didn't know if the treaties specifically addressed half-breeds, but I was going to assume they did. "A taste only. Not a full feeding."

"I do not need to drain you, my dear. I have plenty willing to sustain me."

I didn't like the cockiness of his tone. Was I forgetting something? "Then why ask for my blood at all?"

"I like the taste of Fae blood. It is a delicacy. And your fear will add a spice to the bouquet."

I couldn't deny my fear. No doubt Ignatius could smell it already. I could only show him that I wouldn't let fear control me. Some vampires enjoyed things more when their food was afraid. Or hurting. "No pain either," I said firmly.

"The bite always hurts a little," Ignatius said. The amusement in his voice had eased off.

Yes, he was hoping he could make me scream. "Nothing more than that." I didn't know how I was managing to sound so calm. Inside I wanted nothing more than to run from the room. Run to Guy and let him take me away from the nightmare.

Ignatius bared his fangs at me, clearly displeased.

"Do you agree to my conditions?" I said.

"I will not kill you or hurt you." He nodded. "Is that sufficient to calm your fears?"

My hands had clenched themselves in my skirts in an effort not to reach protectively for my throat. It was only blood, I reminded myself. It would not kill me. And it couldn't hurt too badly or people would not willingly submit to it. I had survived Cormen's beating. I could bear this.

Ignatius circled me where I stood, prowling like a large cat. I felt very much the mouse waiting to be pounced upon. Why had I ever set foot on that damned staircase?

Guy and Fen were both likely to want to lock me up for doing something so foolish.

But they didn't understand. They didn't feel what I felt every time I thought of my mother in Cormen's hands. Picturing her believing whatever pretty tale he'd spun for her. That he had come for her at last, most likely. About to have her heart broken all over again.

I didn't think she would survive it a second time.

And that was the most optimistic scenario.

More likely, he had her locked up somewhere. Had hurt her. She wouldn't survive that either. Not and keep hold of what small parts of sanity she still had left.

I couldn't let him break her completely.

What he might do to Reggie, who meant nothing to him, didn't bear thinking about.

A moment or two of my own pain was a small price to pay for their safety. If I got out of here, I still had a chance to save them.

I cleared my throat, tried to make dry lips move. "Yes. That satisfies me."

"So you agree. A taste in exchange for your freedom?"

"Yes, my lord. I give my consent." There. I had done it now. Spoken the required words and given a vampire leave to drink my blood. Sweet lords of hell, had I lost my mind?

Ignatius stopped his circling, came to stand in front of me. The smile he gave me this time was pure predatory satisfaction. I hoped to whatever gods might listen that he would lose the fight for control of the Blood because his eyes held no lingering traces of humanity. No, this one was all about power and pain and satisfying his own urges. Not the sort of mind you want supposedly keeping the will of the vampires in check so they conformed to the terms of the treaties.

"Very good." He retreated to his chair—throne—no, think of it as a chair, that was easiest. The movement was almost too fast as if one moment he stood before me and then the next he was in the chair. The speed made my stomach lurch.

"Come here, then." He beckoned with one long pale finger.

I walked toward him, fighting for every step. I wanted to turn and run. Run and keep running. The gazes of the other Blood watching me, crushing my lungs. Their hunger—aroused by Ignatius' games—smoked the air. If I tried to flee, I would be brought down in a second.

And who knew what might happen to me then? I had given my word, agreed to what was about to come. Breaking a deal with one of the Blood in their territory could leave me subject to whatever punishment they cared to mete out.

"Kneel," he said when I was directly in front of him.

I frowned. Kneel? How could he feed from me if I were kneeling in front of him? As I hesitated he gestured and suddenly there were two vampires on either side of me. Ready to ensure my compliance. I didn't want to be forced to my knees. Didn't want to give any other vampire an excuse to touch me. So I knelt.

"Very good," Ignatius said. He rolled his sleeve up, baring one wrist.

"What are you doing?" My voice quivered.

"You agreed to a taste. I didn't say who would be doing the tasting."

Stupid, Holly girl. Horror washed over me. He was right. I had agreed. *Oh* so *stupid.* "No!"

Cool hands clamped down on my shoulders as I tried to rise, pinning me in place as effectively as chains. No way to break a vampire's grip. I fought against the rising tide of panic, trying to think. "No. This wasn't our agreement."

"Yes, it was." He glanced around the room. "Anyone disagree that she agreed to a taste?"

Deathly silence.

As if any of the assembled there were going to take my side

of the argument. I struggled against the vampires holding me even though I knew it was futile. "No."

"You must learn to be careful in your agreements, *hai'salai*. Did your Fae father teach you nothing?"

"I didn't agree to this," I said.

"Yes, you did" His voice was triumphant.

"I'll—" I broke off, knowing there was nothing I could do. I could only make it worse for myself.

"Let her go."

I almost fainted at the voice.

Guy.

"Hold him," Ignatius snapped. I tried to twist around, but I was blocked by the vampires holding me. I heard the hiss of metal and several blows amidst grunts and snarls. A voice I didn't recognize cried out once, and then there was a nasty-sounding thump.

"Let her go," Guy's voice repeated, cracking a little, and my heart leapt. Had he won?

Before me, Ignatius grinned viciously. I pulled again against the hands holding me, but their grip tightened painfully.

"So brave and defiant. How charming," Ignatius said. "What do you think you can do about it, Mr. DuCaine? Your Templars won't protect you now."

"I don't need them," Guy snarled. "If you hurt her—" His voice cut off with the sound of flesh striking flesh.

My heart plummeted. "Don't hurt him."

"You are hardly in the position to make further bargains," Ignatius snapped, face twisted in rage.

"Holly!" Guy yelled.

If he kept struggling they would hurt him or kill him. I had caused this mess and I held the only way out of it. Submission. It left a bitter taste in my mouth. "I will do as we agreed, my lord," I said. "But please, don't hurt him. He doesn't under-stand." I twisted again, and this time the vampire to my right moved so I could see Guy.

It had taken four vampires to restrain him. There was a cut over his eye dripping blood. Shit. Fresh blood. That was all we needed to add to this situation. "Guy, listen to me."

Blue eyes snapped frustrated fury at me.

"I agreed to this. He won't hurt me. Everything will be fine. But you have to stop fighting."

He snarled wordlessly but stilled. I nodded at him, mouthed, "Trust me," and then turned to Ignatius. "All right, my lord, Let's get this over with."

He still looked angry as if Guy's arrival had spoiled something for him, and his movements were almost jerky if such a thing could ever be said to be true of a vampire.

He crossed to me and his hand closed into my hair, pulling my head back sharply. It hurt but I hid the wince.

"Open your mouth," he snarled.

I obeyed.

He drew a knife from the sheath at his hip and held it up. The candles flickered off the blade and I shrank away. Vampire blood is addictive over time. Usually it is given a few drops at a time. If he was angry and did something foolish like slashing his wrist over my mouth, then it could be enough to addict me. Bloodlock me. Had that been his game all along?

He stood, staring down at me for a moment. He wasn't looking at my face. I wasn't sure what it was. My pendant perhaps?

"Tell the evening star that he should stop hiding behind the Veil and messengers and come to me himself." He raised the knife and held it against his thumb.

"Drink deep," he said, with vicious satisfaction; then the knife moved and blood welled and he let it fall into my mouth.

For a second all I tasted was blood. Warm salt and metal, but then I felt the flavor change . . . it bloomed and sweetened on my tongue and the room swam around me as pleasure swept through me, turning my limbs to liquid, spiraling into the core of me. "Oh my," I heard myself say in a dreamy voice, and the vampires holding me let me go as I fell forward onto the floor and the orgasm took me.

GUY
✛

I yelled for Simon as soon as we were through the front door of the hospital. My brother didn't miraculously materialize, but an orderly appeared at a run.

"Sir—er, Mr. DuCaine," the man said, eyes wide as he took in the scene. "What happened?"

"Get Simon," I snarled.

Another man, a healer, also appeared. "We should take her into a treatment room."

I tightened my arms around Holly. "No one is touching her until I've spoken to Simon."

"Healer DuCaine is not on duty," the healer—Lorenzo, I thought his name was—said tentatively.

"Then send someone for him," I snapped. *"Now."*

The healer jerked his head at the orderly. "Do it," he ordered. Then he peered up at me. "At least put her down in one of the rooms. She'll be more comfortable. So will you."

I considered. Maybe the man was right, but I didn't want to let go of Holly. She was still pale and motionless; she hadn't stirred since I'd picked her up in the Assembly, surrounded by vampires, and carried her away from Ignatius Grey's laughter. I'd thought at first she'd merely fainted, but surely she should be coming around by now?

If it weren't for the rise and fall of her chest—all too obvious in that damned dress—I would've thought she was dead. I focused on her breathing, willing each breath to be followed by another.

"Mr. DuCaine?" the healer repeated. "She really will be more comfortable."

"All right. But no one but Simon touches her."

"Of course." The healer led the way to a treatment room and I laid Holly down on the bed.

"Can you tell me what happened? Is she hurt?" He hovered near the bed, obviously wanting to do what healers did.

"I'll speak to my brother. She has no wounds that need immediate attention." I hoped that was true. She wasn't bleeding at least. Ignatius hadn't done anything to her that I had witnessed except give her the cursed blood. I felt bile rise in the back of my throat. What in the name of all that was holy had she been thinking to agree to such a thing?

Drinking vampire blood. No amount of information was worth that, was it? She was risking blood-locking or . . . I had a sudden horrible thought. She didn't do this regularly, did she?

What if she was a Nightseeker and she'd fooled me?

Surely not. I wasn't that stupid.

No. I was being an idiot. She was no Nightseeker. A Night-seeker wouldn't fight so hard for her family. Holly might be a spy and a thief, but she had her own code of honor. She wouldn't lie to me about something so vital.

A taste for the blood was a hard thing to hide. Though maybe you could for a short time. After all, I'd only known her a few days. . . .

"Guy?" Simon's voice came from behind me. "What happened?"

"She drank vampire blood," I said, staring down at Holly where I'd placed her. The black satin of her dress fanned over the small hospital bed. Her skin was icily pale against it. I swallowed, hard. Even if she wasn't a Nightseeker, she had tasted vampire blood. What happened if she became addicted?

"Gods and suns," Simon said. He came up beside me, bent down, and took Holly's wrist in his hand. "Why would she do that? Where were you?" He twisted round to look at me accusingly, but he didn't let go of Holly's arm.

"Halcyon," I said, and saw him grimace.

"Why?"

"We can talk after you deal with Holly," I said.

"Yes, I think we will." He focused on Holly. "Whose blood did she drink?"

"Does it matter?" I didn't want to think of Ignatius Grey or I might have to return to Halcyon and do something exceedingly satisfying like beat him to a pulp. Of course, it would also be extremely stupid.

"Would I ask if it didn't?" Simon said. "Who was it?"

"Ignatius Grey." Hell's balls. When was he going to stop talking and fix her?

"Ignatius was there?" This time it was Lily's voice, coming from the door.

"Ignatius was the one throwing tonight's little shindig," I said, still watching Holly and Simon.

"Rising fast," Lily murmured. She came over, touched my face lightly. Which meant she was worried. Lily still didn't touch anyone other than Simon easily. "You're hurt too," she said, stepping back. She stayed close, watching me carefully as though she expected me to fall over.

"I'll live," I said firmly. The cut on my head was throbbing, but it seemed to have stopped bleeding. There was blood on my jacket and splashed across my shirt, drying red brown against the white. Head wounds always make a damned mess. I swiped at my face, with the back of my hand. It came away smeared with half-dried blood. No wonder the orderly had stared.

"What's taking so long?" My gut twisted. Was she really hurt? What if the blood did something to her? "The blood. It wasn't much, I don't think. Will she—"

"She's half Fae," Lily said. Her tone sounded convincing, but her eyes were worried as she watched Simon work. "She'll probably be all right."

"You're half Fae," I pointed out. "Lucius addicted you."

"Not the very first time," Lily said. "How much did Ignatius give her?"

"A few drops, maybe more. But I don't know if this is her first time," I ground out. "Simon?"

Simon was still bent over Holly, doing whatever it was sun-mages did. "She fainted. I'm going to wake her up."

I took a half step forward, stopped when Lily put her hand on my arm. I shook her off. "Is that safe?"

"Guy, this is my job, remember?" Simon sounded exasperated.

I clenched my hands, still overloaded with adrenaline and the need to hurt something. "Yes. Sorry. Do what you think is best."

"Good. Why don't you go and let Bryony look at your head?"

"I'm not going anywhere until I know Holly is all right."

Simon and Lily exchanged a look, smiles blooming on their faces.

"Don't go getting ideas. She got hurt on my watch. She's my responsibility." That was all it was, I told myself firmly. I couldn't afford anything else.

"Whatever you say, big brother," Simon said. He laid a hand either side of Holly's skull and closed his eyes for a moment.

Holly sighed softly and her eyes fluttered open. She looked sleepy, smiling a little as she caught sight of me. "Hello."

"Hello," I said. Relief made my knees sag. I braced myself on the bedstead.

Holly's smile turned to a frown. "Why do you have blood on your face?"

"Holly, you're at St. Giles," Simon interrupted. "Do you remember what happened?"

Her frown deepened. Then her eyes widened abruptly. "Ignatius. Oh *gods*." She buried her face in her hands. "Oh gods. Don't look at me." Her voice was muffled, half-choked. I took another step toward the bed. Lily moved faster than me. She went to the bed, fished a handkerchief out of her pocket, and tucked it into Holly's hand.

Holly's fingers tightened on the square of linen, but she didn't lift her head.

"Holly, it's all right," Simon said. "You didn't do anything wrong."

"I did. I was st-stupid." Her voice trailed away on a sob.

Definitely crying. I wanted to help but didn't know how. Not with Simon and Lily in the room.

"The Blood are treacherous," Lily said soothingly. "The important thing is that Guy got you out of there. You're safe now."

"They hurt him," Holly said. "Because of me."

She was worried about me? Something strange twisted in my stomach. I moved closer still, but Lily shook her head. Simon waved me away.

"Holly, I need to take a look at you," Simon said, as the sobs grew noisier. "Lily will take Guy to Bryony. She'll heal his head. Everything's going to be all right."

HOLLY

"Am I going to be blood-locked?" I asked as the door closed behind Guy and Lily. I was propped up against a pillow, Lily's handkerchief still clutched in my hand. I'd gotten the tears under control, but horror and shame still twisted in my stomach, making the room swim. Worst of all, beneath the disgust, I could feel satisfaction sliding under my skin, as though I'd recently left a lover's bed.

It made me feel slimier than the geas ever had. I'd drunk vampire blood. I'd *come* from drinking vampire blood.

Simon drew up a chair. "It's unlikely. The Fae don't get blood-locked."

"I'm only half Fae."

"Yes. So we'll watch you for the next few days."

I twisted the handkerchief. I didn't have a few days. Guy needed to know what I had learned. And I needed to figure out how to get to Cormen. Behind the Veil, Ignatius had said.

Which meant he was in Summerdale. He had my mother and
Reggie somewhere in the bloody Veiled Court. I had to get
them out. Though how exactly I was going to do that—face him
down on his home ground where human law didn't apply—I
had no idea.

"What happens if I am?" I asked. I knew the answer. There
was no cure for blood-locking. The cravings grew stronger and
stronger until they consumed everything else. Until you died.

"Let's cross that bridge if we need to," Simon said.

It should have made me feel better, but I couldn't help feeling
unclean somehow. I had drunk blood. Ignatius' blood. And it
had felt good. I clenched my teeth so I wouldn't retch, breathed
through my nose a few times until I was sure I could speak.

"Lords of hell," I muttered. For almost the first time in my
life, I wished I were full Fae. Smart enough to stay out of trouble.

Simon patted my arm. "Don't worry. Other than humans, I've
never come across anyone who was instantly addicted. Just
make sure you don't do it again."

"I wasn't exactly intending to do it this time." I didn't want
to explain how I'd gotten myself into this mess. It was too complicated. I rubbed my forehead. Trying to think through the ache
in my head and heart. How was I going to get into the Veiled
Court? How could I get Cormen to see me?

By bringing him what he wanted.

Fuck. I'd forgotten. Simon. I made myself focus. Yes. There.
I could still feel my charm at his side. So he hadn't discovered
it and discarded it. It was still there. Still working. I had to take
it back. Ideally, I'd leave it for longer, but who knew if it would
last? Or if I'd get another chance to be alone with Simon.

My stomach twisted suddenly, and the urge to reach over and
grab for the charm rose within. I fought the sensation, but the
geas fought back, the twisting sensation changing to biting jabs
of pain as I resisted.

I knew it would only get worse. Which meant I really had no
choice at all. I had to do what it wanted. Go after Simon's secret.

Simon who was Guy's brother. Guy who had saved me. Who
trusted me. They all trusted me.

And I was going to have to betray them.

Lords of hell. I felt exhausted, as though Ignatius had drained
my blood rather than the reverse. Sick with what I had done and

what I was going to do. I had no idea if I could summon enough power to glamour Simon.

I had to take the chance. I straightened, pushed my hair back from my face, and winced as the pain jabbed again.

"Does anything hurt?" Simon asked, leaning closer. "You didn't hit your head when you fainted, did you?"

"How would I know?" I asked.

"Good question. Do you feel dizzy?" He peered at me. "Perhaps I should take another look." The pain eased a little as the distance between us lessened.

Now. This time the urge was irresistible. But still I worked to keep control. The geas had no concept of subtlety or safety. Maybe if I hadn't been brought back to the locus of its need, I could have staved it off. But it was too strong.

"Simon." I put my hand on his arm, flesh to flesh. I bit back the tears. I didn't want to do this. But I had to.

I gathered myself and threw the glamour at him. He froze and for a moment I thought I had failed. But then his face went vacant and relaxed.

"Simon, you won't remember this," I ordered softly. "But I need you to reach into your pocket and give me your charm." He did as I asked, face still dreamily empty. Lady help me if Lily came back now and saw what I had done. I didn't have much time. I doubted Bryony would take very long to heal Guy's wounds.

The charm was still warm when Simon handed it to me and I tried not to fumble as I worked at disentangling my charm from his, whispering words of power to speed my fingers and unwind the binding I'd wrought on them. Not to mention keep Simon happily glamoured. It seemed to take forever, but eventually it was done.

I gave the invisibility charm to Simon. "There, you can put it away again now." I tucked my charm into the evening bag, which had somehow made it back from Halcyon with me. There was no way to trigger it now and see if it had recorded anything useful. I would have to wait.

Later tonight. I could see if I'd gotten what I'd come for, if I had a way of getting the information Cormen wanted. If he'd retreated to Summerdale, then my options were rapidly narrowing. I didn't want to help him, nor did I trust him to release my mother and Reggie if I did.

I still wanted to find a way to ruin his plans.

If I could.

If not—if I couldn't find them or if I couldn't resist the geas—I still needed backup to make sure Cormen could be persuaded to release them when I did bring him Simon's secret. Either way I still needed Guy's help.

Needed to keep on betraying him.

Right now I didn't know if I hated my father or myself more.

First things first. I released Simon from the glamour. "My head doesn't hurt," I said, continuing our previous conversation as though nothing had happened.

"Indulge me," he said with a smile. "That way I can reassure my brother your brain is perfectly intact."

"After tonight, I don't think your brother cares all that much whether or not my brain—or any other part of me—is intact."

"I wouldn't be so sure about that," Simon said.

I wanted to ask what he meant. But I wouldn't. I wasn't going to let myself hope. Guy would learn the truth about me soon enough. About what I'd been doing all this time. And once that happened, there's no more laughing knight in my bed. No, I'd be sleeping with guilt and desperation. Which were, at least, fairly familiar bedfellows.

Chapter Eighteen

HOLLY

It didn't take long for Guy to return, his face clean and only a thin pink line showing where the cut had been. It was strange. I still wasn't entirely used to what a healer could do. At the Dove, there were illnesses and babies. Few actual wounds. Somehow making flesh meld with flesh seemed different from curing a cough or making labor go easier.

"Is she all right?" Guy asked Simon.

I couldn't really read his tone. Angry? Scared? About to call the whole thing off? "I'm right here, you know," I said, wishing he'd look at me.

"Is she?" Guy repeated, eyes still on Simon.

All right, so angry had to be part of it, I thought. If he couldn't even look at me . . . Fear gripped my stomach, biting down with icy fingers. If Guy backed out now, then it would be even harder for me to get to Mama and Reggie.

I had to tell him about Henri. If I was still useful to him, he would still help me. Would trust me a little longer. "I'm fine," I said. I stood, wanting to demonstrate. "Fine," I repeated. My voice sounded vaguely distant to my ears. The room swam around me suddenly, the light breaking into little jagged daggers.

Damn. I'd expended too much power. I swayed backward

and someone caught me, lowered me back to the bed. I shut my eyes, willing the dizziness to subside.

"She fainted," Guy said. "That's not normal. Are you sure she's not . . ."

"Healing is draining," Lily said gently. "She just needs rest. She'll be perfectly well, Guy."

I hoped she was right about that, but I couldn't bring myself to open my eyes and join the conversation again. Not quite yet. I needed just a few minutes to breathe. I focused on doing just that while the DuCaine brothers argued over my head. When Guy's voice went icy again, I pushed myself back up to sitting. "I'm all right," I said again.

"Yes, you are," Simon said. "But you need to rest and eat and recover. You should stay here tonight; someone needs to keep an eye on you."

Guy was watching Simon, not looking at me. "I can do that."

A whisper of relief eased the knot in my guts. He wasn't leaving. Not yet. I snuck another look up at those icy eyes. He still wasn't looking at me.

Simon apparently was wise enough not to get in the middle of whatever was happening. "In that case, I'll leave you two alone. I'll get someone to take you to a room."

I blinked. I hadn't really taken much notice of our surroundings, but now that I did, I saw that this was indeed not a proper patient room. It was far too small. Even after Simon left, Guy seemed to take up most of the available space. Even if he was trying to keep his distance.

I pushed myself to my feet, reached up to touch the new scar on his face.

Guy caught my wrist. "Don't."

"Does it hurt?"

"No. But we have things to talk about." His voice rumbled, his anger palpable.

My heart sank. "Yes, we do." My knees wobbled and I sat on the bed. Might as well let him say his piece. In my experience it was simpler to let men blow off steam than try to reason with them. "Go on, then." I folded my hands, waiting for him to start.

Guy stayed where he was, his face twisted in frustration. "I don't know what to say."

"Why not?"

"Mostly because a lot of what I want to say isn't fit language for ladies."

I almost laughed. "I think we've established beyond all reasonable doubt that I'm not a lady."

He blew out a breath, but he didn't argue with me on that point. "Why? Why in the name of—just why?"

"Why what, exactly? Why did I bargain with a vampire?"

"Why were you idiotic enough to go up there alone?"

"I saw a chance, I took it."

His hands flexed suddenly, the snarling beasts stretching as though they were roaring disapproval. I'm sure he wanted to roar his displeasure too. "I was right *there*. My job is to protect you."

"I thought I'd be all right."

"You went to talk to Ignatius Grey in the heart of his little fiefdom and *you didn't think it would be dangerous*?"

Definitely roaring now. I schooled myself not to wince. Or yell back. That would only fan the flames.

"No. I knew it was dangerous. But I thought I could handle it. Anyway, I was looking for Cormen, not Ignatius."

"Next time, my lady, perhaps you'd do me the courtesy of running your idiotic plans past me so I can lock you in the nearest dungeon until you come to your senses?"

"Excuse me?" My own temper, which had been on shaky ground all this time, blown up by nerves and adrenaline and a healthy dose of knowing that I was in the wrong. "Idiotic? It worked. I found out where Cormen was. And I found proof—"

I broke off as the door swung open. A nervous-looking orderly cleared his throat.

"What?" Guy snapped.

"Healer DuCaine said you needed a room. I've come to take you to it."

"Come back in a minute."

I stood abruptly. If we were going to yell, I'd rather do it in a larger room. If only because it might give me more scope to find things to throw at Guy's arrogant head. "No, it's fine. Let's go." I picked up my bag, squared my shoulders, and marched past Guy. The orderly looked at me, then at Guy, and gulped. But he gestured for me to follow him and I did, sweeping out after him into the corridor, trying not to think what I must look like with my hair half falling around my face and my dress wrinkled beyond rescue.

I didn't wait to see if Guy was following me. At that moment I didn't care.

But somewhere in the journey through the endless corridors of St. Giles, my indignation started to fade again, leaving only shame. Guy was right. I did deserve to be locked up. I'd let my concern for my mother drive me to do something reckless. But I'd also survived and as I'd been about to say, I'd gained something from the risk I'd taken. So maybe we were both right.

Not that Guy was likely to see it that way.

The orderly ushered us into a room in what seemed to be a mostly deserted corridor of the hospital. Painted white, it was larger than the room I'd had before. And the bed was big enough for two.

Subtle, that Simon.

Though he was likely going to be disappointed. I doubted Guy would be touching me any time soon.

Besides the bed, there was a small desk against one wall and several chairs for visitors. In the far wall, a window showed the night sky. I had no idea what time it was. The moon was still high in the sky, the stars peeking determinedly through soft clouds.

For a moment I was tempted to climb out through the window, over the roof, and away into the City. Anything to be free of this wretched situation.

But dancing slippers and evening gowns hardly lent themselves to rooftop adventures. And running away wasn't going to change anything.

The door clicked shut and Guy's footsteps crossed the room, then came to a stop. I didn't turn around.

"I did use the charm. I called for help when I needed it."

"A little too late." Guy's voice was somewhat calmer.

"Things happened fast."

"Things usually do in bad situations."

"I know." I did. I'd been in enough bad situations in my time to find out firsthand. But apparently I was a slow learner. Or stupid enough to ignore what I'd learned when enough was at stake.

"Then why," Guy said. "Why risk it? Couldn't you see that Ignatius wouldn't let you out of there easily? Or was that what you wanted?"

"What?" I whirled from the window. Guy's eyes were ice

blue again, cold as they watched me. "You think I wanted anything to do with a vampire?"

"You were quick enough to deal with him. How should I know what you want? As you keep telling me, the Night World is your world. Perhaps you know it a little better than you admit."

There was scorn in his voice now, along with the anger, his words lashing at me until I was sure I might bleed from them. "You think I've been lying to you? That I'm some Night World slut? Quick to spread her legs or offer her throat?"

He didn't deny it, watching me with accusing eyes.

"I was doing what we went there to do," I spat. "I found out something about Henri and Ignatius. And I found out where Cormen is. Where my mother likely is."

Guy clenched his hands. "And is that information worth dying for?"

My hands clenched. "To me, yes. You're right. I'm a thief. And a spy. I grew up in the border boroughs and the Night World. And yes, my mother was a whore. All of that is true. But she's my mother. She and Reggie are my family. I won't let anything happen to them. Anyway, you're the one who wanted to know more about the Beasts and Ignatius. That was important enough for you to risk your standing in the order over."

"I didn't drink vampire blood!" His voice wasn't angry now, more anguished. His hands were fisted at his hips.

"I did that to get out of there. To get us *both* out of there. If you can't handle that, then I suggest we call this off. End the charade."

"I won't leave you unprotected."

My hands tightened further, nails digging into my palms. Impossible, contrary man. I wanted to hit him and kiss him at the same time. "I don't understand you."

His face twisted. "That makes two of us."

I sat down on the bed abruptly, head pounding. I wanted to cry. But there was no time for that. "Do you want to know what I found out about Henri or do you want to fight?"

Guy's eyes were bleak. "I—no, go on. Tell me."

"He was trying to get in and the Trusted turned him away. He was shouting something about being owed. Wanting payment. Said he wanted more for being shot. So it seems Ignatius is the one behind that, at least. I had a hear-me. It should have recorded the whole thing."

"Did he mention Ignatius by name?"

"No. But it's a start. A connection. You can tell the Templars to watch him and Antoine. You can give them the charm. And I can find out more." I looked up at him, set my jaw. "But we need to get Mama and Reggie first."

"You want to just march into Summerdale? Do you even know where she will be?"

"Somewhere in the sa'Inviel territory, I would imagine."

"Which is where?"

I rubbed my head as my temples throbbed. "I don't know exactly, but I'll find out."

"And how will you go about that?"

There was plenty of accusation behind his words. Too much, in fact. I didn't think I could handle anything more tonight. If he stayed, I was going to break. "I want to rest. You should leave now."

"Simon said someone needed to watch you."

"I'm in St. Giles. Surrounded by healers. I don't need you." A lie, but I wasn't sure how much more I could take right now. Along with the pounding in my head, there was still the faintest pulse of heat in my veins, but I didn't know whether that was still the blood or whether it was the ever-present awareness of Guy tugging at my senses. Either way, it did nothing to ease my mood.

"Healers aren't knights."

"No one is going to start a riot here."

"How do you know?"

Fair question. I didn't. "What, then, you're going to sleep across my doorway like a proper knight?"

His mouth flattened and his breath blew out. Amazing. Had I actually pushed him too far this time?

"No." He came and sat beside me. "Actually, I thought I'd do this." He put his arms around me and scooped me into his lap.

The simple gentleness in the gesture undid me. I buried my face in his shoulder and tried not to cry. "I'm sorry," I whispered.

His arms tightened around me. "I'm sorry too."

I lifted my head, not sure what his tone meant. It sounded a little too close to good-bye for my liking. He couldn't leave. Not now. Not when I knew where Cormen was. I couldn't storm the Veiled World alone.

Besides which, despite all my better judgment, despite my certainty that there was no way for things to ever come out right for us, the thought of seeing him walk out the door made my heart clutch.

So I did the only thing I could think of to keep him here with me. Curled one hand around his neck and pulled his head down to mine.

He made a noise of surprise—protest—I wasn't going to stop to find out. I slid my free hand down between us, sliding my palm over him. He was hard. Something in my chest eased a little. There. He wanted me. No matter what else, we had this between us. Need. Longing.

Maybe it would be enough.

Tonight I would make it enough.

I stroked him again, deepened the kiss. Wanting to light the fire that would burn away everything else that had happened.

Guy made another rough noise, deep in his throat, and his hands moved, his grip changing from comforting to possessive, bunching in my skirts and pulling them upward as he lifted me, urging my knees to either side of him.

Oh yes, this I liked.

I helped him, gathering the satin out of my way, then letting it fall so I could maneuver, so there was nothing between us but his trousers. Then I had to grip his shoulders while he dealt with his own clothing. His hands brushed me as he dealt with buttons and flaps, and I shuddered, pressing closer even though I knew that would only delay what I wanted. All the time our mouths still met, desperate hot kisses that might have been closer to a battle than lovemaking.

No matter.

I was beyond caring. All I wanted was the man beneath me. He seemed equally eager. His hands tightened again; then he lifted me and slid home as he let me down again. The pleasure of it was enough to make me gasp, my head falling back as the sensation engulfed me.

Guy moved beneath me again and my eyes snapped open, locked on his. Searching the pale blue fire for any hint of what he was thinking. But then he pulled my head down to kiss me and I couldn't do anything more than let him take me where he led.

*   *   *

I lay sleepless for a long time after Guy fell asleep. So when the door to our room clicked open, I was awake to hear. I cracked an eye open but didn't move, hoping that whoever had come to check on me might leave me if they thought I was actually asleep.

I didn't recognize the head that poked through the door, but the woman wore a healer tunic. It didn't take her long to satisfy herself about whatever she had come to do and the door closed again.

I closed my eyes, trying to find a comfortable position. Sleep still eluded me. The hospital was quiet. Too quiet. Beside me, Guy's slow, even breathing sounded very loud. I didn't know how he could sleep soundly.

My own thoughts were whirling so fast, I wished Simon had given me something to help me sleep.

Simon.

I could feel the charms in my evening bag, buried somewhere halfway across the room under my discarded dress, from where I lay. So much rested on the charm I'd retrieved from Simon and what it might have overheard.

I'd told Guy that I didn't know how to get to Cormen. I hadn't told him that I hoped I could make Cormen come to me. I didn't even know if I could tell him that. Regardless, my plan rested on the charm. What secrets did it hold? Enough to free me? Enough to save Mama and Reggie? Enough to damn Simon? Or make him a target again?

I didn't want to do that, but that was the choice in front of me. Save my family or save Guy's. I couldn't throw my sense to the wind because my heart was foolish enough to want to throw itself under the feet of a Templar to trample. I wouldn't. I couldn't. If Mama and Reggie died, it wouldn't matter what happened with Guy and I. I could never forgive myself.

To save them, I had to know what was on that charm.

Now seemed as good a time as any.

Indeed, it might be the only chance I got. Cormen would, no doubt, hear of my excursion to Halcyon sooner or later. I needed to get to him fast. And I needed my bargaining chip.

Regardless of what that made me.

I slipped carefully from the bed, hovering on the edge for a minute to see if Guy would wake. But he merely rolled toward the spot where I had lain and smiled slightly in his sleep. He looked peaceful. Happy. For a second I almost crawled back in next to him, see if I could wake him and chase reality away a little longer. But no, I couldn't.

What I wanted didn't matter. As usual, it was my job to take care of things, not be taken care of. I would do what I had to do. And I'd bear the consequences.

I moved as soundlessly as I could, putting on the clean clothes left for me. Black trousers, a pale green shirt and vest. Soft black boots.

Lily's doing. Almost as though she knew I would need to be able to move easily. I wondered how many times she'd dressed to do something that made her feel sick inside, creeping through the darkness feeling as though there was no way to win.

More than me, probably.

It only added to my reluctance, the thought that maybe Lily and I could have something in common. That maybe, if things were different, she could be a friend. In that other life where I had no problems and could be the sort of woman Guy might love.

Stop dreaming, Holly girl.

I twisted my hair up, jabbing the lock-pick pins in with more force than strictly necessary, then bent to retrieve the charm from my bag.

The crystals dug into my palm as I stole out of the room, closing the door softly after one last look at the man sleeping there.

Outside, the corridor was deserted, the lamps burning at half strength, so that everything was dim and soft looking. I walked cautiously along it, looking for somewhere private to trigger the charm. I wondered if Simon and Lily shared a room like ours somewhere nearby. Part of me hoped not. If anyone was likely to sleep lightly, it would be a wraith. I couldn't risk any interruptions.

It didn't take too long to find an empty room: what looked like an abandoned office when I peered through the small glass pane in the door. My picks made quick work of the lock and I eased inside. The moon gave me enough light to find my way to a chair. I carefully carried it over to a corner on the same side of the room as the door.

I sat, legs crossed, and stared down at the charm glinting at me in the moonlight. Tears blurred my vision briefly before I wiped them away.

No choice.

I had to do this.

Indeed, now that I was so close to the charm, I had an almost overwhelming urge to listen to what it had to say. The geas at work. There was no other way I could feel so disgusted with myself and so compelled to keep going at the same time. Somewhere in the back on my mind I could hear my father laughing at me.

Get on with it.

I bent my head again, whispered the words to trigger the charm, and began to listen. Simon had carried the charm for nearly two days. A hear-me is activated by voices and I'd keyed this one to him, but a healer has many, many conversations in a day. I gripped the charm tighter, calling my power, going into the half trance I needed to let the charm speak faster to me, almost as though what it carried was dumped directly into my brain. It was an unpleasant sensation, but I gritted my teeth and held the trance, listening for anything that might be useful.

After what seemed like a series of unending medical conversations, interludes with Lily, and Simon talking to himself as he made notes on patients and went about his business—with not a little cursing about his fool brother—I suddenly heard the words.

Blood-locked.

My spine prickled. That was something unusual. Not many blood-locked made it to a hospital. By the time they needed medical care, it was usually too late for their families to drag them away from the Night World. I listened more carefully, but whoever Simon was talking to, the charm hadn't caught all of the conversation. I didn't know whether it was because I hadn't made it properly or whether some other magic wherever he had been was interfering, but I only caught a few words. *Blood-locked* again. And *progress. Patients. Not much longer.*

Lords of *hell.* I had to force myself not to throw the charm across the room in frustration. None of it made any sense. I held the charm closer, increasing the power I fed it as much as I dared. But nothing else came through. Reluctantly, I let the charm go quiet. If I pushed too much power into it now, I could burn it out and not be able to bring it to life again to listen a second time.

My hand curled around it, the glass and metal biting into my palm. It hadn't given me what I wanted. Nothing I could take to Cormen.

Nothing to save Mama and Reggie.

I'd failed.

Part of me was happy. No information meant no victory for my father. But that part was small and nearly drowned by the relentless tide of fear rising in my veins.

I'd failed.

And my family would pay the price.

Chapter Nineteen

HOLLY

I hadn't long crept back to bed, sliding cautiously in next to Guy after finally managing to quell the storm of frustrated tears that erupted after my realization, when the door to our chamber opened once again.

I squeezed my eyes nearly shut, hoping the healer would leave as quickly as the previous one.

Only it wasn't another unknown healer checking on us. It was Simon. I felt the warm hum of his power even before I recognized his profile in the glow from the light in the hall. And more than just his power. Besides the warmth of his magery, there was the familiar chill of the invisibility charm hanging by his hip. Stronger now.

Activated.

I fought to stay still, keeping my breath slow and even.

Where was he going that he needed an invisibility charm ready to hand? He couldn't leave St. Giles, not after he and Lily had claimed haven. I didn't think he'd leave Lily sleeping alone willingly.

Simon's head withdrew and the door shut softly behind him. I lay there for a moment more, heart beating fast.

The Lady had given me another chance. One last opportunity to discover his secret. If I dared to risk leaving Guy a second time.

Last chance. It rang in my head. And suddenly I had to act. Maybe it was the geas seizing my will, but I didn't think any further. I slipped softly out of bed and pulled my clothes on again. Guy stirred once and I froze, but he didn't wake.

I pulled an invisibility charm from my bag, slipping it into a pocket.

After a second's hesitation, I added a hear-me, tucking it inside my boot. I triggered the invisibility charm as I opened the door. Simon's charm left a trail in the air, a tiny fading glow of power that showed me which way he had gone. I hurried silently after him, moving quick and cautious.

St. Giles was quiet this late at night, but it was by no means empty. It wouldn't do to crash into a Fae, or even a human, and reveal myself.

Simon's trail led me to the staircase and then down, as I had half expected, into the tunnels. I didn't see the man himself until I had nearly reached the tunnel with the wards and then I almost ruined everything by skidding to a clumsy halt when I did catch sight of him. He must have deactivated the charm. His sudden appearance surprised me but also made my life somewhat easier.

I moved closer, keeping what I hoped was a safe distance, paying even closer attention to staying silent. He approached the final branch of the tunnels and then, curse it, triggered the charm again, disappearing from view.

But I could still feel it, strong enough to follow. I would have to be careful, beyond careful, to trail behind him when I couldn't see him.

We approached the door in the tunnel and I felt Simon work the wards. This was the tricky point. I had to slip through the door after him without him noticing. Hard but doable. I'd managed such things before and the massive size of the door in question would make it easier. Still, uneasy sweat trickled down my back as the door swung open and I waited a few seconds before making my move, hoping that I wasn't about to ruin everything.

But my luck held and I made it safely through. Holding my breath, I moved a little way down the tunnel, standing as near to the wall as I could to minimize the chance of Simon bumping into me as he walked past. The door closed behind us and I heard his footsteps move past me.

The lamps on the walls bloomed into life and I looked down the tunnel. Another door. Another set of glowing wards.

Damn.

I'd done it once; I could do it again.

I followed Simon, placing each foot with care. A full Fae could walk across the squeakiest of floors and you'd never know. But the blood that meant that I wasn't sickened by the iron we'd passed through also made me more tied to the earth, gave me less of the connection that let the Fae walk so lightly across it. I had to work for my silence, calling on every skill I had learned in all my years of spying.

Muttering silent prayers to the Lady, hoping she'd let the dice continue to fall in my favor a few more feet, a few more steps. One more hour even.

Until I could see what lay beyond the door and fulfill my father's binding. Free myself and my family.

My fingers curled into my palms. Freedom.

A pretty notion. Not one I'd ever known. Not really. Guy said he fought for the humans to stay free, to survive. Who fought for me?

No one.

Stark reality but it didn't stop the guilt curling in my stomach. Whatever secrets lay hidden in these tunnels, the humans obviously valued them. If I turned them over to my father, what was I doing to these people who had taken me in? Who had healed me?

What was I doing to the man whose bed I had stolen from to follow his brother here? My nails bit harder. I couldn't afford guilt.

Inside the second door was a medium-sized room. A desk and a chair sat near one wall, another long table nearby. The table was cluttered with tubes and various things that looked vaguely medical to me.

I frowned, wondering what exactly I was getting myself into. The room was empty, though, and there was yet another warded door in the wall opposite where we were standing.

Simon suddenly blinked into view, stuffing the charm into his pocket. We must be close enough to his destination that he was no longer worried about detection. If I had been able to make a sound, I would've breathed a sigh of relief. At least visible, he was easier to tail.

Simon headed toward the next door and I followed, walking even more cautiously. I didn't want to be detected so late in the game. Even if I had wanted to turn back, I doubted the geas would let me.

Still, something perverse made me stop a moment, test the theory by taking a few steps backward. As expected, the geas bit hard and fast. I clenched my teeth, cursing Cormen in my head, and started after Simon again.

Simon worked the wards on the door and once again, I slipped through behind him, stepping sidewise to press myself against the wall.

This room was larger. What it held made it easy to freeze in place. Row upon row of hospital beds. Filled with mostly still, sleeping bodies, though a few of the occupants moved restlessly, as though they were having a bad dream. Some of the beds were empty. But it wasn't the beds or the rest of the hospital paraphernalia that held me frozen. No, what surprised me was the vampire moving among the rows.

One of the Blood down here? Helping the humans? The shock of it had my blood roaring in my ears, so loud I wondered that Simon didn't hear it.

But he was only human.

Unfortunately for me, the vampire was not.

He lifted his head from where he was bent over one of the beds, then turned toward us. "Simon?" he called. "Who is with you?"

Simon started at the question, turning from the lock he was working to the vampire. "No one," he replied, sounding confused.

The vampire's head swiveled for a moment, then focused unerringly on me. Scars covering his face. Even covered what should have been his eye sockets. Blind.

But lack of sight wouldn't save me. Not when he still had all his other vampire senses.

"You are mistaken," he said. "I hear another heartbeat." Then he moved. Too fast for me to follow. Long fingers grasped my shoulders and fangs flashed in front of my face as he snarled, "Show yourself."

Simon was suddenly beside him, holding a pistol. Around us the room brightened, the gaslights flaring.

The vampire's fingers tightened. He shook me. "Show yourself," he repeated.

I put my hands between us and shoved. "Let *go*." I might as well have shoved a tree trunk.

At my words, Simon's expression darkened. "Holly?" he snapped. "I would appreciate it if you did as Atherton has requested."

So much for prayers. The Lady had chosen to withdraw her favor, it seemed. There seemed to be no way for me to get out of this. Visible or not, I couldn't escape from a vampire's senses and they could keep me down here until my charm wore down. They would know who I was eventually.

"All right," I said. I slid my hand into my pocket and deactivated the charm.

The vampire didn't move, still pressed me into the wall with a grip I couldn't break.

Beside him, Simon looked disgusted. "Guy warned me to watch you."

The words felt like a blow. He had? When? Then common sense prevailed. Of course, Guy had warned him. He was a Templar, dealing with a Night Worlder. This was a reminder that I needed to remember we were both after our own agendas no matter how pleasing he was in bed.

I met Simon's gaze without flinching, but I didn't say anything. The vampire—Atherton—was still far too close for comfort, the gaslights making his pale skin eerily white. His fangs were paler still, glinting at me. He could tear out my throat before I could blink if he chose.

"Would you care to tell me exactly what you're doing here?" Simon continued when it became clear I wasn't going to answer.

I lifted my chin. "How about you tell me what you're doing here first?"

The vampire hissed at me and I flinched.

"Atherton," Simon said sharply. "Let her go. She can't get very far."

No, I couldn't. Nor was I going to try with Simon's pistol pointed with casual ease at my head.

With another snarl, the vampire stepped back.

"Are you armed?" Simon asked.

I shook my head. I hadn't thought to grab even my razor as I'd set out. I hadn't expected to need it. Getting too cocky. Or too driven by the geas into following before I could properly prepare myself.

"Search her," Simon said to Atherton.

I held out my arms and let him pat me down. No point doing

otherwise. To his credit, his hands were coolly professional. He didn't take any liberties.

"Nothing," he reported.

Simon nodded, and then gestured with the gun. "Miss Everton, why don't you take a seat? There are things we need to discuss."

I nodded and did what he asked, choosing a high-backed wooden chair beside the nearest bed. I wasn't looking forward to this next part. I didn't think the geas was going to let me answer any questions, and Lady knew what would happen to me after that.

Simon sat on the bed opposite and the vampire moved behind me, making me wish for eyes in the back of my head.

"So, let's start again," Simon said. "Why are you following me?"

"I—" I tried to answer, but my throat closed over, a wave of nausea gripping me. The geas. My throat burned and tears rose in my eyes. I shook my head at Simon.

He frowned. "Come, now, we have you red-handed. There's no point in trying to protect whoever it is you're working for."

I swallowed and shook my head again, making a slashing gesture across my throat. Let him think I was in fear for my life. Maybe chivalry would make him treat me with some understanding.

"I take it from your silence you are unwilling to name names?" Simon's fingers drummed the barrel of the pistol.

I shook my head again. Not unwilling. Frankly, there was nothing that would please me more than to cast Cormen into the hands of the humans and let them do with him as they would.

I tried again to speak, but as expected, the geas bit again, sending a throb of pain to my head so fierce it made me gasp. "I—" I tried again, not knowing why I was bothering. Other than the fact that I felt more loyalty to the man in front of me and his brother than I did to the man who'd sired me.

Apparently I pushed the geas too far. The next thing I knew I was slumped on the floor, with Simon leaning over me.

"Don't move too fast," he said, sounding exasperated. "You'll faint again."

"I fainted?"

"Yes." His blue eyes narrowed at me. "Though there's no earthly reason why you should have. Which makes me suspect an unearthly one. Lady Bryony is on her way down. Perhaps she'll be able to discern what I cannot."

Lords of hell. That was all I needed. A high Family Fae poking around in my brain. Would she be able to spot the geas? If she did, could she remove it?

Doubtful. Cormen wouldn't have sent me here in the first place if that were possible. Still, a small shred of hope flared within me.

While I waited to find out, I looked carefully at the beds around me but couldn't determine what was wrong with their occupants. Nothing to indicate why they were hidden away down in the bowels of St. Giles, under the care of a sunmage and a vampire. My mind buzzed with possibilities, but I was also more than a little distracted wondering what was going to happen to me next.

Would I be handed over to the human authorities? Sent back to the Night World? What would Cormen do to me? What would he do to my mother? Or Reggie?

I laid my head on my knees for a moment, not wanting Simon to see the despair I felt written on my face.

But I didn't get the luxury of being able to compose myself for too long. The door snapped open again and Bryony appeared.

"What happened?" she said, her gaze fixed on me. I shifted uneasily. The chain around her neck had a dark blue-purple tinge to it. An angry Fae was something to be wary of.

"She followed me down here." Simon plucked the invisibility charm he'd confiscated. "She used this."

The hear-me in my boot felt very hard against my skin. Atherton hadn't discovered it in his search. It shouldn't be noticeable in its dormant state, but who knew what Lady Bryony could or could not sense? I didn't want to give it up.

Bryony took the charm in her hands and studied it a moment. "Nice work," she said, rubbing it between her fingers. "Yours?"

"Yes," I admitted.

Her eyebrows flickered upward. "You could earn a lot of money making charms this strong," she said. "What are you doing sneaking around St. Giles?"

"My charms don't work very well for other people," I admitted. I avoided answering the second part of her question. I really didn't want to faint again.

"I see," said Bryony. "She fainted?" She directed her question at Simon.

He nodded. "Nothing wrong with her that I can see. She was worn out earlier, but we were just talking and then she gasped and keeled over."

Bryony's eyes darkened further. She came closer. "Do you want to tell me what's going on?"

I waited for the grip of the geas, but it didn't come. I nodded my head slowly.

The dark head tilted. "Next question. Can you tell me what's going on?"

I knew the answer to that one. Felt the geas rise within me even as I considered nodding my head again. I stayed motionless, not knowing if even a denial would bring on another fainting fit at this point.

Bryony made a curious humming sound in the back of her throat and then laid a hand on my head. Power swirled around me, invisible but turning the air around me to prickling eddies. Not warm and calm like Simon's. No, this was more like standing on the edge of a summer storm.

"Anything?" Simon asked.

"No. But that's to be expected."

"I don't understand."

"I suspect Miss Everton is under a geas," Bryony said. "The whole point of a geas is that it can't be detected. They've been used for assassinations in the Veiled Court. Not that the assassins usually survive the experience. Those who compel them usually add a command to commit suicide at the end."

I sucked in a breath, ice seizing my stomach. Could Cormen have done that to me? I hadn't heard him say it, but I hadn't understood all the Fae conditions he'd added at the end. Was I going to go through all of this and then kill myself?

Nausea swept through me and I had to close my eyes and breathe slowly not to vomit.

"Though," Bryony added, "that is unusual. It's more likely she was sent to find something out. Would that be right, Miss Everton?"

I risked the merest fraction of a nod. I paid for the small gesture of acknowledgment, though, when my throat tightened painfully, making me fight for air. I bent over, gasping, head throbbing.

"Don't fight it," Bryony said dispassionately. "Do what it wants and it will loosen its grip."

"I was doing what it wants," I said when I could talk again. "They stopped me." I nodded toward Simon and Atherton.

"What do we do now?" Simon asked.

"We should hand her over to the Templars, let them deal with her," Atherton said. His scarred face turned toward me, mouth twisted down. The sense of thunder brewing around Bryony had eased in the last minute or so, but Atherton still seemed poised to strike.

"Doing that entails explaining why we have her down here and exactly what she was up to," Simon said.

My ears pricked up. The Templars didn't know about this place? My stomach coiled. Gods, did Guy not know? What on earth could Simon be doing down here that he would be hiding from his own brother?

I looked at the beds, at all the sleeping patients. Who were still asleep despite the conversation being carried on in their midst. The unease in my stomach deepened. I turned back to the three who were deciding my fate.

Simon rubbed his chin. "Can you undo the geas?" he asked Bryony.

"No. Only the one who laid the geas can do that. Or perhaps the Veiled Queen. If she should choose."

I choked again, this time from surprise. The Veiled Queen could free me? I swallowed. Somehow, doing what Cormen wanted seemed more appealing than begging a favor from the Fae queen.

"Obviously whoever sent her is interested in what you're doing down here," Bryony went on. "You didn't tell her, did you?"

"Nothing was said," Atherton replied.

"I don't know anything," I added, trying to work out how to minimize the damage that had been done. *Talk fast, Holly girl.* "Only that this ward exists."

"That could be enough," Simon added.

"I didn't want to do it," I said, then doubled over, retching again, as pain gripped me.

"Free will or its lack might count for something," Simon said. "But that's not up for me to decide."

I straightened. "Who does get to decide?"

"Given the situation, I think you know the answer to that," Simon said. "I'm turning you over to Guy."

"No!" I sprang to my feet, panic flaring. I couldn't face Guy. Not now.

"Too late for regrets now," Simon said, shaking his head at me.

Bryony suddenly twisted toward the door, a strange expression on her face. "Truer words than you think," she muttered.

Simon turned as well. "What—" His words cut off, his face paling as the door swung inward and Lily and Guy walked through.

Simon moved to block their path. "Lily? What are you—"

"I was looking for Holly," Guy said. "I found Lily down here in the tunnels. She was kind enough to bring me here when I asked where you might be."

"Have you lost your mind?" Simon said to Lily.

Lily didn't blink. Just shook her head, red hair flicking around her shoulders, face set. Even I could tell she didn't mean to be stopped from doing whatever it was she had decided to do. "It's time, Simon."

Simon's eyes flicked from Lily to Guy. "I—"

Lily moved closer to him, put a hand on his cheek. "It's time."

Simon bowed his head, eyes closed. The rest of us were frozen, where we stood, watching the two of them.

"Somebody needs to tell me what the hell is going on," Guy said.

Chapter Twenty

GUY

"I think we'll let Holly explain," Simon said.

I tried to keep my temper as I turned from my brother to Holly. "Holly?"

She stared at me, eyes huge in her face. She looked scared. Scared and guilty. My hand curled around my sword hilt while I waited for an answer. I still wasn't entirely sure where Lily had led me, through the tunnels and two warded iron doors, but it seemed I wasn't going to like it when I found out. Any more than I liked the expression on Holly's face.

My gut twisted. Had she played me? This woman who'd gotten under my skin? Who'd gotten me into her bed and led me into the Night World. I glanced down at the mutilated tattoos on my hands, sickened. Had it all been for nothing? All lies?

Holly folded her hands in her lap, her knuckles white. But she met my gaze. "I was spying on Simon."

I froze. "What?" She was working against my *brother*? My hand tightened until the metal hilt bit into my skin.

"You heard me."

"Why?" It was all I could think to ask, through the fury setting my brain alight.

She shook her head. "I can't answer that."

"Can't?"

"Literally, can't," Bryony said, moving to stand beside Holly. "She's under a geas, Guy."

I blinked. Bryony defending a half-breed? Maybe the world had gone mad tonight. I tried to think through my need to hit something. "Someone is forcing her to spy?" The new scar on my head throbbed. "Is this because of what happened at the Assembly tonight? Is it Ignatius?" Could a Blood Lord compel her through his blood? Please let it be true. I wanted to believe she hadn't been lying to me. That my faith in her had been justified.

"No," Holly said.

Her blunt answer felt like an actual blow. I couldn't breathe. *So much for faith.* I found my voice with an effort. "Then when?"

Holly didn't answer.

Fuck. "This whole time?"

She nodded, not looking at me.

"Fucking—" I swung around to Simon. I wanted answers. Even if I had to pound them out of him. "What was she looking for?"

Simon stiffened. "I don't—"

"Don't lie to me, Simon. If Holly was sent here, then there's something worth finding out. I didn't press you when Lucius came after you, but I'm asking you now. What are you doing that has the Night World up in arms?" I looked around the room, registering the rows of beds with sleeping patients. "What the hell is this place?"

"What makes you think I'm doing anything?" Simon said.

"For someone who isn't doing anything, you're attracting an awful lot of attention lately," I snarled.

Simon folded his arms, not moving. "Are you going to behave if I tell you?"

"That rather depends on what you're going to tell me." I folded my own arms, more to keep my hands away from my sword or my brother's face than anything else.

He was up to something. All this time, through the assassination attempts, through killing Lucius, he'd been up to something. There was a reason he'd been targeted beyond the strength of his magic. One he hadn't told me. The thought of Simon lying to me tore at my guts.

"Sit down," Simon said, gesturing to a chair near one of the beds.

"I prefer to stand."

Simon swore under his breath. He turned to look at Lily. She just nodded at him.

"Any time now," I said as the silence stretched.

"I'm figuring out where to start."

"That seems simple enough. Tell me whatever it is that you're doing that made Lucius want to kill you. People have gone to a lot of trouble for you, Simon. People have been killed because of what you did to Lucius."

Simon's face was grim. "I know."

"So tell me what's so important that you hid it from all of us."

"Bryony knew."

"If you think the fact that you told one of the Fae before you trusted me is going to improve my mood, then think again, little brother."

"All right. I'll tell you. But you have to promise to hear me out."

"No. Don't," Holly said. Her voice sounded strained and she was suddenly gasping, bent over double.

"She's right," Bryony said. "If you tell her, then it may trigger the geas to do Lady knows what."

Holly was still gasping, writhing in place. Part of me wanted to help her. I ignored it. I wasn't going to be fooled twice. "What do you mean?"

"If this is what she was sent to find out about, then once she does, she will most likely be compelled to try and return to whoever cast the geas. She'll fight."

"She can't fight her way past Lily and me."

"Are you willing to cut her down?" Lily said. Her eyes were cool.

I looked at Holly, who stared back, eyes frightened as she gasped for breath. She had betrayed me. But I couldn't kill her. "You can knock her out, can't you?" I said to Simon finally.

"Yes," he replied slowly, looking unhappy at the thought.

"It may be too late already," Bryony said. "She knows about the ward."

"I think we can safely assume whoever is behind this knows Simon's hiding something down here. Otherwise they wouldn't keep coming after him," I said. "Knock her out. We'll deal with her afterward."

I watched as Simon touched Holly's head and the green eyes

slid shut. She slumped over in the chair. Simon lifted her and laid her on an empty bed.

I made myself look away. Ignored the fool part of me that wanted to make sure she wasn't hurt, lying there so still. Simon wouldn't have hurt her. And even if he had, I shouldn't care. "Talk," I said when Simon came back to us.

"You still have to promise to hear me out," Simon said stubbornly.

"I'm not in a promising type mood." I heard the drawl in my voice. Involuntary this time. My grip on my temper was slipping. I gritted my teeth.

Simon let out a breath. "A few years ago I was coming to the hospital, very late. I'd been sent for. I was passing that alley near the east gate and I heard something." He paused, frowned as though trying to find the right words.

"When I went to look, I found someone who'd been wounded. Burned very badly. He'd lost his sight. So I took him in."

I didn't like his tone. Or the lack of information. "Wounded by who?" I asked.

"Lucius, as it turns out."

I felt my hands curl again, reaching for my sword. I couldn't think of many people who'd be likely to survive torture by Lucius. No, that would take more than human strength. "Are you telling me you rescued a vampire?" I heard my voice rasp, hoping my guess wasn't true.

Simon nodded. "Yes. He was hurt. It's my job."

Hell's fucking balls. For a moment the room seemed to close in on me. A Blood. He'd rescued one of those who'd killed our sister. Only my idiot brother would take in a wounded Blood. One who'd escaped from Lucius' tender mercies.

All because of his fucking healer oaths. I tried to remember that those oaths were a good thing. And that to Simon they were as serious as the ones I'd sworn to the order. The ones everybody thought I'd forsaken to chase after Holly. Who had been lying to me all this time.

Don't think about her. I couldn't afford to think about her or the fact that she'd left my bed to spy on Simon. One betrayal at a time. "So this patient is who they're after?"

Simon squared his shoulders. "No."

Perfect. There was more. "Go on."

"I knew that Atherton—that's his name, Atherton Carstairs—would be safer if nobody knew he was in the hospital. So I brought him down here. These are the old quarantine wards that aren't used anymore."

"Without anyone knowing?"

"Initially. But as he recovered and we started talking, I had to tell Bryony."

"Why?" What was there to discuss with a Blood? "Why didn't you send him away from the City?"

"Because he's on our side," Simon said.

I almost choked. "Our side?"

"He told me that there were those among the Blood who didn't agree with Lucius and the way he was running things. That they wanted change. Wanted a more peaceful relationship."

A bark of laughter escaped me. "Peace? With the Blood? I doubt it. Unless they want us peacefully subdued. We're food to them, Simon."

"Not to all of them."

"Don't fool yourself. You have more reason than most to know what they do to humans."

"Not all of us are that way."

I whirled, my sword out of its sheath before I could stop myself. The vampire pushed himself away from the wall. How the hell had I not seen him? I raised the sword, prepared to lunge.

"Guy!" Lily caught my arm, her fingers iron against my skin. "Stop. Simon's right. Atherton is on our side."

"None of them are on our side." I lowered my sword, knowing that Lily and Simon were both stupid enough to try and get in my way if I attacked the vampire.

The vampire came closer, hands raised in a gesture of goodwill. As the light moved across his face, I saw the scars that covered his skin, the empty places where his eyes should have been. Simon hadn't been exaggerating the part about him being badly hurt.

"We do not all want to live in strife," Atherton said. "Don't forget we were human once too. We do not need to kill to feed."

"Plenty of you do."

"Many of us don't."

"No," I said, hands curling tighter around the sword. "You just feed them your blood so they die anyway."

Lily's hand gripped my arm tighter. "Atherton is telling the truth, Guy. I know. I lived in the Blood Court, remember? Not all the Blood treat humans badly."

I looked down, staring into her gray eyes. "How can you say that, after what Lucius did to you?"

"Some of them choose to be different. You once told me that it's the choices we make that are important, isn't that right? Not who or what we might be but how we behave?" Lily said softly.

I pressed my lips together. I had told her exactly that. But the Blood were not the same. They were killers. Preying on the stupidity of humans. I looked from Lily to Simon. My brother. Who had hidden a vampire down here all this time. One of the race that had killed our sister.

Simon seemed to know what I was thinking. He shook his head at me. "Atherton is different. And if he can be, then I have to believe that others can be too."

Madness. "You always were an idealistic fool," I ground out. But Simon hadn't finished telling me the story. Lily and Bryony were watching him expectantly. I needed the rest of the story. Needed to know how deep a hole my fool brother had dug for us all. "What happened next?"

"Atherton healed. I told Bryony he was down here. He claimed haven, so Bryony let me reinforce the doors and the wards so no one else would find out."

Haven laws. Sometimes I thought them one of the most ridiculous parts of the treaty. They meant that anyone could claim sanctuary, could escape the reach of the law or the retribution of those they'd sinned against if they were willing to stay within the walls of Haven indefinitely.

For some they were a true refuge, but there were those who didn't deserve a bolt-hole. I didn't know how Simon put up with it, sheltering some of those who must have claimed haven here. Of course, the cathedral and the Brother House were Havens too, but as far as I knew no Blood or Beast Kind had ever sought haven at either place. We only attracted humans.

"So you built a nice little Blood nest for your tame vampire," I snarled. This story was not going to end anywhere good. I could tell that much from the bleak look in Simon's eyes as he spoke to me. "Then what?"

"About six months later, we had a young man brought into the hospital by his family. They'd taken him out of the warrens.

Bought him actually, from one of the Blood who was tired of him."

"Blood-locked?" I asked, stomach twisting. The locked were beyond saving. The addiction was fatal. Nothing could change that. Those who made the choice—Edwina amongst them—to enter the Night World understood that risk. They chose to pay the price. The way it should be. God gave us free will. To be good, to live a right life was a choice. It was hard work. And sacrifice.

"Yes. Fairly far gone. Not eating. He would have died in days."

"Would have?" I questioned. My guts twisted. I really didn't like where this was going. "Simon, what in hell's name did you do?"

"I thought there was a chance to heal him," Simon said, eyes flashing at me. "To find a cure."

"There is no cure for blood-locking," I snarled.

"Not yet." Simon gestured around the room. "But look around, Guy."

I gazed around the room, at all the beds filled with sleeping patients. Who slept on, despite the argument raging around them. An unnatural sleep. "Simon, what did you do?" Please, God, let it not be what I was beginning to suspect. A cure for something that gave the Blood rights over the humans who fell under their sway. That could throw the whole balance of power in the City into mayhem. No wonder Lucius had wanted Simon dead.

Simon's eyes blazed. "I helped them. All these people. They're blood-locked. But we've kept them alive with Atherton's blood. And when Lucius died, some of them woke up. We're almost ready to send them back to their families. We're on the right track."

It was all I could do to stand still, not to go over and shake him as I longed to do. "But why?"

"What else am I supposed to do, Guy? I'm a healer. Blood-locking kills hundreds of humans. It's one of the few things we can't fix. Of course, I want to find a cure. I don't want anyone else to suffer what we did."

"You think a cure will stop the suffering?" I said incredulously.

"Of course."

"You *idiot*."

Simon took a step toward me, fists clenched. "For fuck's sake, Guy, could you get off your high moral horse for once in your life? How on earth can a cure be anything but a good thing?"

"Because," I ground out, "it makes it easier for people to choose the Night World. What will keep them away if they don't have to fear blood-locking?"

"Common sense," Simon shouted. "People aren't crazy, Guy."

"No? Then why do so many of them become addicted in the first place? I promise you, for each person who has actually done it, there are others who are curious. Who would try a little Night World dabbling if they didn't think the cost was too high. And you want to make it so there's no cost at all." I almost spat the words at him. Hell's fucking *balls*. I'd known we had different views on the Blood, but I'd never thought my own brother would be so stupid.

"But they'll be able to come back," Simon protested. "They won't die. They won't be lost."

"And how do you think the Blood will react to that?" I roared. "Why do you think they are trying to kill you? They'll cause all sorts of havoc in the negotiations if this gets out. We'll have to make all sorts of concessions to get them to agree to renegotiate any of the laws around the blood-locked. They'll hold us for bloody ransom."

And that wasn't all they could do.

The pieces of it all suddenly came together in my head. Ignatius. Cormen—whoever the hell he was—and Ignatius. And the Beasts. Cormen was Fae. Why would a Fae be helping Ignatius, exactly?

It always came down to fucking power. "And they might do fucking worse than that."

Lily spoke first. "What do you mean?"

I looked at Lady Bryony, as all the treaty law and Fae law I'd ever had drummed into me by the order swirled in my head. "Do any of the Fae apart from you know about Simon?"

"Not officially," Bryony said. "Chrysanthe—well, she got herself killed but likely she was working for Lucius. We don't know how he recruited her. We couldn't find anyone else working for him. But there could be others who know. Here or in Summerdale."

"But you don't know for sure?" I asked. "No one from the court knows?"

"We spoke to the Speaker for the Veil about Lucius, after he tried to kill me," Simon said. "But he doesn't know about this."

"As far as we know," Bryony added softly. The chain around her neck was slowly turning gray. She was worried.

"But you're High Family," I said.

"Yes." Bryony's chain flickered as though a spark had run through it, whirling through multiple colors before returning to purple.

"Then it could be enough that you know. The queen is taken under your laws to know what her nobles know, isn't that right?"

"Veil's eyes," Bryony breathed, eyes widening. "I hadn't thought of that."

"Hadn't thought of what?" Simon said. "Someone care to explain for the rest of us?"

"Under Fae law," Bryony said, "the queen is assumed to be responsible for the actions of the members of the Veiled Court—the High Families."

"How does that work?" Simon asked. "I thought the queen administered justice in the Veiled World."

"She does. If those crimes only impact the Veiled World, then those responsible are punished. But if there's a treaty violation, it lies at her feet. She's supposed to control the court, after all," Bryony said.

"Holly"—I forced myself not to look over to where she lay"—and I were working together. I wanted to know who was ordering the Beast attacks on the order." I flexed my hands, staring at the tattoos I'd defiled because I'd trusted Holly. "And she wanted to find her mother. Who'd been taken by a Fae."

"The one who cast the geas?" Bryony asked.

"That seems a safe assumption."

"Anyway, to cut a long story short, it all comes back to Ignatius Grey. Who is suddenly in funds. Funds enough to buy himself a pack of young Beasts to carry out ambushes perhaps."

"What does that have to do with me?" Simon asked.

"I suspect the ambushes are a distraction, a way to scatter our attention," I said. "They wanted the Templars to be drawn thin. And most likely, one of the reasons for that is to keep us away from St. Giles. So that they could get to you. To this—" I waved my hand at the room.

"I still don't understand," Simon said.

"We thought Lucius wanted you dead," I said. "And maybe he did. Because if you were dead, this place would be far less protected. And if I were Lucius and I wanted to gain power, then I would want to destabilize the treaties. To do that, the best way would be to go after those who hold the balance of power."

"The Fae," Simon. "But what—"

"Oh, shit," Lily said beside me. "They want to try and take out the queen."

Everyone started talking at once, making it impossible to decipher any of it. "Shut up!" I said, trying to cut through the chaos.

It worked.

"Good." I rubbed my head for a moment, where the ache seemed to start at the new scar on my forehead and carve a path like a blade through to the base of my skull. "Bryony, am I right?"

Bryony's eyes were stormy, but she nodded, one hand toying with her chain. I'd never seen her look rattled before.

"Bryony?" I prompted.

"The Veiled Queen is the one who forged the treaties," Bryony said. "She brokered the first deals with the humans and the Beasts and the Blood after the Templar Wars. She was the one who decided there should be peace in the first place. She dragged the Fae with her. Much like the Blood, we do not all agree. There are those in the court who might prefer a less constrained existence. But as long as the queen holds the throne, she will defend the treaty."

"And how do you bring down the Fae queen?" I asked.

"If there was proof that she knew about a treaty violation—a serious one—and did nothing, then enough of the court might be swayed to act to remove her. If someone was already laying the groundwork—whispering in the ears of those who are unhappy with her rule—it might work."

"And if Bryony knows. About Simon. About this. Even about me. Plus the Speaker for the Veil has reason to suspect. Either of those could be used to argue that the queen knew."

"And that's enough for the court to remove her?" Atherton asked.

Bryony shrugged. "Maybe not. It's likely that most of the court would want proof of what Simon has been doing. We Fae can't lie, but the rest of you can. There would have to be evidence when so many other races are involved. That's why they need to get to Simon. If they had him—or Atherton—that may be enough to make someone bold enough to try and stage a coup perhaps. Who knows?"

"Someone might be bold if they had the backing of the Blood Lord," Atherton said. "Didn't I hear you mention Ignatius Grey? He has ambition, that one. And lack of sense enough to attempt something this reckless. He wants to be the next Lucius. An offer of assistance from some of the Fae would be very appealing if he thought that what they offered would increase his chances of becoming Lord. And he might be in the position to know some of what Lucius knew. Or suspect it, at least. Enough to be curious about Simon and find allies to help him turn the situation to his best advantage."

An unholy alliance between the most ambitious of the Blood and those of the Fae who chafed under the treaty. Our worst nightmare.

"What we're doing isn't wrong," Simon said. "There's no treaty law against finding a cure for blood-locking."

"Because nobody ever thought somebody would try it," I said. "The law gives the Blood the right to feed amongst the Nightseekers and the right to do what they will with the locked. That's not something they will want to give up. They will absolutely try and strike down a cure as a violation of their rights. If they don't do something worse."

"Such as?" Simon growled.

"If someone like Ignatius becomes Blood Lord, then this would give him the perfect way to break the treaty. Surely you can see that?" He *must* have thought about the implications of what he was doing? Or had he truly let his healer instincts blind him to the consequences?

"The question, then," Lily said, "is how do we stop a plot against the queen and stop Ignatius gaining control over the Blood?"

"We can't go after Ignatius directly," I said. "Not so close to the treaties. Holly has evidence linking Henri Favreau to Ignatius, but we'd need more than that to prove he's behind the ambushes. We have no real proof yet."

"You need the one who set the geas," Bryony said. "He has to be involved. Do you know who it is?"

"If it's the one who has her mother and her sister, then his name is Cormen. That's all I know."

Bryony's eyes narrowed. She turned and crossed to Holly. Bending to the bed, she jerked Holly's pendant free from beneath her shirt. The light hit the gems, sparking black and blue. Bryony studied the jewels with the air of someone deciphering a code.

"Sa'Inviel," she said. She looked down at Holly. "She must be Cormen sa'Inviel'astar's get. These stones are sa'Inviel colors. Or closer to those than any other. And Cormen is not a common name among us."

"You know him?" I asked.

Bryony nodded. "The sa'Inviel are a closemouthed clan. Traditional. I would not have picked them to be involved in this, but the 'astar line is a minor one, without real power. Cormen has always thought himself better than those around him."

"We have to stop them," Simon said.

I scowled at him. "We? You've done enough damage for now, Simon."

He winced. "I'm not letting you charge off alone."

"You don't have any say in that," I said.

"You're not—"

"Guy's right," Bryony said. "Simon can't leave St. Giles. Nor can Lily. It's too dangerous. Plus they will only complicate things where you have to go."

"And where's that?" I asked, though I already knew the answer.

"You and Holly have to go to Summerdale. You have to find Cormen and bring him before the queen."

Chapter Twenty-one

GUY
✠

"No!" The denial rose in my throat automatically. "I am not going to take her. She can't be trusted."

Bryony shook her head. "You need her. She can lead you straight to Cormen."

"How?"

An eloquent Fae shrug. "We wake her up. We tell her what we just told you. And her geas will lead you home."

"Why, in the name of all that is holy, would you tell her what our enemies want to know?"

"There's no choice, Guy." Bryony's chain flashed red. "I cannot go into Summerdale. If I am questioned, I can't lie. If you go alone, you may not even be admitted. Even if you were, you have no chance of finding a Fae who doesn't want to be found on your own."

"She's a spy, a Night World spy. She was willing to betray Simon."

"She was acting under a geas," Lily said.

"Is that an excuse?"

Lily's expression turned steely. "I think I know rather more than you about being forced to act against your will. You said this man has her family. Are you going to blame her for doing exactly what you would do in her place? For trying to save the ones she loves?"

"She lied," I said flatly. Endangered my family. Took me to her bed, smiling sweetly. It was all a lie.

"Ah," Lily said. She shook her head at me. "So merciless."

"Bryony is right," Simon said. "You need her—"

I opened my mouth and he held up a hand.

"You don't have to trust her, but you do need her."

"Says the man who is causing all this trouble in the first place." My head pounded. I felt as if I had walked into a nightmare. Holly had betrayed me. Simon was working with a vampire. And they wanted me to just go on as though nothing were wrong. My hands curled. I wanted to hit something. Anything.

"You swore oaths to protect the City," Bryony said. "Will you forsake them now? Become the forsworn knight everyone believes you to be?"

My fists curled tighter, tighter than the knots in my stomach. No. I would hold to my oaths. That much I had left to me. But I didn't have to like it. "I will do my duty. Wake her up."

HOLLY

I stayed silent while they explained the plan to me. They would tell me Simon's secret so that the geas would lead me to Cormen. Guy would come with me. Bryony and Lily and Simon gathered around me, faces earnest. Guy was halfway across the room, back turned.

It was perfectly clear that he was not pleased with this development. I, on the other hand, felt relief. Here was a way to get to Cormen and to bring him down.

"I'll help you," I said. "But I want my mother and Reggie."

"You're hardly in a position to bargain," Bryony said. Of the three of them, her manner was coolest. Simon was carefully professional. Lily was hard to read, but I thought I saw a hint of sympathy in her clear gray eyes. She'd been a slave once. Maybe she understood.

"We had a deal, Guy and I," I said.

He turned at that. "You lied to me."

I wanted to flinch away from the anger in his eyes. Instead, I lifted my chin. If I had lost any chance with him and if I was going to attempt this madness, then I deserved something at least. "I kept my end of the bargain. I found out about Henri and Ignatius for you. You swore to help me."

Guy turned away again.

Simon started to move, but Lily put a hand on his arm. "I'll do it." She walked over to Guy, said something in low tones. Guy shook his head. Lily spoke again.

Guy turned back to me, face stone. "Very well. Your mother and Regina will be safe if it is in my power to see it so." He spun away again and this time walked out of the room. The door to the outer chamber swung shut behind him with a horribly final sound. Like the cover of a crypt sliding home. Severing all light and air. Severing anything that had been between us.

Stupid. I'd known all along that he could only walk away from me eventually.

If he could be stone, then so could I.

"I'm ready," I said to Simon. "Tell me what Cormen wants to know."

"Could you at least look at me?" I held on to the grab strap as the autocab rattled around a corner and waited to see if Guy would finally respond. He'd yet to address me directly since we'd left the ward. He hadn't listened when I'd tried to explain. To apologize. I needed him to hear me.

Slowly, his head turned and ice blue rage focused on my face.

I gripped the strap more tightly to resist the urge to flinch. He was angry. I couldn't fault him for that. But I wasn't going to cower to make him feel better.

"If you can't talk to me, then this isn't going to work," I said, keeping my tone light, as if we were discussing nothing more complex than the weather. Which was hot. The sun burned high and fierce, turning the sky to a white-blue shimmer. Sweat dampened my prim white cotton shirt and long skirt. The sunlight only added to the ache in my head caused by too little sleep and fear and guilt.

"I'll talk when it's necessary."

The cab jolted again. Unlike me, Guy simply braced himself with a hand against the door. The beasts on his hands were very black.

"It's necessary now," I said. "We have to plan what we're going to do."

"We have a plan. We're going to Summerdale. We're going to find Cormen and bring him to the queen. Make him confess his alliance with Ignatius. Then this will be all over and done with. And I won't have to see you ever again."

I flinched then, cheeks reddening as though he'd slapped me. There. He'd said it. The words I'd known were coming. I clenched my fingers tighter still, willed the bite of the hardened leather to keep the tears at bay. Guy's face was perfectly blank, his eyes looking through me rather than at me.

"I can go to Summerdale alone," I said. "You don't have to come." Even now, I could feel the geas tugging at me. West. Toward the Veiled Court. Toward a distant spark I assumed was my father. I could find him alone, if I could get myself admitted to the Veiled World. I didn't rate my chances of rescuing my mother and Reggie very highly without Guy, but I didn't want him there if he wasn't on my side. At least for as long as it took to accomplish our task.

"Yes, I do. If I don't, then you'll run straight to Cormen and tell him what he wants to know."

I sucked in a breath. He was angry. Angry with me, angry with Simon judging by the snarled interaction I'd witnessed between them back at St. Giles.

Angry with the whole hells-damned world. I kept telling myself maybe he would see reason eventually, but as each word he said to me turned more barbed, cutting deeper, I struggled to believe my own lies.

But I couldn't afford pain and heartbreak right now. So instead I used something else. My own anger. At Cormen. At Simon. At the stupid, stubborn man beside me who could see nothing but black-and-white and didn't care enough about me to give me even the slightest chance to explain. "You know," I said, letting my own voice turn icy, "I was doing something I was forced to do. And if your brother hadn't—"

"We're here." Guy cut me off with a gesture. He was out of the cab almost before it came to a complete halt. I climbed out on the other side. I didn't think Guy would be coming around to assist me. I doubted he'd lift a finger to do anything beyond what he considered to be his duty for me ever again.

Don't think. I lifted my chin and smoothed my skirts while Guy paid the driver, pretending it was the glare of the sun making my eyes water.

When my vision cleared, I took in the sight before me. The Guild of Metalmages was a complex of redbrick buildings, surrounded by an ornate wrought-metal fence. It was said that each class of students added another layer of enchantment and decoration to the metalwork standing between the guild and the rest of the citizens of Silversdown.

I could believe it. The fence was a dense screen of curling and twisted metal. Leaves and flourishes and curlicues chased themselves over and around and between the spiked metal supports, looking like the product of the union between a lace maker and a possessed blacksmith.

But there was no time to admire the artistry of the work. Guy concluded his business with the driver and then marched past me, headed for the main gate.

No rest for the wicked, it seemed.

GUY
✠

The gate guard recognized me and waved us through. I kept walking, not stopping to see whether Holly still followed me. I didn't want to see her. Didn't want to talk to her.

Her or Simon, for that matter. But I'd set out to stop those who wanted to hurt my brother, and I would see that task through. Even if I didn't agree with what he was doing. He had, in a way, betrayed me.

That part made me feel as sick as I did when I thought about Holly. How I'd been taken in by big eyes and easy kisses. *Fool.*

But apparently being a fool didn't stop just because you found out you were a fool. Because every time Holly tried to reach out to me, tried to apologize, I couldn't completely ignore her. It hurt me when I hurt her, cutting her off. Shutting her out.

She hid her pain well, but I still felt it. Or was that my own?

Fool.

We had to wait in the main hall as they sent for Saskia. She appeared quickly enough, moving with authority through the milling students and mages and visitors.

She looked at home here. My little sister fitted in with the other mages, her hair pulled back smooth against her head and soot smudging one cheek and several places on her plain gray dress. Certain of her power. I only hoped hers wasn't going to lead her into the same sort of idiocy as Simon's. But that was a discussion for another time.

"Guy?" She stood on tiptoe to kiss my cheek. "What are you doing here?" Her eyes were curious as they turned in Holly's direction. "Miss Everton."

"Is there somewhere we can talk privately?" I asked before they could get too far into polite female chitchat. We didn't have a lot of time. So far, Holly was resisting the geas, possibly because we were moving toward Summerdale, but Bryony had said that the longer we took, the more likely she would lose control and run.

That only lifted Saskia's eyebrows higher, but she nodded at me. "My workshop." We followed her through the building and out the other side to a set of small one-storied structures set around the garden beyond. Each of them stood slightly apart from its fellows . . . probably to minimize the risk of fire spreading in the case of student accidents. Metalmagery gone awry could produce some spectacular results.

Saskia stopped at the last of the squat little buildings and unlocked the heavy metal door.

I followed her into the workshop. I had no idea what most of the apparatus scattered around the long wooden counters did: strange glass tubes and metal implements, piles of leather-bound notebooks, and two heavy copper sinks. The air smelled of smoke and steam and flames with an acrid tang of chemicals.

"We need weapons. For Summerdale. No iron or anything else that the Fae wouldn't permit," I said when Saskia closed the door.

Saskia's eyes narrowed. "I seem to remember you having a fairly impressive arsenal of your own." She crossed the room and unlocked a chest under one of the windows. She lifted the lid but then turned back to me. "What exactly is this about, Guy?"

"You don't need to know," I said. "Weapons, Sass."

She made a disgusted noise. "I'm getting very tired of you and Simon treating me as though I'm made out of glass, Guy. I'm a metalmage, I'm not helpless. You have the masters here riled up enough that I can't go anywhere without permission, and while I appreciate the concern, I don't want to be left in the dark any longer. Ignorance is more dangerous than knowing what I'm up against."

I scowled at her. "You don't—"

"If you say you don't need to know, then I will hurt you," Saskia gritted. "Tell me what's going on."

"We're in kind of a hurry."

"Then talk fast." She slammed the lid of the chest down, and then sat herself on it. Clearly we weren't getting anything until she was happy.

"It's Templar business," I said shortly, hoping it would shut her up.

Saskia's lips pressed together. "Guy—"

"I can't tell you. Please, Sass. Don't argue."

Her hand stole up to the 'prentice chain at her neck. "Are you just going to Summerdale, or into the court?"

"We may go to court," Holly said. I shot her a look, but she ignored me.

"They might not let you take anything with you," Saskia said.

"We know that," I said. "But we need to try. So we need weapons. No iron. A sword for me. A dagger perhaps for Holly."

"I can use a sword," Holly interjected.

"I might have something your size," Saskia said. "Do you want guns as well?"

"Yes," Holly said.

Saskia rummaged in the chest, produced two pistols. "Here, these are silver and a few other things. They work well enough."

I took the pistols from her before Holly could, felt their weight. Tucked them both into my belt for now. I would give Holly a weapon when I had to. Not before. Not while the geas might still take hold of her. "Swords?"

Saskia bent again. "You're spoiling my surprise, you know," she muttered from the depths of the chest. "I was going to give you this for Hallows' Night. But I guess you need it now." She stood back again, holding a sheathed sword in both hands. "I haven't finished the decorations, but it should still be balanced." She smiled a little lopsidedly at me. "I meant it to be more ceremonial."

I took the sword from her. "Don't worry about me," I said, and drew the sword from the sheath. It was beautiful. The blade glinted a strange pale silvery gold and the hilt was black, padded with leather. I lifted it. It felt true in my hand. Made for me.

"You've been talking to Williams," I said to Saskia as I examined the sword more closely, wondering how she had charmed my preferences out of the closemouthed Templar armorer.

"I was hardly going to guess how you preferred your blades. I wanted it to be a good sword even if you weren't meant to use it." She smiled again, then went back to the chest, coming up with a smaller sword this time.

I took it before she could pass it to Holly. "What are they made from?"

Saskia shook her head. "Trade secret." She grinned at me. "Perhaps not quite as strong as steel, but I'm getting closer. They'll do the job unless you try and chop down a tree or something."

I was hoping we wouldn't have to use them at all. But I didn't like our chances.

HOLLY

The autocab took us to a livery stable next. As Guy handed me silently up onto the gig that appeared, I felt as though I were going to my own funeral.

We drove out of the City in silence and Guy pointed the horses west. It didn't look alarming. No, Summerdale looked much the same as the hills to the east of the City. Except perhaps for the denseness of the forest bordering those hills. But apart from that, the ground above the Veiled Court appeared to be rolling green hills.

Which was true to a point. They were rolling green hills, peaceful and serene.

Because the Fae didn't live on the hills, they lived under them. Or perhaps not even under them. Because from all I'd heard, the geography of the Veiled World bore little resemblance to caves underground. The hills were merely a gateway to their realm.

I didn't understand it, but I did know I felt dread when I looked at them. Dread and an ever-increasing pull from the geas.

I clenched my hands into the leather of the gig's seat. I was doing what it wanted. I would control myself. To bring Cormen down, I would fight.

Guy glanced at me. "Too late for second thoughts."

"The Fae are dangerous," I said.

Guy slowed the horses to turn through the gate. "I thought the Fae courts were meant to be full of beauty."

I fixed my eyes on the road ahead. In this distance, an airy-looking marble tower rose from the base of one of the hills. The Gate. The tower that guarded the entrance to the Veiled World. There was no other way to enter if you weren't Fae. I'd hoped never to come here. "More glamour and intrigue and danger. If you think the Night World is bad . . ." I shivered, wishing I'd worn something warmer.

"The Fae aren't the same as the Blood," Guy said. "They don't turn people. Or blood-lock them." The distaste in the last word made me wince.

I still didn't know exactly what had happened to him to make him hate the Blood so much. Simon had said something about not wanting anyone else to lose someone as they had done, so I had to assume it was tied up with how their sister had died. But I wasn't about to raise the subject with Guy when he was riding a knife's edge just keeping his temper under control.

"The Fae in the City abide by its rules," I said. "But the Fae who spend their lives in the Veiled World? They have different rules there. And if you enter, then you are agreeing to be bound by them."

His expression suggested he wasn't going to be agreeing to anything.

I stifled a sigh. Guy was used to winning his battles with strength and steel. Blood and Beasts could be cut down, driven back. Their magics were specific and limited. I doubt he had any idea of what a Fae Lord or Lady was truly capable of.

We were risking our lives coming here.

If Cormen thought he was about to be exposed, then he wouldn't hesitate to kill me. I was certain of that. Just by stepping into the Veiled World, I was putting myself more under his power. Half-breeds could be claimed as property and had virtually no rights here. If it actually got to the point where I had to tell him what I had learned, then only Guy could save me.

More than Mama's and Reggie's lives were riding on this now. Cormen and Ignatius and those who sided with them could bring the City burning to the ground. With the treaties broken, unrest and war could spread like wildfire throughout the world. And who knew if any humans would be left standing in the end? Or any half-breeds.

But I didn't know how to explain to Guy the parts of this that he didn't already know. Didn't know how to ask him to help me think of a better way. Not when he looked at me so coldly.

So I fell silent again and watched the white tower grow larger as we traveled toward it.

Chapter Twenty-two

HOLLY

Guy's hand was cool around mine as he handed me down from the gig. He let go of me once I reached the ground, pale eyes gazing beyond me to the Gate in front of us.

Up close it was daunting, its walls rising white to tower above us, unbroken by windows. There was one dark door, twice as tall as Guy. The whole place gave off an icy chill of Fae magics.

I wanted to ask Guy if it would be all right. If he was as scared as I was.

But it was too late for that.

The geas was mostly quiet. I still felt the distant spark and the tug toward it, but obviously I was moving in the right direction.

"Ladies first," Guy said, jerking his head toward the tower.

I stared at it for a minute longer. The Gate. Inside those walls was the way to the Veiled World. The way to Cormen. To Mama and Reggie.

I should be sprinting toward the doors, but I also knew that beyond that door lay the end of anything between Guy and me.

A deep price but one I had brought upon myself. I took a breath and walked toward the tower.

*   *   *

My pendant won us admittance through the first door and we were ushered into a round marble chamber, relieved of our weapons, and given tea. Neither of us drank.

I didn't trust myself to be able to swallow. I had agreed to the humans' plan, but now that we were here, my doubts were growing. If we actually went to Cormen, then we would be at a severe disadvantage. I would have to tell him Simon's secret. Guy was relying, as far as I could tell, on being able to overpower him and get him to the queen.

I gathered Bryony had provided some sort of charm to facilitate that part, but that didn't change the fact that Cormen would be in possession of Simon's secret. Or that he could be somewhere well protected.

Surely there was another way? One I hadn't thought of. Something teased the edge of my memory . . . something my father had told me once when I'd been small and he'd entertained me with tales of the wonders of the court. But no, it refused to emerge.

Eventually one of the three doors in the walls opened and a Fae woman came toward us. She wore layers of white and silver, her robes flowing around her like a snowstorm. Her hair was silver too. True silver. I rose and curtseyed. Guy followed my lead and bowed.

"I am the Seneschal," she said, looking at us with disdain. "What business do you bring to the Veiled Court?"

"We seek Cormen sa'Inviel'astar," Guy said before I could speak.

"Has he summoned you?"

"Yes," Guy said.

The Seneschal still looked skeptical. She glanced back over her shoulder toward the door.

A *door*. Memory suddenly cooperated.

"We seek the queen," I blurted.

Guy's mouth opened. "What—"

"Be quiet, Guy." I looked only at the Seneschal. "We seek the queen."

"The Veiled Queen does not speak to *hai'salai*." The Seneschal's tone was icy.

"Holly—" Guy said.

"No." The Seneschal cut him off with a gesture. "If you wish to speak, *hai'salai*, you may appeal to your . . . connections. Perhaps one of them will speak for you."

I straightened, knowing what I had to do, preparing myself for what reaction the geas might have. "No. I do not need anyone to speak for me. I will see the queen. I choose the Door."

The Seneschal blinked. "You—"

"Yes," I said firmly. "Me. Or rather, we. We have that right, don't we? To win an audience?"

The silver head bowed. "Yes. The right exists. You have chosen. Very well." She clapped her hands suddenly. "It is late. You will be shown to a supplicant's chamber. The trial will start at sunrise."

Late? Sunrise? When we'd walked into the tower, it had been a little past noon. Only a few minutes had passed since then. Or had they?

Damned Fae magic. Time moved differently under the hills. I should have remembered that. Perhaps it did in the Gate too. Without windows, there was no way of telling.

"What the hell are you doing? What the hell is the Door?" Guy demanded as the door to our chamber shut behind us.

We'd been escorted here by a stony-faced Fae man who'd instructed us curtly to bathe before sunrise and don the white Fae robes he gave us before he left.

"A way for us to get what we came for," I said, still not quite believing what I'd done. I prowled around the room, still feeling the tug of the geas. So far it hadn't wakened any further. Maybe my gamble had paid off.

The room was not large enough for me to be able to prowl too far. There was one large bed, two chairs, and a table. All beautifully carved from gleaming dark wood. Rich blue tapestries lined the walls, and darker shades were echoed in the rugs. The effect against the marble walls was cold rather than welcoming.

"The plan was to get to Cormen," Guy said. "So give me one good reason why I should do this instead?"

"The Door is a loophole," I said.

His eyes narrowed. "That's hardly an explanation."

I sighed. "Guy, if I go to Cormen, then I'll have to tell him Simon's secret. The geas will make sure of that. But the Door is a greater magic. It's the queen's magic. If you choose the Door, then you are bound to that choice. These chambers are built to stop supplicants from changing their minds. The geas won't be able stop me." Cormen's tales of the Door had been clear on the powers of the Door and the fact that you couldn't change your mind.

"Are you sure about that?"

"So far I'm still standing." Truth be told, I hadn't been sure. But I had no urge to throw open the door and run to my father immediately. My gamble seemed to have paid off.

"That still doesn't explain the Door."

"The queen can refuse an audience. But she can't refuse the right to stand before her."

"I don't understand."

I barely understood it myself. But it was one of the parts of Fae lore that Cormen had taught me. Long ago when I was small and amusing and he was still playing the loving father. When I had believed that one day I might join him there.

Well, now I would. But hardly in the way I'd imagined back then. I doubted he'd imagined it either. I hoped he would enjoy it even less than I would.

I walked to the window, gestured out at the night sky. "The land under the hills, the Veiled World and the court, are . . . alive. The Fae magic is tied to it. It's what makes it so dangerous. The landscapes shift to the will of the Fae, but they also shift on their own."

"I know that much. That's why it's night here but still day back in the City."

"Yes. The land has a mind of its own. And Fae lore says that if the land will let you get to the queen, she cannot turn you away. She has to hear what you have to say."

"I see." Guy's voice was tight. "And the Door?"

"The Door, supposedly, is a path directly to the queen's throne. But the journey is different for everyone. And not everyone makes it through."

Guy shook his head. "You can't do that."

"I have to. There's no other way." I sat on the bed, curling my legs up beneath me. I wasn't sure I could stand now that I was thinking about what I had committed myself to doing. I could die tomorrow. The Veiled Court could swallow me up and no one would ever see me again.

It was Guy's turn to prowl the chamber now. Anger swirled around him. When he finally stilled, his face was thunderous.

"No. You can't do it. It's not safe. Besides, how does getting to the queen help you? We can't tell the queen about Simon."

His voice sounded strained. He was more like his brother than he realized, this man. He too wanted to save people, to keep them safe. Even when he thought he hated them as he did me.

"No. And I won't have to, I hope. Cormen phrased the geas so that I could only tell him. But we can tell her that he's working with Ignatius. We can warn her. And we can tell her that Cormen kidnapped my mother. You can tell her he laid a geas on me. Those things are illegal under the treaties. I'm not full Fae and my mother is human. She'll have to call him to account."

"We don't have proof of that."

"Ignatius recognized my pendant. He talked about the evening star. He told me that Cormen had already sent his regrets. The queen can read that memory from me. It's enough to make her suspect him. It's a better plan, Guy. It's a better chance. Less risk that we have to tell anyone about Simon. I have to do this or the geas . . . I can't trust myself with it. Not here. But the court, in the queen's presence. She can control me, if she has to." I rose on my knees on the bed wondering if I should go to him. "You don't have to come with me."

He shook his head, holding up one hand to cut me off before I could go any further in my protests. Relief welled through me. I didn't want to do this alone. It was unsafe, yes. Deadly even. I needed him by my side. More than that, I wanted him by my side. My knight. One last time.

"I've come this far," he said. "I won't leave you to do this alone now."

In the strange light, the beasts on his hands seemed to flicker and move. I told myself it was a trick of the Fae lights. I hoped it was. Those tattoos bore testament to just how much he had done for me. Thrown his reputation in the gutter for me to walk across. People thought he'd been thrown out of the order he'd given his life to.

No doubt, even some of the brothers believed it. That would leave scars, even after the truth came out. That they had so little faith in him, when he'd given his life to the Templars, would hurt.

And I'd betrayed him too. Yet here he was, prepared to lay down even more.

Or maybe he didn't care what happened. Maybe we'd pushed

him too far. He was at war with his brother, with his order, with me. Every man has a breaking point.

This thought drove me from the bed. I crossed the room, then stopped before I reached him. I had no right to do anything to comfort him. Nor was it likely that he would accept it.

"Don't you do anything foolish," I warned. He stared at me, mouth curving for a moment as if he couldn't believe I was the one warning him when I'd led him here.

"Anything extra foolish," I added. "Don't you go all knight-in-shining-armor on me unless it's absolutely necessary. This isn't the City. Your rules don't apply."

"My rules stopped applying about the time that you fell off that roof," he muttered.

Mine too. I didn't say it. What I had to do would be hard enough to face without actually speaking what was in my heart. Because I'd ruined what was between us. I'd broken it. What right did I have to try and mend things? To ask even more of him? A Night Worlder spy had no place in a Templar's life. I should stay silent, leave him free to walk away from me.

The thought made my heart catch and tear.

So I had to think about something else.

But I couldn't. It was if all I could see was the man before me. The man I'd lost.

I blinked back tears.

"Holly, don't," he said softly.

I turned away. "I'm sorry," I said. "I didn't mean for any of this to happen." The words were muffled, the same words I'd already offered to him. He had no reason to forgive me.

"Holly, I can't—" his voice rasped.

I turned, smiled at him through the tears, seeing his face, those blue, blue eyes waver and blur. "I know. You don't have to." I walked closer, reached up, let myself touch his face one last time. "I'm sorry," I repeated.

"Damn it to hell." He stared down at me, then hauled me to him and kissed me. Kissed me hard enough to make my head spin and my heart pound. Kissed me with a mouth that tasted of regret. Of good-bye. Of longing.

Then he let me go. Stepped back. "Rest now," he said. "I'll watch over you."

*   *   *

Cormen had told me about the court. About the Door. But hearing about it wasn't the same as standing in front of it. A twenty-foot-high shining expanse of black metal. It bore no ornamentation, nothing to distract from its size. Almost unbearable in its purity of line. I could see my reflection, pale and nervous, as I wondered if everything I'd heard was true.

Not all who entered the Veiled Court left it. It was the heart of the Veiled World, most dangerous of all the Fae realms. The seat of the queen's power.

"Are you sure you want to do this?" Guy asked. He looked once more to where the Seneschal and two attendants stood by the far more normal door we'd entered this chamber by.

"What choice do I have?" I met Guy's eyes, but there was nothing more to say. Now it was time to do what I had come to do. Save my mother. Save Reggie. Save the City.

Destroy my father.

I nodded at the Seneschal and she lifted a hand. The vast doors swung inward soundlessly to reveal . . . nothing. A gaping darkness. Well, then, apparently this was the first test. Was I brave enough to step into that nothingness? It wasn't a peaceful dark. No . . . it felt menacing. My stomach knotted tighter, though a minute earlier I wouldn't have thought that possible.

But if I faltered now, all would be for nothing. My mother would die, Cormen would win, and who knew what chaos might be unleashed on the City? Someone had to try and stop it. Apparently that someone was me.

I squared my shoulders, allowed myself one last look at Guy in case I was swallowed by the darkness, and stepped through the Door.

The darkness was cold. A chill that sank into the bone, pain so sharp it felt as though I might shatter.

Sweet Lady, did it hurt this way every time someone entered the court? Or was it because I was half-blood? I had a moment's panicked thought that I should go back, warn Guy. If it hurt this badly for me, what might it do to a human? But the blackness behind me felt suddenly solid, bricks of night forming a barrier to bar my retreat.

The cold intensified as I struggled for each step forward until I was sure my lungs would shatter—breaking to frozen shards. The cold bit at my skin, my eyes, my mouth, slicing at me until I was sure I must be bleeding.

You knew it wouldn't be easy, Holly girl.

But I hadn't expected this. Not endless darkness and pain. I'd thought to face a wilderness perhaps, or a desert blocking my path. Not this horrifying absence of anything alive.

It felt almost as though I'd died already. Only the pain convinced me otherwise as I fought to keep moving. The chill sank deeper into my bones, the pain growing until it was all I knew and I couldn't tell if I was even still walking. Everything hurt. Every part of me. All my instincts told me to stop. To lie down. To do whatever it took to make the pain leave. Instead, I summoned the faces of my mother and Reggie, summoned the image of Guy standing behind me, and took one last step.

Pain speared me again, tearing at me, and I screamed. But then, in the next breath, the aching chill was gone and I stood in the light.

It took a moment to take it in: a moment mostly filled with attempting to convince my lungs that taking another breath wouldn't kill me. I stood in the middle of a vast marble floor, pure white with veins of black that seemed to shift as I watched. The space was empty. Above me a night sky glittered with stars. Not sunrise, even though moments earlier dawn had been breaking as the Seneschal led us to the Door.

The stars were none that I recognized, but then again, the City was hardly a good place for stargazing. The smoke of the factories and houses and railways obscured the night sky.

Despite the sky, there was light around me, as though I stood in bright sunshine. The contrast between the sky and the light made me queasy. But not as much as looking into the distance did. My brain couldn't judge how far the marble reached, but it was a square despite its immeasurable size.

Each edge bled into a different scene. To my right a forest even older and wilder looking than Summerdale's. To my left, an ocean. Behind me, I realized suddenly there was an equal vastness, though I had yet to take a step. At the edge of that was a mountain range, snowcapped and forbidding.

I turned back. In front of me, there was a garden, a vast lawn surrounded by hedges and rioting flower beds filled with flowers I didn't recognize. At the far edge of the lawn was a building. Marble steps and pillars and a pointed roof. I walked toward it, my feet soundless in the grass, until I reached the top of the steps. A huge expanse of white marble lay before me. A chair carved from black stone, delicate and airy, stood in the middle floor.

A throne.

Her throne.

Shit.

Suddenly I wanted to be back in the antechamber with Guy, to take his hand and run. But when I turned, there was no exit. No hint of walls and doors or forbidding darkness. No sign of Guy either, for that matter. If I was going to get out of here, then I needed to approach that throne and hope like hell its owner would appear to hear me. I'd made it this far. That had to be a good sign, surely? I steeled myself and took a step forward.

I had taken maybe ten more steps when I realized that there was someone walking toward me. I froze but the figure kept coming.

It was her. The Veiled Queen. As she walked, her robes moved and fluttered, a shifting mass of color. I couldn't see her face because her head was veiled, as it always would be in the court. The veils moved too, though in a subtly different pattern from the robes, as if a different force moved them. As they rose and fell they seemed sheer. Not enough to hide anything behind them, but nothing could be made of her face but the veils.

I'd done it. The Door—the land—had let me through.

It seemed too fast.

Too easy.

I tried not to give in to the sudden sickening fear as I watched her approach.

At least there was no hint of black in the colors dancing around her. If the Veiled Queen wore black, someone was going to die. That was another part of Fae lore I knew very well. One I'd heard from other sources besides Cormen. All the tales agreed. Black meant death.

I sank to my knees as she approached, bowing my head.

I couldn't hear footsteps, but the soft rustling of fabric warned me when she was close.

"Who seeks me?" she said. The voice was cool and light, beautiful as Fae voices tended to be. Neutral, or so I tried to tell myself.

"My name is Holly Evendale, Lady," I said, hoping my own voice wouldn't betray me.

"Evendale?" She sounded puzzled, but I didn't lift my head.

One didn't look upon the queen until she had given permission. "Ah. I see. The evening sky about the hills."

"Yes, Lady."

"I didn't know that sa'Inviel had acknowledged any by-blows," she said smoothly. "Or invited them to court."

"I am not here under sa'Inviel's aegis, Lady," I said.

"Oh?" The rustling increased and I tried not to picture robes and veils moving with greater agitation. Or darkening. "Then why are you here? Look at me," she added impatiently.

I raised my head cautiously. No black, though my mind insisted the mix of colors was more somber than it had been previously. "I bring information, Lady."

"What information does a *hai'salai* bring that is of interest to the court? And what do you hope to gain from giving it to me?" She beckoned me closer. She didn't wear a Family ring, I noticed. Instead her fingers carried bands laden with jewels of every possible color.

A sign of her hold over all the Families?

Now was the time for the truth. If I could speak it. There was still the geas to overcome. "No price, Lady."

"No? That seems unlikely. But tell your tale, little *hai'salai*. You have come this far and the Door did not dissuade you. Perhaps it shall prove a worthy journey."

I took a breath, hardly knowing where to start. Then I remembered Guy. "Your Majesty, I had a companion. He was going to come to the court with me. But I have not seen him since I passed through the Door. Is he . . ." What? Alive? Unharmed? I didn't know what to ask.

The queen shook her head, veils fluttering. "I do not control the land's will, child. Not when it comes to the Door. He will appear when he is meant to. If he does at all. Say what you have come to say."

I swallowed against the fear that Guy was lost somewhere in that darkness behind me. I couldn't waste this chance. Couldn't waste his sacrifice, were it true. "My lady, I believe there is a plot against you. A plot to break the treaties, to bring down the peace between the races."

The veils swirled for a moment, colors deepening still. "Oh? And who is it that you think works against me, *hai'salai*?"

I opened my mouth to tell her and my throat clenched, pain gripping me. No sound came out.

The queen's veils darkened further. "I need a name," she said. "Or else I will have to believe you are wasting my time. I do not look kindly on those who waste my time, little halfling."

I struggled to speak. Struggled to breathe. Nothing came out. The queen straightened, started to turn away.

"Cormen sa'Inviel'astar." Guy's voice came from behind me. "He is the one plotting, Majesty. Against you, against the treaty. He has formed an alliance with one of the Blood. He has bound his daughter to do his work for him and she cannot speak the truth."

The queen turned. The veils grew still, which was even more unsettling than their constant movement. "A geas?" She reached toward me. "Let me look at you."

I forced myself to stay still when I wanted desperately to turn, to see if Guy was all right.

The queen's hand raised my chin and I felt a wave of power wash over me. Her hand dropped away. "If there is a geas, I cannot sense it."

My heart sank.

"But then, they are bound by blood. I cannot interfere in such ties." Her attention moved beyond me. "What proof do you have, Guy DuCaine?"

"I believe that he—and perhaps others in your court—have formed an alliance with Ignatius Grey. Someone is funding Grey anyway. The Templars, and others, have been subject to Beast attacks recently. I believe Grey is behind that."

Guy's voice was blunt. Dispassionate. The tone, I imagined, he'd adopt giving a report to Father Cho or another superior officer. I wished I could see him but didn't risk a glance.

"And why would Ignatius Grey be willing to do such a thing? What can he gain?"

"He wants control of the Blood Court. There is more, but if I tell you what, I may be aiding their cause."

The veils moved again as the queen's head tilted. "Then it seems we have a dilemma before us. One that requires a solving." She snapped her fingers and a huge bronze bell suddenly appeared beside her, hanging in the air with no visible means of support.

"My lady, what are you—"

"Hush, child. There is only one way to proceed. Before the court." She snapped her fingers again and the bell moved, tilting swiftly until it rang, an ominous shimmering note that vibrated around us like a warning.

Chapter Twenty-three

HOLLY

🔑

Before the sound of the bell had faded, everything changed. Only the throne and the queen stayed the same. Around us, the roof filled with the Fae Court, hundreds of Fae appearing, as though all the invisibility charms in the world had failed at once. Behind the queen, a row of Fae, veiled like she, appeared. And to each side of us, Fae guards, armored and armed, stood in rows.

But apart from the last dying tones of the bell, there was no sound.

I kept my gaze on the queen. She was the most dangerous thing in the court, after all. So much power.

From behind me, I heard the Seneschal's voice. "The court has been summoned. Hear the will of the Veiled Queen."

The Fae sank into obeisance, in a thousand whispering rustles of silk and linen and whatever other fabrics made up the shimmer and shine of their clothing. I hastily followed, curtseying awkwardly in the voluminous robe. I had no idea if Guy followed my example, but I didn't dare look away from the queen to see.

"Cormen sa'Inviel'astar, come forth," the queen said, her voice ringing like the bell.

There was a murmur from the crowd as they all rose. Then I

heard the precise click of boots crossing the marble. My father's footsteps.

Cormen came level with me, shot me a glance full of menace as he bowed again. "My queen?" He straightened, his gleaming bronze robe shining in the sunlight.

The queen's veils floated and shimmered, moving through blue before settling on gray. A shade too close to black for my comfort.

"Cormen, I have heard a tale today that does not please me."

He bowed his head. "I am all sorrow to hear that, my Queen. Perhaps if you tell me this tale, I can find a way to mend it."

"Perhaps." The queen lifted her hand, gestured at me. "But first, I would have you remove the geas from this *hai'salai*."

Cormen's face twisted in rage before smoothing again, so quickly I thought I had imagined it. Would he risk arguing with the queen or do as she asked?

I had my answer soon enough. He gestured toward me and the room suddenly spun around me, nausea driving me to my knees as the binding unwound itself from my flesh.

"The *hai'salai* is insolent, my Queen. I merely sought to ensure her obedience in a matter of no interest to you." His tone was smooth, but I heard the edge of malice.

Could he hurt Mama and Reggie? From a distance? Quite possibly. I had to make sure they were safe before this went any further. I pushed to my feet, still fighting dizziness. "He has taken my mother, my lady. And the one who stands as sister to me. They are in danger."

"They are perfectly well, my Queen," Cormen protested.

"That may be," the queen said mildly. "But you will be so good as to produce these two humans. They can confirm what you say, no doubt. The *hai'salai* seems concerned and we would not want to break the bonds of our treaty."

This time my father wasn't so good at controlling his expression. He scowled at me, then gestured and my mother and Reggie suddenly stood to one side of us. Reggie looked exhausted, dressed in the same blue work dress I'd seen her in last. Beside her, my mother, wearing a pale blue Fae robe, looked confused and thin.

Alive. They were alive. It took a wrenching effort not to run to them, to touch them. But I couldn't risk upsetting the queen with a breach of protocol. Instead I just smiled at them, blinking back tears.

"Holly," Reggie cried. "Thank God. You found us."

The queen's head tilted toward Cormen. "That does not seem so willing. Still, we will deal with the humans later." She turned her head to one of the veiled attendants. "Take them somewhere safe."

The attendant bowed and Reggie and my mother were escorted away. I took a half step toward them as Reggie twisted to look at me, her eyes wide and frightened.

"Now," said the queen. "Let us deal with the matter before us. Cormen," she said casually. "You stand accused of treason against the throne."

"The *hai'salai* resents me," Cormen snarled. "She cannot be trusted."

"That may be true," the queen said. "Yet I cannot let such an accusation lie. Perhaps if you told us what task you had set her on that required a geas?"

Cormen went pale. "That is a personal matter, Majesty."

"I am your queen, Cormen. You should have no secrets from me. Tell me. Else I shall think you guilty."

I felt a surge of glee. There. She had asked him a direct question. A Fae cannot lie. Cormen would have to tell the truth.

Cormen turned and glared at me, hatred clear in his face. My hand dropped to my side, seeking the weapons I no longer carried. It was probably good that I was unarmed. Shooting my father dead in front of the Fae Court wasn't exactly a way of guaranteeing my long and happy life. We stared at each other a long moment, then Cormen smiled.

My stomach turned over, my confidence sinking. I knew that look. It boded nothing good.

He turned to the queen. "My Queen, I claim trial by combat. I will prove my innocence on the blood of this *hai'salai*."

Lords of hell. I froze. Trial by combat would clear the name of an accused. But only by the death of the accuser. Cormen meant to kill me.

"She knows how to fight, my Queen," Cormen continued. "It's a fair match."

The Seneschal stepped forward. "Trial by combat has been claimed. Shall we proceed, Your Majesty?" Her icy expression looked almost anticipatory. I doubted she was on Cormen's side, not if she was a true servant of the queen, but no Fae would be troubled overmuch by the death of a half-breed.

There was no way out. I had to fight him.

"I need a weapon," I managed through numb lips. "I had a sword." I trusted Saskia's blade more than any that the Fae might provide for me. I might not be able to defeat Cormen. He outweighed me and had the greater reach. Plus he was an excellent swordsman. But with Saskia's blade perhaps I could hurt him before he killed me.

"No." Guy's voice came from behind me. "You don't. I do."

I turned then, saw him come to stand beside me. His face was bloodied, his clothes slashed. Whatever he had faced on the journey from the Door to the court, it had been different from my trial. He looked as if he'd fought an army to reach me. Blood crusted his hands, almost obscuring his tattoos. He stood awkwardly as though favoring one leg. My throat closed with fear. He was hurt. How could he fight?

"Guy—"

"You would stand champion?" the queen asked.

Guy nodded. "Yes, Your Majesty."

"Very well. This is allowed. Trial by combat. Someone bring Sir Guy his sword. Cormen, you may arm yourself as well. Blades only." The queen turned, walked to her throne, settled into it. Then her head lifted. And her veils turned black.

It felt as though I had forgotten how to breathe. Pain stole my breath, warring with the terror freezing my mind. Worse than any thing the geas had ever done to me. One of the queen's attendants took my arm and led me to stand beside the throne. All the better to see Guy die?

Cormen was Fae. Hundreds of years older than Guy. Guy was a warrior, but he was human. He'd barely slept in days. And he was hurt. How could he win?

Another of the faceless attendants glided from the crowd, carrying Guy's sword. He took it from her with another bow, wincing slightly as he grasped the hilt.

A tear slid down my cheek, but I didn't brush it away. I would witness what was to come. If Cormen won, I didn't care what might happen to me; I would kill him.

Cormen looked relaxed as he waited for his own sword to be brought to him. When it came, he lifted the jeweled hilt and saluted the queen with a bow. I didn't turn my head to see if she reacted.

"Trial by combat ends with death," the Seneschal said, her voice ringing out over the expectant buzz of the crowd.

I could feel their anticipation. Nasty, like the bloodlust of the vampires at Halcyon. Waiting for blood to be spilled. Waiting for a spectacle. Did any of them care about the treason? Were any of them part of Cormen's plot? I saw no nervous faces.

A buzz of anticipation drew my attention back to Guy and my father. There were to be no polite preliminaries, it seemed.

Only a battle to the end.

My hand stole to my pendant, gripped it as if I could strangle Cormen. I had no reminder of Guy. Nothing of his to send him my strength. Only my will to stand here and watch him fight.

And fight he did. I had never really seen him in action. I'd been too terrified at Halcyon to notice what was happening around me. Plus he'd been outnumbered quickly.

But here, in the Fae Court, one-on-one and fighting for his life—and mine perhaps—I watched him do what he was meant to do.

A Templar knight fighting to protect the things he believed in. His family. His city. His God.

Not me.

I knew I wasn't the reason he'd stepped forward. No, he'd done it to stop Cormen. To do his duty. As he would have done no matter who stood in my place.

The key bit into my hand, and I felt blood run onto my palm. Good. If Guy was to bleed, then so would I.

He had no armor, just a plain white shirt and gray trousers—he must have kept them on under his robe. No Templar cross to mark what he was, but it was unmistakable.

His blade gleamed brilliant silver as he raised it to face Cormen. Cormen's hilt shone with jewels and the blade was chased with gold. Far more impressive looking than the elegant sword Saskia had made for her brother. Could the work of a metalmage withstand that of the Fae smiths?

I held my breath as the two of them circled, feinting for position. It was Cormen who attacked first, moving forward with a slashing blow. Metal clashed, sang, parted as Guy parried and broke away.

He fought well, my knight. Brilliantly. Cormen was fast—Fae fast—and strong and he attacked relentlessly, but Guy held him off and counterattacked savagely. Both of them collected wounds.

I smiled savagely when the tip of Guy's sword sliced across Cormen's face, prayed it would leave a scar to make his pretty facade reveal the rot within. But my triumph was short-lived when Cormen scored a hit to Guy's arm. And then another to his thigh.

Guy's breath was coming fast, too fast, rasping loud enough to be heard over the clash of metal and the slap of feet against the marble. He was tiring against Cormen's unrelenting assault.

He fell back, circled, trying to catch his breath. For one moment he was opposite me and his eyes met mine.

Guy.

My hand went to my mouth and he nodded, just slightly. Then he smiled, not the wicked smile I'd learned to love in such a short time. No, this was something far more unsettling. The smile of a man at peace with the path he'd chosen.

And I suddenly realized that there didn't have to be a victor in this match. That Guy could bring Cormen down by sacrificing himself.

In fact, as I watched him move more slowly, I had a horrifying sense of certainty that was what he meant to do. He moved differently now. Not attacking, rather drawing Cormen in, baiting him to attack. To get closer. To get careless.

I knew enough about fighting to see him doing it. Cormen apparently was too arrogant to see what I saw, to think that a human might outsmart him. He was falling for Guy's ploy. His blows grew bolder, encouraged as Guy retreated. He cut Guy again on the same arm and Guy's sword dipped to the floor, striking the marble with a screech of protesting metal before he raised it again, arm shaking.

Cormen laughed and pressed the attack, and as I watched, wanting to scream in protest, to throw myself between them to stop what I knew was about to happen, I saw Guy drop his guard, toss his sword to his left hand, and let Cormen's sword bite deep into his side.

Those blue eyes went wide as the blade hit him, his face twisting in pain. But his sword didn't falter. It arced around and struck, biting through my father's shoulder and down at an angle to his heart.

Cormen's face went strangely blank and his hand dropped from his sword, leaving it half embedded in Guy's side.

His head swiveled toward the queen, lips parting, and then he fell, crumpling against the marble, a rapidly spreading pool of red running away from him as his eyes went sightless and blank.

Dead.

My father was dead.

Grief caught at me. Unexpected. Unwanted. But unavoidable. My father was dead.

I stared at his body, waiting to see if I were wrong. If he would rise and claim victory somehow. But he was still. So still I couldn't take my eyes off him until another movement caught my attention.

Guy.

His hand clapped to the sword in his side, he staggered a step toward the throne.

"Guy!" I didn't care about protocol anymore. I broke away from the attendants and ran. But I was too slow. Because I was only halfway there when his knees buckled and he too sank toward the floor.

Too late, Holly girl.

"Guy, no!" I was crying now as I reached him, skidded to a halt, then dropped beside him, then realized with horror that I had no idea what to do. I couldn't help him. "He needs a healer," I screamed. The Fae around me were standing still, varying shocked and uncertain expressions on their faces.

Guy's chest still rose and fell. Just. He was bleeding, though the blood collecting beneath him was not nearly the size of the pool surrounding my father's corpse. I had to stop the bleeding. I tore frantically at my robe, but the silk resisted. "Somebody fetch a healer," I said again.

"Come away, child." It was the queen's voice. "We will attend to him."

"You have to save him," I said brokenly.

"We will do what we can." Her voice was still cool, unfeeling. I wondered if she felt anything at all. Ever. "Attend to the victor," she said to someone behind me, and then someone lifted me to my feet, arms around my shoulders guiding me away. I looked back to see Guy, but he was surrounded by Fae, hidden from view.

I couldn't stop crying. Tears streamed down my face no matter what I tried to do. I couldn't see, couldn't think. The arms at my shoulder tugged at me and I followed blindly. The noise of the court vanished suddenly and someone passed me a handkerchief.

I mopped at my eyes, hiccupping in the effort to stop my sobs. When I could see enough to take in my surroundings, I saw the queen watching me, her veils white and sheer.

I could see her face, finally. Her eyes were a deep green, like the needles of a Hallows tree. And her hair, what I could see of it, gleamed bronze like the streaks in mine. She looked more like me than my own mother.

I squeezed my eyes shut, unable to process anything more. I felt dizzy, sick from fear and grief, my eyes burning from the tears.

"Is there something we can get you, Holly?" the queen asked gently.

"Yes," I gulped against another wave of rising tears. "I want my mother."

"Mama," I said from the doorway.

Reggie turned from her seat by the bed. "She's asleep." She blinked tired eyes at me and once again I was struck by the thought that Reggie resembled my mother far more than I.

Fair and girlish. Nothing like me.

I watched Mama sleeping. Spoke softly to Reggie while we waited, apologizing to her. The Fae hadn't let me see them immediately; they had wanted to see to Mama and to Reggie. And they'd done something to me that had sent me into a deep sleep when I couldn't stop crying. I slept for two days.

When I woke I asked again for my mother. And for Guy. Guy, I was told, was still being treated for his wounds. That started the tears again. Any wound that took several days for the Fae to heal was near fatal.

I wanted to be happy he was still alive, but I couldn't help dreading that he would still die. Even if he lived, I had lost him.

Mama stirred on the bed, lifted her head, pale blond hair tumbling down around her face. Though really it was now more silver than blond, I saw with a pang. Only seventeen when she had had me. Only just forty-two now. Too young to look so old.

Her face was horribly thin, the lines around her mouth and eyes standing out starkly. Her cheeks were pale and her eyes reddened, as mine were, from crying.

"He's dead, isn't he?" she said, and the pain in her voice tore at me. Too close to the pain in my own heart. All these years and it seemed I hadn't really learned the most important lesson I should have learned from her. Not to fall in love.

"Yes, Mama," I said gently, walking to her. Reggie relinquished the chair and I sat and took my mother's hand. "He is."

Sticklike fingers tightened on mine and tears bubbled over. I didn't know what to say. Didn't think there was anything I really could say. She had lost the man she loved, and whether I thought him worthy of love or not, that hurt. As I was discovering.

I held her hand and stroked her hair and eventually the sobs stopped and she slept again. At some point Reggie had slipped away. I was alone in the room by the time I'd stopped watching Mama's chest to make sure it still rose and fell.

Or rather, not quite alone. The queen stood by the bed, gazing down at my mother. Her veils were white. Near transparent. I could almost see her face unobstructed. Still too beautiful to look at for long.

"How sick is she?" I asked.

"Very. Your father . . ." She paused, seemed to reconsider. "The last few days have been very hard on her."

"Can't you heal her?" The queen had the power to do almost anything. I had brought Cormen's plot to her attention—telling her what I knew of his connection to Ignatius and the attacks on the Templars. How he'd set me to spy on Simon. What I had discovered. Simon and Guy might hate me for that last part, but I had decided that the truth was required. The queen had a better chance of defending herself if she knew what might be coming. She was the only one who knew I'd found anything at all. She was even now, no doubt, working on finding out who my father's fellow conspirators were.

Politics. I was sick to death of politics. I wanted to go somewhere where no one cared about politics, buy the little house I'd always wanted. Take my mother home. Surely the queen owed me that much. She could give my mother back to me.

"Not if she doesn't wish to heal. Her heart is broken. I can mend her body, but it won't help if her mind wants to die."

And there was the thing I hadn't wanted to face. Could my mother live with Cormen gone? "Broken because of *him*." The words were sour in my mouth.

"Yes." She paused again, and then sighed, the sound a breath of silk in the air. "We are an arrogant race, Holly. We live so long, it's hard to be otherwise."

"It doesn't make it right. To treat people as though they're worth nothing."

"My court is fickle and I have been binding them to my will, to this treaty, for a long time. There are some smaller fights I cannot fight while that is so."

"My mother's life is a smaller fight?"

She nodded. "To me, yes." Her tone was implacable.

"The greater good," I said wearily. I was sick to death of the greater good. It had lost me everything.

"Yes."

"Can I take her home?" I didn't want to leave her here, amongst those who thought her nothing important, merely a human, gone in a fleeting moment.

"She won't last long. She doesn't want to."

"I know." I bit my lip, breathed deep before I continued. "But she'll be loved." My voice cracked on the last word.

"There's an alternative," the queen said.

"Oh?"

"Leave her here. She can sleep a long time here and not grow old."

"How long?"

"I can't tell you that. If her heart mends, she will wake up. If not she will sleep until she fades away."

"So lose her now, have her perhaps wake in a hundred years after I am gone, or die even longer from now than that? How is that better?" I fought against the tears that threatened yet again. Mama would be lost to me either way. All that I'd risked and fought for and I was never going to have what I wanted. The home with the peaceful garden. Mama healthy and happy, smiling at me.

The man.

"Her dreams will be happy, I can promise you that much."

Happiness. There'd been little enough of that in my mother's life since Cormen left us. Could I really be selfish enough to deny it to her now? Surely she deserved that much?

Surely I deserved to be happy too, part of me protested. To have my mother with me, even for a short time?

I blinked away tears. More tears. I felt as though I'd cried more in the last few days than I had in the last ten years. Then I looked up at the queen. "Can you wake her up for me?"

She nodded. "Of course." She leaned forward, touched Mama's forehead lightly, then drew back.

My mother opened her eyes, the faded blue lighting a little when she saw me. "Holly," she said softly. "My Holly girl."

Then I saw it, memory flooding across her face. Loss. Pain. I couldn't hold her to that. I clenched my jaw, willing the tears away, leaned forward, kissed her cheek. Her skin was wrinkled—more than it should be at her age—but soft, and the scent of her filled my lungs. My mother. My throat ached. "Mama, I have to go. But you can rest here for a while, if you want."

She smiled again, touched my cheek. "All right. I'm tired, Holly." Her fingers closed around mine. "You're a good girl. I always loved you, you know."

The tears rose again, my throat tightening more than it had when the geas had ridden me. The pain was worse too. "I love you too, Mama. You rest now."

I looked around to the queen, eyes beseeching. Then held my mother's hand while her breath gentled to the slow rhythm of sleep and her grip loosened around mine. "Sweet dreams, Mama."

When I stopped crying, the queen was still there, her veils floating around her. Her expression, what I could see of it, was gentle.

Reggie touched my shoulder. "She looks peaceful," she said.

I nodded, reached for her hand. "I want to go home now."

"You can stay here. You are both under my protection, but Summerdale is the safest place for you."

I shook my head. "Thank you, but no. My life is out there." I rubbed my throat where the absence of my father's chain still felt strange. I'd been able to take it off after his death. I'd given it to the queen to be buried with him. I didn't want any reminder of him and what he'd done to me.

I stared down at Mama. My life. What was left of it anyway. Reggie squeezed my hand and I forced a smile. *Nothing for it, Holly girl.* I had to go on. Or I'd be the one who might as well sleep forever. "Besides, we have a diva waiting for her clothes."

The queen smiled at that. "Very well. Is there anything else I can do for you, Holly Evendale? I am in your debt still."

"Yes," I replied, and then I told her what I wanted.

Chapter Twenty-four

GUY
✠

Getting information out of the Fae was somewhat akin to getting blood from a stone. I knew Cormen was dead, but no one would tell me anything about Holly or her mother.

Or even when they might be letting me go home.

For all I knew, the City could have burned to the ground, news from outside Summerdale being another thing my Fae healers didn't wish to discuss.

The healing wound in my side still hurt, which I took to be a measure of how lucky I was to be alive. A week in Fae care and I was still in pain.

I should probably be dead.

I was starting to feel as though I would die from frustrated boredom when the door to my sunny little prison cell of a room opened and the queen walked in.

I tried not to gape. I hadn't expected to see the Veiled Queen again any time soon. I bowed my head. "Forgive me if I don't get up, Your Majesty. Your healers have threatened me with dire consequences if I rise from bed without their permission."

I kept a wary eye on her veils, but today they were yellow and green and pale pink. Like spring. They were almost transparent, revealing her face and green, green eyes.

She came toward the bed, sat in the chair the healers used.

This close, the power around her made the air buzz against my skin. The hairs on my arms stood on end.

A cozy chat with the Fae Queen? Perhaps I should've let Holly's bastard father kill me after all.

"Perhaps I can do something about that," she said as I stared at her expectantly. "After you and I discuss some things."

I managed not to wince. Just. "Your Majesty?"

"Holly has told me of your brother's activities. His and the vampire's," the queen said.

I nodded. I'd expected that much. You didn't lie to the Veiled Queen if asked, and I hadn't expected the queen wouldn't ask. "She told you the truth. He's looking for a cure." My fool brother. How much of this lay on his head? How much on Lucius'? How much on those foolish enough to think the four races could live in peace in the first place? Like the woman seated beside me.

"The treaty negotiations start in a few weeks. You tell the sunmage to be ready."

Ready for what? To present his cure to the world? As far as I knew, he didn't exactly have one yet. If he said that, then the Blood would be even more eager to kill him. "Yes, Your Majesty." There wasn't anything else to say.

Her head tilted. "You don't approve of what Simon is doing?" She sounded surprised.

"No. I don't."

"Why not?"

"Because I think it will cause more trouble. I don't think we should be doing anything that will encourage people to choose the Night World."

"You think that's what a cure would do?"

"Yes. If you take away the consequence that frightens people, then I think more of them will be stupid enough to give in to their curiosity. And that won't be good for anyone."

"You and your brother have different views of the world," the queen said, her voice curious.

"My brother's an idealist. I have more sense than that."

Her head tilted, veils fluttering. "Strange words from a man who's dedicated his life to protecting people."

"That's not idealism. It's practicality. Someone has to stand between the Night World and the humans."

"Yet you believe in the possibility of a better world."

"I believe that that's most likely to be in the next life, my lady." Though I found myself curiously happy that I hadn't yet discovered if that theory was true or not. My world was fucked up, sure enough, but I wasn't ready to let go of it yet. Not while there was still work to do.

"You don't have much faith in people themselves, then?" She sounded amused.

"I've seen a lot of people not worthy of faith, Your Majesty." Including the man I'd killed in front of her. But Cormen was just the latest in a long line. A line I was growing weary of.

"I see. Then perhaps, I can do a little to restore some of your faith," she said. "Hold out your hands, Guy."

I looked down at my hands where they rested on the counter-pane. My journey from the Door—of which I now had only the haziest memory—had torn my palms half to shreds. Cormen had added to the tally of scars on my body. But the hells-damned beast tattoos had somehow survived intact.

"Hold out your hands," the queen repeated. Her voice commanded obedience.

I lifted my hands. She took them in hers. "I bring you a gift, Guy," she said.

"Oh?" For some reason my heart was hammering, blood roaring in my ears. "From whom?"

"From one who could have chosen to use the gift for herself," the queen said gently. "She could have chosen my protection or my favor."

"Holly?" I said somewhat stupidly. Holly, who always had one eye on the deal, who knew how to make the best of a situation for herself? Why would Holly turn down the Fae queen's gift? "Is she still here?"

I didn't know what I wanted the answer to be. Did I want to see her? I'd been so angry. I'd hurt her. Part of me was still angry, but killing Cormen had gone some way to assuage my rage.

"She and Regina have returned to the City."

"Only the two of them? Where's her mother?"

"Her mother will stay with us for a while. She took the death of the sa'Inviel hard." The queen's voice hardened on Cormen's name. "She does not want to live without him."

Holly's mother had stayed here to die? Hell's balls. She'd done everything she could to save her mother and now she was losing her anyway? I closed my eyes for a minute, thought about Edwina, lost so long ago, and yet still the hurt seemed new.

Now Holly was going through that same pain.

"I don't want it," I said suddenly. "Whatever she asked for. Heal her mother."

"I can't do that," the queen said gently. "I cannot change a person's will to live. And the boon is Holly's to give, not yours."

I was the one who'd bloody well killed the traitor. Where was my fucking boon?

The queen laughed suddenly, as though she'd heard my thoughts, the sound beautiful as a spring day. "Let us proceed."

Her hands tightened around mine. Warmth flowed over me, and the air suddenly filled with the smell of every good thing I knew. My vision blurred, colors flashing before my eyes as though I were crying, though there were no tears. It felt very different from Simon's healing. Different even from Bryony's. Vaster. As though it could sweep me away in its tide.

"There," the queen said. She let go of my hands as my vision cleared.

I stared down at my hands where my crosses glowed, fresh and red and unmarred, looking as though nothing had ever happened to them. "Bryony said tattoos couldn't be removed," I said, wondering if I was seeing things.

"I didn't remove them. I restored them." The queen flicked one of her floating veils back with the snap of a hand, the gesture reminding me suddenly of Bryony tossing her head in irritation.

I hid a smile.

"Besides, Bryony sa'Eleniel is not Queen of the Veiled World."

"No, Your Majesty," I murmured, still staring at my hands. My side didn't hurt. "Holly asked you to do this?"

"She was most insistent."

"But why?" I didn't understand. Why would Holly choose this over protection for herself and Reggie? I was a means to an end to her. A way to get to Simon. A tool to help her save her mother. Or was I?

The queen shifted in her chair, her veils turning even brighter shades of spring. "She said she wanted you to have your life back."

HOLLY

The return to warmer weather hadn't improved the smell in Seven Harbors any. The smell of rotting food and unwashed bodies and other things I didn't want to think about carried on the warm night breeze and seemed to settle around me in the little sheltered niche I'd found between two gables.

Nor did warmer weather really make hanging around on rooftops at midnight any more comfortable. Though at least now I could be happier with my client. I'd chosen a side. Maybe a foolish choice, but the last few weeks had changed me. The treaty negotiations would begin soon and the City was going to change one way or another.

I wanted it to be for the better. Even if that made life more dangerous for me. Besides, working like a madwoman kept me from thinking too much about Guy.

Or rather, I hoped that it would . . . eventually. Hanging around on rooftops involved entirely too much time to think. To remember. To regret.

I knew Guy was back. That he was alive. But I hadn't seen him. Hadn't tried to see him. And he hadn't come looking for me.

That told me all I needed to know.

One day it might not hurt so damned much. I wiped my face as I stared down at the windows I was meant to be watching. This time, I hadn't been so lucky. The shutters were closed. But my charms were in place and hopefully recording the words being spoken between one of Ignatius' circle and one of Henri's little conclave of disgruntled Beastlings. The Veiled Queen might be perfectly capable of hunting out the traitors in her court, but I—and Father Cho—wanted to know exactly how far the plot reached.

Whether Lucius' attack on Simon was the beginnings of it or whether the Blood had formed a new plan after Lucius had died. Knowledge was power. And the humans would need power at the negotiations. I didn't know if Simon was going to come forward with his research, but I wanted to help arm those who would support him if he did.

Which was why I was up here on another rooftop, soaking up the reek of Seven Harbors, at Father Cho's direction.

Working for the Templars, Holly girl. Who would've thought it?

I smiled bitterly. I was working for the Templars, yes, but the only one of their order I wanted to see was forever out of my reach.

Something creaked above me and I glanced upward. A man's silhouette loomed on the rooftop. I started and almost lost my footing. But I'd learned my lesson and I was firmly tied in place. Of course, that meant I couldn't get away quickly if I needed to. *You're invisible,* I reminded myself, staring up at the figure. *He can't see you.*

Then something arced through the air toward me. I put out a hand and caught it by reflex. Felt the buzz of the charm. Felt my own charm stutter and die. Saw my hand blink into solidity in front of my face.

Lords of hell. He'd killed my charm. I tugged at the knot at my waist as my pulse sped.

"Good catch, darlin'."

I froze. I knew that voice. Though a roof in Seven Harbors was about the last place I'd ever expected to hear it.

I pitched my voice low. "What the hell are you doing here?"

"Looking for you," Guy said. "Come on up."

I felt my jaw drop, closed it with a snap, reached for the razor in my boot, and sliced the fool rope. Knots be damned. I felt my way up the roof to the ridge where Guy perched.

"Are you trying to get us both killed?" I demanded in a whisper. "Anyone could see us." I tried not to stare at his face, not to drink him in. "How did you know where to find me anyway?"

Guy pushed back the hood covering his pale hair. Making us even more visible. I fought the urge to slap him. Or kiss him. Or both.

"There's a window open on an empty room on the other side," I said. "Follow me. And be careful. There's no one to catch you."

His soft laugh made my heart clutch. I told myself not to be foolish. Father Cho had probably sent him to give me another mission.

Still, my hands shook a little as I swung down to the railing outside the window and slid myself through to safety. I stood in the dark room, heart pounding, waiting for Guy to follow.

It didn't take him long. Apparently it wasn't his first time climbing on a roof judging by the ease with which he came through the window.

He moved easily, more confidently than I had. He must be fully healed. My heart clutched again.

"Are there lights in this place?" Guy asked.

I nodded, stupid when he probably couldn't see me. I had a lantern stashed by the door. I lit it with unsteady fingers and carried it to the middle of the room, hanging it from the rope I'd used to ensure that the window stayed open.

Only then did I let myself turn and look at Guy.

Whole.

Here.

"I asked how you knew I was here." There. That sounded suitably detached. My voice hadn't wobbled.

Guy smiled. "Father Cho told me who your targets were. Fen helped me with the rest."

"Fen?" That explained the charm killer at least. But as to what in hell Fen thought he was doing sending Guy my way, I had no idea. But we would be discussing it later.

"So you're here. What do you want?" I hoped my voice wouldn't betray how much I wanted to know the answer to that question. Wanted him to tell me so I could get over this foolish flare of hope already, and leave him again.

"I came to ask you a question," he said.

"It couldn't wait until daylight?"

"It took me a while to wear Fen down," Guy said. "And I was in a hurry once I did."

"Well, then, ask away."

He held out a hand. "I came to ask you about this." He twisted his wrist, so I saw the tattooed cross. Clean and whole.

"She did it," I breathed. Thank the Lady.

"Yes, she did," Guy agreed. "The question is why you asked her to."

I looked away. I wasn't going to answer that. Because the answer didn't make any sense. Why did I still love a man who didn't love me? How had I fallen in love with him so quickly anyway? People didn't fall in love in days. Did they? "You were almost killed because of me. The least I could do was give you your life back. You are back in the order, aren't you?"

"Yes," he said.

"And things are all right?"

He looked down for a moment. Then shrugged. "It's not perfect. But it's a lot better than it would have been if I'd shown up with those beasts on my hands."

"That's what I thought," I said. There. I'd answered his question. He could go again.

"But," Guy said, "there is another problem."

My heart sank. "There is?"

He nodded. "Yes. You see, I'm back in the order. A Templar. The famous Guy DuCaine."

"Yes?" I wished he'd get to the point. Then he might leave.

"Knights are meant to protect those they care about."

My stomach rolled, dipped. "Did something happen to Lily or Simon?"

He laughed. "No. Nothing like that. But there's someone else. Someone who put herself in danger because of me. Someone who could have had the Veiled Queen's protection but turned it down."

Me? He was talking about me? But hadn't he said someone he cared about. "I—"

"You turned it down, darlin'," Guy said. "And that means someone else has to protect you."

"I'm fine," I said automatically, my brain still not making sense of the words I was hearing.

"But I'm not," he said. "You gave me my old life back, Holly Evendale." His eyes seemed very blue in the lamplight as he smiled at me again.

"Isn't that what you wanted? You can go around saving people like you always wanted."

"But who's going to save me?" he said softly. "That's what was missing in my old life." His hand reached for mine. "Save me, Holly. Give me another chance."

"But I betrayed you—"

"Shut up," Guy said. "And make sure you don't let anyone put a geas on you ever again." His hand fingers tightened on mine, drawing me toward him.

"Guy, you don't want me. I'm not right for you. I'm—"

"You're you. I'm not exactly perfect myself. And I get to choose who's right for me," he said.

A smile crept across my face, happiness bubbling through me. "What about what I choose?"

"Well, darlin'," he drawled, "I figure we have plenty of time to discuss that. But right now can we talk about something else?" His free hand crept around my waist, pulling me closer still.

"Like what?" I asked

"I thought we'd start with this," he said, and his mouth came down on mine and I tasted home.

ABOUT THE AUTHOR

M. J. Scott is an unrepentant bookworm. Luckily she grew up in a family that fed her a properly varied diet of books and these days is surrounded by people who are understanding of her story addiction. When not wrestling one of her own stories to the ground, she can generally be found reading someone else's. Her other distractions include yarn, cat butlering, dark chocolate, and fabric. She lives in Melbourne, Australia.

CONNECT ONLINE

www.mjscott.net
twitter.com/melscott
facebook.com/authormjscott